THE RING

FLORENCE OSMUND

ISBN-13: 978-0-9998074-3-9
LCCN: 2020925948

Cover: Tugboat Design, https://www.tugboatdesign.net/
Formatting: Anessa Books, http://anessabooks.com

ACKNOWLEDGMENTS

When I was in the checkout line at Kohl's one day, the name on the cashier's nametag intrigued me, so I asked her about its origin, which turned out to be a derivation of her parents' names. I told her I was a novelist always on the lookout for unique and interesting names for my characters, and she graciously agreed to my using her name for one of the two main characters in this book. Thank you, Jessivel!

The ring on the cover of this book belonged to my father, Walter Osmund Sr. He wore it every day as far back as I can remember. When I inherited it, I had it resized so I could wear it myself. It is something of his I will cherish for the rest of my life. The wallet on the cover belonged to Roland Lundstrom, the late father of my childhood friend Vineta Lundstrom Ochsner. Vineta was kind enough to let me borrow it for the photo shoot. I'm afraid there is no personal significance to the watch on the cover, at least not for me. This I found in a thrift store. Thank you Deborah Bradseth of Tugboat Design for utilizing my photo in the cover design for *The Ring*.

Thank you Carrie Cantor for your editing talents. Once again, not only were you instrumental in making my writing more accurate, clear, and credible, but you helped me take it to the next level. For this I am grateful.

I owe a huge measure of thanks to my two Beta readers. To my sister Marge Bousson, Beta reader extraordinaire, thank you for catching technical errors in the manuscript I had missed and providing constructive feedback on the content as well. Your tireless efforts are much appreciated. And to Deborah G. Lynn, thank you for pointing out areas that needed clarification and consistency as well as raising some psychological issues that only someone with your background could contemplate.

And finally, thank you to Meredith Bond of Anessa Books for your extraordinary skills in producing all the file formats required for publication of *The Ring*.

CHAPTER 1

Paige struggled to stay attentive during the eulogy as the funeral home director's calm voice droned on.

"Devoted husband, loving father of two daughters, Ryan West was an ardent provider for his family. He was a humble man, often putting the needs of others before his own."

It was somewhat disheartening to listen to a man, who had barely known her father, talk about him as though they had been friends. The words he spoke originated from what they had provided to him, not from his heart. The substantial gold watch she cradled in her hands provided some comfort, the mere feel of it reminding her of happier times when it had graced her father's virtuous wrist.

She fidgeted on the unyielding bench next to her mother, the tightness in her chest unrelenting. At forty-two, she had been to enough memorial services to know how her mind and body would react. But this one was different—this was her father they were mourning.

She glanced sideways at her mother, dressed in a black St. John knit suit, a veiled pillbox hat atop her head, her face still except for one tiny muscle pulsing in her jaw. Her stiff, frail body looked as though it would instantly shatter if someone were to tap her on the shoulder.

"Could these seats be any more uncomfortable?" Paige whispered. When her mother didn't respond, she clutched the watch a little tighter.

The gaudy floral carpeting provided a welcome distraction as Paige half-listened to the man at the podium still speaking—it had now been over twenty minutes—until the muted French mauve lilies appeared to grow before her eyes. She blinked away the moving images and shifted her gaze to the wall behind the podium where a glassy-eyed figure of

Jesus loomed over the room, until she couldn't tolerate another second the sight of the spikes pounded into his flesh.

Paige turned her focus to the blown-up photo of her father resting on the easel beside the memorial urn that contained his ashes, a photo she had picked out for the occasion, one she had taken the previous year when she and her father had gone to see *La Traviata* at the Lyric Opera of Chicago. Happier times.

"And he served his country well too, with active duty in the Army for four years." Word-for-word what her mother had given the man days before.

The comingled aromas of cut flowers and the perfumes, colognes, and body odors of at least a hundred people in the room made her feel lightheaded. She closed her eyes, wishing the service was closer to its end rather than the beginning.

"Let us pray," the funeral home director said midway into the service.

As the balding, emotionless man at the podium recited the prayer, Paige reflected on her father's life. A salesman of large medical equipment, he had traveled extensively throughout his career, sometimes overseas, making a substantial income. She wanted for nothing while growing up, except perhaps more of his time.

"Born to second-generation immigrant parents, Ryan worked his way through school and was the first in his family to attend college."

Her father had often told her that education had the power to change one's life. It had undoubtedly changed his—without a college degree, he likely wouldn't have had such a successful career.

"Ryan West was a charitable man, giving of both his time and money. He gave so generously to Lakeside University that they named their science lab after him. And when he was in town, you would often find him volunteering in one of many neighborhood soup kitchens." What her mother had provided verbatim.

Paige had often joined her father in the kitchens and planned to continue going. She had loved watching him interact with the patrons like they were his long-time friends. She aspired to be more like him in this respect.

"He leaves behind his loving wife, Elaine Forrester West, and daughters, Paige Cushman West and Natalie West." Paige's sister Natalie was, unsurprisingly, not in attendance.

Upon hearing the name Cushman, her former married name, Paige realized she had failed to contact Leland about her father's death. Her father had liked Leland and was disappointed when they divorced. When she had been married to him, Leland and her father had gone on twice-yearly fishing trips and the occasional outing to an Indiana riverboat casino.

The thought of her ex-husband conjured up the mournful memory of their daughter, Briana. Rarely a day went by when she didn't think about her and her tragic death from a congenital heart defect when she was only eighteen months old—an agonizing loss with rippling effects that Paige suspected would linger over the course of her lifetime.

"The family has asked that donations be made to the Huntington's Disease Clinic at Midwest Memorial Hospital. As you may know, Mr. West died of complications from this disease."

Paige was actually thankful that pneumonia had set in before the often-lingering disease had a chance to take its final toll. Because the illness was genetic, with a 50/50 chance of passing from parent to child, Paige was tested as soon as her father was diagnosed. Fortunately, the results had come back negative. Natalie had refused the test.

"Let us pray for others who have been afflicted by this disease."

She had wept all she was going to over his death—one good cry at first, followed by many sorrowful moments in the days following. Despite his frequent travel, she had been exceptionally close to him, and it was difficult to imagine life without him.

At the end of the service, the funeral home director asked if anyone wanted to share memories about the deceased. Her father's long-time golf buddy and CEO of the company where he had worked spoke first.

"I loved playing practical jokes on Ryan," he said, "and the best one I ever played on him was when I had a plaque made that said A BAD DAY AT GOLF IS BETTER THAN A GOOD DAY IN THIS LOUSY OFFICE. I sent it to him anonymously…at work. After he opened it and set it on his desk, I walked into his office and pretended to be outraged by it. I think I may have even fired him. Of course, when he realized the joke was on him, he threw it at me. And…I guess I deserved it. We laughed about it afterward. We laughed a lot, Ryan and me. I miss that. I miss him."

When the man finished, Paige walked to the front of the room, her taller-than-average, slim figure standing erect behind the podium. The prepared words had long since flown from her mind, so she went instead with what came to her spontaneously.

"For those of you who don't know me, I am Paige West. Ryan West was my father. And as I am standing up here today, I realize how fortunate I was to have him as my father, my mentor, my hero really.

Losing him has been painful, and I don't think I'll ever be the same without him.

"Dad was a hard worker—I'm sure most of you know that. And while he traveled a lot in his job, his time at home was always devoted just to us. His work stayed at work." She gulped back the emotion that clogged her throat. "Whenever he was going out of town, he'd say to me, 'Look for that star tonight, sweetie.'" Now unable to hold back her sobs, she choked out, "Because he'd told me when I was little that he'd wished on a star for me to be born."

It didn't matter to Paige that he had missed most of the milestones in her life—her first day at school, many birthdays, her prom, high school graduation, seeing her off to college. When he was around, he made her feel as though she was the only thing on his mind and the most important person in his life.

"I don't have words to express what an influence he has had in my life." Paige glanced at her mother. "Along with my mom, the examples they set for me, the values they imposed upon me, and their knowing advice are why I am the person I am today. I can honestly say my dad was everything a daughter could ask for—someone to look up to, someone to respect, someone to listen to and learn from, and someone most of all to go to when I needed him. I know nobody is perfect, but my dad came as close to it as a dad could come. He taught me so much, but two things stand out for me. One is that if you really put your mind to it, anything is possible. And the most important thing you can give to another person is your respect."

Her father was the most nonjudgmental person she'd ever known. He was a good listener, had empathy for everyone, and never put another person down. Respect for others, in his mind, was the most important virtue a person could have.

"My father was a strong man—in body, in spirit, and in commitment. As he faced his final days, he may have lost some of his physical strength, but he displayed not one moment of self-pity. The day before he passed, when the nurse asked him how he was doing, he gave the same answer he gave every day. 'I'm doing fine, and you?'"

"To say I loved my dad would be an understatement—to say I'm going to miss him would be even greater."

On the way back to her seat, Paige surveyed the sea of vacant-faced guests, tears partially blurring her vision. Most of the mourners were her and her father's business associates. Few relatives on either of her parents' side of the family were in attendance—two nephews from

Indiana whom Paige hadn't seen since she was a child and a great aunt neither she nor her mother had ever met.

Seated together, near the front of the room, were "the girls," Gayle, Sandy, and Valerie. A close circle of friends for many years, the four of them supported each other and had each other's back no matter what the circumstances. Paige walked by them as Gayle appeared to be comforting Valerie who was known to cry easily, even at certain TV commercials.

Paige rejoined her mother in the pew, grateful they had waited a month after his private funeral to hold this memorial service. Otherwise, she wasn't sure she could have held it together as well as she had among all these people.

"I wish Natalie was here," her mother whispered as Paige settled back into her seat. Natalie, who lived less than twenty miles from her parents, had been made aware of their father's illness and eventual death, and their mother had even offered to arrange for an Uber to pick her up and drive her to the funeral and memorial services. Her absence from both was surmised to be due to lack of sobriety.

After the last person had said a few words, Paige and her mother stood at the head of the long receiving line. As she had suspected, it proved to be a test of endurance. And while pretty and appropriate, the music didn't help. "Morning Has Broken," "Amazing Grace," and "Love Lives On" were painful to withstand, but she had no one to blame for the song choices but herself.

Mourners repeated the same few sentiments in the receiving line, until Paige silently screamed *I know you're sorry for my loss. That's why you're here!* Honestly, who wouldn't hope a person hadn't suffered in the end? And whether he was "in a better place," or not would be something she could argue either way.

Halfway through the receiving line, a woman she didn't recognize told her she knew what Paige was going through because she had lost her dog the previous month. *Are you kidding me?* Before she could think of a response, a thunderous clatter from across the room drew her attention toward the stand where her father's memorial urn containing his ashes was displayed along with a flower arrangement and the large, framed picture of him. A woman—rather short with a dark shawl wrapped tightly around her head and shoulders—dashed away from the stand, which now lay on its side, with everything once on it strewn on the floor.

Everyone in the room stopped talking and watched the woman hastily exit out the side door. Paige looked at her mother, who shook her head but continued the conversation she was having with one of the mourners as if nothing had happened.

Paige called for the director, but by the time he arrived, the woman was gone. He and another person attempted to put the items back on the stand, in the same manner in which they had been originally displayed, but when they were done, it didn't look quite the same.

When everyone had been through the receiving line, Paige took her mother aside.

"Did you see what that woman did?" Paige asked her. "Do you know her?"

"I didn't see her face." She took a step forward. "Let's go over to the remembrance table one last time."

Paige grasped her mother's arm. "Mom, I think she deliberately knocked over the stand with Dad's ashes on it. Why would she do that?"

"I'm sure it was just an accident, Paige."

"If it was just an accident, why would she have run out of here like that?"

"She was probably embarrassed. Wouldn't you be?"

Paige didn't accept her mother's explanation for the incident but knew it would be pointless to discuss it with her any further. She led her to the remembrance table where more than a hundred pictures of her father were displayed—ones from his childhood, her parents' wedding, his army tour, Paige's childhood, golf outings, and family vacations—a visual tribute to him and his life. The commemorative display drummed up images of her father helping her with homework, supporting her through her difficult teen years, and walking her down the aisle at her wedding. A small, vacant place on the display marked the spot where a photo of her father holding Briana on his lap on her first birthday had originally been pinned. Paige had later removed it due to the uncompromising feelings it evoked with the reminder of her daughter's short life and eventual death. Now, she didn't know which was more painful to look at—this photo or the empty spot it had created by her removing it.

The table beneath the photo board displayed the many sales awards her father had won over the years. An expansive arrangement of purple irises, his favorite flower, adorned the center of the display. She found their subtle but sweet, fruity fragrance to be soothing.

Within a couple of hours, the chapel thinned out to a few remaining mourners.

"It went well, I think. Don't you?" she asked her mother.

"Mm-hm," she said as she swept a strand of Paige's curly auburn hair away from her forehead. "You have his eyes. I never knew what *he* was thinking either."

"You look troubled. What's wrong? Is it about that crazy woman who came in here?"

"No. I'm just thinking back to his funeral and what happened while we were here. It makes me not want to go home."

Paige's mother's house had been burglarized the previous month while Paige, her mother, and a few close friends had attended his funeral. Afterward, Paige had had a more sophisticated security system installed at her mother's home, and as an added precaution today had arranged for the local police to keep an eye on the house during the memorial service.

But Paige suspected there was something else her mother was still upset about regarding her father's private funeral. Her mother's estranged sister, Bernice, and Bernice's daughter, Wanda, had shown up…uninvited. Her mother had asked them to leave for reasons unknown to Paige. All Paige had heard of the conversation was her mother saying, "You know damn well the reason why." While she was dying to know what had caused the interminable rift between the two sisters, Paige knew this to be too sensitive a subject to bring up with her mother…ever.

"It won't happen again—the police are watching out for us," Paige said, referring to the break-in.

"I hope so."

"I'm still freaked out about the woman with the shawl on her head," Paige said. "Why would she do that?"

"I wouldn't worry about it. Like I said, she probably just bumped into it and got scared or embarrassed and left without saying anything."

"I don't know."

"When it's just you and me left, how about we go home and have a drink?"

"Good idea," Paige said, troubled by the woeful expression on her mother's face. "What are you thinking?" she asked.

"I don't know. The service stirs up so many memories."

Paige put her hand over her mother's. "Fond memories."

"Mm-hm."

Paige and her father often took the train to downtown Chicago to see live theater, go shopping on Michigan Avenue, or visit a museum—always followed by a fancy restaurant where they would talk about where they had been, what they had seen. She remembered one time when she was thirteen and they had shopped at Marshall Fields for a birthday present for her mother. Afterward, they went to the top of the Hancock Center for lunch. That day, they talked about her future—what she wanted to be when she grew up. Inspired by the panoramic view of the city from the top of the skyscraper, she had told her father she might want to work in real estate. Years later, she ended up doing just that.

"Someone from Dad's office asked me how long you two were married. Forty-three years, right?"

A flush crept across her mother's face.

"You okay?" Paige asked.

"It's been a long day, that's all."

"I sure do miss him."

"Me too," her mother said behind a pained smile. "I have to go to the restroom before we leave. I'll meet you back here."

Paige watched her mother walk toward the stairs, her flexed posture and deliberate stride jarring Paige with the realization that her mother could become more dependent on her as she aged. With little time to herself amid a hectic work schedule, Paige wasn't sure how that would play out.

She walked toward a small seating area to wait for her mother to return when a woman barged through the door, almost running into her, mumbling something about being too late. Paige watched her enter the chapel, then turn around and approach her.

"Everybody's gone?" the stranger asked.

Paige took stock of the woman. She was her own age or maybe a little older. Her outfit was casual, more so than what most people would wear to a memorial service.

"Just my mother and I are left. And you are?"

"I was looking for my sister," the woman said.

"This is the memorial service for Ryan West. Is that—"

"Yes, I know," she said as she headed toward the door.

Paige's mother joined her. "Who's that, dear?" she asked.

"Not sure."

Before leaving, the woman snatched one of Paige's father's memorial cards from the sign-in stand, glanced down at it for several seconds, then looked up. She stood there for a long, uncomfortable moment staring at Paige and her mother before leaving.

CHAPTER 2

"What do you mean he's dead?" Jessivel got up from the kitchen chair, almost knocking it over, the numbness in her chest giving way to rage.

Jessivel's mother, Crystal, a compact woman in her fifties almost a foot shorter than her, took a step backward. "Calm down, Jess," she said. "Give me a chance to explain."

"I think you just did," she said, rolling her neck in a manner she knew her mother hated. "Dad died last month, and you're just telling me now? What the—"

Jessivel's twelve-year-old daughter Kayla entered the room. "Mom, what's going on?" she asked.

"Nothing, sweetie. Go to your room and play."

"But I need to—"

"Go to your room!"

Kayla left the kitchen on the verge of tears. "And do what?"

"Anything. Do something with your hair," Jessivel shouted after her, her arms flailing. "It's a mess."

"You better get a grip on it," Jessivel's mother advised her. "She don't deserve that. You talk about Kayla's hair. Look at yours. And can't you ever wear something besides sweats and a t-shirt?"

Jessivel sat down hard on the kitchen chair. "Dad is gone," she said. "And you're ragging on me about what I'm wearing? How the hell can you be so calm?" She stared at the red, white, and blue Chicago Cubs mug sitting on the kitchen counter, the one her father always grabbed first for his morning coffee. "What's that thing doing out?" she said.

Her mother picked up the mug, swung open a cupboard door that was half off its hinges, and placed the mug inside. "I was shocked too when I first heard. But now… He's gone. We just have to accept it and go on from here." Her mother twisted her body away from Jessivel, one of her signature moves when she didn't want to show emotion. "You better tell Kayla."

"What do I tell her? How did he die? Where is he now? You haven't told me shit." Jessivel loosened the fist she hadn't even realized she'd made.

"I don't know exactly how he died, but both of us noticed he wasn't himself lately. Remember us talking about that?"

"Not himself and dead are two different things."

"And he had several doctor's appointments in the last month that he downplayed."

"He didn't look sick to me."

"We didn't see him for ten days. He could have gotten sicker during that time."

"How did you even find out about this?"

"I called his work when he didn't come home after his last trip and didn't return my calls. They put me through to Human Resources, and that's when I was told."

"So, some random person tells you Dad is dead, and you say 'Thanks, have a nice day'? They didn't call you when it happened? What's wrong with these people?"

"We talked, and she—"

"Where is he now? Who's planning the funeral? Who's his doctor? Let's call *him*."

"The funeral already happened, and I have no idea who his doctors were. He kept that to himself. He kept a lot of things—"

"How the fuck can you say this with a straight face? We're his family!"

"You watch your mouth." Her mother's eyes ping-ponged about the room as she talked, landing everywhere but in direct contact with Jessivel's. "I think there are some of those vanilla coffee beans left. Can you make a pot and add that flavored syrup you found?"

"How can you think about coffee at a time like this?"

"I'm trying to stay calm. And you're not helping matters. Are you going to make the coffee or not?"

Jessivel slammed her fist on the table. "No! Not until I get some answers."

The look on her mother's face told Jessivel she wasn't going to say anything more about her father's death, even though she was sure her mother was holding back. She had to have been.

Jessivel closed her eyes for a moment, inhaled deeply, and let out a long sigh before continuing the discussion. "Why didn't they call you right away? And why did you wait so long to tell me?"

"I just didn't…" Her mother sat down across from her. "I just didn't, that's all. You better tell Kayla."

"Where is he buried? Do you even know that? And who would have made the arrangements? Paid for it. We're his family. This is all so bogus. He may not even be dead! How do you know that for sure?"

Her mother attempted to smooth the wrinkles of her dress with the palms of her hands before responding. "I don't know. Maybe…"

Jessivel shot up from her chair. "This is crazy! And you don't even look concerned."

"Don't get that way with me, Jess. This isn't *my* fault. It isn't *anybody's* fault. He's gone. He didn't plan on it. He didn't die on purpose. It just is what it is."

Unable to think of anything more to say, Jessivel left the kitchen to seek out her daughter. She found her lying on the bed in her room.

"Kayla, honey, there's something I have to talk to you about." She looked past Kayla to the colorful walls that had been defaced with crayons and markers during various phases in her daughter's life, walls her father had recently said he'd repaint for her birthday.

"What are you and Nana fighting about now?" she asked, hugging a worn stuffed teddy bear.

"We're not fighting," Jessivel said as she sat down on the bed and put on her best game face. "Poppy is in heaven, sweetie."

"Why?"

"Because he got sick…and he died." Jessivel struggled to keep her emotions from showing on her face, not knowing where these feelings came from since the main thing her father had provided for them for as long as she could remember had come out of his wallet, not his heart.

"How?" Kayla asked.

"How what?"

"How did he die?"

"I don't know. We weren't told."

"When Katie's poppy died, she had to go to his funeral, and it was awful. She had to look at him while he was dead and everything. Will I have to do that?"

"No. You won't." Another thing that angered Jessivel—no funeral. This was her father, for God's sake. Her mother's husband. Well, not really. They were never married. But he had lived with them forever, so it was like they were married. They should have been the first to be notified.

"So, we'll never see him again?" Kayla asked as she fidgeted with her hair. "I thought he was just on another trip for work."

Her father's job had required him to travel to various construction sites around the country, and he was often absent for long intervals.

"That's right, Kayla. We'll never see him again." Jessivel shut her eyes while trying to quash confusion, resentment, and anger at the same time.

"So now you don't have a daddy either," Kayla said.

Jessivel had never told Kayla that Kayla's father, Jason, had vanished upon learning she was pregnant. She had lied instead and told Kayla he had died in a car accident before she was born.

Unable to contain her emotions, Jessivel jumped up, ran into her own bedroom, and slammed the door. She buried her face in her pillow before collapsing into a ball on her bed while she attempted to sort out her thoughts, the acrid smell of the pillowcase reminding her that it should have gone in the wash days earlier.

"Jess?" her mother said through the closed door.

"Go away."

"Come help with dinner."

"I'm not hungry. I need to be alone right now."

"Suit yourself, but no matter how you feel, you still have to eat."

"Later."

She got up and grabbed from atop the dresser the beat-up Care Bear her father had given her after she had threatened to run away when she was in the second grade. She took it back to the bed and curled up in a fetal position, eventually dozing off.

A knock on the door awakened her.

"I'm not hungry!"

"It's me, Mom," said Kayla.

Jessivel contemplated whether to respond.

"Can I come in?"

She caved, knowing she'd hear crap from her mother later if she didn't let Kayla in.

"C'mon in."

Kayla opened the door, sat on the edge of the bed, and stared at her.

"What?"

"When are you coming out?"

"When I feel like it."

"I think you better feel like it soon."

"Says who?"

"Says Nana."

"She's not the boss of me."

Kayla got up, put hands on her hips, and said, "Okay. Have it your way, but I know Nana, and I think you'd best be coming out of your room…like now."

"I'll come out when I'm good and ready."

Kayla stomped out, and before she disappeared around the corner, Jessivel's mother appeared.

"We can talk in here or at the kitchen table. Your choice."

"I'm grieving. Leave me alone."

"We need a plan."

"For what?"

"For how we're going to live. That's for what."

"Why? Like Dad didn't leave us with anything?"

"Right."

"Right what?"

"He didn't leave us with anything."

"Like he didn't have a will or something?"

"Not that I know of."

"This is so— Dad dies, we're not told anything, and now we're left out in the cold. We don't even know where his body is. How are we supposed to live?"

"That's my point. We need to support ourselves now."

"Just like that."

"Just like that."

"Well, you need to talk to the right people and find out what he left us or who inherited all his money when he died, instead of us. Something."

"I'm going on the assumption he didn't leave us anything. Let's start there. And don't you think it's about time you found a job anyway?"

Jessivel's mother worked part-time cleaning houses for a living, but Jessivel had managed to avoid work her entire life, using her pregnancy and then raising Kayla as excuses. Her mother had given up nagging her about it since they had always been able to make ends meet, and she liked having her daughter and granddaughter around.

Jessivel could feel the heat flushing through her body. "What?"

"You heard me. You need to get a job."

"Doing what?"

"Whatever you can. What I earn cleaning houses won't support me, let alone you and Kayla."

"Well, you won't find me cleaning up someone else's shit. Why would you—"

"There's nothing wrong with what I do, Jess—it's an honest way to make a living." She stood with her hands locked on her hips. "What are you going to do?"

"I don't know. What am I supposed to do? I don't have any skills. Who would hire me?" The thought of having to go to work scared her. "He must have had a will, Mom, or life insurance or something."

"Jess, we're on our own now. You need to get a job and support yourself. I couldn't support us in this house by myself even if I went full-time. Not even close."

"No way," she said, tossing back her hair. "I'm a stay-at-home mom."

"Not anymore, you're not."

"Why don't you want to fight for what's ours? It seems like you don't even care. Call a lawyer or something."

"Look, Jess. We were never married. There's no will to take care of us. And I can't afford a lawyer. I don't even have enough money for next month's rent."

"How can you get over this so fast? It's like you don't even care he's gone."

Her mother stood firm and responded in a purposeful voice. "Oh, I care he's gone, alright. For close to thirty years, that man took care of us, paid most of the bills. You bet I care. But he's gone now, and so is all the money. What am I supposed to do?"

"What about a checking account? Savings account?"

"I never had access to them. He handled all his money."

"So you have nothing."

"I have whatever's in my purse right now, and that ain't much."

"Are you kidding me? What are we going to do?"

"I just told you—you need to get a job. I'm going to look for something else too. Maybe find a job that includes room and board."

"Living in some mansion, cleaning up after rich people?"

"Whatever."

"Nice. Real nice, Mother. Well, I need to stay at home. Kayla can't come home from school to an empty house."

"Other kids do."

"Well, not my kid!"

"You look here, Jess. You have got to pull your own weight. How you do it is up to you. I'm going to start looking for another place to live because I can't afford to live here."

"And what am I supposed to do?"

"How many times do I have to say it?"

"This is insane. *You're* insane."

"It's time to grow up, Jess."

"*You* grow up. I'm not ready yet."

CHAPTER 3

"What was *that* look for?" Paige's mother asked when she witnessed the unfamiliar woman grab one of her late husband's memorial service cards.

"She came in all flustered, looking for her sister," Paige responded.

"Who's her sister?"

"No idea."

Her mother picked at an imperceptible fleck of something on the lapel of her suit. "Probably just some mistake on her part," she said.

But the incident bothered Paige, especially given the earlier mishap that had taken place inside the chapel. "Wait here a minute," she said. She walked out the door in time to see the woman in question driving rather erratically through the parking lot toward her. Paige waved her down.

The woman rolled down her window.

"Something seemed to surprise you back there. I'm curious what it was."

"Nothing. I just thought I'd find my sister here, at Wayne's memorial service. That's all."

"Wayne?"

"Did I say Wayne? Sorry, I meant Ryan."

"I see. Well, I'm sorry you—"

Before she could finish the sentence, the woman drove off.

Paige went back inside and repeated the conversation to her mother. "Does that name mean anything to you? Wayne?"

"Not a thing. Let's go home."

Paige drove to her mother's historic brownstone home in Lake View, an upscale neighborhood of Chicago where Paige had done most of her growing up. Paige led the way, opened the front door, and made sure everything was intact before summoning her mother to come inside.

"We shouldn't have to do this," her mother said.

"I know."

The police had convinced Paige the break-in had been an isolated incident, but that didn't keep her from worrying about her mother living alone. The list of missing items her mother had given to police was relatively short—two small flat-screen TVs, a hundred dollars cash, a bottle of Glenlivet scotch, and her father's diamond ring. The missing ring was particularly upsetting—he had worn it every day for as long as Paige could remember. She chuckled to herself while thinking about how she had been so impressed with the ring when she was a child. Not until adulthood had she realized how modest its carrot weight actually was. Still, the ring held sentimental value, and she was unnerved over its disappearance.

They talked about the memorial service over a glass of wine. After an hour, Paige got up to leave.

"Do you have to leave so soon?" her mother asked.

Paige knew that was coming.

"I have a company to run, Mom. I've got two big deals going on that could change things dramatically for my business."

Paige owned Castle Realtors, a successful real estate brokerage firm that she had bought after ten years of selling for them as an independent agent. The firm specialized in retail transactions but also handled commercial, industrial, and residential properties. She had grown the firm substantially since she had purchased it, primarily by having a keen sense of the ever-changing real estate market and the ability and forethought to tweak business strategies accordingly. The previous year, Castle Realtors had been recognized as the largest female-owned real estate brokerage firm in Chicago, a personal goal she had achieved a year ahead of her five-year plan.

"But you have staff to do everything, right?"

She had indeed an ample, capable staff, but that didn't keep her from being involved in the daily grind. "Yes, of course, but not—"

"How many satellite offices do you have now? Fifteen? Twenty?"

"Twelve." The offices were small with most of her agents working remotely.

"Enough to have the staff do the work."

"I'd like to think I play some role in the success of my company..."

"Why don't you stay a few days with me. I don't get to see you that often anymore."

Paige owned a home in Winnetka, a posh suburb less than a half hour north of her mother's home. She typically visited her parents—now just her mother—once a week.

She stared down at her shoes, a pair of black Louis Vuitton slingbacks she had just purchased. "I'll come back one day during the week, Wednesday maybe."

"You need to take off more time for yourself. You work too hard," her mother said, the words carrying more than just a whiff of disapproval.

"I'm fine, Mom."

"And you need to relax more. You remember what your father used to say. 'Slow down and enjoy life.'"

"Dad never said that, nor did he do that himself. What he used to say was 'Choose a job you love, and you will never have to work a day in your life.'"

A work schedule that often took up more than sixty hours a week bordered on insanity, she knew, but the work was something Paige excelled in, loved, and found necessary to maintain her status in the industry—and, to her thinking, be happy. Whether she was single because she was so immersed into building a successful company in a male-dominated industry or so into her career because she was single was a debate she had often had with "the girls" over a glass of wine or three.

"You work too hard. When are you going to slow down?"

"Never, I hope."

"Is that what you really want out of life?"

"Yes. That's what I really want."

"Whatever. Do you see my purse anywhere?" her mother asked.

"You didn't bring it with you this morning?"

"No."

"Where did you leave it?"

"Right here, where I always keep it, on this dining room chair…or so I thought."

"Maybe Natalie came after all."

Paige's younger sister had a history of stealing.

"Paige!" The tightness in her mother's expression told Paige she shouldn't have said it.

"Well, she's done it before. And she knows where the spare key is."

"After the funeral incident, I hid the key in a new place. And she wouldn't do that anyway."

"Did she not steal your wedding ring and pawn it?"

"We have no proof of that."

"C'mon, Mom, we both know she did."

At times, Paige agreed with her mother and stood behind Natalie, even when they knew she'd done wrong. Other times, she wasn't so forgiving.

"Call her then," her mother said. "Ask her about it."

"Like she's going to admit it."

"When something goes missing, you can't automatically assume Natalie had something to do with it."

Paige had initially assumed her sister had burglarized their mother's home the previous month. She thought differently only after Natalie's name was cleared by the police.

"Right. I'll keep that in mind," Paige said with an eye roll. "And chocolate milk comes from brown cows."

"Don't be absurd."

"Mm-hm."

"It's unfair to Nat."

"Mm-hm."

Her mother let out a shallow sigh. "I remember a time when you two were so close."

"That was before she became an addict."

"She needs medication because of the accident."

"I agreed with that…at first."

"And now she needs us, more than ever before."

"She needs money to buy alcohol and drugs more than ever before. And don't you give her any more. You're enabling her."

"She uses it for food and gas and other things."

"More chocolate milk ideology. She's a master at manipulation, and you know it." Something small and black sitting next to her mother's favorite living room chair caught Paige's eye. "Is that your purse, Mother?"

She glanced in the direction of Paige's pointing finger. "Oh, dear. I must have put it there and forgot," she said in a thin, transparent voice. "You'll come by Wednesday then?"

"Yes, I'll be here."

Paige drove home thinking about her sister. She felt bad for her—it had all started with a serious accident many years earlier when a car carrying a mother and her ten-year-old son ran a stop sign and t-boned Natalie, who had just left a bar after having had several drinks. Natalie had suffered severe spinal disc damage and subsequent unbearable pain. The oxycodone prescribed afterward, in Paige's opinion, not only numbed her physical pain but got her through the emotional pain as well—the little boy hadn't survived the collision. And while the accident was not deemed to be Natalie's fault, she had never gotten over the trauma of the boy's death and wondered if she hadn't been drinking that maybe the outcome would have been different. In time, she became addicted to the pain pills. Adding to the problem was her habit of drinking to excess. The combination created a vicious cycle of abuse.

Her mother had been right about happier times with Natalie. Less than three years apart in age, they *had* been close growing up, and Paige had enjoyed being Natalie's big sister. But those days had ended a long time ago.

Paige entered the Georgian-style home she had purchased five years earlier. The 3,000-square-foot house—complete with all the traditional architectural trims and arches, two fireplaces, and an indoor atrium—was too big for one person, but she had been drawn in by the coziness of it, lush gardens, and expansive patios. She had justified the extravagance by thinking of the resale value, if nothing else.

The first thing she did was check her voice-mail messages. There was just one.

"How dare you accuse me of stealing Mom's purse. Go to hell!"

CHAPTER 4

"We have to be out by the end of the month," Jessivel's mother told her a few days after informing her so casually of her father's death.

"Says who?" she asked.

"Says me. I can't pay the rent. I lost three customers this month, and money is really tight right now."

"Well, they're going to have to kick me out. I'm staying."

"Don't be a fool, Jess. You know you can't stay here. Don't wait to be evicted."

"Dad had to have stashed money somewhere. C'mon, Mom. He always had money to buy stuff," Jessivel said. "And what about life insurance?"

"Accept it, Jess. He's gone, and we have nothing."

"So where are you going?"

"I haven't figured that out yet. All I know is I can't—"

"I know. I know. You can't be there for me. You've said it enough times. Neither could Jason. Dad was the only one who was ever there for me." She turned her back on her mother. "And now even he bailed."

Two weeks later, Jessivel's mother informed her that she had landed a job as a live-in maid for the Perlmans, an older, presumably rich couple on the south side of Chicago. She told Jessivel that she planned to stay there until she could figure something else out.

Believing her mother would soon wake up and realize she needed to include her and Kayla in her plans—maybe when she discovered her father had left them something after all—Jessivel stayed in their home. When that didn't happen days later, she spent the better part of her time blaming her mother for abandoning her and breaking up their family.

Almost thirty years old and never having lived by herself, Jessivel wondered how anyone could expect her to make it on her own. She had come close to leaving home at sixteen when she had become pregnant and counted on her boyfriend Jason to take care of them. When that premise failed, she had reached out to his parents, but they were unsympathetic and unwilling to help, telling Jessivel that their son told them the child wasn't even his. Eventually, Jason and his parents moved, never to be heard from again. Jessivel's father's indifferent attitude on the matter and her mother's "you made your bed, now lie in it" philosophy only made matters worse.

"It's all your fault," she had said to her mother. "If you had told me about sex and having babies, this never would have happened."

Jessivel's rude awakening came when the police showed up at her door. They explained that if she didn't vacate the property, she would be charged with criminal trespass.

"You can't do that!" she told them. "Don't I get some kind of notice?"

"You're not on the lease, Miss. The landlord is within his rights. Make it easy on yourself and leave. That's our advice."

"But I have nowhere to go."

"Have you got a friend, a relative?"

"How long do I have?"

"Forty-eight hours if you don't want to be charged."

She replayed the scene repeatedly in her head until reality finally set in. Leave or get arrested. And then what would happen to Kayla? Not much of a choice. Now, being pushed into a situation she didn't want but was unable to escape, Jessivel couldn't envision her and Kayla's future.

When it came to friends, Jessivel had none. As soon as she had become pregnant and dropped out of school, her friends had dropped out of her life in turn. After Kayla was born, she tried reaching out to them, but without success. Their ambivalence caused her to lash out at them on social media, hindering the possibility of ever restoring the relationships.

Jessivel called Marcy, the former friend she had antagonized the least and the one she believed to be the most kindhearted. She asked if she and Kayla could hang with her and her family for a while until she could figure things out. Marcy agreed.

Jessivel sold some items on Craigslist that her mother had left behind and pocketed a few hundred dollars before moving out. She then loaded up her ten-year-old Honda Civic—paid for by her father but in her mother's name—and headed to the near north side of Chicago where Marcy lived.

Marcy arranged to have her girls sleep in the same room so Jessivel and Kayla could share a bedroom. Living with a twelve-year-old in a small room filled with all their belongings was worse than Jessivel had imagined. Marcy worked days, and her husband Kerry worked third shift, leaving little time when she and Kayla had the house to themselves. When home, Marcy was too busy with the kids and household chores to spend much time with Jessivel. Worse still, Kerry gave Jessivel a bad vibe, so when he was there, she and Kayla mostly kept to their room.

After they had been there for a week, Marcy took Jessivel aside.

"Um…Kerry wants to know how your job search is coming."

Jessivel—still holding out for her mother to come to the rescue even though the few conversations she'd had with her hadn't gone well— admitted that she hadn't made any attempt to find a job.

"I guess we figured you'd be working on getting your own place. And since you aren't looking for a job or anything, well, Kerry—"

"Wants us to leave?"

"You understand, with three kids and—"

"Fine."

"Well, don't be mad at me. We really tried to—"

"I know."

Feeling powerless to do anything else, Jessivel called 3-1-1 for help. Next, she loaded up her car with their belongings for the second time and drove herself and Kayla to a state-run women's shelter on the outskirts of Chicago where they were each given a bed, two meals a day, and a place to shower. The beds—cots would be a better description—were narrow and hard. Breakfast consisted mostly of Starbucks bakery goods that hadn't sold the day before. Dinner included items that had been donated by a local food depository.

Whether she wanted to or not, Jessivel got to know the shelter's other inhabitants through their public conversations with each other, most of whom weren't shy about telling their stories to anyone who would listen. She didn't seem to fit in, as most of the other women appeared to be ex-cons, addicts, abusees, and run-aways. Weekly AA meetings were held in one of the conference rooms, and therapeutic counseling for other issues was provided to those who wanted it. She and Kayla kept to themselves.

The main room in which everyone stayed was overcrowded and oozed a stench of alcohol that presumedly crept out of the pores of the women with drinking problems. Even though an off-duty policeman worked security there 24/7, Jessivel didn't feel safe given the amount of shouting and scuffling among the residents. Many spoke a foreign language, and so she didn't know what the arguments were about some of the time, but she soon learned that the f-bomb was recognizable and conveyed the same hostility regardless of dialect. The police and/or paramedics were frequently called to remove someone who was obviously high or otherwise causing trouble.

Rarely did Kayla sleep in her own bed, and she would visibly shake when anyone came too near to them. She asked multiple times per day when they were going to leave, a question for which Jessivel had no answer.

When it got close to the thirty-day limit for her stay at the shelter, Jessivel was told she would have to talk to someone from the Department of Child and Family Services the following week. Instead of waiting around for that discussion, she and Kayla left.

"Where are we going?" Kayla asked once they were in the car.

When Jessivel didn't respond, Kayla raised her voice.

"Mom, where are we going?"

"I don't know!"

"Don't yell at me. It's not my fault."

"You think it's *mine*?" Jessivel snapped back.

"Well, if—"

"Look Miss Twelve-year-old-who-thinks-she-knows-everything, we wouldn't be in this mess if it weren't for your grandparents. Everything was going just fine until he died, leaving us with nada. No notice, no nothing. And he had money, money we were entitled to. I know he did. And don't even get me started on Nana."

Jessivel had had several phone conversations with her mother while in the shelter, leading her mother to believe she was still living with Marcy. Thinking back, she realized it might have been better to tell her the truth about moving into the shelter—maybe then she would have felt more obligated to help them.

"Whatever. But I still want to know where we're going."

They continued the drive in silence until Jessivel pulled into the back of an all-night gas station and convenience store where she and Kayla spent the first night of their total independence—in the circumscribed space of Jessivel's car.

Well into the night, bone-weary, Jessivel was unable to fall asleep behind the steering wheel. She slouched down in the car seat, staring at a dumpster overflowing with garbage, several gluttonous grey pigeons blending in seamlessly with the asphalt beneath it, cooing to one another as they scrounged the pavement for scraps of food.

Jessivel was surprised at how little time it took to feel hopelessly alone—lost and unwanted—drained of any hope for something better.

CHAPTER 5

Paige entered Tracy's Backstreet Kitchen, located on the outskirts of Chicago's Hyde Park neighborhood, for the first time without her father. Two months had passed since his death, and even though she yearned to get back into a comfortable routine, one of the things she'd avoided since his death were the soup kitchens where they had volunteered, expecting that being there would stir up wistful memories of when he was alive and they had worked there together side by side.

More than just a soup kitchen, Tracy's offered classroom and hands-on cooking training for participants who wanted to better themselves and one day live independently. Those who wanted to work for their meals could tend the large garden in the back, weather permitting. Most impressively, Tracy's treated the less fortunate who walked through the door like restaurant patrons—they were greeted, seated, and waited on, the food served on nice dinnerware.

For some of the physically and spiritually hungry patrons within the community who patronized Tracy's, it was much like being at a big family gathering, the reunion atmosphere allowing people to chat, reconnect, and share stories. Some of them had been coming here for years.

This Wednesday started out no differently from others Paige had experienced with her father. She arrived in time to help with the early meal of the day and reviewed her assignment on the work-duty sheet posted in the kitchen. Today, she was one of the serving staff.

Her first table included two brothers—regular customers for as long as she had been working there—both quiet and reserved, almost shy, never ones to interact with the other patrons. She knew one brother to have been an electrical engineer in better days, the other a wounded Viet Nam veteran.

"How are you today, my friends?" she asked as she placed plates of meatloaf, corn, and mashed potatoes in front of them. When they didn't answer, she inquired as to what they wanted to drink. Still no answer.

"Coffee?"

She accepted their barely noticeable nods as a "yes."

Paige waited on table after table until her shift neared an end. Her last customer, a thirtyish woman whom Paige had not seen before, walked in with her head hung low. The greeter seated her in Paige's section.

"Hello. My name is Paige. What's yours?" she asked the woman.

Without lifting her head, the woman said, "Could I just get some food, please?"

"Of course," Paige said. Being destitute could make a person act in unexpected ways, and it was not unusual for patrons to avoid conversation, to be rude even. "I'll bring it right away. What would you like to drink?"

When the woman didn't respond, Paige told her the drink options.

"Water," she mumbled.

Paige served the woman her food and then busied herself in the kitchen for the next fifteen minutes. When she looked up, she caught sight of the woman talking to another volunteer through the service window.

"She said it's for her daughter," the volunteer said to Paige after fixing the woman a to-go box of food. "But who knows."

The week flew by, and before Paige knew it, TRACY'S appeared on her calendar again. She considered not going, as she was in the middle of implementing a new marketing strategy for her company, one that required a large chunk of her time and concentration. Competition in the real estate industry was fierce, and it took a fair amount of insight to even stay afloat, let alone quell the competition. Nonetheless, she put it all aside for the day—a commitment was a commitment.

When she arrived, the kitchen manager asked Paige if she would help unpack several boxes of donated food that had been delivered by a nearby grocery store that had gone out of business. The hours dragged as Paige emptied numerous cartons of canned and boxed food items, paper goods, and toiletries. Tracy decided to give a toothbrush and tube of toothpaste to each customer on this day until the supply ran out, and Paige welcomed the opportunity to do the handouts.

"Could you use either of these today?" Paige asked the woman she had served the prior week—the one who wouldn't look at her—as she held out the toothbrush and tube of toothpaste.

"No, thanks," the woman said without making eye contact. She hurried past Paige and out the door, but not before Paige caught a glimpse of a gold chain around her neck—something notable since most of the patrons did not wear nice jewelry. What she couldn't see was what was on the end of the chain that was heavy enough to pull it down to form a V.

Paige went back to the prep room after the last toothbrush had been given away and continued to help put away the donated merchandise. Tracy joined her.

"We miss your father," she said to Paige.

"Me too."

"I'm so glad you decided to continue here. I know how busy you are with your business."

"You couldn't keep me away. Coming here has actually changed me for the better." Paige's soup kitchen experience had stopped her from taking anything she had for granted and made her more self-conscious about wasting any resources. She knew that but for her parents and upbringing, she could be the one coming to Tracy's for a meal. Her volunteer work gave her a sense of purpose beyond her real estate business.

"I sent your mother a thank-you letter for the generous donation she made in his name, but I want to say 'thank you' to you as well. You know what I was thinking of doing with it?"

"No, what?"

"Creating an outdoor eating area, so in nice weather we can accommodate more people."

"I think he'd like that."

On the drive home, Paige reflected on her self-imposed busy life— her thriving business, prominence in the community, and reaching career goals—all the things she had planned and worked hard for since her divorce, things she associated with success and happiness.

She considered her married days, back to when she'd first discovered she was pregnant and the moment she'd told Leland about it.

Their marriage had been decent, but she'd hoped a baby would make it better. Based on his reaction to her pregnancy, Leland did too.

But their daughter, Briana, had been born with a congenital heart defect, and even though they had performed surgery on her at fourteen weeks that had saved her life, the doctors said she would not likely live past her first birthday. A stubborn child in every sense of the word, she made it to eighteen months. Paige's unavoidable postpartum hysterectomy meant no more children, and this added to the heartbreak.

Paige couldn't accept the way Leland dealt with their daughter's death, even after reading many articles on the subject. She had wanted to talk with him about what she had been feeling, wanted his support in her grief. But he kept his emotions bottled up inside, preferring to "get over it and move on." In time, while her husband's grief appeared to be decreasing, hers was on the rise.

The differences in how they grieved wasn't the only thing that pulled them apart. They had ostensibly become different people after their daughter's death and were in a marriage that no longer worked—finding it difficult to talk about things, to think things through together, and to come to terms with what had happened. They argued over the most trivial issues—whether to go out to eat or dine in, who left the patio door open, and who was supposed to have made a hotel reservation. Paige saw negatives in Leland that she had never seen before. Adding to their dysfunctional relationship, sex became nonexistent.

After having been married ten years, they divorced—only ten months following Briana's death.

CHAPTER 6

Jessivel struggled to stretch out her legs without interfering with the car's foot pedals, nightmares having disrupted the little sleep she managed to get the first night camped out in her car. A whiff of the previous night's fast food, whose rancid odor permeated the vehicle, caused her to crack open a window to allow fresh air to drift in.

Kayla awoke minutes later complaining about the cramped sleeping quarters. Part of the back seat, as well as the trunk and front passenger seat, served as storage space for their belongings, leaving little room for the two of them.

"Before you go on about our living arrangements, keep in mind this is temporary," Jessivel told her. "Nana's going to get us out of this…somehow."

"I have to go to the bathroom."

"So do I," Jessivel said as she glanced at the gas station in the middle of the parking lot. "I'll drive closer so we don't have to walk so far."

"Mom."

"Just do what I say. We'll get through this."

"Right."

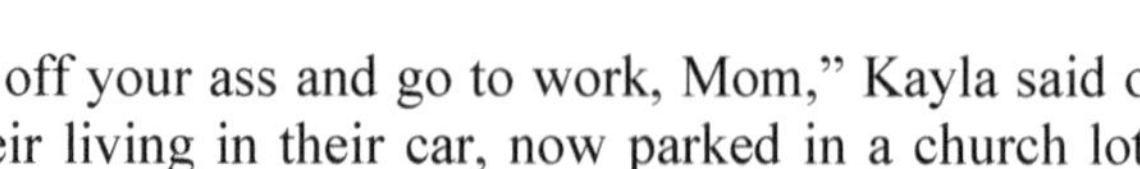

"You need to get off your ass and go to work, Mom," Kayla said on the second day of their living in their car, now parked in a church lot. She swiped at the tangled knots of hair that had formed in her sleep, which immediately fell back into her face.

"How dare you talk to me like that!"

"Well, somebody needs to. We can't keep living like this forever."

"I hate your grandfather right now."

"Nana seems to have figured out how to live."

"I hate her right now too."

"What are we going to do, Mom? What about school? Have you even enrolled me for this year?"

"I have no money for school, Kayla. And it's not only the registration fee. You need supplies, clothes, and who knows what else. I have no money for anything. Don't you get that?" Jessivel was aware that keeping Kayla out of school was illegal but clung to the notion that it was just temporary and she could make up the time.

"Get a job, Mom. Don't you get *that*? Nana's doing it, and she's got a place to live!"

"Cleaning up after people is all she knows. And it's not for me. Besides…"

"Besides what?"

"Nothing. I don't know. Stop grilling me!"

"Are you gonna go into that soup kitchen we passed by yesterday or what?"

"I said I would."

"When?"

"When they open."

"Well, I'm hungry now." Kayla opened the car door.

"Where do you think you're going?"

"Geez, Mom. I gotta pee."

Jessivel watched Kayla march toward the church. When she returned, Jessivel took her turn.

Once Jessivel was back in the car, she drove past the soup kitchen they'd previously seen, her fingers nervously drumming on the steering wheel. The line outside was long, and she couldn't picture herself standing in it with all these other people.

"Let's wait until the line goes down," she said to Kayla.

"Fine."

"I know you're mad at me, mad at the world probably, but I'm not in the best of moods either."

"But you can do something about it. I can't."

"You could help me by dropping the attitude."

"Right. As soon as we have a place to live and—"

"Fine. Don't help me then."

A few minutes later, when she had mustered the courage to go in, Jessivel got out of the car and headed toward the building. She knew that inside she'd see pathetic vagrants—people unable or unwilling to fend for themselves, people who up until now she had managed to keep in her peripheral vision.

Now she was one of them.

The next morning, Jessivel woke up tired and her daughter cranky. Daylight had just begun when Kayla bolted out of the car.

"Where are you going?" Jessivel shouted after her.

"I gotta go!" she said as she ran toward the church. When she emerged from the building, Kayla headed in the opposite direction of their car.

Jessivel rolled down her window. "Now where are you going?"

"Anywhere but here," she shouted.

Jessivel went after her, and when she caught up to her, she grabbed her by the arm.

"Get back in the car."

"I'm going for help!"

Kayla shook herself free from her mother's grip, but Jessivel was quick enough to get ahold of her again, this time by the back of her shirt. Kayla fought to get free, and in their struggle, the two of them fell to the ground.

"You're still my daughter, and until you turn eighteen, I can tell you what to do," Jessivel said as they wrestled. "Now, get up and get back into the fucking car."

"Let go of me, and I will!"

The two of them walked back to the car, where they sat in silence for several seconds.

Finally, Kayla broke down crying. "This sucks! You have to do something, Mom," she said, her voice tight with emotion.

The dense feeling that had been building in Jessivel's chest worsened. She squeezed her eyes shut and pictured her father's face—an

image she now despised. Jessivel's fist came down hard on the dashboard, causing Kayla to jump. "Damn him!" Jessivel shrieked.

The next morning, a painful cramp in her neck roused Jessivel from sleep. She attempted to rub it out with her fingers. "Hey, where's my necklace?" she yelped. "Where's my goddamn necklace?"

Kayla groaned. "Stop yelling, will you?"

Jessivel clutched her throat. She hadn't taken it off—her father's ring that hung on a chain around her neck—since he had given it to her weeks before he died. At the time, she didn't know why he had given it to her—a gold band with a small diamond mounted on it surrounded by four smaller diamonds, one he had worn every day. Now she understood that maybe when he was sick, knowing he was going to die, he had wanted her to have it to remember him by. Another convenient gesture of his giving her something material instead of his time.

"Put your seatbelt on," she screeched at Kayla.

"Where are we going now?"

"Never mind, just buckle up."

Jessivel drove to the back parking lot of the nearby Walmart, threw the car into park, and turned to face Kayla.

"Get out. I'm going to empty the car. The ring has got to be in here somewhere."

"Mom, get real. I'm not—"

"Get out of the damn car!" Jessivel shouted. She opened the door and started pulling things out one by one as she searched for the necklace. Clothes, empty food containers, and garbage bags filled with other miscellaneous items came flying out onto the pavement. When she had the front seat emptied, she started on the back seat where Kayla had been sleeping.

"Stop, Mom," her daughter said. "Calm down, for God's sake."

"I won't calm down until I find it. Get over here and help me look."

Kayla did as told, mumbling something under her breath that Jessivel didn't care to comprehend as her sole focus was on finding the ring.

"Keep looking! It's here somewhere."

Kayla stopped what she was doing. "When did you see it last, Mom? You're always fiddling with it. When do you remember touching it last?"

Jessivel stopped long enough to ponder Kayla's question. "In the church parking lot last night. I remember fingering it when we were parked there."

"Maybe it came off when you tackled me like a madwoman."

"Put all this stuff back in the car. We're going back there."

"Mom…"

"Move it!"

Jessivel drove over the speed limit through two neighborhoods until she reached the church where they had stayed the previous night. She parked the car and then ran to where she and Kayla had scuffled the day before. She paced back and forth, examining every inch of pavement.

"It's not here. Fuck!"

Kayla caught up with her. "Mom, this is a church."

"I don't give a—"

"Look! Over there." Kayla pointed to the right of where they stood, toward the bushes. "Is that your chain?"

Jessivel rushed to the item in question, picked it up, and hugged it to her chest. "Help me find the ring."

The two of them combed the area. No ring.

"It has to be here. Keep looking. I've got to find it."

"Maybe someone else found it and turned it in to the church."

"That's it. I'm going in there. You keep looking."

"Let *me* go. Please?" Kayla scrutinized the length of Jessivel's body. "You're a mess."

Jessivel gave in. It was hard to admit that lately her daughter had more common sense than she did.

Ten minutes later, Kayla emerged from the side door of the church with a somber expression on her face. "No one turned anything in, Mom."

Jessivel walked toward the car, wishing she could retreat inside herself so as not to have to deal with the loss. Her father had wanted her to have the ring. It was all she had left of him. It was all she had left of anything.

When they were settled back in the car, Jessivel drove back to Walmart and searched through the dumpster, hoping to find something not too disgusting for them to eat, feeling in the moment as discarded as the two pieces of rotting fruit lying on top of the garbage heap, the slimy residue on them glistening in the sun.

She returned to the car. The vibration caused by her slamming the car door shut made the dream catcher hanging from the rearview mirror sway back and forth. Jessivel stared at the swinging object, grabbed it, and stuffed it in the glove compartment. The dream catcher clearly wasn't doing its job.

The next day, Jessivel positioned herself first in line at Tracy's, waiting for them to open so she could use their shower facilities. She hadn't showered since her last day at the shelter, and washing up in Walmart's restroom wasn't cutting it.

Inside the shower room, Jessivel turned on the spigot and waited for the pipes to stop moaning before she found the perfect water pressure and temperature, her toes flinching as they touched the chilly ceramic floor. She closed her eyes and allowed the steady stream of warm water cascade down her body and massage muscles long past cramped, while the steam and heat soaked into her skin, melting away the tension.

When finished, she hastily dressed in order to trap the warmth between her skin and clothing. On her way out, she asked if she could have two plates of food to go.

CHAPTER 7

Paige watched the people who had lined up outside the soup kitchen file in and wait to be seated. Many of them, she assumed, were mentally unstable and unable to work to support themselves, but many others she thought were people who had fallen on hard times and needed temporary help. Most of them, she speculated, did not have stable housing nor money to purchase their own food. Tracy's and other similar facilities allowed them to be in survival mode, a grim situation at best.

She prepared a boxed meal for the woman she had seen here for the past several weeks. There was something about her that intrigued Paige, made her wonder about her story, which category she fell into. The hollow, unexplained feeling that bore into the pit of her stomach whenever she saw her confused her, making it difficult to get the words out as she spoke to her today.

"Here you go… What's your name, dear?"

Without making direct eye contact, the woman said, "Um…Margo."

Paige handed her the box. Her gaze went straight to the woman's neck—no necklace this time.

"Can I get a box for my daughter too?" the woman asked. "She's in the car."

Paige prepared a second box to go.

"How old is your daughter?" Paige asked when she handed the box to her.

The woman glanced up at Paige without answering her question and left. Something she saw in her eyes concerned her.

"Hard to tell who it's for," said Tracy, who stood within earshot. "Could be for her daughter, like she said, or it could be a second meal for herself for later, or maybe a friend."

"Sad either way."

"I saw that she used the shower room," Tracy said. "Excuse me while I go tidy it up."

As Paige finished up her shift, she couldn't stop thinking about Margo. She didn't have that seasoned, worn look about her that most of the other patrons had, and her clothes looked better than the majority of the other people who frequented Tracy's.

"Has she been coming in here for very long?" Paige asked Tracy in the food-prep area a little later. "The one who asked for the second boxed meal to go. She told me her name is Margo."

"No, she's fairly new. Comes in every day and then asks for an extra meal."

"Hmm."

"Why do you ask?"

"Just curious," said Paige. "She seems to stand apart from the other customers."

"I know what you mean, but sometimes it's hard to tell by someone's outward appearance what they're going through."

"I suppose. Hey, what's this?" Paige picked up a ring that was sitting on the ledge over the sink.

"Oh, I found it in the shower room," Tracy said. "Looks like a man's ring."

Paige stared at the ring in disbelief, then examined it more closely including inside the band. "This is my father's ring!" she said, catching her breath.

"Your father's? How could *that* be? I just found it today. Just a few minutes ago."

She showed Tracy the inscription, her father's initials.

"Well, I don't know how something of your father's could have gotten there. I sweep those rooms every day, the bathroom and the shower room, and I have a cleaning service come in once a week to scrub them down. Your father hasn't been here in how long? Over a month?"

"It's been over two months. He wore this ring every day."

"Did you see it after he died?"

"No, that's just it. We couldn't find it after my mother's home was broken into while we were at his funeral service. We assumed it had been stolen."

"Could you have put it in your pocket at some point, forgot about it, and now it dropped out of your pocket or something? Maybe it hadn't been stolen after all."

"No, I would have remembered doing that. And I obviously wasn't in the shower room today. Where exactly did you find it?"

"On the floor, under the bench, peeking out from under the common wall to the bathroom. There's a half-inch gap between that wall and the floor, so I think someone could have dropped it in either room the way it landed. Did you use the restroom today?"

"No."

"If it was between the two rooms, like you say, under the partition, could you or the cleaning people have missed it when you cleaned?"

"Not the cleaning people. They use a wet mop on the floor and it goes under the partition. I've watched them."

"What about when you sweep?"

"I suppose it's possible, but not very likely. I run a push broom along all the edges of each room before I sweep the middle. I'm pretty sure I would have come in contact with it on at least one side."

Paige's mind went straight to Margo—the only person she had seen use the shower room this day—before her thoughts froze.

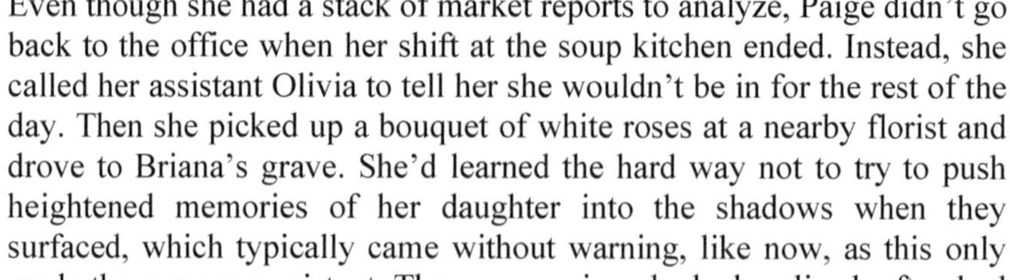

Even though she had a stack of market reports to analyze, Paige didn't go back to the office when her shift at the soup kitchen ended. Instead, she called her assistant Olivia to tell her she wouldn't be in for the rest of the day. Then she picked up a bouquet of white roses at a nearby florist and drove to Briana's grave. She'd learned the hard way not to try to push heightened memories of her daughter into the shadows when they surfaced, which typically came without warning, like now, as this only made them more persistent. These memories, she had realized, often had a life of their own.

The weather, always unpredictable this time of year, had suddenly turned cold. Paige turned up the collar of her Hermés jacket to keep the chill in the air off her neck as she walked toward her daughter's grave. She sat down with the flowers in her lap, ignoring the cold dampness of the bench.

Silence hung in the cemetery air until eventually broken by the melodious notes of a lone warbler. Seeing her daughter's headstone brought back a flood of emotions. Her heart swelled with an overwhelming sense of emptiness. She closed her eyes and allowed her mind to wander until she saw a vision of how Briana might look today as a pre-teen. When she opened her eyes, she uttered aloud her name, and despite her tears and broken heart, smiled.

Paige drove to her mother's house, feeling better for having made the visit. She found connecting with Briana's grave comforting, even though all it held were the decomposed remains of her little body.

Her mother's clenched jaw told Paige she was upset about something—most likely the number of days that had elapsed since her last visit.

"Everything okay?" Paige asked her.

"Yes. Fine. Everything's fine. Why wouldn't it be?"

"Just asking. You look like you're upset about something."

"How about you? I missed you last week," her mother said, changing the subject.

"I was here last week. On Monday, I think."

"Monday. Today's Wednesday."

"I would have come over Monday, but—"

"No problem," her mother said as she retreated to the kitchen.

Nine days instead of seven. *So shoot me.* She had been chin-deep in reviewing critical sales statistics for two days straight, but no use telling her mother this.

She followed her mother to the kitchen and, before sitting down in her usual chair, picked up a crumpled piece of paper next to the trash can. Just as she was about to toss it away, she recognized the handwriting as her father's.

"What's this?"

"That belongs in the trash. Give it to me."

Paige backed away from her mother and smoothed out the wrinkles on the paper so she could read the words. When her mother moved closer to try to grab the paper, Paige backed away even more.

She read the first two lines before her hand rose to her throat. "It's a letter from Dad. Why did you throw it away?"

"Give it to me, Paige."

"No. I want to read it."

Her mother stopped moving. "Go ahead then," she said in a weakened voice. "Read it."

Paige read it aloud.

My Dearest Elaine,I write this as my days are numbered. With any luck, you won't read it until I'm gone. Shows what a coward I really am.

Paige looked at her mother. "What's he talking about?"

Her mother sighed. "Keep reading."

I did the best I could to provide for you over the years, and I hope you've been reasonably happy. And while I admit to having told a long river of lies over the years, I'm not lying when I say I've always loved you. No matter what you learn after I'm gone, please never forget this. And that goes for Paige and Natalie too. You three have always been first and foremost in my heart.

Ah, the power of secrets. Maybe you'll never find out about the rest, and I will have written this letter for naught. But if you do, please forgive me.

Love,

Ryan

Her father calling himself a coward and asking for forgiveness for lying conflicted with everything Paige knew and felt about her father. A big, deep-voiced bear of a man, he had always been gentle, kind, and caring. It was he who had taught her the importance of honesty. She had looked up to him her whole life in part because of his integrity.

Paige glanced up from the letter and shook her head. "I don't get it."

"I don't either," her mother said unconvincingly, her expression unreadable. "Just toss it."

Paige read from the last paragraph. "'Maybe you'll never find out about the rest,' means you know something already. Why did you crumple it up?"

Her mom shrugged.

"Mom, what do you know?"

"Nothing. I know nothing." Her tone was confident, but an underlying uncertainty sent a different message. "Nothing for sure."

"Well, what do you know 'not for sure'?"

Her mother sat down and put her hands on the table, methodically folding one over the other.

"I'm not sure which lies he's talking about."

"Which ones? He told that many?"

"We all lie now and again. It's human nature."

Stunned by her mother's response, Paige asked, "What kind of lies?"

"I don't know, Paige. Little white ones, I suppose."

"Like what?"

"Like where's he's been. Mostly that, I guess."

"For his work?"

"There were times I knew he'd lied about being at work."

"How long was this going on?"

"Always, I guess, now that I think about it, but more so after you and Natalie left home."

"What makes you think he wasn't telling you the truth?"

"I don't know. A gut feeling. Sometimes you just know when someone is lying."

"Like he said he was in one city on business, and you thought he was somewhere else?"

"Something like that."

"Did you just find the note?"

She nodded. "In one of my dresser drawers."

"Well, let me add a little tidbit about Dad. I found his ring."

"Where?"

"At Tracy's."

"The soup kitchen?"

"Yep."

"What was it doing there? Did he take it off one day and leave it there?"

Paige told her mother about the strange woman Margo, and how Tracy had found the ring.

"You think this homeless woman had something to do with your father's ring?"

"I *know* she did."

"Paige, you said yourself that it was feasible that someone dropped the ring in the bathroom and it rolled toward the shower room wall. Slid underneath. It could have been anyone."

"No, I'm convinced it was her."

"You think she's the one who broke into the house and stole it?"

Paige shook her head. "I don't know, but I intend to find out."

"What about Natalie?" her mother asked.

"What about her?"

"Don't you think you owe her an apology?"

"I wouldn't if you hadn't gone and told her I suspected she took it."

"Makes no difference. She was so upset about it."

"Fine. I'll call her."

"And you might want to think this through, sweetie, trying to find out about the ring, that is. It could lead to something…well, that you don't want to know. Take it from me."

"You know me better than that, Mom. I can't let go of things I don't understand. And certainly not this. If she stole it, the police should be told about it. They'll investigate."

Her mother's grimace was telling.

"What's the matter?" Paige asked. "We need to find out the truth."

"That, my dear, is what I'm afraid of."

CHAPTER 8

Jessivel considered changing soup kitchens—they were getting to know her at Tracy's, and she didn't like it. She didn't like what it said about her—that she was either lazy, crazy, or couldn't afford to buy food for herself. But after thinking about it more, she decided the same thing could happen at any kitchen, and pretty soon she'd run out of places to eat. Besides, Tracy's was different—they seemed to care about the people who went there, which was a huge bonus on one hand, but also a double-edged sword. And they had a not-so-bad shower room.

That woman who said her name was Paige had shown an interest in her, always on a Wednesday. She seemed nice enough, but it was hard to tell where the "helping the needy" façade ended and the real person began. She didn't like her eyes. She couldn't tell what she was really thinking, which is why she had felt compelled to give her a fake name the previous week. The woman always asked how she and her daughter were getting along, and that was none of her business. She looked like she came from money—likely a rich woman trying to feel good about helping poor fools like her.

Still bummed about losing her father's ring, Jessivel had scoured the church parking lot twice since finding the chain, but with no luck. She was angry with Kayla—if she hadn't bolted like that, she wouldn't have lost the ring.

Today, having decided to stay with Tracy's for the time being, she went early to avoid the crowd. She went in alone as usual, not feeling comfortable bringing Kayla inside, as she had never seen a child in the place. She threatened Kayla that if she didn't stay in the car while she got their food, she would be in big trouble. Kayla, of course, resented this treatment.

To Jessivel's relief, a volunteer other than Paige greeted her at the door and showed her to a table. Someone else quickly served her a plate of turkey, stuffing, and green beans. When she was finished, she walked up to the service window, like she always did, and asked for a plate to go for Kayla.

A few feet from the car, she felt a tap on her shoulder. When she turned around, she stood face-to-face with Paige.

"Can I talk to you for a minute, Margo?"

"Why? What did I do?"

"Nothing. I just want to have a word with you."

Jessivel took a step back.

Paige took a step back herself. "I'm sorry. I didn't mean to startle you. Maybe we could sit for a minute…and talk?" She pointed to a nearby bench. "Over there, perhaps?"

"I have to get back to my daughter," Jessivel said before she turned toward her car.

"Please?"

Jessivel didn't want to talk to her—didn't want to deal with her beyond getting a free meal—but she knew that if she continued to come back for food, it would just be a matter of time before Paige said whatever it was she wanted to say. *Okay, let's get this over with.*

"Let me give this to my daughter first."

She opened the car door to a pouting Kayla. "Why do I always have to stay in the car?"

"Because… that's why."

"Who's that lady?"

"Just someone from inside. I'm going to talk to her while you eat, okay?"

"Why did she call you Margo?"

"Never mind. Eat your meal. And roll up this window."

"Fine."

Jessivel sat down on the bench as far from Paige as she could get.

"I was wondering if this looked familiar to you," Paige said, holding a ring in the palm of her hand.

The sight of it made Jessivel gasp. "Where did you find it?"

"The owner found it in the shower room after you left last Wednesday. I wondered if maybe you had dropped it."

Jessivel went to pluck the ring from Paige's palm, but Paige closed her hand before she could reach it.

"That's my ring. Give it back to me," Jessivel said, the tightness in her chest causing her to feel unsteady even in a seated position. "That ring belongs to me!"

"May I ask you where you got it from?"

"Why do you need to know that? It's mine."

"How long have you had it?"

Uncertain of where Paige was going with this line of questioning, Jessivel hesitated long enough to collect her thoughts. "Look, that's my ring. I lost it last week, and I want it back."

"This was my father's ring," Paige said, the change of pitch in her voice noticeable. "His initials are engraved on the inside."

"Bullshit. That's impossible. Now, give it to me." Jessivel grabbed the ring out of Paige's hand and ran to her car, not caring what Paige thought of her. Within seconds, she was accelerating down the street away from the soup kitchen.

"What was *that* all about?" Kayla asked as she clung to her box of half-eaten food.

"Nothing."

"Can you slow down? We're going to get into an accident. Who was that woman?"

"I told you, she works in the soup kitchen. And look! She found Poppy's ring." She held up her hand for Kayla to see.

"Where?"

"I must have dropped it when I was in there last week. Yes, that's it! When you and I were fighting in the parking lot, the chain broke, and the ring must have gotten stuck in my clothes somewhere. Then, when I undressed in the shower room, it fell out, but I didn't notice it."

"They have a shower in there?" Kayla asked, her eyes wide.

"It's not for kids."

"Why not?"

"It's just not."

"I'm tired of washing up at Walmart. They have a shower in there?"

"It won't be for much longer."

"I saw you grab the ring from that lady, you know."

"No, I didn't. She gave it to me."

"Didn't look like that to me."

"Well, that's the way it happened."

"Where are we sleeping tonight?"

"Walmart."

"I hate Walmart."

"Well, it's all we have for now."

"When is this going to end, Mom? We need a home."

"I know, sweetie. I know."

"Promise me we're going to find a home."

Jessivel didn't respond.

As she and Kayla bedded down for the night in the back of Walmart's parking lot, Jessivel tried to make sense of the conversation she'd had with Paige earlier in the day. She checked the inside of the ring for an engraving and found the initials RAW, not her father's initials WS. But it didn't make any difference—that ring had been her father's regardless of the engraving. She considered calling her mom, but discarded the idea, thinking it would be better to talk with her about the ring in person.

She couldn't quite figure out Paige and wondered if she might be a little "off." Like maybe when she saw the ring, for some weird reason, she made up the story about her own father. Or maybe the ring *had* belonged to Paige's father a long time ago, he'd lost it, and her father had found it. Or maybe Paige's father had pawned the ring, and her father had bought it.

While any number of things could explain it, none of them made perfect sense. And it looked like now, thanks to Paige, she had no choice but to change soup kitchens.

CHAPTER 9

Paige watched as Margo drove away, confident that she knew something more about the stolen ring than what she had said. But it was more than the ring that drew her to the woman—exactly what, she wasn't sure. She memorized her license plate number and then called her mother to tell her about the encounter.

"I wouldn't… Paige, I would forget about it if I were you. Let her have the ring."

"Aren't you curious how she got it? Maybe we could find the thugs who broke into your house."

"Perhaps she lost a ring that looked a lot like Ryan's. She was mistaken, that's all."

"Way too coincidental. I'm not giving up on this—there needs to be justice. That ring means a lot to me. He let me try it on when I was little. It's a piece of him I would want to keep near me for, well, forever."

"Forget about it, Paige. You said this woman was eating at the soup kitchen. That means she needs it way more than you. Did you hear about the new antique store that opened on Fourth Street? We should go in there sometime."

"You're changing the subject, Mom."

"I know. Someone had to. You're becoming obsessed with something so trivial that—"

"Well, it's not trivial to me, and I'm not going to have any peace of mind until I know how she got Dad's ring."

"Don't do anything you'll later regret."

"What do you mean by that?"

"I have to go, dear. Someone is calling me on the other line."

Her mother's unwillingness to discuss the matter only incited Paige to dig further.

It was no surprise when Margo didn't show up at Tracy's the following Wednesday. Paige asked Tracy if Margo had come in during the last few days.

"I haven't seen her, and I would remember it because she always asks for a meal to go. Why do you ask?"

"Have you noticed anything…different about her?"

"Not really. Why?"

"I don't know. Just wondering. I'm concerned about her. I got to know her a little and—"

"They come and go, Paige. We can only hope she got back on her feet and doesn't need our help anymore."

"I suppose."

With her new business model well under way, Paige turned her focus back to normal work issues but found that Margo was on her mind in between each meeting, phone call, and real estate deal. To maintain her sanity, she had to convince herself that curiosity and not obsession fueled her motivation to find out more about her.

A client of hers, a detective with the Chicago Police Department, was interested in buying a small storefront in the Washington Park neighborhood. She decided to give him a call.

"If I were to give you a license plate number, could you tell me anything about the owner of the car?"

"If you mean as a personal favor, I'm not supposed to. What are the circumstances?"

Paige explained the situation.

"What's the number? I'll see what I can find out for you."

She waited while he searched for the information.

"Here's what I can tell you. The car is registered to Crystal Kick, born March 30, 1967, no criminal history, no traffic violations."

"Do you have an address for her?"

He gave Paige the address.

"The house is owned by Walter Emery, who lives in Denver, Colorado."

"You would know if this car was stolen, right?"

"Only if someone reported it. Now, you can't tell anyone where you got this information, right?"

"Not a soul."

A birth year of 1967 didn't jive with Margo's appearance—she looked to be in her late twenties or early thirties, not fifties—so Paige ruled out that Margo was really Crystal Kick. Apparently, she was using a borrowed car. But who was Crystal Kick?

That evening, with the last glimmer of daylight lingering low in the sky, Paige drove to the address the detective had given her—a blue-collar, middle-class neighborhood on the near west side of Chicago. The house, a nicely maintained brick bungalow sandwiched between two other similar homes, had a FOR RENT sign out front.

She walked up to the door and rang the doorbell, not knowing exactly what she would say if anyone answered. She rang it a second time and waited a few minutes before turning to leave.

"If you're looking for Crystal, she moved," said an elderly woman sitting in a rocking chair on the porch next door. Bent over a large bowl in her lap, she appeared to be pinching off the ends of string beans, which she continued to focus on as she talked.

"Excuse me?"

"I said Crystal don't live there anymore."

"Do you happen to know where she moved?"

"Somewhere on the south side I heard, but her daughter and granddaughter are living out of their car somewhere." She shook her head. "Poor thing. Can't see bringing a child to live in some old car. Just not right."

"How unfortunate. Do you know where she keeps the car?"

The woman glanced up at Paige. "Who are you, Social Services?"

"Oh, no, I'm not. I'm…a friend."

"Nope. Don't know. Shame about the old man though. He wasn't that old."

Did he die?

"Old man?"

"Jess's father."

"Jess?"

"The daughter." The woman gave her a quizzical look. "I thought you said you were a friend."

"I am. I just didn't know… When was that?"

"When was what?"

"About Jess's father."

The woman shrugged. "I don't know when it happened. Haven't seen him around here for a while. But that ain't unusual." She peered at Paige over her spectacles. "Doesn't sound like you know these people."

"Yes, of course I do. They lived here for such a long time," Paige said on a whim.

"Longer than us, and we've been here twenty-one years."

"I never knew him. Only Jess and her mother. What did you say his name was?"

"Wayne. I don't know his last name." She lowered her voice. "I don't think they were married."

"Do you know if—"

"Katy!" a voice shouted from inside her house.

"What?" she yelled back.

"Com'ere."

"Gotta go." The woman looked up at Paige. "I hope you find them. That young child needs a real home."

As she walked back to her car, Paige pondered the name "Wayne" and didn't know why it nagged her so.

CHAPTER 10

Jessivel awoke to find her daughter bending over the front seat, staring at her. Kayla's messy hair covered much of her face, and the smell of her stale breath made Jessivel cringe.

"What's wrong?"

"Really, Mom? What isn't wrong? How long are we going to live like this?"

"I don't know."

"You should. You're the adult."

"Stop being such a nag. You sound like Nana," she said as she stretched out her arms and legs to relieve the unforgiving stiffness.

"Someone needs to. I'm hungry."

"We have to wait for the soup kitchen to open. What time is it?"

"Who knows? We don't even have a clock."

Jessivel glanced at her phone. "It's only eight o'clock. None of them open until ten. And I'm not going back to Tracy's. We'll have to find a new one."

Kayla wriggled in her seat. "I have to go to the bathroom."

"I'll drive closer, and we'll go into Walmart."

"I'm tired of having to go to the bathroom in Walmart," Kayla yawped. "They always stare at me when I leave without buying anything."

"Lower your voice, will you. This car is too small for yelling."

"This car is too small for *anything*."

"Look, I don't like it any better than you."

"Well, do something about it!"

"What do you want me to do?!"

"Find somewhere we can live. Get a job!"

"Who do you think you're talking to?"

"Someone who needs to get their shit together, that's who."

Jessivel ignored Kayla's language and disrespectful attitude. Instead, she broke down and sobbed, the stink of dirty clothes and leftover food in the car making her cry even harder.

The respectable, loving relationship she once had with her daughter was shattering before her eyes. She knew Kayla needed her now more than ever, but how could she give of herself when she had nothing to give? She was failing as a mother—a shameful offense.

The concept of trying to find a job terrified her. Who would hire someone with no work history? Could she make enough to support the two of them? And even if she miraculously found some crappy job, she'd be going in on the first day not knowing anyone, or how things are done, or who to talk to. What if they didn't like her? What if she wasn't good enough? And what if she messed up? What then? It all seemed so out of the question.

"I really have to pee, Mom. Like now."

"Can you walk there by yourself?" she said through her crying.

"Fine."

Jessivel tilted her head back on the stiff headrest and stared up at the ceiling of the car, without the energy to do much more than focus on the cracked lens cover of the yellowed dome light.

How did this get so screwed up?

She closed her eyes and allowed memories of better times fool her into a peaceful sleep.

The sound of someone rapping on the car window woke Jessivel with a start. The face of a female police officer peering in startled her even further.

"Wake up, Miss Salter," she said.

She shook off the grogginess from her short but deep nap. What would the police want with her? She wasn't doing anything wrong, was parked in a legitimate Walmart-customer parking place, minding her own business. When she sat up, she saw that the officer had Kayla by the arm. She rolled down her window.

"What's going on?" she asked.

"Your daughter was caught stealing, ma'am."

"Stealing? That can't be. My child has never stolen anything in her life."

"Well, she has now."

Jessivel glared at Kayla, who was hanging her head. "You stole something?"

Kayla shrugged.

"What?"

Kayla shrugged.

"What did you steal?"

"She stole some food," the officer told her.

"What?" Jessivel got out of the car and stood close to her daughter. "Are you kidding me?"

"She said you two were homeless."

"We are *not* homeless. We're just in between—"

"Mom, get real. We're homeless."

"Look," the officer said, "since the store called me, I have to follow through on this."

"What does that mean?"

"I have to take you both down to the station."

"Then what?"

"She'll likely be charged with a juvenile misdemeanor—retail theft—and released into your custody." The officer turned her back on Kayla and said in a quiet voice, "If it's her first offense, they'll go easy on her—counseling, probation, a stern warning. She's banned from this store, by the way. And Walmart can still sue if they want. I've never seen them do it, but they can."

"What about my car? I have to leave it here?"

"Can you call someone to come pick you up at the station to bring you back here?"

"No."

"If you need help—public assistance, housing, Medicaid, food stamps, whatever—there's someone at the station who can help you with that."

"We're fine."

"Okay, ma'am, but—"

"We're fine!"

"Can I give you some advice?"

Jessivel stared at her until she continued.

"Face whatever situation you're in. Accept help. Just don't let it define you, and you'll do fine." She paused, and when she didn't get any reaction from Jessivel, she continued. "I'll see if someone can drive you back here after you're done at the station."

Jessivel pondered the officer's advice. Did she even have kids of her own? Could she possibly know what Jessivel was going through?

The policewoman ushered them to her car. Once in the back seat, Jessivel took Kayla's wrist and squeezed it hard. Kayla winced.

"If you ever pull a stunt like that again," Jessivel said under her breath," I'll take you to the police station myself and leave you there."

"Good. At least I won't be sleeping in a car," she whispered back.

Jessivel squeezed her arm a little harder.

"You're hurting me!"

The policewoman glowered at them from the rearview mirror.

"Sorry, officer."

Jessivel dialed her mother's phone number. When she heard it go to voicemail, she threw her phone back into her purse. Waiting on dear Mrs. Perlman was obviously more important than picking up the phone to talk to her. Her mother either didn't care, or she was forcing Jessivel to handle things on her own. Either way, she didn't like her mother for it.

When they arrived at the station, Jessivel and Kayla were escorted to a small windowless room that reeked of cigarette smoke. A male officer joined the three of them. Following a brief discussion, Kayla admitted to the charges.

"Why did you do it, Kayla?" the policeman asked.

"I was hungry."

"When was the last time you ate?"

"Yesterday."

"What did you have?"

"Soup kitchen food."

"What does this have to do with the charges?" Jessivel asked. "She admitted to it. Why can't you just give Kayla her punishment and let us go?"

"It's not that easy, Miss Salter. Kayla is a minor, and right now we're concerned about her health and safety. Living out of your car and eating at soup kitchens may not be in her best interest. Is she in school?"

"Well, no, we haven't—"

"She has to be enrolled in school. That's the law."

"So what are you saying?"

"I'm saying one of two things needs to happen. Either I put you in touch with a representative from the Chicago Department of Family and Support Services and you follow their recommendations, or I call Child Protective Services."

"I am not going to—"

"I'm afraid those are your only two choices. Look, we're on your side. There are services in this city to help you, and it seems to me like you need help right now."

"I'll have you know that I lived my whole life in a nice home, with plenty of food on the table, and anything else I needed. I'm not some stupid person who can't live on their own."

"But you *are* homeless now, and I'm telling you that we can help you with that."

"What about Kayla? What about the charges against her?"

"She'll be charged with retail theft and have to appear in juvenile court for her arraignment."

"If you want to help so much, why not drop the charges? She won't do it again." She turned to Kayla. "Will you, sweetie?"

Kayla didn't respond.

"Once the store involves us, we can't drop the charges. That's up to the juvenile system judge. And to tell you the truth, I'm more concerned about her general welfare than these charges. Yours too."

The two officers arose from their chairs.

"Who should I call? CDFSS or CPS?"

"What's CDFSS again?"

"The Chicago Department of Family and Support Services."

"You're not giving me much of a choice."

"Which one?"

"The family one."

"Good choice."

CHAPTER 11

"Could you do another look-up for me, Gary?" Paige felt awkward about badgering her detective client, but she couldn't rest until she knew more about the woman taking up so much space in her thoughts.

"You'll owe me."

"I know. Can you see what you can find on Crystal Kick?"

"You want to hold while I do it?"

"Sure."

While retrieving the information, Gary passed the time by telling her his favorite cop jokes.

"Did you hear about the crime spree going on at our local IKEA?"

"No."

"The cops are having a hard time putting the pieces together."

Oh dear.

"You'll like this one. What do you call a snobbish, negative criminal walking down the stairs?"

"Do tell."

"A condescending con descending."

"Is that the last one?"

"I have more."

"Maybe some other time?"

Having to listen to Gary's corny jokes was a small price to pay for the information he was about to give her.

"Here it is. Crystal Kick. We already know she was born in 1967. In Chicago. I gave you her address. Married to Dillard Kick in 1985. Widowed in 1986. A daughter named Jessivel Salter born in 1988. No criminal background on Crystal. Previous employers include Merry Maids, McLean's, and KMB Cleaners."

"Previous employers. Nothing current?"

"The most recent was KMB—she left there in 1988. Almost thirty years ago. Since she's worked for cleaning service companies, she may also clean people's houses for cash. A lot of them do, and we wouldn't have a record of that. Oh, and her maiden name is Scott."

"But her daughter Jessivel's last name is Salter?"

"That's what it says. I suppose you want me to look her up too?"

"Could you?"

"This is really going to cost you."

"Dinner?"

"No, my girlfriend wouldn't go for that."

"Bring her along!"

"You don't know my girlfriend. You don't want to know my girlfriend. Here she is. Jessivel Salter. It appears to be the name she was given at birth."

"How could that be? Her mother's name is Crystal Kick and before that, Scott?"

"I'm just reading what I'm seeing. Born in 1988. Never married. No work history. No criminal record, just a string of traffic violations. Daughter Kayla Salter, born 2006. Now, *she* was recently arrested for shoplifting."

"Who?"

"The daughter, Kayla. Awaiting arraignment in juvenile court. Jessivel's address is the same as her mother's, Crystal Kick."

After they hung up, Paige reviewed her notes. She Googled KMB Cleaners—they cleaned commercial office buildings but were no longer in business. Crystal had stopped working for them the year Jessivel was born. So her husband died, and shortly afterward she got pregnant by some guy whose last name might be Salter. She reflected on her conversation with Crystal's former neighbor. Could the husband's name have been Wayne Salter? *Wait a minute!* Wayne was the man's name the woman in the funeral home parking lot had given her before she corrected herself. *What the—*

She called Gary.

"More background checks?"

"Please?"

"That property in Washington Park—get me a good deal on it."

"You have one of my best agents working on it, Gary, but I think the owner is holding at $399."

"You can do better than that. Pull out your big guns."

"I'll see what I can do. The name is Wayne Salter."

"Hold on. Hmm, nothing is coming up. Are you sure about the first name?"

"Kind of. I've never seen it in print, just someone saying it."

"I'll try a few different ones—Duane, Lane, Shayne. Nothing is coming up."

"Interesting."

"Nothing in the local database is coming up on Salter at all, except for Jessivel and Kayla, of course. Anything else, Paige?"

"What about in the not-so-local database?"

"I'll do the state of Illinois. Okay, three came up—Martha, June, and Emily."

"Can you tell by whatever you're looking at how old they are?"

"Martha is 76. June was born last year. And Emily is…looks like Emily died in 2001. She was 83. Will that do it for now?"

"Yes, and I don't know how to thank you."

"Negotiate that price down."

Paige hung up the phone more bewildered than before and determined to get to the bottom of how Margo came into possession of her father's ring. She called her mother and filled her in on what she had learned.

"Why are you even spending time on this, Paige? Don't you have better things to do?" She paused. "I've been thinking about buying a second home, somewhere warm year-round. Marina Del Rey maybe. Or Palm Springs. Can you put me in touch with a good realtor there?"

"Why are you thinking of doing this now?"

"Because your father would never go along with it when I wanted to, and now I can."

"You're changing the subject. You're good at that."

"Then you could go there too, to visit, get away from it all every once in a while. Meet new friends. Or maybe you'll go in on it with me?"

"What's wrong with my friends?"

"Nothing. I was thinking of male friends. Find yourself a man and start a new life. You're still young. You—"

"I don't need a man, Mother. I don't *want* a man. I'm very happy being single."

"I'm just trying to help you expand the scope of your life a bit."

"You're trying to get me to stop trying to figure out who broke into your house."

"Quit wasting your time…and mine. So, will you go in with me on the condo?"

"I don't know. I'll think about it."

But Paige didn't think about going in with her mother on buying a condo in sunny California. Instead, she focused on what she had learned from Gary. That, and the offhanded comment she'd made to her mother about not needing or wanting a man in her life.

———◇———

Paige's mother had to know something she didn't want Paige to know—otherwise, she wouldn't keep discouraging her from finding out about the break-in…or was it the ring? The ring seemed to be a trigger for her. Perhaps she was protecting Natalie from something again. She texted her friend Sandy and asked her if she was in the mood to meet for a drink. Minutes later, their other two friends, Valerie and Gayle, agreed to meet them later at Rigo's, a Mexican restaurant they often frequented.

"The girls" had been friends for a long time and were not shy about disclosing with each other everything that was going on in their lives. Sandy and her husband owned a downtown hair salon that catered to certain well-known Chicago figures…some upstanding and others not so much. Sandy had shared details for more than a few shady deals that had gone down there over the years. Valerie—married four times and now a fifty-five-year-old widow and the oldest in the group (but, thanks to a few plastic surgeries, looking every bit the youngest) was raising three grandchildren after her son and daughter-in-law were killed in a car accident when the youngest was just two years old. Gayle, Paige's former college roommate and a reasonably successful author of romance novels, was single and seriously looking. At forty-two, Paige was the youngest in the group.

This evening, they clinked their margarita glasses to good health before Paige breathlessly began her story.

"Sounds like a real mystery to me," Sandy said after hearing about the ring and the strange woman who claimed it. "What other clues do you have?"

"I wouldn't go there, Paige," Valerie said. "Let sleeping dogs lie, my mother always said. Just like what I'm doing with what I just learned about my dead daughter-in-law. Some things are best left alone."

"Tell me more about your father's ring," said Gayle. "Maybe he and this woman had a secret romance going on?"

"First of all, Gayle, I don't want to think that about my own father. You've written too many romance novels! And Val, I can't let it go. I must know. So what *did* you find out about your daughter-in-law?"

"For another time. Let's get back to you."

"Any other clues you can give us, Paige?" Sandy asked again. "You have to find out why she had the ring, but you've got so little to work with."

"I know. That's the problem."

"So why do you think your mother is being so secretive? Is this the first time she's acted this way?"

"Pretty much. Mom doesn't confide in me on everything, I'm sure, but I never knew her to keep significant secrets from me either."

"Sounds like she is now," said Sandy. "I'm excited about it. How can we meet this woman? Things at the shop have been so boring lately."

"Come to my house with two teenagers and an eleven-year-old who's madly in love with Ethan Wacker," said Valerie. "I promise you won't be bored."

"Ethan who?"

"Are you kidding me? The raddest boy on the face of the earth? Bernie on *Bizaardvark*?" Valerie said with dramatic flair.

"I don't think kids use *rad* anymore, Val."

"I was going to say *gnarly,* but I knew that was wrong."

"How about *bitchin'*? Can we still use that one?" asked Sandy.

"Only when you're feeling *dope*. And Paige?"

"What?"

"We missed you at our last two get-togethers."

"I had work conflicts."

"In the evening?"

"It's real estate. All hours of the day and night."

"You know what they say about all work and no play."

"Will only make you sad and gray?"

"You got it, girlfriend."

They parted ways, with Paige promising to keep them up to date on the Margo conundrum. She felt bad about missing out on seeing them the last two times, but when it came to sealing a deal versus having a few drinks with friends, she chose the deal every time. Who wouldn't?

Later, lying in bed that night, with a mid-summer night's deep rumble of thunder and driving rain beating down on the skylight in her bedroom, Paige replayed in her head what she knew about Margo.

Margo drove a car owned by Crystal Kick but wasn't connected with Crystal in any of Gary's searches. She claimed the ring to be hers—obviously, a lie—and that she had lost it. But why did she claim that instead of just saying she'd found it somewhere or that someone had given it to her? And then she had said that it couldn't have been Paige's father's initials engraved inside the ring. She had seemed so adamant, like she really believed it, not like something she had come up with in the spur of the moment during their conversation. It just didn't add up.

Paige recalled what she had learned about Crystal Kick. She gave birth to Jessivel Salter in 1988. A man going by the name Wayne Salter was presumably Jessivel's father, lived with them, and may have died—according to their neighbor—but Wayne Salter was nonexistent, according to Gary, at least in Illinois. So maybe he was linked to somewhere outside of Illinois. Did any of this pertain to Margo? She wished she had access to the same database Gary did so she could conduct her own research and stop pestering Gary.

Erratic thoughts and images wandered through Paige's head for a while until she glanced at the clock—three A.M. A distant train whistle penetrated the sound of the rain, instilling in her a brief sensation of melancholy. When the sound of the wind and rain weaving through the trees reminded her of a baby's frantic cries and prevented her from falling asleep, she finally gave up, turned on the bedside light, and started jotting down what she knew about Margo.

She wrote a few things down before tossing the paper and pen aside. The rain had stopped. She opened a window, and fresh air enveloped her in momentary calm—her favorite Rachmaninoff CD would do the rest. Lying back down, she concentrated on her breathing as the music filled the room, thinking about the busy day at the office that lay ahead with three new major listings to market.

Paige stared blankly at the ceiling, a soft flicker of moonlight streaming through the window bringing transitory comfort to her dazed frame of mind, until none of what she'd been agonizing over made any sense. She then closed her eyes and focused on relaxing her body like she'd been taught in yoga class years before, tensing each major muscle and then relaxing it until it became loose and limp. Entering a dreamlike state, she pulled in one more deep cleansing breath before drifting asleep, her last thought that there had to be connections between Margo, Crystal Kick, and her father—unfathomable as they may be.

CHAPTER 12

Jessivel dreaded meeting with CDFSS, the agency that dealt with wretched homeless people who couldn't fend for themselves. She wasn't *like* them.

She dropped Kayla off at the local library and drove to their offices where a frumpy middle-aged woman named Cassandra, whom Jessivel immediately disliked, greeted her. Cassandra led the way to a small, dreary conference room, void of any furniture or décor except for a table and four chairs.

"How are you today, Miss Salter?"

Jessivel didn't answer—too dumb of a question.

"Okay, let's talk about your living situation. I understand you need housing."

"Exactly where would this housing be?"

"We'll get to that, but first I need to ask you—"

"Because I'm not going to live in some dilapidated government housing. I'm used to—"

"Look, I'm trying to help you here. If you would just let me do my job, we'll get through this a lot faster."

"Fine."

Cassandra asked many questions, which Jessivel answered honestly, albeit reluctantly.

"Where is your daughter right now, Miss Salter? Is she in school?"

"Well, no. She's with… I mean she's at the library."

"By herself?"

"Of course not! There's always other people at a library."

"So she's not in school. She's at the library with whoever happens to be there this morning."

"She's in good hands. It's a library, for God's sake."

"Miss Salter, the library is a public place where anyone can go, those with good intentions and those with bad. It is not an acceptable place for an unsupervised twelve-year-old. Someone could take her, or she could leave on her own at any time. Right now, you have no idea if she's there or not."

"She wouldn't leave."

"You probably didn't think she'd steal anything either, but she did."

The woman stared at Jessivel for a prolonged moment without blinking, the impact of her gaze unsettling. "What are you afraid of, Jessivel?"

Feeling the conversation going down a path she didn't care to travel, Jessivel shifted in her chair as her pounding heartbeat grew loud in her ears. "I'm not afraid of anything, and I don't need anything from you or this stupid department." She got up to leave.

"You leave here, and CPS will get involved. That I can promise you."

"You can't take my daughter from me!" she shouted.

"It doesn't appear to me that her basic needs are being met—adequate food, shelter, supervision, schooling. Look, I'm mandated by the court to report this. And that's what I am prepared to do, unless you take advantage of the social services I can offer you. And this, by the way, includes job training so you can get out of this situation and support yourself and your family."

The woman's calm demeanor and precise word choices annoyed Jessivel further. "I can find a job on my own."

Cassandra gave her a guarded smile before saying, "Sit down."

Jessivel remained standing.

"Sit down!"

"Fine."

Cassandra leaned back in her chair and glared at her for an instant. "I broke my arm last year. My right arm. Couldn't do even the most basic things. If I hadn't been able to rely on my husband and children for help, I don't know what would have happened to me. I couldn't write, get dressed, cut my own meat, or even go to the bathroom without a struggle. Do you know how humiliating it was to have my husband help me go to the bathroom?" She paused. "We all need help at some point in our lives. And right now, you need it. The more receptive you are, the quicker you'll be able to be on your own. I don't want to see your daughter taken away from you—she needs you—but that's what will happen if you don't let me help you."

"Fine," Jessivel said in a tone she knew indicated otherwise.

Why it was so difficult for her to ask for and accept help, Jessivel hadn't a clue.

Jessivel wanted to break out of her situation, but not by taking a handout from social services and joining the ranks of pathetic welfare recipients. She decided to make a last-ditch effort to get her mother to move out of the Perlman palace and go back to living together as a family. She asked her mother if she could pick her up on her supposed day off and go out for breakfast.

"You look terrible," were the first words out of her mother's mouth when she entered Jessivel's car two days later. "And this car smells like…I don't know what."

"It's nice to see you too, Mom."

Her mother turned around toward the back seat.

"Where's Kayla?"

"I dropped her off at the library."

"By herself?"

Jessivel held back from lashing out at her mother, despite the pain grinding into her temples—pain she thought might make her head explode without some form of release.

"She's fine. There's a workshop she's attending—"

"A twelve-year-old needs better supervision than that."

"She's being supervised. She's fine. Really, Mom?"

"I never left you alone at that age. I would have—"

"She's not alone!"

"What's all this stuff back here?"

"Just some of our things that didn't—"

"You have to keep this stuff in your car? I thought you said Marcy had plenty of room for you two."

"I did. She does. It's just that—"

"You're still there, right?"

"I said I was."

Her mother took a closer look at the items in the back seat. "Tell me you're not living out of your car."

"Of course not."

"Then where are you living?"

"I told you, with Marcy and her family."

"How long are you going to be there? What have they said to you?"

"Would you stop with the third degree?"

"Calm down, Jess. And be careful! You're going over the yellow line."

Jessivel said nothing more until they were seated in the restaurant, where the pleasant aroma of fresh-baked bread helped to alleviate the tension that had built up inside her.

"We can't go on living like this. I want us to be a family again. I'm willing to get a job to help with living expenses."

"What's changed your tune?"

"I just said that I want us to be a family again. Live together, so Kayla has her nana back. She misses you."

"And what else?"

"What do you mean 'what else'?"

"You're living out of your car, aren't you?"

"No. We're—"

"Admit it, Jess. You and Kayla are living out of your damn car!"

Embarrassed by what the people at nearby tables might think, Jessivel asked her mother to lower her voice.

"Admit it," her mother whispered.

"It's temporary. I was hoping you would consider—"

"I don't have enough money saved up to put down a deposit on an apartment yet. I can't do anything right now. I'm in survival mode."

"What do you think I'm in?"

"There's one big difference."

"What's that?"

"I'm surviving."

CHAPTER 13

This day at the office should have flown by, given Paige's full agenda of working with her IT specialist on a website revamp, preparation for an Illinois Realtors board of directors meeting, plus consideration of a new satellite location in Streeterville. But her heart wasn't in it, and by four o'clock, she'd lost all ability to concentrate and canceled her last two appointments.

Thinking back to her suspicion about her father and Margo, she had a hard time picturing him as someone who was deceptive, doing unconscionable things behind their backs, and even more disturbing, having some kind of liaison with a woman half his age. In her mind, he was nothing but trustworthy, virtuous, and sincere, the man who would wake her up after returning home late from one of his business trips to give her some trinket he'd bought for her. The man who had given her horsey rides and read bedtime stories to her when she was little. Was there a side of him she hadn't known? She reflected on the tribute to his life at the memorial service. Had all those laudatory remarks been a sham? And her own eulogy—the accolades she had given him and the tears she had publicly shed for him. Had she been that ignorant? Had there been people in attendance who knew a different Ryan West than she?

Paige recalled being suspicious of her father once before following an incident she had never been able to get out of her mind. It had happened the summer following her senior year in high school. Paige and a few of her friends were coming home from the mall in the red Ford Mustang Paige had received from her parents as a graduation gift, when she spotted her father's car parked on a road adjacent to a park. It had been odd to see it there because she knew her father to be out of town, which meant his car would have been at the airport. But she was sure it was his vehicle due to a rather large dent on the driver's side door that hadn't been yet repaired. She drove around the block to see if she would spot him somewhere, but when her friends in the car became restless, she moved on. Days later, when he came home, she overheard him telling her mother all about his trip.

And then, of course, there was the crumpled-up note.

She considered sharing her suspicions with her mother, but it never seemed to be the right time. And there would likely never be a right time. She figured she had two choices—take her mother's advice and forget the whole thing or continue pursuing her father's indiscretions without her knowledge. The latter option felt far more satisfying.

Still conflicted about what to do, Paige drove to her mother's house to see if she could surreptitiously extract information from her. She practiced her spiel during the car ride—knowing her mother was not one to be easily fooled.

For the first half hour of their visit, Paige was upbeat as she tried to get her mother to talk about old times, especially her marriage. And to a point, her mother was receptive. But this didn't last very long.

"What are you up to, Paige?" her mother finally asked.

Unable to hide her ulterior motive any longer, Paige brought up all the little things her father had done or said that may have led to his having a secret life—vague explanations about his trips, missed family events, sudden changes in his schedule, things he said in the letter.

"A secret life? That's ridiculous," her mother said.

"He traveled so much, Mom. Did his job really require him to be gone that often and for long periods of time? And on weekends? And you said yourself that you didn't always know where he was."

"I didn't *have* to keep up with his schedule. If I needed him, he was a phone call away."

"And how did Margo end up with his ring?"

"It was stolen, remember?"

"We don't know that for sure. That's just when you noticed it missing."

"Maybe you should join your author friend in the fiction-writing business. You have quite the imagination."

"Where did he get that ring anyway?"

"I don't know. He wore it for as long as I can remember."

"Probably meant a lot to him then."

"He could have misplaced it, thought it would eventually show up."

"Then how would she have gotten hold of it?"

"I don't know! Stop with the ring already."

"And here's another thing. Remember that woman who came to Dad's memorial service looking for her sister?"

"Not really."

"It's just one more thing that makes me think... I'm going to get to the bottom of this."

"No, you're not," her mother said with more conviction than Paige had ever heard from her. "You're going to drop this nonsense. In fact, I forbid you to take this any further. Your father was a good provider. He was always here when we needed him. Let him rest in peace. And me too. Let me get on with my life without him. This hasn't been easy for me, you know."

"I know that."

"And what if you're wrong? What then? How many lives are you going to destroy? You have no proof to back up anything."

"Not yet. And I'm not going to destroy lives, Mother. That's being a bit melodramatic, don't you think?"

"I'm warning you—be prepared to ruin someone's life."

"And just how would I ruin someone's life?"

"Anything can happen when you start digging into someone's past. And what about me? Do you even care about what your snooping might do to me? Think about it, Paige. Bringing up painful memories only brings up pain."

"I'd want to know the truth, if I were you."

"Well, you're not me."

Paige drove home, and on the way she tried to understand the situation from her mother's perspective. She had been happy in life with her husband, at least it had appeared that way on the surface. He died, she was still grieving, didn't want to tarnish his name, and wanted to remember the good times. She got that. Surely, her mother's sensibilities had to be considered. But waiting until a more appropriate time to discover the truth seemed counterproductive. Yet, if she continued with her search and found nothing to corroborate her theory, then she and her mother could rest easy. She didn't believe the latter to be very realistic, but she had this to consider too.

Paige arrived home and checked in with her office before preparing a list of all the soup kitchens within a ten-mile radius. Then, she drove to each facility to see if she could spot Margo's car. Having had no luck with this undertaking, she retraced her steps and visited each one again just to make sure. Still nothing.

She sat in her car at the last soup kitchen thinking of ways to find Margo when her phone rang. The sellers had finally accepted Gary's offer for the Washington Park property. She called him.

"I knew you could do it," Gary said.

"Thanks to Melodi. She did all the negotiating. On another subject, how do you go about finding someone who doesn't want to be found?"

"There are ways. It depends. Who do you want to find?"

"Someone who is homeless."

"A family member?"

"No. Why?"

"It's easier when it's a family member because government agencies are more likely to offer assistance. So for you, it's just a matter of looking in the obvious places."

"Like?"

"Like churches, bus stations, shelters, community health centers, soup kitchens. Even college campuses and libraries. Under viaducts. Anywhere they can get food and shelter."

"That could take forever."

"Did they do anything to break the law?"

"Not that I know of."

"So we can't do a BOLO on them."

"BOLO?"

"Be on the lookout. Are they over twenty-one?"

"Yes."

"Then you can't force them to do anything. What do you want with them?"

"Just talk."

"Good luck."

"You can't help me with this, can you?"

"Officially, no."

"How about unofficially?"

"Do they have a car?"

"Yes."

"I can keep an eye out for the car. Is it by any chance the one registered to Crystal Kick?"

"Yes."

"When do I get possession of the storefront?"

"It's empty, so as soon as you close. The attorneys will work that out."

"See what you can do to speed it up, okay?"

"I'll do my best," Paige responded, knowing there was probably nothing she could do. "What are you going to do with this building anyway?"

"You ever heard of PAL?"

"No."

"The Police Activities League. LA started it, I think. Policemen get together with kids, usually in poorer neighborhoods, for a variety of activities. If we reach them early enough, we can make a difference in the community. It's what I want to do full-time when I retire."

"Nice."

Paige hung up with a new admiration for Gary.

On an exceedingly wild hunch, and to remove one specific outlandish notion from her mind once and for all, Paige drove to the address at which Jessivel and Crystal Kick had been living, hoping to see the same neighbor sitting on her porch. When she didn't, she parked her car and knocked on the neighbor's door. The same woman answered.

"Hello. You may not remember me. I was here a while back looking for—"

"I remember."

"May I show you something?"

"Sure. Go ahead."

Paige pulled from her purse a recent photo of her father and showed it to the woman. "Do you recognize the man in this photo?"

"Sure. That's Wayne from next door. I thought you said you didn't know him."

"You're sure."

"Looks just like him."

"Thank you." She wanted to keep the conversation going, but the impact of the woman's response kept her from delivering any more words. She turned and mindlessly walked down the front steps toward her car. Once inside, she sat for a long minute, staring straight ahead at nothing in particular.

That's Wayne from next door.

Paige drove home—a swarm of unconnected thoughts running through her mind. Once there, she poured herself a glass of wine, settled into her favorite chair, and attempted to pull it all together.

It didn't take long for enough of the puzzle pieces to fit for her to understand the essence of the picture, and while disconcerting, seeing the pieces come together was extremely satisfying.

CHAPTER 14

Jessivel and Kayla drove in silence to the west side of the city where she was to meet with the "HOW" representative, short for Housing Opportunities for Women. This being the third government do-gooder she was forced to reach out to, Jessivel felt like just one more loser being jerked around by the "social services system."

They scurried two long blocks from a remote parking spot through the depressed neighborhood and entered the storefront building under the guttural cooing of several pigeons that had congregated on the low roofline. Jessivel whisked Kayla through the door—the last thing she needed was having to go through this lousy ordeal with bird shit in her hair.

Jessivel flipped through the "Help is Here" brochure while they sat in the dismal waiting room. She tried not to focus on the dusty French fry lying under one of the folding chairs nor the crumpled up, fast-food sandwich wrapper next to it.

"You qualify for our FIT program," a woman named Phyllis Paredes told her in a room separate from where Kayla met with another counselor. "Families in Transition. I have an opening in Englewood, a two-bedroom apartment in the same block as an elementary school."

"Englewood? That has to be the worst neighborhood in Chicago!"

"Well, not quite. Anyway, I'll be the first to admit there are bad parts of Englewood, but we have found this building right by the school to be safe. I wouldn't send you and your daughter to an unsafe area."

"I'm not living in Englewood."

"That's the only opening we have right now for you."

"Well, I'm not going there."

The woman's pinched expression revealed her obvious annoyance with Jessivel. "What do *you* see as your options, Miss Salter?"

Jessivel stared at the woman before speaking. "There must be other places for me to live…temporarily."

"There are a number of shelters, but not for women with children."

"Well, you're wrong there, because Kayla and I were in a shelter together."

"You were at St. Mary's Family Safe Haven, a state-subsidized shelter where you had a maximum of thirty days to find more permanent residency. Do you have a job lined up?"

"No."

"When do you foresee getting one?"

"I have no idea."

"I can help you there too. We have counselors who will assess your skills, help you with a resumé, locate opportunities, and help you with the interview, clothing if you need it," she said in a matter-of-fact tone.

"Look, lady, I haven't worked outside of my home a frickin' day in my life. I have no skills. Who's going to hire me?"

"We help people like you every day of the week. Don't sell yourself short. In all likelihood, you have skills you don't even realize you have. That's another service we provide—job training. And as far as someone hiring you, we work with many companies who don't care what your background is. All they want is a reliable worker who can do the job."

"Fine," Jessivel responded. This woman had an answer for everything.

An hour later, Jessivel had three more appointments lined up—one of which was with someone about renting an apartment in Englewood, Chicago's murder capital from what Jessivel had heard. Reluctantly, she drove there with Kayla.

"Looks boring, but at least we'll be able to sleep in a bed," her daughter said when they arrived at the sprawling faded-red brick structure.

They walked together toward the stark building, void of any landscaping, careful to not trip on the crumbling sidewalk. The main door had a bullet hole in the lower right panel. *So much for the safe neighborhood, HOW lady.*

Once inside, they located the office where a young man greeted them. Shorter than Jessivel and fifty pounds lighter, he introduced himself as Hercules Popovich.

"I know. I know. You're wondering where I got my name," he said laughing.

She wasn't really. She just wanted to get this over with.

"My mother was obsessed with Kevin Sorbo before I was born."

Jessivel and Kayla stared at him.

"Kevin Sorbo…Hercules, the TV series."

"Sorry, don't know him."

"You have to look him up! What a dude."

What a dork.

"Could we just get on with the tour?"

Hercules explained details about the building and the neighborhood and continued his pitch while they rode a slow elevator to the fifteenth floor.

"It's one of the nicer buildings, and safe too," he said. "You won't have to worry about going to your car at night here. Well, I guess you have to be careful wherever you are, but not any more so here. And if I'm around, I don't mind walking girls to their cars."

He didn't appear to be capable of fending off much.

"We have a laundry room, vending machines, and a community room where we show family-oriented movies every night. I'll show you all this after we see the apartment."

Jessivel couldn't find too much wrong with the apartment—the rooms were small but clean.

"It comes furnished?"

"Yes. Kayla, would you like to see your bedroom?" he asked.

Kayla's face lit up. "Sure."

While Hercules showed Kayla the smaller of the two bedrooms, Jessivel scanned the apartment. She couldn't ask for anything more for the money—which was zero for the first three months. Feeling more trapped than comforted, a veil of numbness swept over as she stared out the narrow living room window that overlooked a parking lot. Several people were leaned up against cars, smoking cigarettes, frequently gesturing while they talked. She wondered if she would eventually become one of them—nothing more than some sorry-ass projects dweller, unable to escape the maze of poverty.

Still not over the fact that her father had left them nothing, Jessivel wondered now more than ever how she could find out what he was worth and who got it. He always had money to buy them things. And what about his car, his brand-new SUV? Who got that?

"He said we can move in right away, Mom," Kayla said upon entering the living room. "Can I have my old TV in my room again?"

"We'll see."

After he showed them the building amenities, Jessivel signed the contract: ninety days free rent and 30 percent of her adjusted income afterward. Then she and Kayla made several trips from the car to the apartment to transfer their belongings to their new home.

"What's the matter?" Kayla asked. "You look sad, but you should be happy. No more living in our car. Yea!"

"I'm happy, sweetie. Happy as shit."

"Hercules said Jennifer Hudson was born right here in Englewood."

"Well, goody for her."

That night, Jessivel lay on her new lumpy mattress between sheets she wished she had replaced with ones she had packed from her old bed. The dark brown stain on the ceiling forced her to think of several disgusting things that could have caused it. Despite this, her thoughts brought her back to happier times, when she was sixteen years old and lying in bed next to her boyfriend, Jason—cute, charming, and attentive Jason. She felt safe with him, proud to be seen with him, proud to be his girl. Then she got pregnant.

Jessivel had stupidly thought Jason would have been happy about the pregnancy, supportive. Instead, he had ghosted her as soon as he found out. For the next few months, she tried numerous times to get in touch with him. When she had finally reached his sister through social media, she told her that Jason was living with another girl who was also pregnant with his child. Jessivel asked how she could get in touch with him, but all his sister would tell her was that he was in a different state. Further attempts to reach him through his family failed.

Jessivel's parents had considered Jason a "bad-ass boy" and discouraged her from chasing him down, her father telling her that he'd take care of Jessivel and her baby. Ultimately, she succumbed to their wishes, but only after her attempts to reach Jason proved futile.

Jessivel had gone into a long slump after that, wallowing in the hurt and humiliation, too embarrassed at first to reconnect with her school friends who had moved on with their lives without her. Feeling alone, ashamed, and worried about what lie ahead for herself and a baby, she spent the better part of her pregnancy stowed away in her room. Looking back, she was sure she had been experiencing some level of clinical depression, although she had never been diagnosed or treated for it.

Now, under different circumstances, she felt just as low as she had back then.

CHAPTER 15

Paige drove to Tracy's Backstreet Kitchen marveling over her recent investigative accomplishment. "Margo" was actually Jessivel Salter. And Jessivel's father Wayne Salter and her own father Ryan West were one in the same. Sufficient time had now passed to allow this to sink in—she and Jessivel were half-sisters. And all or most of her father's long and frequent so-called business trips had likely been spent with his other family.

She walked in the door, checked out the day's schedule, and went to work. Tracy's was exceptionally busy this Wednesday, and she had a hard time concentrating on what she was doing given her recent revelation. Tracy pulled her aside after they had served dessert.

"Anything wrong, Paige? You don't seem yourself today."

Without divulging too many details, Paige explained that she desperately wanted to find the woman who called herself Margo.

"They come and they go, Paige. You've seen that over the years."

"I know, but I'd really like to help her. It's become personal."

"Our goal here is to feed people in need regardless of their circumstances, to view them as individuals and treat them with respect. But we can't go chasing after them to do it."

"I understand. But could you text me if she comes in here again?"

She hesitated. "I suppose I could do that."

Paige gave Tracy a hug. "Thanks."

"Be careful, hon."

While driving back to her office, Paige reflected on Jessivel's usual demeanor—quiet and self-conscious, but easily provoked. And she had an unfriendly and ungrateful attitude about her that she found puzzling. Made her wonder how two people raised by one same parent, in this case their father, could be so different. Not unlike she and Natalie, now that she thought about it, and they had been raised by *two* same parents.

She considered confronting her mother again now that she had more information. She wanted her mother to know her father had been leading a double life. She wanted her mother to know the truth.

Olivia greeted Paige at her office door with a pained expression on her face.

"We need to talk," Olivia said as she followed Paige into her office.

"What's up?"

"It's your mother. She's in the hospital."

"Why? What happened?"

"I don't know much because they wouldn't tell me anything, not being related and all. But your mother gave them this number to call, and, well, I didn't want to call you on your cell, in case you were driving or something. Anyway, I hope I did the right thing by—"

"Of course, you did. What hospital?"

"Midwest."

"I'm on my way," Paige said as she darted out the door.

Once in the car, she called the hospital.

"My name is Paige West. What can you tell me about my mother, Elaine West? How is she?"

"I'll connect you to a nurses' station."

Paige repeated her query to the nurse.

"She's in serious but stable condition. We can tell you more in person."

"Okay. I'm twenty minutes away."

Paige couldn't imagine what had happened to her mother. Her health was good, and her checkups had always gone well—some arthritis in her back, high blood pressure for which she took medication, other normal aches and pains for someone her age. Nothing ever serious.

Once at the hospital, Paige rushed to the Emergency Room and inquired about her mother's condition. She was asked to wait for a doctor.

She stared out the window at the sizable parking lot as a train of rampant thoughts roared through her head. She wasn't ready to lose her mother, who had just turned sixty-four, so close to her father's passing. It just wasn't fair.

"Miss West?" the relatively young man in blue scrubs asked as he approached her.

She stood up. "Yes."

He led her into a private area.

"Your mother is stable."

"Can I see her?"

"Yes. I don't see why not."

"What happened?"

"Apparently, she was experiencing chest pains and shortness of breath and called 9-1-1. The paramedics found her vital signs to be unstable and brought her here. She has what we call hemodynamic instability, the long way of saying erratic blood pressure."

"They told me on the phone that she was in serious condition."

"Serious in that her vital signs are still unstable. Hemodynamic instability doesn't happen on its own—something caused it. That's what we're trying to figure out."

"What are your initial thoughts, doctor?"

"We haven't ruled out heart attack yet. Many signs are pointing in that direction. And if that's what it was, it was fairly mild."

"Heart attack? I never—"

"She's in good hands, I assure you. We'll figure it out and treat her accordingly. Would you like to see her now?"

Paige followed the doctor to a small cell inside the Emergency Room. When he pulled back the curtain, the smell of disinfectant overwhelmed her, and the sight of her frail-looking mother hooked up to numerous cables and machines made her gasp. She touched her mother's arm on the only surface that didn't have something connected to it.

"Mom?"

Her mother scrunched up her face as if in pain.

"Are you okay?" Paige asked.

Her mother nodded.

"Can you open your eyes?"

Her mother strained to open them.

"I'm fine, dear. Just a little indigestion."

"Well, I think it may be a little more than that, Mom. They have to figure it out."

"Not to worry about me, sweetheart. How was your day?"

"Not important. We need to focus on you right now."

A smile tugged at the corner of her mother's mouth. "Look what it takes to get you to come visit me."

"That's not funny, Mother."

"Wasn't meant to be. Your father died in this hospital."

"Yes, I know. But let's not—"

"Room 229."

"I know, but—"

"I told them not to put me in Room 229."

"Good thinking."

A nurse walked in to check on her. She introduced herself to Paige and, with a twinkle in her eye, softly said, "Your mother has been very clear with us on what she expects while she's here."

"I'm sure she has."

"That's okay—shows spunk. We like spunk."

Despite her tiny frame, her mother generally had a huge presence wherever she went.

"Good, 'cause *that's* what you'll get."

Paige left the room as soon as her mother appeared to have drifted asleep, touching base with the nurses' station on her way out to give them her cell phone number.

She drove back to the office via a longer route than necessary to allow time to process this new turn of events. The more she thought about losing her mother, the more somber she felt.

Intellectually, Paige knew that everyone had a finite amount of time in this world. But emotionally, she was frightened by the prospect of being alone. First losing her daughter, followed by her divorce, then losing her father, now Mom. Paige prided herself on being positive and disciplined when it came to the business of real estate, but she could not say the same when it came to matters of the heart.

She tried to release the thought of losing her mother in favor of something else, anything else, but to no avail.

CHAPTER 16

"You don't know what it's like to be in my shoes," Jessivel said to Kayla a few days after they had moved into their new apartment. "And stop being so damned judgmental. Poppy provided for us our whole lives, and then that stopped without any notice. It's not fair, so quit blasting me for something that isn't my fault."

Jessivel didn't feel comfortable in the new neighborhood and didn't care much for living on the fifteenth floor of a massive building, like shelter animals stacked in cages. And the furniture that came with the apartment, while functional, wasn't great, not like the furniture that had come with the house she and her parents had rented.

She had ninety days to come to terms with an occupation that hopefully she didn't hate, get training, find a stupid job, and start paying rent—a daunting list for someone who had relied on others her whole life.

"It doesn't matter whose fault it was, Mom. *You* have to take responsibility for it now. Today is now. Don't you get that?"

"Look, no twelve-year-old is going to give me advice on what I'm supposed to do, so shut the hell up. I have enough people bossing me around."

That afternoon, she had a meeting with a CDFSS counselor to discuss her skill set, a meeting she was not looking forward to. At least it would be short, she thought to herself. There was nothing to talk about.

"I have no skills," she told the middle-aged woman as they sat across from each other in a small, windowless room. The nameplate on the desk read SOFIA FLORES.

"Yes, you do. You just don't know it yet."

They discussed what Jessivel had been doing for the past several years, her likes and dislikes, and her personality traits. Then the woman told her she had a job in mind for her.

"A barista? What the hell is that?" Jessivel asked.

"It's something you know a lot about already."

"I don't even know what it is, lady. You just wasted an hour of both our times." She rose to get up.

"Sit down," the woman said, her fixed expression telling Jessivel she meant business. "First of all, my name isn't 'lady.' It's Mrs. Flores. You may call me Sofia if you like. And secondly, I don't appreciate you not at least hearing me out before you so rudely get up to leave." She leaned in toward Jessivel, her eyes narrowed. "Something I don't think you understand even a little is that we're here to help you. And if you'd get rid of that big chip you have planted on your shoulder, maybe you'd realize that."

Jessivel sat back down with a thump. "Go on."

"And I don't appreciate the eye roll either."

"Sorry."

"You told me you like experimenting with coffees, that your father would bring home different kinds of beans he'd find when traveling for his work. And you would blend different ones together, add flavorings, experiment. You mentioned using a Moka pot, something I had never heard of. Perhaps I read between the lines, but it seems as though you enjoyed doing this."

"So?"

"What do you think a barista does?"

"I have no clue."

"They make specialty coffees."

"Like in Starbucks?"

"Yes and no. They make specialty coffees, but you have more knowledge than that kind of job requires. I'm thinking beyond that. But here's the thing. While you have excellent coffee knowledge, you have a long way to go when it comes to customer service skills. I'm going to be brutally honest with you. You have a look—like the one you're giving me right now—that you don't like me and don't want to be here. When you wait on customers, you must portray a person who is there to, and more importantly, *wants* to help them. You're there to make their day better. It's part of good customer service."

"Humph."

"You have a sandpaper exterior and an unhealthy mindset, Jessivel, but I know that's not what's on the inside." She leaned back in her chair and faintly smiled. "Do you know what it means to create meaning for yourself?"

Jessivel shook her head, not wanting to know what it meant.

Sofia pointed to a sign hanging on her wall.

LIFE ISN'T ABOUT FINDING YOURSELF.
LIFE IS ABOUT CREATING YOURSELF.

"George Bernard Shaw said it, but that's not important. What he was getting at is that your life shouldn't be decided by someone else or some outside circumstances." She paused and looked past Jessivel for a few seconds. "Think of yourself going through life in a small boat on a river. You can let the river decide where you're going, or you can direct the boat to where you want it to go. It's up to you."

That is the stupidest thing I've ever heard.

"I can read your facial expression, and I see you're not on board with this. But I'm here to tell you that life should be about discovering what you're capable of and evolving into the person you aspire to be, rather than waiting for someone or something else to decide for you and then settling for it. Do you get that?"

"Sort of."

"Whether you realize it or not, every choice you make shapes you into who you are. It's up to you to decide to face the things you're unhappy with in your life and either accept them or change them. And most things in life can be changed."

"So it's *my* fault I am where I am today. That's what you're really saying."

"I never used the word 'fault.' You weren't listening. Jessivel, I'm willing to work with you on this." She leaned forward and focused with intent into Jessivel's eyes. "I do this for a living, and I know what it takes to turn things around. I can put you in touch with hundreds of success stories if you want. But first, you need to decide whether you are willing to do this for yourself. And more importantly, are you willing to do this for your daughter?"

"A barista."

"It would be a solid job doing something you love. With your subsidized housing, you could easily support yourself and Kayla."

"Dealing with a bunch of people who know nothing about coffee."

"See, this is where you need to change your way of thinking. That mindset of yours is a critical weakness for you. Think of it as you'd be helping people who would benefit from your knowledge of coffee. Do you think you could do that?"

Jessivel shrugged. She doubted it.

"You would just need some coaching on how to approach people, how to support them in their decision as to what coffee they want. Good customer service is vital to the store owner."

"Right. The store owner. The rich store owner. Be friendly, polite, and smile at the a-hole customers so he can make money."

"There goes that attitude again. Look, the owner making money is part of it—they're certainly not in the business to lose money. But there's more to it than that. I know the owner of The Busy Bean in Lincoln Park. Extremely nice woman. And talk about a success story. Audrey grew up in extreme poverty, in a gang-infested neighborhood on the west side, where it isn't safe to sit on your own front porch and you risk your life waiting at a bus stop. She grew up scared but determined to break the vicious cycle that had plagued her family for generations. Her first job was at a chicken processing plant. Can you imagine what it's like to work all day on an assembly line in an unairconditioned factory, expected to break down scores of slaughtered, defeathered chickens a minute, with the stench of chlorine and ammonia so thick in the air that it's hard to breathe?"

"No, I can't."

"She did this for four years, until she had enough money saved to move her and her mother out of that neighborhood and eventually start the coffee shop business."

The chicken story got to her.

"The Busy Bean would be the perfect place for you to work—she's always experimenting with coffees. But I couldn't present you the way you are. We'd have work to do. What do you say? And don't say 'yes' unless you're going to buy into it all the way. Don't waste my time."

Jessivel took a moment for reality to set in.

"Lincoln Park?"

"You said you have a car, right?"

"It's a long drive."

"What do you consider a long commute?"

"It would take me twenty minutes to drive there, and then where would I park?"

Sofia shot her a disapproving look.

"Okay, I'm in," Jessivel mumbled.

"Could you show any less enthusiasm?"

"It's going to take a while for me to get used to this."

"You can do it, Jessivel. I know you can. I have faith in you—more than you have in yourself right now."

Jessivel hadn't been prepared for being put in her place by the likes of a social services counselor. But she had been, and while it was not easy to take, she had to admit that it was almost gratifying to have someone stand up to her. She also hadn't been prepared to like anything she had to offer. But if she was honest with herself, the idea of being a barista was somewhat interesting—if only she didn't have to deal with people she knew she wasn't going to like. That part terrified her. Sofia had referred to things like point-of-sale systems, inventory management, and teamwork. So many scary concepts.

She had ninety days to prepare for being the sole supporter of herself and Kayla. That in itself was a terrifying concept, but not even close to having to work in a chicken processing plant.

CHAPTER 17

Paige drove from the hospital back to her office, assured that her mother was in good hands though she couldn't wrap her mind around a heart attack. She knew of no one in her family who had ever had heart trouble.

Once in her office, after an hour of unsuccessfully trying to reconcile the current month's dip in operating cash flow, she logged into the company's central database and electronically earmarked a raft of new listings she needed to review, and then headed home.

She thought more of her mother's lifestyle as she sat at a red traffic light—her relatively healthy eating habits, a good sleep routine, and physical exercise—when the blasting car horn behind her snapped her back to reality. She glanced in the rearview mirror to see who was being so impatient and was shocked to see Jessivel behind the wheel in the car behind her.

Paige released her foot from the brake pedal, but before she stepped on the gas, she changed her mind and swiftly put it back on the brake. The maneuver caused Jessivel's car to rear-end her with an ugly-sounding impact, making Paige's body jerk forward, but luckily not with enough force to cause the airbag to inflate.

Paige put her car in park and proceeded to open the door. But as soon as she did, Jessivel backed up, pulled away, and sped down the street.

Paige slammed her door shut and took off after her.

The two women made numerous left and right turns down dozens of narrow side streets, blowing most of the stop signs, until they wound up at a dead end not big enough to make a quick turnaround. Paige had Jessivel trapped.

They stayed in their respective cars glaring at each other for several seconds. Jessivel, wide-eyed and red-faced, appeared to be screaming something at her. Paige cracked her window and caught a few words.

"You stupid bitch. Leave me the hell alone."

Paige slipped the gear into reverse but kept her foot on the brake while she vacillated between confronting Jessivel and fleeing the scene. In business, it would be a no-brainer—she never backed down from confrontation—she was wired for it. But when it came to personal matters, she tended to respond in the opposite way.

Paige could feel her heart rate increase, and her entire body went tense. Continuing with this confrontation would only make her feel worse...physically. But if she backed down now, it would in all likelihood hinder her search for the truth. Or even worse, completely end it.

As soon as she was able to focus on the payoff of a confrontation, Paige was able to assuage her initial weak-kneed reaction. At least, she hoped. She put the car in park just as Jessivel jumped out of her car and barreled toward her.

"What the hell do you think you're doing?" she shouted, standing less than three feet from Paige's car door, her arms flailing. "Are you crazy or something?"

Paige rolled down her window a bit more, trying to appear calm on the outside. "You hit me back there," she said. "Why did you run off like that?"

"I barely touched you, and you're the one who caused it. I doubt if there's even a dent on your fancy car."

"Well, you didn't give me much of a chance to check it out."

Jessivel inched closer to Paige's car, causing Paige to fear what the woman was capable of doing. She considered her surroundings—no visible sign of another human being within shouting distance.

"I checked. There's no damage," Jessivel said through clenched teeth, her facial muscles noticeably tight.

"How could you have checked? You've been standing here the whole time."

Jessivel swiped at Paige's car window with an open hand, a combative gesture that caused Paige to recoil.

"I saw there was no damage right after it happened, stupid," Jessivel said. "Now move your damn car so I can get out of here."

"Can we talk?" Paige finally asked, suddenly having the wherewithal to do what she thought would defray the hostility of the situation.

"We just did."

"I mean about your father. I have some information you might find useful."

"You know nothing about my father! Now, move your damn car and let me out of here before I call the police." When she grabbed the door handle, Paige instinctively clicked on the "lock doors" button inside her car to ensure her safety.

"C'mon, there's no reason to call the police. And keep in mind that if you do, and they hear you hit me from behind, you'll likely be the one to get a ticket."

"And I'll tell them you've been stalking me!" she said with her hands on her hips. "You're really crazy, you know that?"

"I've been trying to talk to you, that's all."

"Don't you get it? I don't want to talk to you. We have nothing in common. Nothing to talk about. You annoy me. Now back up your rich-ass car and let me out of here."

Paige stared into her eyes for a brief moment before reaching into her purse and pulling out the photo of her father. She rolled her window all the way down and, undeterred by the tremor in her hand, showed it to her.

Jessivel's body appeared to freeze in place when she saw it.

"Now can we talk?" Paige asked.

CHAPTER 18

Jessivel walked around Paige's car at a slow, deliberate pace before she opened the passenger door. Then she slid partway into the seat, one foot remaining outside of the car, firmly set on the ground. "What are you doing with a picture of my father?" she asked without looking at Paige, her rage subsided from a moment earlier. When she didn't get an immediate response, she turned toward her.

Paige met Jessivel's gaze and stared into her eyes longer than was comfortable. "Jessivel..." She paused, taking a hard, obvious swallow. "He's my father too."

She had never told Paige her real first name. A heaviness expanded within Jessivel's chest in the space of seconds, rendering her speechless. She gulped down a swig of air to relieve the knot that had tightened in her throat.

"That's bullshit."

"His real name is Ryan West. He was married to my mother for forty-three years when he died in May."

"It's not the same man," she said with determination. "He lived with *us* my whole life."

"Was he there every day?" Paige asked.

"No, he traveled in his work."

"A lot?"

"Yes...a lot."

"Sometimes for a week at a time?"

Random thoughts swirled through Jessivel's head, thoughts that had nothing to do with the subject at hand—leftovers in her fridge, the heartbreaking episode of *Grey's Anatomy* she had watched the previous night, Kayla's math homework. "Yeah," she finally said. "Sometimes even longer."

"Same here." Her eyebrows squeezed together, almost becoming one. "As hard as it is to say this, it looks to me as though our father was leading two lives. Was he married to your mother?"

"No…but it was like he was. We were a fam—" She stopped talking when her voice cracked.

"I know. Same here. I never would have dreamed he had even cheated on my mother, let alone lived with another woman at the same time. As far as I knew him, he was a good man."

"Everyone has a twin. So…maybe the two men just looked alike. Or maybe they were real twins. That's it. They could have been twins."

"And his ring? How do you explain that?"

Jessivel reached up to clasp the ring through the fabric of her blouse. "I don't want to hear any more of your crap," she said, her hand still on the door handle. Her mind told her to go, but her body froze.

"I understand your reaction to this, Jessivel. Believe me, I do. Can you at least take my phone number and call me when you're ready to discuss it further?"

Jessivel turned toward Paige and snapped, "Why? You've said your piece. Story over."

"Don't you want to know more? Aren't you curious as to how he pulled this off?" She paused. "It appears we're half-sisters. Couldn't we get to know each other a little?"

Now with both legs out of the car, Jessivel turned toward Paige.

"No…to all three."

Jessivel exited Paige's car and got into her own. She waited for Paige to back up and drove off.

She hated Paige. They couldn't possibly be sisters. That fancy hairdo and clothes and car and her know-it-all attitude. She rolled her window all the way down to let the wind brush against her face, breathing in the sweet aroma of a nearby chocolate factory. How dare that woman butt into her personal life, especially now when she was at an all-time low, struggling to keep a roof over her and Kayla's head. *Who does she think*

she is? And what was her deal anyway? What did she want? She wasn't reaching out to her from the goodness of her heart. She had to be looking for some kind of payoff. And it couldn't be money. That was the scary part.

It was all some big mistake. It had to be.

Now that she was receiving food stamps, she didn't have to go to soup kitchens anymore and run the risk of running into her—that was a relief. She didn't have to go anywhere these days, for that matter. Except for the grocery store. And barista classes. She'd enrolled in a five-day course at the Chicago Barista Academy, paid for by Audrey Russo, owner of The Busy Bean. Apparently, Mrs. Flores had done one helluva sell job on her.

When Jessivel arrived home, she called her mother and asked if they could meet somewhere after she got off work.

"I never 'get off work,'" her mother said. "I'm on call here around the clock."

"No time off? What kind of slave drivers are they?"

"The kind that provide a place for me to live, that's what kind. What is it you want to talk about?"

"Dad."

"There's nothing to talk about, Jess."

"Yes, there is. I just found out—"

"Gotta go. I'll call you later."

"But—"

Her mother had already hung up.

"Where were you?" Kayla asked as she entered Jessivel's bedroom. "How long can it take to pick up something for dinner? What did you get?"

Jessivel had forgotten all about the reason she'd been out and about.

"Sorry. I forgot."

"Forgot what?"

"Dinner."

"How could you forget? Where were you all this time?"

"Never mind! Leave me alone."

"Geez, what a grouch," Kayla muttered on her way out.

The pre-teen attitude and smart mouth were unbearable. Jessivel had enough on her mind without that. And as far as her mother, what was she hiding?

Paige had stuffed something into Jessivel's purse. She hoped it was the supposed photo of her father so she could study it, recognize his shirt or something. She grabbed her purse. The photo wasn't there but Paige's business card was. OWNER, CASTLE REALTORS. *How nice.* One sister owns her own company. The other is going to barista school so she can wait on rich people…rich people like her sister.

Perfect. Just perfect.

CHAPTER 19

"You need a better social life, Paige. You can't work *all* the time. What happened to all your friends?" her mother asked from her hospital bed on one of Paige's daily visits. Her mother had undergone numerous tests before being diagnosed with a pulmonary embolism and put on blood thinners. Her condition remained serious but stable.

"I *have* friends. I was just with Sandy, Gayle, and Valerie for dinner last weekend. I do okay."

Most days, her mother didn't talk much—often complaining of fatigue and light-headedness. So as much as Paige wanted to pump her for more information about her father, she knew it would upset her, so she didn't, figuring her blood pressure was erratic enough. Consequently, on these visits, Paige gave her mother updates on work and her social life, such as it was.

"You need a man."

"No one really *needs* a man, Mom."

"One day, you'll realize I'm right. And it doesn't matter that you can't have children. You can have a happy marriage without children, you know."

"I know, Mom."

On the sixth day of her mother's hospitalization, her condition worsened. It happened while Paige was in her room when she witnessed a bluish tint permeate her mother's face accompanied by a noticeable shortness of breath. Paige rang for the nurse, who appeared so quickly that Paige figured she must have seen something going wrong from the nurses' station monitor as well. More hospital staff arrived. They ushered

Paige out of the room and transported her mother to the ICU while Paige waited nearby.

Paige fidgeted in the waiting room chair, adjusting the settings on her phone, catching up on Facebook postings, her attention snapping at every sound and movement in the immediate area. After what felt like too long of a time, the doctor came out to talk to her.

"Your mother has developed epiglottitis, a fancy word for inflammation of the tissue that covers her windpipe. We have her on a breathing tube, humidified oxygen, and antibiotics."

"How serious is it?"

"It's treatable. We'll want to keep looking for any sign of infection—that can complicate things."

"Can I see her?"

"Let's give her some time for her vitals to come down a bit. Then you can see her."

An hour passed before a nurse came out to tell Paige she could see her mother.

Even though she had been warned about the breathing tube, still she was taken aback by the bulky apparatus covering her mother's nose and mouth. She approached her bed and peered down at her.

"How are you doing, Mom?"

Her mother looked up at her and rolled her eyes. She held the briefest of smiles, just enough to accentuate the deep lines around her mouth.

"Can I get you anything?"

Her mother pointed to the door.

"I'm not sure what you mean."

Her mother's first words appeared to get caught in her throat.

"I wish I could help you, but—"

When her mother mimed writing something down, Paige pulled out a pen and pad from her purse.

Home, she wrote.

"I'm afraid you're going to be here for a while."

Her mother let out an impatient snort. *Dead plants,* she wrote.

"What plants? Your houseplants?"

Her mother nodded.

"They need watering?"

She nodded a second time.

"Can the cleaning lady water them?"

She shook her head.

"Okay. I'll go water them then. I'll take in your mail, too. Anything else I can do while I'm there?"

My will, she wrote, then looked up at Paige, the emptiness in her eyes disquieting.

"Mother, you're not dying," Paige said with no conviction.

Her mother's look signaled she needed to say no more and do as told.

Paige felt uneasy being alone in her mother's house. Even with her permission, it seemed like she was invading her mother's privacy, sneaking around behind her back.

She walked through each room with an increased awareness of her mother's possessions as she watered the houseplants, observing her belongings as if she were there for the first time. Her mother's penchant for neatness and classic taste in home décor made her house looked staged, ready to be put on the market. Paige stopped to inspect things as she went from houseplant to houseplant, opened drawers and cabinets, and peeked under things. Her curiosity didn't stop until she had examined every room in the house, even those without houseplants in them.

One thing surprised her—none of her father's personal belongings was in sight. Her mother had either discarded them, gave them away, or hid them somewhere. Paige wondered what she would have done under similar circumstances—keep certain things around for sentimental reasons or get rid of all the distressing reminders. Her mother hadn't asked her if she wanted anything of her father's, and that bothered her. She hoped her mother had just stashed everything away until she was emotionally ready to deal with it.

The more she reflected on the request from her mother to bring her will, the more Paige questioned it—she and Natalie were her only heirs. Sure, some distant relatives existed out there, but no one her mother had kept in touch with except for weddings, funerals, and the annual Christmas-card exchange. And then there was her mother's sister and niece with whom she had no relationship.

She went to her mother's desk where she thought she'd find the will and, in the process of looking for it, found a savings account book. She opened the faded front cover and saw the account was in her mother's name and had a balance of slightly over $20,000, the only deposit of $50,000 dating back to before Paige was born. A dozen or so withdrawals ranging from one to five thousand dollars had been made during the last fifteen years.

After a short hunt, Paige located the will in another drawer. Her mother hadn't told her *not* to look at it, so she did. A quick glance proved nothing out of the ordinary. She put it in her purse and took one last look around the front room before watering the last plant, locking up the house, and proceeding to the hospital.

When Paige entered the ICU, she was happy to see her mother wearing a less cumbersome breathing apparatus—one that covered her nose but not her mouth.

"Feeling better?" she asked.

"Have my plants been watered?"

"Yes."

"Did you bring my will?"

"Yes."

"Then I'm feeling better."

Paige handed her the will.

"No, you keep it. Keep it until I'm in a regular room. I can't do anything with it while I'm in here."

She wants to alter it?

"Okay," Paige responded. Had her mother finally come to her senses about Natalie's addictions, enough to place conditions on her share of the inheritance?

They chatted a while until a nurse came in and told Paige that they were going to take her mother down to the lab for more tests.

"I'm going to go now," she told her mother. "Do you need anything? Anything else from home?"

"The cleaning lady comes on Tuesdays, nine o'clock or so. Can you let her in?"

"Sure, Mom," Paige said, despite knowing of an important meeting with her accountant that had been scheduled for that time. She leaned over her mother and kissed her forehead. "Love you." That was something they didn't normally say to each other. Not because they didn't love each other. Because they just never said it. Her mother didn't offer a reciprocal response, which was neither surprising nor upsetting. Still, Paige was glad she had said it.

On her way home, Paige wracked her brain trying to figure out how her mother might change her will. The current wording indicated that she and Natalie were the sole heirs. She considered the other components covered in her will. She had no debt, so that wouldn't be an issue. It stated that her assets would be evenly distributed between her and Natalie. Her mom wanted a simple funeral. And Paige had been named the executor. She couldn't imagine any of this changing. She figured it must have something to do with Natalie.

Paige spotted the blinking light on her answering machine as soon as she walked in the door. Only two people other than annoying marketers ever called her on her landline—her mom and Natalie.

"You won't let my plants die after I'm gone, will you, dear?"

CHAPTER 20

Jessivel called her mother for the third time in as many days, this time insisting on seeing her.

"Meet me on the patio in the back," her mother told her. "Mrs. Perlman doesn't like outsiders in the house."

"Are you kidding me?"

"Just do it, Jess."

She found her mother on the patio when she arrived.

"Maybe we should meet behind the pool house where no one can see us," Jessivel quipped. "Behind that clump of trees over there."

"Don't be smart."

The one-story contemporary house wrapped itself around a large kidney-shaped pool—complete with a waterfall—the water a tranquil shade of aqua that shimmered under the strong sun. The pool house on the far side of it was larger than their old house.

Jessivel joined her mother at the table adjacent to an expansive outdoor kitchen. The cushioned swivel lounge chair she plopped herself into was more comfortable and likely more expensive than any piece of furniture her family had ever owned. She placed her knock-off Coach purse on the glass tabletop next to a shallow porcelain bowl of colorful succulents.

"If you want to talk about what I think you want to talk about, save your breath," her mother said in a hushed tone. "He's dead. Let's move on."

"Why won't you talk about him? What are you afraid of? What are you hiding?"

"I'm not hiding anything. You seem to want to dig up dirt about—And let me remind you that he took care of us ever since you were born. Good care of us. Let it be."

"Do you know Dad had another family, a rich one?"

Jessivel's mother rose from her chair. "I've heard enough."

Jessivel stood up, walked to her mother, and put her hands on her shoulders. "No. You're going to listen to me," she said as she gently pushed her mother back into her seat. "Not only did he have another family, but it looks like I have a half-sister. Did you know that?"

Her mother stared at Jessivel without so much as a blink for a long, uncomfortable moment, biting her bottom lip, her distorted face almost unrecognizable.

"Yes, I knew that." She shook her head. "Maybe not for sure, but I had reason to suspect it. I would've had to have been deaf, dumb, and blind not to. Is her name Paige?"

"Yes. How did you know that?"

"I've seen the name in a few places."

"So you've known about her all this time?"

"For a while, yes."

"And you were okay with it?"

She shrugged. "I had no choice."

Jessivel thought about her mother's response. She obviously had choices. She stayed with him for a reason—financial support, companionship, or perhaps fear of raising a child alone. Looked like she and her mom had more in common than she'd previously thought.

"So how did all this happen? You met him, got pregnant with me. Not planned I assume."

"Mm-hm."

"He was married at the time?"

"I didn't know it at first, but yes."

"How did it happen?"

The dazed expression on her mother's face didn't require an accompanying response for Jessivel to realize how stupid the question sounded.

"Okay. Where did it happen? How did you even know him?"

"Do we really have to talk about this, Jess? It's all past history."

"Not for me, it isn't. Where did you two meet? I know you didn't hang with the same crowd." She paused a moment. "Or did you?"

"No, we didn't."

"How then?"

"I cleaned his office."

"What?"

"I was working for KMB, and his company was one of their clients. His office was assigned to me."

"You cleaned his office. While he was in it?"

"He often worked late."

"So one day you were emptying his waste basket and you ended up sleeping with him?"

Her mother's body froze in place, her look unforgiving.

"So you must have known his real name. It's not Wayne Salter. You know that, right?"

"I do know, but I didn't for a long time."

"But you cleaned his office…when he was in it. What did you call him?"

"I called him Wayne. He told me that was his name."

"So how did it happen? I don't get it."

"You know, I don't owe you any explanation."

"Well, I think you do!"

"Lower your voice, will you? I don't want Mrs. Perlman to hear us."

"I don't give a—"

"Who do you think you're talking to?"

"A big frickin' liar, that's who!"

A petite older woman with bleached-blond hair, dressed from head to toe in white, emerged from around the corner. "Is everything alright out here?"

"Yes, ma'am. We'll be done soon."

"Well, you need to keep it down." She flicked a strand of hair off her forehead. "And another five minutes should do it, Crystal. Don't you think?"

"Yes, ma'am."

"Are you kidding me?" Jessivel whispered when Mrs. Perlman had disappeared.

"Keep it down. Do you want to get me fired?"

"Well, you wouldn't catch me working here."

"Apparently, I wouldn't catch you working anywhere."

"Good one, Mom."

"How's Kayla? Does she like your new apartment?"

"She's fine, and don't change the subject. I'm here to talk about Dad."

"But I miss her."

"And she misses you too. If you had a day off once in a while, we could see each other more. So what about Dad?"

"I told you everything."

"No, you haven't." Jessivel threw her hands in the air, ready to give it to her mother with both barrels when a new tactic came to mind. She breathed in deeply before continuing. "Look, I'm sorry. I just want to know more about the man I called Dad my whole life. Is that asking too much?" she asked.

Her mother stared at her through what appeared to be weary eyes.

"Could you get away for a half-day?" Jessivel asked. "I want you to see my apartment and spend some time with Kayla."

"I have Tuesdays off."

"You could have told me that before."

"You're right, I could have."

"But?"

"But I was afraid you were going to ask me the very questions you just asked me, so I didn't want you to know that."

"Really, Mom?"

"You have no idea how upset this discussion is making me."

"Can I pick you up next Tuesday then? Ten o'clock?"

"Fine."

"Crystal? Are you just about finished with your little visit?" Mrs. Perlman asked from the open French door.

"I'd slap her," Jessivel mouthed to her mother.

"Ten o'clock Tuesday. Don't be late."

Chapter 21

"You're not dying, Mother." Paige had arrived at the hospital to find her mother in a fatalistic mood. "The doctors say you'll be fine."

"Well, it feels like I'm dying. And what do they know about how I'm feeling? They whisk themselves in here when they have a minute, half of them I don't even know, probably charging a few hundred dollars for the pleasure of their brief company, and before I've had enough time to formulate a question, they're gone. Damn hospital. I hate it here."

"From what I understand, you're going to be here for a little while, so you need to get used to it."

"How are my plants doing?"

"They're doing fine." One of them had a few fuzzy spots of something grey on its leaves, and another one looked to be in premortem condition, but Paige wasn't about to tell her that.

"Even the Staghorn fern?"

"Which one is that?"

"The one hanging on the wall in the family room."

"That's a real plant?" Paige asked.

"So you haven't watered it?"

"Sorry. I thought it was artificial."

"It started to decline when your father died, and it's taken me this long to get it back to—"

"I'll water it today, after I leave here."

"It'll be dead by the time I get home. Another one dead."

"I'll buy you a new one."

"I've become rather attached to that one. Like your father."

Give me a break.

"I want to talk to you about him when you're home and feeling better."

Her mother closed her eyes and shook her head.

"All I want to talk about is—"

"No."

"I don't see why—"

"Can I have my will dear?" she asked, eyes still closed.

Here we go.

"I didn't bring it with me. Do you want to wait until you get home?"

"If I ever come home."

"You're coming home, Mom. The doctors say you'll be released within the week if everything goes well." She hadn't planned on telling her mother this, in case it didn't happen that soon.

"I doubt it. I'll probably die in this godforsaken room." She glanced around. "Some flowers would be nice. Nothing extravagant."

Paige patted her hand. "You're going to be fine. Trust me. And if you need help with anything when you get home, we'll hire someone."

Her mother's face perked up. "What? A caregiver? Not on your life!"

"Why not? At some point, we all need—"

"What's wrong with *you*?"

"Me? Well, of course I can do some things for you, but—" A blurred vision of her business sliding out from under her swept through her mind.

"But what?"

"But nothing. I'll do whatever I can. I was just saying—"

"No outside caregivers."

"Okay. No caregivers."

"And no more talk about your father. I need closure."

"Yes ma'am."

Her mother gave her a look that caused Paige to snicker.

"And stop smiling."

"Yeesh. I can't even smile."

"You know what I mean."

Paige stopped by the hospital florist before leaving and ordered a spring bouquet for her mother's room.

Mothers could be so trying.

Paige's thoughts were on Jessivel and her father's disease that ultimately would have killed him. The child of someone with Huntington's had a 50-50 chance of being similarly afflicted. Early detection could provide a means of treatment that would slow down the progression of the disease. If Paige were Jessivel, she'd want to know. Even if Paige failed at any other communication, she wanted to have this discussion with her. Jessivel deserved this.

But getting Jessivel to listen would be a problem, and Paige knew that it would take some doing—some creative doing—to get and then keep her attention long enough to talk to her about it.

The next day, Paige called Gary, who now had a new address for Jessivel.

"Tell me you're not going to do anything foolish…or unlawful," he said.

"Of course not. It's not illegal to park on her street and observe her comings and goings, is it?" she asked, thinking a little judicious snooping might be beneficial.

"Would you like me to read you the official definition of stalking?"

"Please."

Gary read her the definition and relative punishment.

"I think I'll be okay," she told him.

"Do you want to tell me what you intend to do?"

"No. I wouldn't want to implicate you."

"That you used the word 'implicate' scares me."

"I'll be good."

She hung up, got in her car, and went to Jessivel's new residence, which she knew by the address to be government housing. After observing Jessivel's car in a numbered parking space, she found an unobtrusive place to sit in her car and watch the doorway.

She sat for a few minutes until she had to admit to herself how ridiculous it was to sit there wasting valuable time when she should have been analyzing the latest real estate market reports in her office. Waiting for Jessivel to emerge—especially when she didn't have a sensible plan on what she would do if she did appear—made no sense. There had to be a better way. If only she had something Jessivel wanted, or a peace offering of sorts. She searched her mind for a plausible scheme.

An idea came to her. The market reports would have to wait.

Paige knew someone at CDFSS she had helped a couple of times when subsidized housing had been at maximum capacity. Time to call in a favor.

"Hi, Cassandra. Paige West here."

"Hi, Paige. What can I do for you?"

"I'm not sure if you can do anything, actually, but I'm going to ask anyway. There is someone I know who recently went into government housing. Her name is Jessivel Salter. I got to know her when she came into the soup kitchen where I volunteer. I would like to help her in some way. I'm not sure how exactly—she's not one who is very receptive to help. Scared, maybe. I know where she lives, but I don't want to just knock on her door out of the blue. Do you know her by any chance?"

"You know I can't talk about my clients, Paige."

"I know, but—"

"You could try contacting people in the area who have entry-level job openings."

"Okay," Paige said, thinking she knew where Cassandra might be going with this. "Can you recommend anyone in particular?"

"Do you know Audrey Russo?"

"Owner of The Busy Bean?" Paige and Audrey had met at various Chamber of Commerce meetings. Nice lady.

"That's the one. She often has openings."

"Are you saying—"

"I can't say any more, Paige. Good luck."

Cassandra had come through.

Chapter 22

Jessivel arrived at Mrs. Perlman's home promptly at ten o'clock the following Tuesday, expecting her mother to be waiting outside. When she drove into the circular driveway past the massive front door and didn't see her, a heaviness swept through her. Her biggest fear was that she'd been too aggressive with her mother the last time she had seen her when trying to glean information about her father, and now she'd lost her. She half-expected to see Mrs. Pearlman come out the door and shoo her away.

"Where is she?" asked Kayla from the back seat.

"She'll be here," Jessivel said with hope in her heart.

A long couple of minutes passed before her mother appeared from around the side of the house.

"Are you kidding me?" Jessivel asked her mother when she got into the car. "You couldn't have come through the front door?"

"Just leave, Jess. Mrs. Perlman doesn't like cars parked out front."

"You know what I would do if—"

"Yes, I do. Now drive."

"Hi, Nana," Kayla said.

"Oh, dear Kayla. How I've missed you."

"Me too, Nana," Kayla said as they drove away from the house. "This is some mansion you live in."

"It's some mansion she slaves in, you mean. What's your room like, Mom? Where is it, in the basement?"

"Not in front of the child."

Crystal turned around to face Kayla. "Never you mind your mom, sweetie. I have a good job and a very nice room."

"Maybe we could move in with you," Kayla said.

Jessivel let out a snort. "That'll be the day."

"All I have is one room, dear. And what's wrong with your new apartment? I hear you have your own bedroom and everything."

"It's okay. You'll see it. It's okay."

Jessivel parked in her assigned spot before they walked the short distance to the building's back door.

"Welcome to the dump," Jessivel said to no one as she opened the door and led the way inside. "It's only fifteen flights up, Mom."

"We have to walk up fifteen flights of stairs?"

"Not if the elevator is working."

Once inside her apartment, Jessivel walked to the kitchen and pulled a soda from the fridge. "Want anything?"

"Nothing right now." She looked around the room. "This is nice, Jess. Are you going to show me the rest of it?"

"Kayla, give Nana the grand tour."

Jessivel formulated her thoughts while Kayla showed her mother the other half of the apartment. She had to remind herself of her plan to be a kinder and gentler daughter, to get on the good side of her mother so she would be more forthcoming about her father.

"I don't know what you're talking about, Jess. This isn't so bad," her mother said as she entered the living room.

"And we even have Hercules here to help us with stuff," Kayla announced.

"Hercules?"

Jessivel explained Hercules's position.

"Can't ask for more than that, right?" her mother said.

"Not until you go outside these walls and see all the 'hood rats roaming the halls. Other than that, and the panoramic view of a parking lot we have from the only two windows in the place, it's just heavenly in here."

"You can work your way out of here, you know."

"Mm-hm. In the meantime, I have to live among the wretched."

"In the meantime, you *are* one of the wretched. Don't forget that."

"Thanks for the reminder."

"When do you start your barista job?"

"Monday."

"That's great!"

"It's just a stupid job."

"The sooner you change that attitude of yours, the better. Don't be such a fool, Jess."

"A fool? Is that what I look like to you?"

"Look like one? No. But you're acting like one."

"Kayla, go to your room. Nana and I have to talk."

Jessivel waited for the sound of Kayla's door closing before she continued the conversation.

"You try living here and—"

"What are you so angry about?" her mother asked. "Sassy, rude, mad at the world. No one wants to be around an angry woman. Trust me. Especially a child."

"Now you're telling me how to raise my child?"

"I'm telling you that if you kick a stone in anger, you'll only hurt your foot."

"Great. Now here come the sayings."

"They're sayings because they have meaning. It would do you some good to think about them once in a while."

"I'll tell you what will ease my anger, and that's knowing more about Dad. Do you know what it's like to one day have a decent life and then—"

"No, tell me about it."

"Mom?"

"Hmm."

"When are you going to open up and tell me about him?"

Her mother didn't flinch.

"At least tell me something. He had another family for Christ's sake!"

Her mother slumped down in the chair and went quiet for a moment before speaking. "Your father hid a lot from us. There's so much we don't know about him."

Finally.

"More than his other family?"

"Yes."

"Like what?"

"Like he had a dishonorable discharge from the Army."

"Really?"

"And he never graduated from college."

"How did you find out about these things?"

"Aunt Hannah, mostly."

Hannah was Crystal's younger sister. Once a vivacious and active woman who had flown private aircraft for a living, she had suffered the past fifteen years with multiple illnesses, including two bouts of breast cancer, COPD, and an anxiety disorder. She had stayed with Jessivel and her family a few times over the years while recuperating from the worst of her afflictions.

"Aunt Hannah?" Jessivel braced herself for how her aunt fit into the picture.

"She was suspicious of Wayne from the get-go. He made her uncomfortable, didn't like him much, and so she did some digging."

"And?"

"She told me things about him, some of which I just told you, that I didn't believe…at first anyway."

"Like that he had another family?"

"Yes. She was the one who told me that."

"Was there more?"

"She told me that Wayne Salter wasn't his real name."

Jessivel let that sink in for a moment. "So Salter isn't my last name?"

"That's what's on your birth certificate, but as far as I know, it's a made-up name."

"So I don't even have a legitimate last name? That sure stinks!"

"You can have it legally changed if you want."

"To what?"

"To his real last name I would think. He *is* your natural father. Or to my last name. We'd have to check out the legalities."

"What about Kayla?"

"Same thing."

"And you knew these things all along?"

"She told me a bunch of stuff years ago, but I didn't believe it, wouldn't believe it, for a long time."

"And you never confronted him on any of it?"

"No."

"Why not?!"

"I was in denial I suppose. And he was supporting us, financially. We couldn't live on what I made. Not like we did with him. He served a purpose."

"How do you know he doesn't have other families too, besides Paige?"

"Actually, he…" She paused. "I don't know. Maybe he does." She gazed into Jessivel's eyes for a long moment, adjusting herself in her chair before speaking. "Let's just say your father had a problem keeping his you-know-what in his pants."

"Mom!"

"Well, it's the truth." Her mother leaned back, closed her eyes, and sighed before continuing. "There were times I knew he'd been somewhere other than where he said he'd been, and I suspected he was with another woman, but I refused to think about it. Every once in a while, he'd slip up and say something that…well, confirmed he'd lied to me earlier."

"I wouldn't have put up with it."

"You don't know what you'd put up with in that situation, trust me."

"I'd haul his ass off to jail or something."

"Jess, we weren't married. He was taking care of us. We always had food on the table. You went to decent schools. He could have walked out at any time."

"Why didn't he?"

Her mother looked past her, obviously lost in thought.

"Why didn't he?"

"Well, I…"

"You what?"

"At one point, I sort of held it over his head. He knew I could expose him, and he was so well-connected and known around town, around the country really, that it would have destroyed him, his job maybe, and his other family."

"So you threatened him with this?"

"No words were ever spoken or anything. It was a silent agreement of sorts. He knew that I knew. We just never talked about it."

"And that's the reason he supported us? To save his ass?"

"I don't—"

"What a bastard!"

Her mother's face reddened. "Don't talk about the dead like that. He did what he had to do for as long as he could, and that was that. Actually, I feel grateful—he could have left us high and dry from the beginning."

"Grateful?"

"And you should, too. You had a pretty good life…because of him."

As hard as it was to let go of the ridiculous suggestion that she feel grateful, she did. Her mother was on a roll revealing some of the deep seeded secrets about her father, and she didn't want to prevent her from continuing.

"So I could have other half-brothers or -sisters out there."

"Wouldn't surprise me."

"That explains why we didn't know about him dying right away, doesn't it?"

Her mother nodded.

"How *did* you find out about it?"

"I called his company—the one where Hannah said he worked—and asked about him. I pretended to be his sister and got information about his funeral and memorial service."

"But we couldn't go, of course."

"Actually, I did go. Not to the funeral. I didn't know about it in time. But I went to the memorial service, sort of."

"What do you mean 'sort of'?"

"I slipped in an hour or so after it started, when people were just standing around talking, and I…"

"You what?"

"I don't know what I was thinking, what was going through my mind at the time." She laughed. "I really don't. But I ended up tipping over the table with the urn of his ashes on it. I was so mad at him."

"You gotta be kidding. Did anyone see you?"

"I don't know, and I didn't care at the time. I did it, and I left. It made quite the crash, and it did make me feel better in the moment."

"So you did it on purpose?"

She nodded. "Hannah tried to talk me out of going there. And then she actually came herself to try to stop me, but she got there too late. The damage had been done."

"Geesh. I can't get over this. So he has this other family, but he comes home to us from his so-called business trips, all smiles, bringing stupid gifts, like he'd missed us. Did he really inspect construction sites for a living?"

"No, he sold medical equipment. High end stuff."

"More lies." Jessivel shook her head in disbelief. "All this bullshit about being away on business when he'd really been with his other family or hookin' up with someone else." Jessivel slapped the palms of her hands on her lap. "Well, you know something? I'm glad he's dead."

Her mother massaged her forehead with her fingertips. "So maybe he betrayed us, both of us. But that doesn't take away from what he did for us your whole life, Jess."

"If it hadn't been for you getting pregnant with me, you would have been nothing more than one of his flings."

Her mother's glare softened to a polite smile that soon fell away. "You can drive me home now."

CHAPTER 23

Paige didn't have to ponder for long about Cassandra's cryptic comment regarding Jessivel's whereabouts. Once in her office, she attended to the most important phone calls and e-mail messages before Googling trendy coffee flavors and heading for The Busy Bean.

The café was large compared to other neighboring storefronts. Inside she noted two long bar-height tables in the center, several bistro tables scattered throughout the space, a few conversation pits, and a bar that would seat a dozen or so people. She walked toward the ORDER HERE sign and looked at the confusing menu board, glad she had researched coffee before arriving. Not much of a coffee enthusiast, she settled on a caramel macchiato.

Paige waited for her order to be ready and then sat at a small table in the corner where she had a good view of activity in practically the whole place—people ordering their beverages, others sitting at the tables conversing, couples holding hands at the bistro tables, laughter and conversation humming throughout the room. She estimated thirty to thirty-five patrons in all. Her "business" mind compelled her to perform quick math in her head—open ten hours a day, each coffee $3.50 to $4.00, pastries, coffee beans, teas, and lots of unconsumable branded merchandise. If this volume of customers were steady throughout the day, and depending on overhead and operational costs, one could make a lucrative living this way.

Paige's attention perked up when she saw Audrey emerge from the back room. And when she saw Jessivel following close behind her, she felt her mission had been accomplished. Careful to remain unnoticed, she observed what appeared to be Audrey showing Jessivel around, explaining things. When the two women returned to the back room, Paige got up and discreetly exited the café. She needed to think about the right way to approach Jessivel—what to say that would get her attention, be non-alienating, and possibly build some goodwill.

Soon after she walked back into her office, Paige got a call from the hospital to learn that her mother was having emergency surgery. When she asked for details, she was told it would be better for her to come to the hospital.

"I'm on my way," she told the nurse. She offered up a crude prayer asking for her mother to be okay, and then felt guilty about praying only when she needed something.

At the hospital, Paige approached the nurses' station on shaky limbs.

"I was called about my mother, Elaine West. Can you tell me what's going on with her?"

"Why don't you have a seat, and I'll let the doctor know you're here."

She's dead.

Paige moved to the farthest corner of the waiting area to avoid being around other people, the only distraction a plastic ficus tree that had obviously seen better days. The more she stared at it, the more she wanted to grab it, march out the door, and throw it as far as she could. When it finally dawned on her that getting upset over a fake plant was ludicrous, she tried to focus on something else. Couldn't do it. The damn ficus tree bothered her.

Her mind raced through erratic possibilities of her mother's condition while trying to avoid thinking about worst-case scenarios. Memories of better times floated through her mind—how proud her mother had been when Paige graduated college summa cum laude, married someone she actually liked, and bought her own business. Things that made her smile.

She was about to get up and revisit the reception desk when a tall, lanky man in scrubs approached her.

"Miss West?"

"Yes."

"I'm Doctor Ahsan," the man said as he reached for her hand.

"How's my mother?"

"She's in surgery right now. Her pulmonary embolism progressed to CTEPH, chronic thromboembolic pulmonary hypertension, which means high blood pressure in the arteries in her lungs. She was a good candidate for PTE surgery."

"PTE?"

"Pulmonary thromboendarterectomy. It will remove the blood clots that are causing this high blood pressure."

"How dangerous is it?"

"There's risk, of course, but we are fortunate to have a surgeon on call who is trained specifically for this type of surgery, so I can assure you she's in very capable hands."

"When can I see her?"

"She went in around ten o'clock. She won't be out for a while. With this type of procedure, they lower the body temperature—drastically, I'm afraid—to perform the surgery. Afterward, it will take some time to rewarm her to normal. Then she'll go to the ICU where she'll be on a breathing tube and remain asleep throughout the night. I would recommend you go home—there is nothing you can do here. Someone will call you when she's out of surgery to give you an update and an indication as to when you can see her."

Overwhelmed by the amount of information she had been given in the span of less than three minutes, Paige thanked the doctor and watched him disappear through the swinging double doors. She remained seated for a brief time, now finding some solace sitting next to the dismal ficus tree.

The next day, Paige sat in a chair at her mother's bedside in the ICU listening to the symphony of beeping sounds emanating from the patient monitor. The large digital screen displayed all of her mother's vital signs in vivid colors, but without knowing what was normal for most of them, Paige didn't know whether to be content or concerned. Heart rate, blood pressure, respiration rate, temperature, oxygen saturation. She Googled each of them. Her mother's heart rate and blood pressure were above the normal range according to her quick research. Her temperature was 95.2 degrees, only slightly above the hypothermia zone.

Why aren't alarms going off?

Online research from her phone revealed what happens to your vital signs when you are subjected to extreme cold. Temperature decreases, obviously, and heart rate and blood rate increase. She felt better knowing what her mother was going through was probably normal.

Her mother's arm moved, then her foot.

"Mom?"

No response.

Paige checked the monitors. Her temperature had risen almost a degree since she had arrived, not back into the normal range but going in the right direction.

Her mother stirred, her face flushed, and her forehead puckered before she opened her eyes.

"Bring me my will," she bellowed. Paige jumped up from the chair, amazed at the volume of her mother's voice, given the ventilator tube in her mouth.

"Calm down, Mother. There are sick people here."

"Can't you see I'm dying? Get me my will!"

"You're not dying. Anyone with lungs like yours right after surgery is a long way away from dying."

"What's this thing in my mouth? I can hardly talk."

"It's a ventilator tube. To help you breathe."

"And what are these tubes coming out of my chest?"

"They're for drainage, Mom. They need to stay there for a few days. The ventilator, I would think, could come off soon though. I'll check with the nurses."

As if on cue, a nurse approached them. "Everything okay in here?" she asked.

"We were wondering when she could come off the ventilator," Paige told her.

"We were thinking the same thing, so what we're going to do is remove it and see how her breathing is on her own. Would you mind giving us some privacy while we do this? We'll come get you when we're done."

When Paige reentered the room several minutes later, she was relieved to see the tube gone from her mother's mouth. "You look good, Mom. Feel better now?"

"Where's my will?"

"I have it at home."

"Where are my other things?"

"I have them in my car. They gave me everything."

"See, they didn't think I'd make it either."

"That's not why—"

"Bring it to me."

"What?"

"The will."

"Okay. I'll bring it tomorrow."

After battling with the sheets and blankets all night, Paige got up the next morning thoroughly exhausted from lack of sleep. When she checked in with her office before setting out for the hospital, Olivia said someone called her earlier who left only the name Jessivel and a phone number.

"No message, just the number?"

"I didn't take the call, and that's all that's written on the message pad. Do you want me to look into it further?"

"No. Just give me the number."

Paige entered the number into her phone's contact list. She popped a couple of antacids, grabbed her mother's will, and drove to the hospital.

"Did you bring it?" her mother asked as soon as she walked into the room.

She didn't recognize her at first, thought she may have entered the wrong room. She walked toward her for a closer look. A vacant aura appeared to drape itself across her mother's face, something Paige had never witnessed before. Maybe she *was* dying.

"Hi, Mom. How are you feeling?"

"Did you bring my will?"

"Yes, I brought it."

"Give it to me."

Paige handed her the ten-page document, which her mother flipped through as though she knew exactly what she was seeking.

"Give me a pen."

"Are you feeling better, Mom?" Paige asked as she handed over a pen.

Ignoring the question for the second time, she wrote something on the document and handed it back to Paige.

"Don't read it now. Read it later. After I'm dead. Now, if you don't mind, I need my rest."

"Are you—"

Her mother closed her eyes. "Please, Paige. I'm tired. I'll talk to you when I wake up. If I wake up."

Paige left her mother's bedside, frustrated at being shut out but trying to be empathetic. Once in the visitors' lounge outside of the ICU, against her mother's wishes, she sat down and flipped through the will looking for handwriting in the margins. There it was. Added to the Beneficiaries section were four names—Emma Osterman, Jessivel Salter, Tamir Noor, and Wanda Forester—each followed by "5%."

Paige stared at the page for a long moment, tuning out everything else in her immediate surroundings. Her mother had added Jessivel to her will as a beneficiary, meaning she'd probably known about her all along. But it surprised her that she had added Wanda, her niece, but not her sister, Wanda's mother. *And who's Emma Osterman and Tamir Noor?*

She put the will in her purse and headed out. Life had been so much easier before all of these equivocal family issues had surfaced.

<h1 style="text-align:center">CHAPTER 24</h1>

Jessivel had decided to call Paige at her office to show her she wasn't the only one who knew shocking things about their father. When she was told that Paige wasn't in the office, she left a message for her, then soon regretted it and hoped she wouldn't return the call, now questioning why she would involve herself with Paige at any level. A day passed without a return call, so Jessivel figured she'd gotten her wish. Still, she was insulted Paige hadn't had the decency to return the call.

She flopped down on her sofa, sinking down into the dreaded low spot. Maybe her mother was right—the past needed to be left where it belonged. Nothing good would come out of digging into the sins of her father. She should be concentrating on her barista job, getting her personal life on track, and removing herself and Kayla from the ugly stigma of public housing.

Her phone rang.

"Hello, Jessivel?"

"Yes." She didn't recognize the voice.

"Paige West here."

Oh, it was *her*. So formal sounding.

"I, uh…"

"You called me. Is there something you want to talk about?"

"No. Um, it was nothing."

"It must have been something or you wouldn't have called me. Does it have anything to do with our father?"

"My mother wants me to leave it alone."

"I hear you. Mine too."

Now Paige's voice sounded more human to her, relatable.

"Really?"

"Really."

"I think if I don't give it up, my mother may disown me," Jessivel said.

"Do you think she would actually do that?"

"I don't know, but if she did, my daughter would lose her nana, and I don't think she would want that."

"My mother asked me to stop looking into it…her dying wish, so she thinks."

"Your mother is dying?"

"The doctors don't think so," Paige said. "But Mother does. You know, based on what she told me, there may be other siblings of ours out there."

"Mine thinks the same thing."

"My mother added the names 'Emma Osterman' and 'Tamir Noor' to the beneficiary list in her will," Paige said. "So I'm assuming they're two of them." Paige didn't mention Wanda's name that had been added to the will since she was her cousin and had nothing to do with their father. No use muddying the waters any more than they were already.

Jessivel wanted to know if her name was also on the will but was afraid to ask. "Wow. Hard to believe. But maybe not, based on what my mother says."

"What all did your mother say? Wait a minute. Could we talk about this in person? Wouldn't that be better?"

"You mean today?"

"If you can."

"I have to be at The Busy Bean in a bit, but I'm off at three."

"How about if I come by at three then?"

"Okay. You know where it is?"

"Yes. I know where it is."

Jessivel's day at The Busy Bean dragged. And when the end of her shift neared, the rocklike feeling she had in the pit of her stomach told her she may have made a mistake agreeing to meet with Paige. But by the time

Paige walked through the door and waved at her, it was too late to slip out the back door.

They drove in separate cars to a nearby park. Jessivel tried to ignore the physical signs of her nervousness, becoming more apprehensive about the meeting with each passing minute. She had to remind herself more than once to drop her shoulders and loosen her neck muscles to relieve the tension.

At the park, she handed Paige a raspberry-infused espresso—a drink she had created herself for The Busy Bean.

"Mmm…this is really good," Paige said.

Jessivel smiled to herself and nonchalantly thanked her. It had always been difficult for her to receive compliments.

"The way I see it," Paige began, "our father had several affairs in his life, and as a result—"

"Affairs? He lived with us! I think that was more than just an affair. And you say it like it's expected, like it's okay for men to cheat on their wives."

"Well, statistics do show that—"

Jessivel was stunned by Paige's remarks and dug in her heels. "I don't care what statistics show, he was a cheatin' son-of-a-bitch who didn't have sense enough to use a cock sock when he was screwin' around."

Paige's eyes went wide as she leaned back a couple of inches. "Must you be so crass? There's no reason to infuse vulgarity into this discussion."

"And how about if you try to talk plain English?"

Paige remained silent before appearing to relax. "Okay. You've made your point. I see now that we don't view our father in the same way, that's all. For me, despite his indiscretions, he was a loving man who was always there for us, even when he traveled."

"You still feel that way, after knowing he was sleeping with my mother and who knows who else?"

"That doesn't change what he did for us."

"Not me," Jessivel snapped, annoyed that Paige thought just like her own mother. "That's not how I see it."

"Can we agree to disagree then and go on from there?" Paige paused, apparently waiting for a response, but got none. "There are some things I want to share with you, and I'm interested in knowing more about my father from your experience with him and your mother's perspective. If we share what we know, we'll have a better picture of what really went on."

"I don't give a rat's ass about getting a 'better picture,' if that's what you want to call it. I'll leave that to you and your high-and-mighty world." She shifted in her seat. "You know what I care about? Not being left with a penny after he died. He lived with us my whole life, provided for us, and when he died—and I found out about it long after he was dead and buried, by the way—we were left with nothing. My mother is living in some rich bitch's mansion cleaning toilets, and I'm in government housing. That's what I care about."

Paige sat motionless while Jessivel talked, the cup of coffee beside her getting cold.

"I'm sorry you had to go through all this, Jessivel. I really am. I can't justify or condone what my father, *our* father, did to you and your mother. But if we work together, maybe I can help you in some way."

Jessivel stood up. "I don't need any handouts from you or anyone else. You can take your 'searching for a better picture' and shove it. As far as I'm concerned, our father was a no-good, lyin', cheatin' bastard who deserved to die!"

Her anger only escalated as she headed for her car, not just toward Paige but more importantly toward herself for not handling the situation better. This wasn't the first time she had lost control when something didn't go her way. But this time was different. This time she regretted her ill-mannered behavior.

CHAPTER 25

Paige arrived at her mother's house for her semiweekly visit to take in the mail and water her plants and was shocked to discover the front door unlocked. She'd been fastidious about securing the house each time she left, especially after the break-in. When she gently pushed open the door and peeked inside, she was struck by the silence. She waited to hear sounds, any indication that someone was inside.

"Who is it?" a female voice shouted, causing Paige to jump back.

"Who's here?" she shouted back.

Natalie, whom she'd not seen in more than a year, emerged from the hallway—her hair a chaotic nest of knots, her eyes glowing with a psychotic, watery shine. She appeared thinner than Paige remembered, unless it was just the ill-fitting clothes.

"What are you doing here?"

"And how nice it is to see you too, Paige."

"I thought someone had broken into Mom's house, so excuse me for neglecting the pleasantries." She checked the security system panel, which was in its normal position. "How did you get in here without tripping the alarm?"

Natalie shrugged.

"Mother gave you the code?"

"It's my house just as much as it is yours."

Paige didn't believe their mother would have given Natalie the code, but how else would she have gotten in without triggering the alarm? On second thought, her mother had the bad habit of using her birthday for all her passwords, so perhaps Natalie had taken a lucky guess.

"Fine. So what *are* you doing here?"

Natalie's posture stiffened. "I could ask *you* the same question? And where's Mom?"

"Mom's in the hospital. I'm here to take in the mail and water the plants."

"No one told me about Mom."

"I tried calling you. Apparently I have an old cell phone number for you."

"What's wrong with her?"

"She just had surgery to remove blood clots from her lungs."

"Is she okay?"

"She will be…hopefully. And *you*?"

"What about me?"

"Why are you here?"

"Mom told me I could stay here."

"When?"

Natalie shrugged. "A while ago."

Paige walked past her sister into the living room.

"Go ahead. Check everything out. Be sure to go into every room. Make sure I haven't stolen anything."

"That's not what I'm doing."

"Like hell it isn't."

"How about a truce here?" Paige asked. "Mom's in the hospital, and I'm sure she wouldn't appreciate us fighting in her house. So when did you and she talk about you staying here? She didn't mention anything to me."

"And you would know, wouldn't you? You stick to her like goddamn glue. Always have."

"What are you talking about?"

"You think I don't know how close you and Mom are? And I know you're the executor of her will, so…"

"So what? And why are you bringing up her will right now?"

"I'll probably get cut out of it, if you have anything to say about it."

"Don't be ridiculous. We get everything fifty-fifty. Well, maybe not now."

"I knew it."

Paige sat down on one end of the living room sofa. "I wasn't going to say anything until I had this all figured out, but Mom recently added four names to the inheritance section of her will."

"Great."

Paige had no intention of telling Natalie about what she'd discovered about their father, but now that she'd said this much, she felt she had no choice.

"We have half-siblings, Natalie."

"And I'm the one whose brain is supposed to be fried from drugs and alcohol. Ha!"

"I'm not kidding. I know of three."

"You're batshit crazy."

"Fine." Paige got up from her seat and walked toward the kitchen. Natalie followed her.

"Okay, so tell me what you're talking about," Natalie said, her words getting more slurred with time.

"What are you on?"

"Nothing...out of the ordinary."

"I'll fill you in when you're sober," Paige said, knowing Natalie's concerns didn't go much beyond her next pill or drink when she was like this.

"Stop with the pompousassness."

"That's not a word. Try pomposity."

"You're proving my point, big sister."

Uncertain where to take this conversation, Paige busied herself with filling a watering can for the plants.

"So tell me the family dirt," Natalie said.

"Ask Mom. I told you all I know."

"Liar."

"Okay, so I'm a liar. Now why don't you go lie down and sleep off whatever it is you're on."

"I'm on prescription meds, if you must know."

"Mm-hm. If you ask me, it looks like they need to adjust the dosage some."

"Well, no one is asking you."

"Are you still with what's-his-name?"

"His name is Derek."

"Sorry. Are you still with Derek?"

"No. We broke up. That's why I'm here."

"That doesn't explain why you're here."

"I was living with him. I have no place to go."

"Do you have a job?"

"No, I don't have a job!"

As soon as Natalie turned sideways, Paige suspected the worst.

"You're pregnant, aren't you?"

"No."

"Yes, you are. I can tell. Anyone could tell, Nat."

"So what? That does happen, you know."

"So now you think you're going to move in with Mom so she can support the two of you?"

"None of your business."

"Will you stop with the attitude? Just so you know, if you could only get your act together, this could work out. Mom may need someone to take care of her when she gets out of the hospital. That someone could be you," Paige said, trying to be optimistic about Natalie's personal issues.

"Not me!" She let out a belly laugh. "I can't even take care of myself."

Paige refrained from saying what she really wanted to say, knowing she'd regret it later. "Well, you may have to put on your big-girl pants when she gets home. Start making yourself useful. Get off the meds and become a productive member of society."

"You know I need the meds."

"Really? Or is it just an addiction?"

"*Just* an addiction. For someone who's so smart, you are so frickin' stupid."

"You've seen an obstetrician, right?"

Natalie didn't respond.

"Right?"

"I'm not that far along."

"You need to see one as soon as possible."

"Didn't do you much good, did it?"

Silence filled the room before a sudden sensation of cold expanded inside of her. Paige turned and walked toward the door, almost knocking over a plant stand on her way out.

She sat in her running car for a few minutes before putting it into gear, vacillating between disbelief, hurt, and rage brought on by her sister's comment. Eager to be alone in the comfort of her own surroundings, she backed out of her mother's driveway and drove home.

<h1 style="text-align:center">CHAPTER 26</h1>

Jessivel stomped back to her car and drove away, fuming over her encounter with Paige. She talked about their father as if he were some kind of saint who just made a couple of minor mistakes in his life. But wasn't that the way it was in this unfair world—a man's "rich" daughter is left in a field of sunshine and roses, while his "poor" one is clawing her way out of a garbage can. She fondled the ring on the chain around her neck, confused as to how she regarded it anymore.

The next day at The Busy Bean, Jessivel immersed herself in making coffees for an endless stream of customers. Close to two o'clock, when it finally died down, Paige walked into the shop.

What the hell is she doing here?

"May I have another one of those raspberry coffees?" she asked.

Something inside of Jessivel began to quiver as she took her time making the coffee, not wanting to have to turn around and face her again. *Calm down,* she told herself. *Treat her like any other caffeine addict with enough money to blow a fiver on a cup of joe.*

"Here you go, ma'am. May I get you anything else today?" *Like a punch in the face?*

Paige stared into her eyes for one agonizingly long moment without saying anything. "No, that will be it." Then she stepped closer to the counter and leaned in. "Except I really need to talk to you," she whispered.

Ignoring her comment, Jessivel rung her up and quickly moved on to the next customer while Paige took a seat at the bar. It was one thing dealing with her outside of work where she could walk away, but in here, she had to endure her presence, and she was proud of herself for handling it so coolly. When she had waited on the last customer in line, she glanced down the bar. Paige was staring at her.

"What are you staring at?" she mouthed.

"What?"

Jessivel walked to where Paige was sitting. "I said, 'Stop staring at me.' Okay?"

"I just thought we could talk for a minute. Do you get—"

Jessivel walked away from her.

"Oh, Miss?"

That did it. With her heart picking up speed in her chest, Jessivel marched down to where Paige sat and faced her.

"Look, you tight-ass bitch," she said, her arms flailing and her insides pulsating with rage. "If you don't stop stalking me, I'll call the goddamn cops. Not that they'd do anything to a privileged piece of shit like you. Why don't you take your—"

"Jessivel!" Audrey shouted at her from the doorway to the back room. "Come back here…now."

Ignoring her boss's demand, Jessivel threw off her apron, grabbed her backpack from under the counter, and stormed out the front door. Once outside, she bolted to her car and drove away, heat rising from within her body and up her neck, into her cheeks. Now that godawful woman had gotten her fired. *Damn bitch.*

When she arrived home, she found Kayla busy at the kitchen table doing her homework.

"You're home early," Kayla said.

"So?"

"Geez. Sorry I said anything. But now that you're here, can you help me with something?"

Getting stumped by one of Kayla's homework questions was the last thing she needed. "Go ahead. What is it?"

"We're studying the Declaration of Independence and we have to write a paper on what 'All men are created equal' means. I'm stuck on this."

"It means shit. That's what it means."

"Mom, I can't write that."

She sat down to join Kayla. "All it means is that at birth, we're all the same. It doesn't mean we're treated the same afterward. It should read all *rich* men are created equal."

"But it says here we all have the same rights."

"Sure we do, but that doesn't mean we're all going to be able to get the same things in life. Oh, we all have the same rights alright—what we have to work our ass off for, others are handed. Does that help?"

"Not really. If I wrote that, I'd probably get a 'D'."

"Sorry. I'm not in a 'created equal' kind of mood."

Jessivel went into her bedroom, slamming the door behind her. She rubbed her throbbing forehead and fantasized about how an unfortunate downfall for her irritating half-sister Paige would have such a satisfying outcome. Like losing her business or something. Might be enough to even the playing field. Or maybe having her house burn down. Or being attacked by a pack of rogue coyotes. Show her how it feels to struggle for everything you have. Course she probably had a ton of money in the bank, and her father's inheritance, so it wouldn't make any difference anyhow. And she was sure her name wasn't in Paige's mother's will. Otherwise, Paige would have said something.

After the self-pity started to wear off, Jessivel winced every time she thought about her hysterical behavior in the coffee shop. She had overacted when she'd lit into Paige. She should have done it outside of work or better yet, not at all. She, "the help," should have shown restraint when provoked, suppressed her anger, just like all the good little poor folks are expected to do.

"C'mon in, Kayla," she said responding to the knock on her door.

Kayla peeked inside her room. "Is it safe?"

"Come here, kiddo. I'm sorry for snapping at you. It's not your fault."

"What's not my fault?"

"That I'm in such a shitty mood."

"Whose fault is it?"

"Mine, sweetie. All mine." She stroked Kayla's hair. "It's just that I'm so frustrated these days."

"With what?"

"Everything. Everyone. But not you. And I need to learn not to take it out on you when I get this way. There is no reason for you to feel the way I do when you had nothing to do with it."

"Okay."

"Am I forgiven?"

"Yep."

"C'mon," Jessivel said taking Kayla's hand. "Still want help with your homework?"

CHAPTER 27

Paige stayed seated at The Busy Bean while rehashing Jessivel's reaction to her wanting to talk with her—Jessivel's resentment glaringly clear but not understandable. But despite everything, surprising even herself, she still wanted to help her.

Paige had never viewed herself as a snob. In fact, she considered herself much like her father who was the most down-to-earth, unpretentious person she'd ever known. Apparently, Jessivel had a different perception, and since she knew that someone's perception was their reality, this unsettled her.

Audrey came over to apologize for Jessivel's behavior.

"Don't be too hard on her, Audrey," Paige said. "She's obviously got issues and a lot going on in her life."

"No one talks to my customers that way," she said.

"Can you give her a break on this one? Give her a second chance?"

Audrey hesitated. "I'm sorry, but I can't take the risk that she'll do it again. She has to learn how to control her emotions, but not on my watch."

"How was her work otherwise?"

She shrugged. "Great. She caught on quickly and even had a few good suggestions, ones I implemented. That raspberry-infused coffee you have in front of you? That's *her* concoction. We sell a lot of it."

"Did she have any specialized training?"

"I paid for her training at the Chicago Barista Academy."

"Interesting. Maybe her outburst was singular? Never to happen again?"

"I hear ya, but I'm not willing to take a chance on her. Sorry."

"I appreciate your stand on this. I honestly do. I just wish the whole incident had never happened. I feel like I'm responsible for it."

"You did something to provoke her?"

"I came in here."

"Not enough. She's gone."

The unfortunate scene replayed itself the whole way home, like a relentless video in Paige's head that she couldn't turn off. She pictured in her mind her father's two families, wanting to understand the differences. Paige's family had lived in a three-story brownstone in an affluent neighborhood with wrought-iron fencing surrounding a sizeable yard complete with multiple flower gardens, two patios, and a fire pit. She had gone to a private college-prep high school and then Northwestern University where she had earned a double-major bachelor's degree in business and finance while maintaining a 4.0 grade-point average. Once she had decided that real estate would be her lifelong career, she earned a master's degree in sales and marketing.

Jessivel, her daughter, and her mother lived in a modest brick bungalow in a lower middle-class community. With Jessivel's father no longer there to support them, they had lost their home, with Jessivel first ending up homeless and now in government housing.

Justification for such bitterness? Paige wondered.

Maybe.

Probably.

Likely.

Paige pondered her next move. Staying away from her newfound half-sister—away from all the hostility, anger, and drama—would be the safest and easiest thing to do. Jessivel hadn't given her even the slightest opportunity to become a kindred spirit, even though in some ways, they were going through the same things, and it should have been clear to Jessivel that Paige was trying to help. Turning her back on her seemed like the wrong thing to do, but maybe the time had come for Paige to call it quits on her.

She recalled a quote she'd heard years earlier: "You live in the image you have of the world." Maybe Jessivel was doing just that.

And now Jessivel had lost her job. Paige understood enough about public housing to know she had three months' free rent where she resided before she'd have to pay a percentage of her income. Jessivel needed another job, and the likelihood of her getting a good referral from Audrey was uncertain at best.

She called Cassandra at the CDFSS offices and asked if she knew of any other coffee shops besides The Busy Bean that were willing to take a chance on someone who didn't have much of a work history.

"Are we talking about Jessivel?"

"No, just a hypothetical question."

"Mm-hm. I'll find out sooner or later, you know."

"I'm banking on later."

"You're pretty funny."

"I try."

"I can't think of any other shops offhand, but she could call Renaldo Vargas over at Goodwill Industries. He might be of some help."

Paige thanked Cassandra and called Renaldo, who gave her the name of the owner of a coffee shop just outside of Jessivel's neighborhood that had hired inexperienced workers in the past, even ones with criminal backgrounds.

"Do you have any openings for an entry-level employee, someone who's gone through training at the Chicago Barista Academy?" she asked the owner of The Daily Grind.

"Part-time, I do."

"She could come in and fill out an application any time?"

"We're open from six A.M. to three in the afternoon. Tell her to ask for me."

That was the easy part. The hard part would be getting the information to Jessivel without antagonizing her.

<hr>

"You're not going to die, Mother," Paige said. "Your doctor is saying you'll fully recover from this."

"He doesn't know, not for sure."

"Well, I guess one could say that no one knows anything for sure when it comes to life. But the odds are in your favor."

"Have they told you when I can go home? They're not telling me anything."

"As soon as your vitals are stable."

"And when will that be?"

"We don't know—it's a wait-and-see thing."

"How many of my plants have died?"

"None." Two were on the brink. "Have you been in touch with Natalie since you've been in the hospital?"

"No. Why do you ask?"

"Because she's at your house."

"Oh?"

"Mm-hm. I'm not sure how she got in though. Do you have any idea?"

"What is she doing there?"

"I was going to ask you the same question. She led me to believe that you and she had an agreement that she could stay there."

"She must have found the key under the fake rock by the back door."

"You removed that when the house was burglarized, remember?"

"I put it back. You never know when—"

"Then, how did she know how to disarm the security panel?"

Her mother didn't respond.

"Did you give her the code?"

"It's her house too."

"I know. And I'm fine with that. I just thought since I'm taking care of it while you're here, you might have mentioned it to me."

"Is that worthless boyfriend of hers with her?"

"She said they broke up."

Her mother closed her eyes.

"Mother?"

"I'm tired now. Can you come back some other time? If it's not asking too much."

"There's something you need to know about Nat."

"What's that?"

"She's pregnant."

Her mother's eyes flew open. "No."

"She is."

"That's the last thing she needs."

"Tell me about it."

"How far along is she?"

"I don't know, but she hasn't been to a doctor, so…"

"She needs to get to one."

"I agree. Maybe she'll listen to you."

"You can handle it," she said closing her eyes.

"I don't think—"

"I'll talk to you later."

Paige drove to her mother's house speculating what it must have been like for Natalie during the last years she had lived at home. She had to have felt very alone with their father gone so much, their mother heavily involved in charity work, and Paige in college. Natalie's accident just weeks before her high school graduation was a huge setback and the beginning of her downward spiral. But neither Paige nor their parents realized until much later the long-term effect it would have on her.

Today, at thirty-nine, Natalie had been an addict for so long that even though she might have been able to overcome the physical part of the addiction, Paige thought it would be difficult for her to unlearn the bad behavior that had gone along with it.

And now, a baby? How could she possibly fit a child into her life?

She found Natalie asleep on the sofa when she arrived at their mother's house and quietly went about the business of watering her mother's plants and going through her mail. When a knock on the door interrupted her chores, Paige went to answer it and found two young men dressed in suits and ties standing before her. She pointed to the NO SOLICITING sign.

"Did you not see this?" she asked them.

"We're not soliciting," the taller of the two said. "We're looking for Elaine West."

"She's not here. How can I help you?" she said while lessening the space left by the open door.

"My name is Tim Noor, and this is my brother Hank."

Their nationality wasn't readily apparent—the one doing the talking had a heavy accent which could have been East Indian, and each had a similar tawny-brown skin tone. While the name 'Noor' sounded vaguely familiar, their presence didn't feel right to her, and she promptly closed the door in their faces.

"Ma'am, please don't shut us out," the man said through the closed door. "We just want to talk to Mrs. West. She was married to the late Ryan West, our father."

CHAPTER 28

The way she had left The Busy Bean gnawed at Jessivel and caused conflicting emotions. She knew what she'd done had been wrong, but no matter where she was or what she was doing, she wasn't going to put on airs for anybody. *I am who I am.* Then she recalled something her mother had told her about her own job—it's something I have to *do,* not something I have to *love.* She considered the alternative—going back to living out of her car; lack of private bathroom facilities; wearing wrinkled, dirty clothing; not feeling safe; and putting Kayla into that unhealthy situation again.

She swallowed her pride and called Audrey.

"I appreciate the apology, Jessivel, but you have to control yourself at all times in front of customers, even if you don't like—"

"Look, I was..." Jessivel caught herself from getting defensive. "I'm really sorry that happened. It won't happen again."

"I have no tolerance for that kind of behavior, and don't forget that you walked off the job. That's when your employment here ended. Learn from the experience, Jess. I wish you well in the future."

Jessivel clicked off without saying anything more, then flung her phone down on her bed, where luckily it stayed—she couldn't afford to replace a busted phone. She figured it would only be a matter of time before Cassandra at the CDFSS office found out about her losing her job, since she and Audrey knew each other. She'd been in the apartment a month and expected to pay rent in sixty more days. *Damn rules. Damn father. Damn life!*

Her phone rang.

"Jessivel? This is Marlene from work. I only have a minute. I'm on break. Listen, we heard about you losing your job here, and we're all so sorry that happened. We really liked working with you. But here's the thing. That lady you yelled at? Well, I overheard her asking Audrey to take it easy on you. She didn't want you to lose your job over it. I just thought you'd like to know. That's all."

Stunned, Jessivel was speechless for several seconds before she responded. "Thanks. That's good to know. Hey, do you know of anyone else hiring?"

"Not really. But if you want to use me as a reference, you can. You know your shit. Hey, you taught me how to do latte art without any splitting. I was terrible at it before. Oh, and something else. I understand getting mad at the customers—some of them are *so* rude. But you gotta learn to hold back when you're waiting on the public. Take a deep breath. Kill 'em with kindness if you have to. I make a game out of it. That's how I get through it."

"This wasn't just a rude customer, Marlene. It was personal."

"Well, all I know is that woman was sticking up for you. Just sayin'."

Jessivel hung up and flopped down on her bed, tired of having to deal with things that were out of her comfort zone. Marlene had some nerve telling her to calm down when she didn't know the circumstances. She called her mother.

"I'm on my dinner break. What is it, Jess?"

"Just wondering how much longer you're going to be living there."

"As long as it takes. Why?"

"Well, how long is that?"

"I don't know. Maybe forever. It's not so bad here."

"Forever? I thought your plan was to save enough to rent an apartment of your own, so we could be a family again."

"So I could support you? Is that what you mean?"

"I'm working! Well, I *was* working."

"What happened?"

"You know how unfair bosses can be."

"What did you do?"

"Nothing. How's Aunt Hannah doing?"

"She's upset that her driving privileges were taken away. Other than that, she's hanging in there."

"It's about time. Her driving was horrible. How's her heath these days?"

"Not good. It hasn't been for quite a while. Why do you ask?"

"I was thinking maybe she has enough room for Kayla and me and wouldn't mind the company."

"She has a live-in caregiver now, so that would never work. Look, I need to tell you something, and I don't have much time."

"What's that?"

"There may be someone trying to find us."

"Like who?"

"He's, well, he's Dad's son."

"What?"

"Your father has a son. He supported him and his mother when the boy was younger. He's grown now."

"What? How do you know this, and why would he be looking for us?"

She talked fast. "Years ago, I found part of a letter from this woman to Wayne. It wasn't hard to read between the lines. There was even a photo of the three of them."

"What the—"

"Your father joined the Army when he was eighteen," she whispered. "There was a war going on at the time, between India and some other country—Pakistan, I think. Anyway, he met this woman there. Fathered a child. Tamir is his name."

"Do you still have the picture? I'd like to see it."

"I don't know where it is now. I pretended I never saw it."

"So why would he be looking for us? Does he know Dad is dead?"

"When Wayne died, I went through his things and found Tamir's address. I wrote to him. Once. To let him know his father died. It seemed like the right thing to do."

"You wrote him?"

"And he wrote back saying he wanted to meet us. I never responded. He'll never find me here, and maybe not you either, but I thought you should know just in case."

"I don't understand how—"

"I don't have time to explain. Just be careful who—"

"Maybe I *want* to meet him."

"Forget it, Jess. You have more important things to worry about."

"It's not that easy for me. You're telling me I have a brother out there somewhere. And let's not forget about Paige."

"Leave them both 'out there somewhere,' as you put it. That's where they've been all these years, and that's where they need to stay."

"What does he look like?"

"He's from India. His mother is dark, but his skin tone is lighter."

"He's Indian?"

"He and his mother moved from India to San Francisco when he was pretty young."

"How do you know this?"

"It was in the woman's letter. I didn't have the whole story but enough to piece a lot of it together."

"I wish I could read it."

"I put it back where I'd found it, and it disappeared from there."

"So when were you going to tell me this?"

"I wasn't."

"So why now?"

"I just got to thinking, and with your connection with Paige and everything. I was afraid he'd find you and you wouldn't be prepared for it."

"Does he know we moved?"

"No."

"Do you have his phone number?"

"Yes."

"Have you called him?"

"No."

"Are you going to call him?"

"What do I want with Wayne's other child? I've tried all these years to forget he had another life. I don't owe him anything."

"He's my half-brother."

"So what? He means nothing to you either."

"How does he know about me?"

"I assume Wayne told him about both of us."

"And you kept all this from me."

"It was his other life. It had nothing to do with you."

"You don't get it, Mom."

CHAPTER 29

Had she heard him right? Paige took a step back while the shock of the man's statement settled over her. Her father's two sons were standing outside her mother's door?

She reached for the doorknob, not sure what words would come out of her mouth when she looked at them again. After a long deliberate moment, she opened the door and invited them in, cell phone in hand in case they tried anything.

"Follow me, please," she said as she led them through the house, past sleeping Natalie, to the patio. "We can talk out here. I don't want to disturb my sister." What she really didn't want was for them to be in the house.

A low-lying fog throughout the property and the cawing of a distant crow created an eerie mood for this meeting. Paige studied the men's stoic faces as they approached her. Both were nice-looking and well-groomed.

After everyone had been seated, Paige introduced herself as Elaine and Ryan West's daughter.

"I am Tim, and this is my brother Hank," the man who had spoken to her at the door said. "Let me begin by saying we are very sorry for your loss."

"And you as well," said Paige, uncertain why she had acknowledged their relationship to her father so early in the conversation.

"Allow me to begin," said Tim. His English, despite his heavy accent, was impeccable.

"Before you say anything more, how did you know to come here, to this address?"

"There were many letters from your father to our mother. We read some of them. His name and address were on the envelopes."

"Really." Paige found it hard to believe her father would have been so transparent about his real identity. "Go on."

"Our mother, who is Indian, was a nurse employed at a small American camp on the Pakistan-India border that, according to our father, was put there by the CIA to investigate Russian activity. There was a war going on between India and Pakistan at the time, and our father was periodically sent to this camp in his capacity as an intelligence officer. That's where they met and eventually had a relationship."

"My father went into the military right out of high school," Paige added.

"That's what we understand as well. Anyway, according to our mother, sometime after they shut down the camp, she discovered she was pregnant but didn't tell our father because by that time his orders had been changed, and he was to finish his military tour in the U.S."

"What year was this?" Paige asked.

"I was born in April of 1972, so she must have gotten pregnant in June or July of 1971," Tim said without making eye contact.

Paige's parents were married in 1975 in Chicago.

"And your brother?"

So far, Tim had done all the talking. "Hank, would you care to continue the story?" Tim asked.

"Our mother told us—"

"Sorry to interrupt, but is your mother still alive?" Paige asked.

"Yes, she is," Tim quickly added. "She went back to India last year, to be with her ailing sister." He glanced at his brother. "Please continue, Hank."

"She told us that she was prepared to raise Tim on her own, even though it meant leaving India, since it was too shameful for her to be an unwed mother there. So she moved to London where she gave birth to Tim. Afterward, she took a job again as a nurse, this time at a U.S. military base outside of London where she met a man named Bernard Novander."

This name was familiar to Paige. Her father had talked about this old Army buddy many times before.

"Well, it turned out that in the course of one of their conversations, Bernard told him about this nurse he'd just met. When Dad realized who it was, and Mr. Novander mentioned she had an infant son, our father came to London and they reunited. And then I was born."

"What is your mother's name?"

"Qudrah. Qudrah Noor."

"And when were you born?"

Hank hesitated, ever so slightly. "December 1973."

Both men came across as unusually articulate—well-spoken, confident, and polite. Almost too much so, she thought. Their guard appeared to be up, and it was impossible to read their faces.

"Okay. Go on."

"The way our mother told it, Father was engaged to another woman—someone from the States, someone we now know was your mother—whom he intended on marrying. Regardless of this, he offered to fly us to the U.S. and support us."

She tried to remember if either of her parents had ever mentioned when they'd met—all she knew was they'd had a long engagement before marrying, which fit in with what they were saying. She made a mental note to ask her mother.

"So you had an ongoing relationship with him?"

"Yes, of course."

"Tell me about it."

"He was in and out of our lives. Perhaps we saw him once a month. One time, when we were much younger, he took us to Disneyland. Another time on a cruise to Cozumel."

"Are you aware of his other children?"

"Not other than you and your sister," said Hank.

"How did you become aware of us?"

"Our father told us about you."

"But he didn't tell you about the others?"

"He may have. We were young and perhaps we don't remember everything."

She didn't respond right away, but instead stared at Hank for a moment while contemplating her next question.

"So, why did you come here? What do you want from us?"

Mid-sentence, Natalie emerged from inside the house, her clothes askew and her hair mussed from her nap.

"Well, well, who do we have here?" Natalie asked.

"Please join us, Natalie." Paige gestured to the nearest chair. "The short version of this story is that these two gentlemen are our half-brothers. Our dad and their mother met in India, where their mother is from, while Dad was in the service."

"Get outta here," Natalie said with a smirk. "Excuse me for a minute." She came back with her phone and pointed it at the two men. "Say 'whiskey'."

"What are you doing?" Tim asked.

"If you're family, we need a photo for the album. Now, smile for the camera."

The two men gave halfhearted grins while Paige looked on in disbelief. If it hadn't been uncomfortable before the photo shoot, it certainly was now.

"Before you walked in, Natalie, I was asking them why they're here." She turned toward the two men. "Is there something you want, something you wish to accomplish?"

Tim responded. "The main reason for our coming here…has to do with a ring."

His response caught her off guard. "A ring," she repeated, a fine layer of goosebumps skittering up her arms.

"Our father wore a gold ring for as long as we can remember. His initials were engraved on the inside of the band. Had a small stone in it. Our mother gave him that ring as a thank-you gift for bringing us to America. Are you familiar with it?"

It took some time for Paige's breathing to return to normal. Undecided at first whether to admit awareness of the ring, she ultimately nodded. Any doubt she may have had believing their story had greatly diminished. "We're familiar with it."

"That is all we want of his. It doesn't hold much monetary value—the stone was quite small—but it has sentimental value for our mother. She's not well. I hope you understand."

Paige was rendered speechless for several seconds—how could one small piece of jewelry mean so much to so many?

"So it's your mother who wants the ring back?" Paige asked.

"It would mean very much to her."

"And she's ill, you say?"

"Heart problems."

"I thought you said it was her sister who was ill."

"Neither is in good health I'm afraid."

"We'll have to talk about the ring at a later time," she said after thinking it over. "There are other people involved, including *our* mother."

"That's fair enough," Tim said. "I am going back to San Francisco Sunday morning, and it would be nice to have this resolved before then, but if not, my brother can handle things from here."

A new wave of suspicion swept through Paige's mind. "Tell me, Hank, what do you do for a living?"

"I teach biochemistry at the University of Illinois."

"And you, Tim?"

"I'm a pediatrician."

"You two don't have very Indian-sounding names," Natalie blurted out.

Leave it to Natalie.

Tim uttered a suppressed chuckle. "In fact, we do. I am Tamir, and this is Hanik. We find it easier to go by our American nicknames."

Tamir Noor—the name her mother had written on her will.

"I see," said Paige as she rose from her chair. "Is that all then?" she asked, suddenly feeling uneasy about their presence.

Tim eyed his brother before rising. "Yes, I suppose it is," he said.

They exchanged cell phone numbers before the four of them left the wet blanket of fog that had settled on the patio and walked through the house to the front door.

"We want to thank you for your hospitality, Miss Paige, and we look forward to hearing from you in the near future."

They all shook hands.

Paige closed the door, leaned up against it, and sighed.

"Okay," Natalie said, "tell me what the hell is going on here."

CHAPTER 30

Jessivel pulled Paige's business card from her purse and dialed her cell phone number. When Paige answered, she didn't waste time on pleasantries.

"So, Paige, do you know about our half-brother from India?" she said louder than she had intended.

"Hello, Jessivel. I'm glad you called. I wanted to—"

"Our father had another child you know…in India. The way I figure it, he's in his mid-forties by now."

"Where did you hear that?"

"My mother told me. Apparently, Dad was stationed there when he was in the Army and got her pregnant. And he wants to meet with Mom and me. What do you think of that?"

"Will you meet with him?"

"I don't know. Maybe."

"I've already met him…and his brother."

"What?"

"They came to my mother's door recently, and we had a long talk. Would you like me to fill you in?"

Jessivel couldn't find the end-call button on her phone fast enough. How dare Paige one-up her news about their supposed brother.

Within seconds, she saw Paige's name flashing on the phone screen. She ignored it.

Never had she felt so out of it when it came to her family—her mother knew things, Paige knew things, and the new Indian brother likely did too. Or was it brothers? Her mother had mentioned just one. She'd been kept in the dark her whole life. But why?

The hell with all of them.

"No, I don't have $125, Kayla. I barely have enough money for this week's groceries," Jessivel explained to her daughter. "Thanks to Princess Paige, I lost my job."

"But I need it for school, Mom."

"That much money! For what?"

"To join the basketball team."

"No."

"Why not? The coach really wants me to join. He said I have the height and the potential."

"You may have all that and more, but you don't have $125."

"But Mom."

"And then there will be money for the uniform and shoes and God knows what else. The answer is no."

"It's called a jersey."

"I don't care what it's called, we can't afford it."

"This stinks."

"Tell me about it."

"Why don't you pawn Poppy's ring? I bet you could get $125 for it."

"Don't tempt me."

"When are you getting another job?"

"Whenever."

"Have you even tried to find one?"

"Look—"

"I'm just askin'."

A ping from her phone alerted her to a text message.

u might try goodwill industries in yr job search

The message was from Paige. Attached to it was something she didn't have the slightest idea how to open.

"Doesn't that wacko ever give up?" Jessivel shouted.

"Who are you talking about, Mom?"

"No one. Never mind," Jessivel said, tossing the phone onto the sofa.

Kayla grabbed the phone. Jessivel tried unsuccessfully to get it away from her.

"Mom, someone's giving you a lead on a job!"

"I'm not interested."

"Well, you should be."

"Look, who's the kid and who's the parent here?"

Kayla stared at her mother. "You tell me."

"Go to your room."

As much as she hated to admit it, Kayla was right. Jessivel had to find work, and if she was being honest with herself, working wasn't so bad, even if it meant waiting on people who didn't know what it was like to be in her shoes. And there had been a few feel-good moments at The Busy Bean when she'd given Audrey and others tips she'd learned in class as well as ones she'd learned on her own.

She called Cassandra at CDFSS to let her know she needed another job. When asked, Jessivel explained what happened at The Busy Bean.

"It doesn't sound like that woman did very much to provoke you," Cassandra said.

"You don't understand. This woman is stalking me, insisting on helping me."

"Which is it? Stalking or helping?"

"Both."

"And?"

"And I don't want her help!"

"Why not?"

"I just don't."

"Like you didn't want my help in the beginning."

"Exactly."

"And now here you are calling me for help."

"You're different."

"How?"

"You don't have a hidden agenda."

"And she does?"

"Of course she does. Why else would she be trying to help me?"

"What is her hidden agenda?"

"I don't know, but there's got to be one."

"You're making judgments based on what you don't really know. Maybe she just has a good heart."

"Bullshit. Sorry, I shouldn't have said that."

"Want to know what I think?"

"Go ahead," she said through a sigh.

"Before you write her off, understand where she's coming from. And then, if you still think she's got an ulterior motive, avoid her."

"We have nothing in common. She's rich, and I'm not."

"So? Look, I'm not here to tell you what to do about this woman or any other person in your life. That's completely up to you. I'm just saying, it will always have a better outcome if you take time to understand people. If they're truly up to something, at least then you'll have given them a chance and a concrete reason for avoiding them."

Cassandra gave Jessivel two contact names for job leads—one of whom was Renaldo Vargas with Goodwill Industries.

Get to know Paige better—right. She knew all she had to know. As far as she was concerned, there was nothing positive about knowing her—the little interaction she'd had with her had only made her feel worse, not better. Paige West was not someone she wanted or needed in her already screwed-up life.

CHAPTER 31

Paige filled Natalie in on the beginning of Tim and Hank's story. They sat in the living room and talked without any negative discourse—something Paige felt very satisfying.

"So how do you think they knew about the ring?" Natalie asked.

"You heard them. Their mother gave it to Dad."

"You believe that?"

"How else would they know about it?"

"I don't know, but I don't trust them. And did you catch that one of them kept referring to the ring as having a 'stone.' That was a diamond in that ring."

"Even so, it's pretty small. I can't believe it's worth that much…like he said."

"And one is a doctor and the other a college professor? Really?"

"It could be true. They seemed well-educated," Paige said, not knowing why she was defending them.

"So you believe them about Dad being their father?"

"They knew an awful lot about him. Like his old Army buddy's name. How else would they know that? And knowing what I now know about Dad, yes, I do."

"What do you know about Dad that I don't know?"

Paige filled her in about Jessivel, the letter their father had written to their mother before he died, and the elusive Emma.

"You're frickin' crazy. Dad wasn't like that."

"Apparently, he was, and the ring proves it."

"Where is it now?"

"Jessivel has it."

"Why does *she* have it?"

"According to her, Dad gave it to her sometime before he died."

"Why her?"

"I don't know."

"And now these two jerks want it."

"Natalie, they weren't jerks. They were very polite and appeared sincere to me."

"You've always been the gullible one."

"What are you talking about? I am not gullible."

"If you believe this Jezebel character and those two Ayrabs—"

"It's Jessivel, and those two gentlemen have names."

"Gullible *and* polite. Woo hoo!"

"Whatever."

"Well, I find their story a little hard to swallow," Natalie said with her arms crossed. "You can believe what you want. So, what are you going to do now? Hand the ring over to them?"

"I can't. Jessivel has it. And besides, it was a gift—first to Dad and then to Jessivel—so legally, it's hers."

"If you believe *her*."

"Why would she lie about it?"

"'Cause she needs the money, stupid. She probably stole it."

So much for having a constructive conversation. Paige stared at her for a moment while she counted to five in her head. "She keeps it on a chain around her neck. And even though she could have, she didn't sell or pawn it."

"Go ahead and keep believing these characters, big sister. See where it gets you."

"What do you *expect* me to do?"

"Do whatever you want to do, and I'm sure you'll end up on top…like always."

"What's that supposed to mean?"

"C'mon Miss Paige Perfect West." Natalie spat the words out as she rose from her chair. "You know damn well what I mean. Mom and Dad worshiped you. You were always their favorite."

"What are you talking about now?"

"Give me a break. You were the one in the school plays, on the cheerleader squad, straight A's. How could I compete with that when I could do nothing right?"

"Since when was it a competition?"

"No matter what I did, I would always look bad following you."

"I don't know where you—"

"And do you think for a minute I wanted to wear all your stupid hand-me-downs? Yeah, right. *That* was special," she said. "No wonder I'm the way I am today," she said walking away from Paige toward the stairs to her old bedroom where she'd taken up residence.

"I had to be that way," Paige said. "I had no choice."

Natalie spun around to face her. "Now, what are *you* talking about?"

Paige looked down at her lap and thought through what she was about to tell Natalie—a story she had never shared with anyone before.

"There was nothing I wanted more as a kid than to spend time with Dad. I did everything I could to get his attention and his approval," she said, trying to suppress her emotions. "I can still remember bringing home straight-A report cards and waiting for him to see it—sometimes for days. And then one time I got a 'B' in fourth-grade history. Mr. Krueger's class. I hid the report card under my mattress. Never showed it to anyone because I was so devastated by it, ashamed of it, and I thought he would be, too. The next day, I overheard Dad say something to Mom that I will never forget. 'A son wouldn't have…' I can't tell you the rest of his sentence because I ran into my room and cried my eyes out. From that point on, I vowed to myself that I would never fail at anything. I would never make Dad wish he had had a son instead of me."

Natalie's facial expression softened as Paige told the story. "The rest of his sentence may not have had anything to do with you," Natalie said. "He could have been talking about anybody."

"In my nine-year-old mind, it had everything to do with me. After that, I worked my ass off at everything to please him, because I knew I couldn't live with his disappointment." She paused to reflect on what she'd just said, something she'd never said out loud or even admitted to herself. "And if that made your life difficult, I'm sorry. It certainly wasn't intentional."

Paige got up and quietly left her mother's home. Once in the seclusion of her car, she cried, not understanding in the moment exactly why.

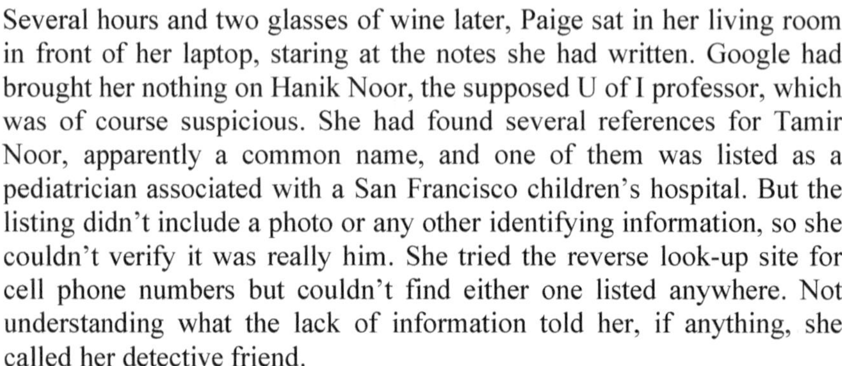

Several hours and two glasses of wine later, Paige sat in her living room in front of her laptop, staring at the notes she had written. Google had brought her nothing on Hanik Noor, the supposed U of I professor, which was of course suspicious. She had found several references for Tamir Noor, apparently a common name, and one of them was listed as a pediatrician associated with a San Francisco children's hospital. But the listing didn't include a photo or any other identifying information, so she couldn't verify it was really him. She tried the reverse look-up site for cell phone numbers but couldn't find either one listed anywhere. Not understanding what the lack of information told her, if anything, she called her detective friend.

Gary laughed. "I'm going to have to start charging you," he said after Paige explained what she wanted.

"And that would be okay," she responded. "Although I don't know how your department would feel about that."

"Hold on a minute. I can check something really quick for you." They chatted while he hunted for the phone numbers. "Well, it looks like both phones are burners, and most resellers don't keep track of their inventory."

"English please."

"Burners are prepaid disposable cell phones. You can buy them anywhere, even the Dollar Store carries them. But retailers typically don't keep track of who they sell them to. Too much paperwork with no real benefit to them."

"Why do people use them?"

"For anonymity mostly. They're virtually untraceable."

"Great."

She pondered Tim and Hank's motive while in bed that night. It had to be more than her father's ring like they said. Unable to fall asleep, she went back to her computer and keyed in the surname "Noor." Over two hundred thousand hits. Tamir had to be her father's son. Her mother wouldn't have added his name to her will otherwise. And he knew too much. Of course, that didn't explain Hanik. Perhaps her mother was unaware of him.

The two men could easily have been of mixed race, adding to their credibility. But all they wanted was the ring, they had said. They didn't want to know more about their father, which now that she thought about it was strange. And their speeches seemed like they could have been rehearsed.

Realizing that she was now overthinking the situation, she put it aside, but not for long.

The following day, she set up a group FaceTime call with "the girls" and told them the latest.

"You have got to start writing mysteries, Gayle," Valerie said. "You can't make this stuff up, and Paige is giving it all to you for free. Are you taking notes?"

"I know. I only wish it were steamy sex stuff I could use."

"Stop."

"You mean with lots of stroking, rubbing, and moaning?"

"You guys are incorrigible. Now what do you think about how these guys knew about—"

"Don't forget to throw in strong fingers. I love when you do that."

"Does anyone care about me and my problems?" Paige asked.

"Make it happen, Big Boy! Remember that line?"

"I'll never forget it! And what about 'His lips found pleasure in myriad places'?"

"I'm hanging up now."

"Ha! How about 'the fleshy mounds of juicy desire'? Did y'all like that one?"

"All I remember is when I read the line in your last book about the guy describing 'the sweetness of her nectar,' I didn't know if I had the urge to have sex with my husband or prune the peach tree."

"'Bye, girls."

In her office the next morning, just as she was about to dial the hospital, Paige's phone rang.

"Thanks a lot for letting me know Ryan died," the man said, the voice unmistakably belonging to her ex-husband Leland, whom she hadn't seen or spoken with in several years.

"Hello, Lee. I'm fine, thank you, and you?"

"I loved that man. He and I got along like brothers. The least you could have done was let me know he died."

"I'm sorry. I thought of it too late."

"Really? Well, how about if you had called me when you *did* think about it? Would that have been so hard?"

"I said I was sorry."

No response.

"Lee?"

"I'm still here."

"So how did you find out?"

"Natalie called me."

"Natalie?"

"Your sister. Remember her?"

"Don't be a smartass. When did she call you?"

"About ten minutes ago."

"I see."

"She also told me about the two Indian dudes who are claiming to be your half-brothers."

"She did, did she."

"Don't trust them."

"That's what she told you?"

"She didn't have to. I know a little about them, well, one of them."

"What do *you* know?"

"Your dad and I were close, remember? He told me things."

"He told you things, and you didn't tell me? When was this?" she asked, feeling a bit betrayed, something she had never felt during their ten years of marriage.

"After you dumped me, so it doesn't actually count."

"I didn't *dump* you."

"Call it what you want—from this end, it felt like I was dumped."

His words brought a flush of shame to her cheeks. She took a moment to unburden the guilt before responding. "So what did he tell you that you didn't feel the need to tell me, even if we were divorced?"

"You're upset with me for not telling you, aren't you?"

"I'm not upset. What did he tell you?"

"I think you are."

"Would you just tell me?" she shouted.

"Calm down, sweetie. He told me about this son."

"What did he tell you about him?"

"That he met his mother in some sleezy bar in Mumbai, I think, when he was stationed over there. Got her pregnant, felt guilty about it, and then kept sending her money over the years until the boy was eighteen."

"There weren't two boys?"

"He only told me about the one—a kid with striking blue eyes I remember him saying. Natalie said the guys you met had dark eyes, almost black, so something is fishy."

"Did he tell you his name?"

"If he did, I don't remember it."

"Okay, go on."

"Have dinner with me."

"Very funny."

"I'm not being funny. I don't like telling you this over the phone. And besides, it would be good to see you again."

Stunned on two levels—that her ex-husband knew personal things about her father that he hadn't shared with her and that he seemed sincere about dinner—Paige mulled over the right response. She had initiated the divorce, claiming they had married young and grown in different ways, making them incompatible. While not the real reason, it had been accepted by everyone in her circle of friends and apparently even Leland—he had never fought the divorce, hadn't even hired an attorney.

"I'm interested in hearing more about what you know about my father, so, yes, let's get together."

"How about tonight?"

His eagerness made her nervous. "Okay. Are you still downtown?"

"Yes."

"Still at MacComb and Little?" Leland had worked in the company's accounting department during their marriage.

"Yes, but now I'm their controller."

"Impressive. We can meet somewhere downtown, if you like."

"No, I'll come to you. How about Michael's? Seven o'clock?"

Michael's, a French restaurant they had enjoyed on special occasions, was out of the question.

"How about Nick's? We can get in there without a reservation." And it's less romantic, she thought.

"We already have a reservation at Michael's."

Really?

"I prefer Nick's if you don't mind."

"Nick's it is. I'll see you there."

CHAPTER 32

"You don't know what it's like to be me in this school, Mom," Kayla said to Jessivel. "They look at me like I'm from some other planet. I'm such an outcast."

Kayla's father had a Caucasian/Black mother and an Asian father, giving him and now Kayla an intercontinental look that most people couldn't readily identify. Jessivel had not explained her multiracial lineage with her as yet, thinking she was still too young to fully understand it.

"I think you're overreacting a bit. They're probably looking at you because they're jealous that you're so pretty."

"Right. Even if they were, which they're not, I'm the only one who looks like me in the whole school."

"I find that hard to believe." They lived in a very diverse neighborhood.

"Well, I am."

"Even if you are, there's nothing wrong with that."

"Yeah? Try eating lunch all alone every day. At least the other kids have phones they can pretend to be looking at. I don't even have that. I don't want to be different, Mom—I want to fit in. And then *you* make it worse by not letting me do anything."

"Like what?"

"Like I told you the basketball coach said I was a natural to play, and you wouldn't let me."

"Because it costs money—money I don't have."

"And look at these clothes. I'm the worst-dressed kid in class. They're all laughing at me."

"They are not."

"How do you know? You're not there."

"Aren't there any kids from around here, in this building, in your class?"

"Not that I've ever seen, and how would I know they lived here anyway?"

"Well, you're going to have to deal with it. Make some friends."

"It's not that easy, Mom."

"Just walk up to someone and start talking. You're making a big deal out of nothing," Jessivel said.

"I wouldn't know what to say. I'd sound stupid."

"Say, 'Hey, I like your backpack. Where did you get it?'"

"That sounds lame, Mom."

"So, come up with something else then. It's not that hard."

"Right. You do it, if you think it's so easy," Kayla said before retreating to her room.

Jessivel pushed Kayla's concerns aside for the moment to focus on herself. Cassandra had given her two contact names for job leads. She called the job-placement agency first and made an appointment to fill out an application. Then she called Renaldo Vargas at Goodwill Industries and did the same thing. Both indicated that while barista openings were rare, they did come up periodically. When asked if she would consider another type of job, one that required few skills and experience, she responded in the negative, as she feared that could mean becoming her mother and cleaning toilets for a living.

Disheartened and depressed, Jessivel gave serious consideration to her situation and whether she would find it better elsewhere—some other city, state, or even country—away from her nagging mother, snobby coffee drinkers, pain-in-the-ass Paige, and the constant reminder that her father wasn't around to care for her anymore. She pictured herself driving on a wide-open road with Chicago disappearing in her rearview mirror, the breeze from an open window blowing the past out of her hair.

The confrontation with Kayla weighed heavily on her mind. "You do it, if you think it's so easy," she'd said. Maybe she had something there. Maybe being around some fun people for a while, having a few drinks, would get her mind off things, at least for a bit. It wouldn't have to be for long. It couldn't be for long—she was not a big consumer of alcohol ever since she had gotten completely wasted once as a teenager, passed out for hours, and awoken covered in vomit in unfamiliar surroundings. This experience had scared the bejesus out of her, and she hadn't overindulged since then.

As long as she drank responsibly, getting out and socializing with people her own age sounded like a good plan, better by the minute.

She waited until Kayla went to bed before trying on the one outfit she owned that was suitable for a club—a black pantsuit with a lacy pink camisole. She dabbed on a little makeup to finish off the look.

In case Kayla awoke while she was gone, she scribbled a note to her saying she'd be back shortly, then headed for Doubleday's, a neighborhood bar she had passed numerous times and thought looked decent from the outside.

Jessivel was not an experienced club-goer, and when she walked into the lounge at Doubleday's, she was petrified. Without making eye contact with anyone, she made a mad dash for the bathroom and slipped into a stall.

"I can do this," she whispered and then froze when she heard the bathroom door open. As she stood there—facing the toilet, listening to the person in the next stall pee—she recalled the Nike slogan "Just do it."

"What are you doing over there?" the voice in the next stall yelped at her. "If you're some male weirdo, you need to use the other bathroom."

Jessivel realized what it must look like from the other side with her standing facing the toilet for so long. "I'm a girl, you idiot!" She turned around, pulled down her panties, and squatted, but as hard as she pushed, nothing came out. She waited for the sound of the door closing before leaving the stall and the rest room.

The lounge seemed more crowded than when she had arrived. She scanned the patrons, most of whom appeared younger than she. She had twelve dollars in her purse—the maximum amount she could spend for the evening. She inched toward the bar with the intention of ordering a gin and tonic when she sensed someone's stare from her left. She glanced over to find a tall, thin man with dark greased-back hair ogling her. His devilish smile sent her off to the other end of the bar where she focused on getting the bartender's attention.

The bar was crowded. She squeezed in between two people seated there to avoid coming face-to-face with creepy guy again. Right after she ordered her drink, she felt someone pressing up against her backside. She waited—frozen in position and afraid to turn around—for the bartender to hand her the drink.

"It's been taken care of," the bartender told her.

"By whom?"

He nodded toward a place behind her. She turned to see creepy guy's grin.

"I don't want it," she said and bolted from the bar without looking back.

Jessivel walked as fast as she could toward the door when she found herself on the dance floor. A tall, good-looking man about her age grabbed her by the arm and swung her around.

"Care to dance?" he asked her.

Jessivel contemplated running in the opposite direction, but the man's playful grin drew her in.

"I'm Andrew," the man shouted while dancing in front of her. "And you are?"

"Jessivel," she said as she blended in with his dance moves.

"Nice to meet you, Jessivel."

They danced until the end of the song when another man came up to them.

"Can I have the next one?" he asked.

Before she could answer, she was dancing with man number 2. Then number 3.

By the time Jessivel stepped out with number 7, she was attempting to do the Floss with a drink in each hand. She searched for a place to set the drinks down and take a break when creepy guy walked toward her. Her "buzz off" glare didn't stop him from approaching her.

"Looks like you need a breather, honey."

Jessivel ignored his comment and continued to try to find somewhere to sit.

Creepy guy took her arm and tried to guide her off the dance floor.

She jerked her arm away from the man, spilling her drink on the woman next to her.

"What the—" the woman yelled.

"I'm sorry," Jessivel said as she dropped the now-empty glass and headed toward the door.

A man snatched Jessivel's arm. "You apologize to my girl, ya hear?"

"You're hurting me," Jessivel said as she tried to pull away from him. "And I did apologize, you fool." She threw the drink she still had in her other hand into the man's face.

A large, heavily-tattooed man with a bulldog look about him took the empty glass from Jessivel's hand and escorted her to the door. "You're through here, girl" he said as he hustled her out the door.

The man's shove caused Jessivel to stumble, and in her attempt to keep from falling, she turned an ankle. She limped to her car as the pain shot through her foot and leg, got in, and locked the door. Feeling a little tipsy, and her ankle now pounding with pain, she slithered down into the seat and closed her eyes.

CHAPTER 33

Paige surveyed the clothes racks in her sizeable walk-in closet before choosing the right outfit for her dinner with Leland—one that was flattering but conservative. She drove to Nick's, curious and nervous about the meeting.

She had met Leland in college and dated him once. He never called for a second date, and she soon forgot about him. A year later, both attended the same Bears game at Soldier Field, and when Leland saw Paige's face on the jumbotron, he spent the rest of the game searching for her in the stands. This time, for some reason, they made an immediate connection and married a year later.

Paige liked taking her clients to Nick's where the food was good but not overly expensive, the atmosphere relaxing, and the lighting not so dim that you needed a flashlight to read the menu. Perfect for her and Leland.

She found him waiting for her in the lobby when she arrived. He wore a blue blazer over a paler blue dress shirt and a pair of khakis—a handsome look on him. His broad, sweet grin brought back memories. He went in for a kiss. She turned her head, causing his lips to land on her cheek.

He took a step back. "You look great, champ." She had always hated it when he'd called her this, assuming he was ridiculing her "achieving" personality. "I see you're still wearing those turtlenecks."

She ignored both remarks. He looked good, even though he had put on a few pounds and a bit of grey now peppered his temples. He still had those soft lines around his piercing blue eyes that deepened when he laughed or smiled—the ones that looked sexy on a man but could age a woman ten years.

"Shall we go in?" she asked.

They slid into a booth. It seemed surreal sitting across from him after so much time had lapsed—a stranger, yet quite familiar to her. The way her body reacted to his presence made her self-conscious.

Paige didn't waste any time getting to the business at hand once they perused the menu and ordered.

"So, tell me what else my father told you about his life beyond my family."

"I'm fine, and you?"

Paige inhaled a large breath of air and let it out slowly as she collected her words. "I'm sorry. It's just that I'm anxious to hear what you have to say about him. There's a lot at stake here. How have you been?"

"I've been fine."

"That's good. How's your family?"

"We're all good. Including Sadie."

"Sadie?" Paige knew from a mutual friend that Leland had remarried to a woman named Arlene. She was not aware that they had had kids together and was surprised to hear this.

He took out a photo from his wallet.

"Oh, how cute!" Yorkies had always been her favorite breed, but Leland had been against getting a dog when they were married. "What made you change your mind about a dog?"

He shrugged. "I don't know. Maybe the timing was right."

"How long have you had her?"

"Just got her."

Paige didn't understand his "timing" remark but decided not to pursue it.

"Okay. Anything else new with you?" She smiled. "Except for your haircut, that is." Leland had always worn his hair a little longer than Paige would have liked, his way of exhibiting non-conformity in his "corporate accounting" world at work.

"You don't like it?"

"Actually, I do. You just didn't wear it that way before."

"Speaking of then, I ran into Ron Bowman the other day. He bought our old house."

"No kidding." Ron had been Leland's best man at their wedding. "What a coincidence."

"So I went there to see him and his new wife, who's expecting by the way." His words drifted off, and so did his gaze. When he focused back on Paige, he said, "We made some good memories in that house."

She nodded. While it was true, she didn't want to unduly acknowledge it to him or herself. Not now. And some sad memories had also been created in that house. Seeing Leland today reminded her how much Briana had looked like him. She suddenly recalled her pale, lifeless face with utter clarity, how she looked while she held her for her last breath in the hospital room, stroking her tufts of blond hair in her final minutes. Thinking about her brought sadness that she was gone but also the sweet, wonderful feeling of her presence. She searched her heart for something to block out the memories and keep the tears from coming.

"I think I know what you're thinking, Paige. I miss her too."

She tried not to lose herself in the tenderness of his eyes and was grateful for their food arriving.

"I heard you got married," she said once the waiter had left.

"I did…but it was never much of a marriage. We divorced last year."

"I'm sorry to hear that."

"You never remarried, right?"

"No."

"Why not?" he asked.

"Oh, I don't know. I seem to do better on my own, I guess." The words had come out way too fast and sounded insidious, even to her.

"I always thought it had something to do with Briana."

"That too."

"Why is that, do you think?"

"Why is what?"

"Why you seem to do better on your own."

Paige had no intention of explaining her wanting to be a member of the "single by choice" club to Leland, especially when she didn't fully understand it herself. Years after her divorce, she had tried being in other relationships, but whenever it got close to serious, she would push the man away, likening being in a new relationship to leaping off a second-story building and hoping someone would be down there to catch her.

"I don't know. I'm just happier being alone, I guess."

"Thanks a lot."

"Nothing against you. It would have happened no matter who I was married to."

"You really know how to make a guy feel special."

"Is that what this meeting is about? Making you feel special?" More regrettable words.

"I didn't know it was a meeting. I thought we were having dinner together."

"Are you going to tell me more about what you know about my father?"

"Are you happy?"

"Yes, I am happy," she said, her patience close to running out.

"Define happiness."

Paige leaned forward. "Look, Leland. This has gone on long enough. We were married for ten years. It ended…twelve years ago. Now we're just two people who haven't seen each other in a long time. You're asking inappropriate questions."

"Eleven years, ten months."

"Whatever."

"Excuse me for caring."

"I never remarried, Lee. I never intend to remarry. I never intend to be in another relationship for that matter. I moved on…to being single. I'm wedded to real estate. That's what I love. That's what makes me happy."

"Really?"

"I thought you had moved on too. And if you aren't going to share with me what you know about my father, we can end this get-together, or whatever you want to call it. Are we clear?"

"I see you're still that independent woman I knew. Taken any vacations lately?" He didn't give her a chance to respond. "I didn't think so." He glared at her before continuing. "You're so self-sufficient that you don't need anyone in your life. And you sure as hell don't need me."

She had watched a host of emotions play across Leland's face as he spoke, until his expression culminated into none at all. He got up from his chair, raked his fingers through his thick ash-blond hair, and said, "You might want to check out the teddy bear…hon."

"What teddy bear?"

"The one she sent him from India," he said before walking away.

She watched him leave until he was no longer visible.

I *am* happy. I love what I do, and I'm good at it. Of course, he didn't give me any credit for that. Never did before either. Some things never change.

What teddy bear?

Leland clearly had more than one thing on his mind for their reunion, one of which she foolishly hadn't prepared for well enough. Had it been a business meeting, she would have had a better plan in play to achieve her goal—it was considerably easier for her to master the art of real estate negotiations than those involving affairs of the heart.

He could have at least picked up the check, she thought as she nibbled on the last of her coconut fried shrimp.

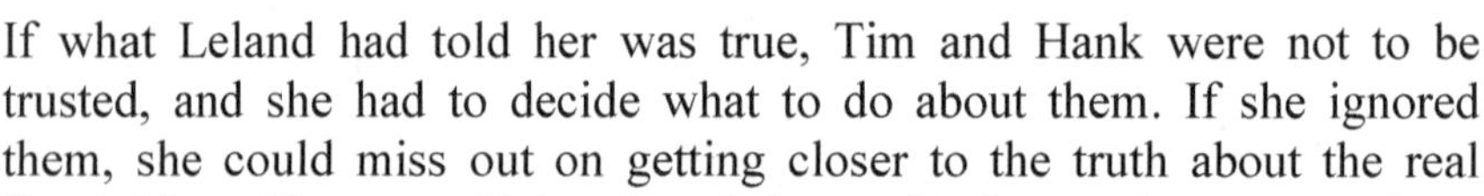

If what Leland had told her was true, Tim and Hank were not to be trusted, and she had to decide what to do about them. If she ignored them, she could miss out on getting closer to the truth about the real Tamir Noor. However, if she played along with them to learn more about the truth, it could mean trouble.

Before she decided which way to go, she wanted to do a thorough search of her mother's house for a teddy bear, thinking that Leland wouldn't have brought it up if it didn't have something to do with her father. She decided to bring Natalie in on it—pretty much had to because Natalie was living there and didn't leave the house long enough for Paige to pull it off by herself.

She approached Natalie the next day and told her what Leland had said about the teddy bear.

"You mean *my* teddy bear?" Natalie asked.

"No. I told you—one that this Indian woman sent to Dad."

"I know what you said. Don't you remember the whole teddy bear incident with me and Dad?"

"No," Paige said, wondering where her often-confused sister was going with this.

"I had this teddy bear—dark brown with blue-and-white-striped pants. And it had blue glass eyes. I found it in Mom and Dad's closet one day and started to play with it. After a while, I figured finders keepers and kept it in my room."

"I don't remember that."

"I kept it hidden. At least *some* thing that wasn't yours first. Know what I mean?"

"Go on."

"Anyway, one day Dad caught me playing with it and took it away from me. I never saw it again."

If it hadn't been for Natalie's detailed description of the teddy bear, Paige wouldn't have believed a word she'd said.

"So, let's go look for it. We know it didn't go to his grave with him, so it's got to be here somewhere."

For the next two hours, they searched every room, closet, drawer, and shelf to no avail.

"I wish we hadn't looked in her drawers," Natalie said.

"I know. Like we were invading her privacy."

"And I didn't have to see she had a dil—"

"Shut up! I don't want to hear it."

"Moms aren't supposed to have those things."

"Eeww."

The conversation flowed easily—they talked about old times, fun times, and laughed until their sides hurt—something they hadn't done in ages.

"Maybe he kept it in his office at work," Natalie said.

"Someone brought over all his office stuff, so I don't think so."

"If Mom found it, she may have thrown it out."

"Good point. I'll ask her today when I go see her. You haven't seen her since you've been here. Do you want to go with me?"

Natalie didn't respond.

"Yes? No?"

"I'll take a pass."

"The two of you never talked about you staying here, did you?"

Natalie stared past Paige for a few seconds before mumbling a response. "Not really."

"Well, she didn't say much when I told her I found you here. Do you want me to say anything about you when I see her today?"

"Would you?"

"Sure. What do you want me to say?"

"Just make sure it's okay if I stay here for a while."

"Anything going on that we should know about?"

Natalie shrugged.

"Natalie?"

"What?"

"Like why did you and what's-his-name break up?"

"What difference does it make?"

"If you're going to live here, I think we need to know everything."

"What do you mean 'we'? Mom, maybe."

"Did it ever occur to you that maybe I could be of some help? Did it ever occur to you that once everything is out in the open, things could go smoother? You can't shock me, Natalie. And unless you've killed someone or committed some other heinous crime, I won't hold whatever trouble you're in against you."

"I haven't killed anyone."

"That's good to know."

"I owe someone some money though."

"How much money?"

"A little over five thousand."

"What?"

"I thought you said nothing would shock you."

"I lied. You owe someone five thousand dollars? For what?"

"What do you think?"

"Drugs?"

When Natalie didn't respond, Paige went down a different path, knowing that she risked being shut off by Natalie and that would accomplish nothing. "Have you thought about what you're doing to your unborn child with the drugs and alcohol?"

"Do you think I'm stupid? Of course I have."

"So what are you doing about it?"

"I can't afford to do anything about it. I have no money, no insurance."

"Will you let me help you? You can't do this to an innocent child."

Natalie shot up from her chair. "And let big sister bail me out? Not on your life!" she shouted before retreating to her bedroom.

So much for the amicable sisterly discourse.

Paige gave her mother's plants a quick watering before leaving for the hospital. On the way there, she pondered her sister's resentment toward her. That brought her to thinking about Jessivel's hostility toward her and, more recently, Leland's. What was she doing so wrong?

Natalie's addictions were worrisome. Google research on pain-pill addiction brought more than 15 million results, telling her that Natalie was far from being alone. Once she'd read a few articles on the subject, Paige knew that helping her sister in any meaningful way was out of her league—it would take a team of professionals. But having a better understanding of her condition was another matter and something she mentally committed to do.

Jessivel was more difficult to understand. If she could figure her out, she might still have a shot at helping her—something she wanted and felt obligated to do.

As for Leland, Paige regretted the way she had interacted with him—he'd done nothing more than show an interest in seeing her again. Without leading him on, she would have to make it up to him, especially if she wanted more information about her father.

Between Natalie, Jessivel, and Leland, she wasn't sure who would turn out to be her biggest challenge.

CHAPTER 34

Jessivel awoke to someone knocking on her car window.

"Are you alright?" the male voice asked.

She took a few seconds for her eyes to adjust and to realize her whereabouts. Then she sat up in the car seat and rolled down the window a crack. The cool, damp air swept across her face, forcing her to fully wake up.

"I think so. What time is it?" she asked the same man who had shoved her out of the bar earlier.

"Four o'clock. The bar is closed, and you have to—"

"Four o'clock! I have to go," she said as she fumbled for her keys.

"Are you sure you're okay to drive?"

"I'm fine."

Jessivel backed out of the parking space and drove as fast as she dared toward her home, a mile away. When she arrived, three police cars blocked her from parking in her assigned spot at her building. She pulled into a guest spot and hobbled toward the building, nursing her injured ankle. A police officer stopped her at the door.

"May I have your name?" he asked her.

"Jessivel Salter. What's wrong? What are you doing here?"

"Let's go into your apartment where we can talk."

Jessivel followed the officer to her apartment—her ankle hurting worse with each step—thinking the worst of what could have happened to Kayla. Inside were two other male police officers, two women, and Kayla, all seated in the living room.

"Kayla…are you okay?" Jessivel asked as she rushed to her daughter. "What's going on?"

"I'm sorry, Mom. I didn't know what to do," Kayla said through tears.

One of the women rose and said, "Kayla, let's you and I go into your bedroom and let the adults talk for a while."

Once Kayla was out of sight, Jessivel demanded to know what was going on.

"Miss Salter, your daughter called us when she woke up to an empty apartment," one of the officers said. He looked her up and down before continuing. "She was worried that something had happened to you."

"I left her a note. I just went out for a bit."

He glanced down at a pad of paper in his hand. "Your daughter called 9-1-1 at three-o-five."

"She doesn't have a phone."

"She called us from your neighbor's."

At a complete loss for words, Jessivel waited for someone to say something more.

"Where were you?" asked the woman who had remained in the room.

"Who are you?"

"I am Hazel Beckworth from DCFS. We were called when the officers found your twelve-year-old daughter here in the middle of the night, scared about what had happened to you. Now, I'll ask you again, where were you?"

"I went out, just for a little while, but I hurt my ankle, and I sort of fell asleep in my car and…"

"Here's what's going to happen Miss Salter. We've interviewed your daughter and inspected your home, and now that you're here and we've met you, we don't believe there is any immediate threat to her safety. But we will give our findings to an internal investigator who will do a much more thorough analysis."

"For what purpose?"

"To determine if there is likely to be any future threat to the child's safety."

"That's—"

"After all the information is gathered and analyzed, the investigator will write a report and provide a recommendation that will be reviewed by a panel of DCFS supervisors. If they find everything to be in order, the report is filed with the agency, and you will be notified of what further steps, if any, will be taken." The woman's rote explanation was one she had obviously spewed many times before.

"Like what steps?" Jessivel asked.

"That depends on the findings."

"Like what's the worst that could happen?"

"Your daughter could be removed from your home and placed in foster care."

The statement hit like a punch to the face.

"I'm not saying that will be the case. You asked what was the worst that could happen."

The woman and the officers got up to leave.

"Do you have any questions, Miss Salter?"

Jessivel shook her head, wanting most of all for them to leave.

"Good night then."

The woman who had gone off with Kayla must have been within earshot of the conversation. She emerged from the hallway and left with the others.

Jessivel sank down into the sofa, emotionally spent. After a few minutes, she went to her daughter's room and peeked inside to see Kayla in bed with her back to her.

"Kayla?"

"What?"

"Are you okay?"

"Mm-hm."

"I'm sorry this happened. I hurt my ankle and… Anyway, I'm sorry. Whose phone did you use, by the way?" Jessivel asked.

"Mrs. Harding from next door. She told us that one time if we ever needed anything to just ask."

"I know."

"She was real nice about it."

"That's good."

"I called you first, but it went to voicemail."

Jessivel looked at her phone and saw there were two unopened voicemail messages. "I guess I didn't hear the phone. Maybe the music…"

"It's okay, Mom."

Jessivel quietly closed the door and went to bed herself, mad at the world, but mostly at her father, followed closely by her mother.

"You've got to get a place of your own. I can't keep living like this," Jessivel told her mother over the phone the next day.

"I can only talk a minute, Jess. I'm busy here. What's wrong with where you are?"

"Haven't you saved up enough for an apartment or something?"

"No, have you?"

"If I don't have a job soon, I'll be kicked out of here."

"Then find another job. What's the problem?"

"You're no help, you know that? I suppose you *want* to see Kayla end up in foster care."

"Of course, I don't. Are you looking for another job?"

"You know how hard it is to find a barista job near me? Do you know—"

"How hard are you trying, Jess?"

"I thought I'd at least get some sympathy from *you*."

"That will come only after you tell me you've exhausted all efforts in finding another job."

"I've looked, okay?"

"How hard?"

"Never mind. You know what? If I—"

"You're acting like a victim, Jessie, and you're angry. There's no one more helpless than an angry victim. And you can change both. I have to go. She's having ladies over for brunch. I'll talk to you later."

"You could at least—"

Her mother hung up before Jessivel could finish her sentence.

If she couldn't rely on her mother, she couldn't rely on anyone. *Except herself,* she knew some people would say. Like Dr. Phil. And pain-in-the-ass Paige. And Cassandra from the land of the I'm-glad-I'm-not-in-your-shoes social services office. She could rely on her father and did so her whole life until he died. Maybe Paige did too and was still depending on him with whatever she ended up with after his death, which was probably a bundle.

She loathed her mother's so-called wise sayings. "There's no one more helpless than an angry victim." Right. Easier said than done. That was her own wise saying.

Jessivel stared at the pathetic furnishings in the living room of her apartment—a worn brown sofa that sagged in the middle; two blue side chairs, one with a hideous stain on the seat; a floor lamp from the eighties; and a lopsided coffee table that someone had tried to fix with slices of a wine cork held on with packaging tape on one leg.

She pictured Paige's living room—a white leather sectional, matching ottoman, crystal lamps on glass-top end tables, fancy artwork on the walls.

She glanced up at the only thing hanging on her wall—a framed print of a bunch of weird-looking people milling around on a pristine lawn under some trees, some with umbrellas, even though it wasn't raining. One woman with a huge butt held on to a monkey on a leash. She'd seen the same picture hanging in doctors' offices and other public places her whole life. The original was probably worth millions and hung in some fancy museum she'd never visit. Her cheap print had a tear in the lower right-hand corner that someone had patched with now-yellowed cellophane tape over the monkey's ass.

Despite her current terrible state of affairs, something gave Jessivel reason to feel a little sunny inside—Doubleday's the night before. Some of the men she had danced with had been totally fine and seemed like decent guys who knew how to treat a girl. Having been without a man since her boyfriend left, she could still remember the feeling of being held, kissed, and told "I love you, baby" at the most unexpected but welcomed times.

But, damn, she had gone out for a little fun just one time, and it had turned into a disaster. If only her mother wasn't so tied to her employer, she could have baby-sat for Kayla, and none of this would have happened.

It was time to get dressed for the back-to-back job interviews she'd scheduled, even though she knew they were going to be a waste of time. Even if there were open barista jobs out there, the employers would call Audrey to inquire about her work history, and Jessivel was fairly sure she wouldn't give her a good referral, thanks to Paige.

She drove to Goodwill Industries. "I wish you had come a few days earlier," Mr. Vargas told her. "The Daily Grind is near you, and they had a part-time barista opening. It's been filled now. Barista jobs don't come up too often, at least not in your area. I see you worked for The Busy Bean in Lincoln Park? Would you consider going that far again?"

"It took me forever to get to work every day. I was hoping for something closer," she told him.

He told her he would contact her if he heard of anything.

Next was her appointment at the agency Cassandra had told her often placed people with little or no work experience. She filled out a long application and waited to speak with one of their placement advisors.

"Under 'Skills' you listed barista. Do you have any other skills?" the woman asked.

"Not really. That's the only job I've ever had."

"You've been trained at the Chicago Barista Academy. That's excellent. And you were at The Busy Bean, let's see, three months?"

"Yes."

"And why did you leave there?"

Jessivel wasn't prepared for this question. "I, uh, was being harassed by a customer and didn't handle it very well."

"Did you quit, or were you fired?"

"I walked away from the incident, and the owner thought I'd walked out on the job, so…"

"I see. Would you be willing to work downtown?"

All that way and where the worst of the coffee snobs are?

"I'd rather not. The commute would be a killer and expensive."

"I see. Well, if anything comes up, I'll contact you, but I can tell you that barista positions don't open near you very often, so you might want to rethink your commute restrictions. I could send you on two interviews right now if you'd consider downtown."

"I'll let you know," she told her.

Jessivel drove home and stewed over what the agency woman had told her. Why should she have to travel two hours a day to get to a stinking job where she'd be treated like shit by people who lived like kings and queens? That was her mother's life, not hers.

CHAPTER 35

"My mother was transferred? Why didn't anyone tell me?" Paige asked the nurse. She had driven to the hospital to discover her mother had been released the day before.

The nurse focused on her computer screen. "It says here that you were notified."

"I was *not* notified. Where did you say she is?"

"At Waldon Rehabilitation Center. In Evanston."

"This is preposterous. No one said anything to me. How did she get there?"

"They have a service that—"

"Give me the address of the place," Paige said with a tone she soon regretted. "I'm sorry. I know it's not your fault. But can you imagine how I feel about this?"

"You might want to talk to her primary."

"Oh, you bet I will."

Paige called her mother's doctor while in the car on her way to where her mother now resided. When the woman who answered the phone said the doctor was currently with a patient, that she would give him the message, Paige lost it.

"You get him on the phone *now!* I don't care who he's with. My mother and I both signed a consent form after her surgery that stated no changes to her treatment would be initiated without my approval. Now she's been transferred without any discussion with me. This is completely unacceptable."

"Hold, please."

Paige waited on hold for fifteen minutes, her anger rising with each passing minute.

"Miss West?" the doctor said.

"What happened to my mother? She's no longer at Midwest."

"I spoke with you on Monday about this. You agreed with my recommendation to transfer her to a rehab facility. You don't remember our conversation?"

"No, I don't. Because we never had it."

"I have it here in my notes. I made the call at 1:15 P.M., on Monday. She was transferred yesterday."

"Well, it wasn't me you talked to. What number did you call?"

The doctor read the number to her.

"That's my mother's landline. Why would you call that number?"

"It's the one I have on file for you."

"That's ridiculous. I don't even live there." She gave him her cell phone number. "Do not call any number but this one from now on. Is that clear?"

"Perfectly. I'm sorry for any—"

"How long will she need residential physical therapy?"

"At least two weeks. We can see how—"

"Thanks. I'll let you know what I think after I see her."

Paige hung up without saying goodbye, disappointed in herself for not handling it better with the doctor and incensed with Natalie, who had likely taken the doctor's call. Still twenty minutes away from the rehab facility, she called her mother's home phone and forced herself to calm down while the phone rang.

"Hello," the voice on the other end said.

"Who is this?" Paige asked, not recognizing the high-pitched female voice.

She laughed. "It's me, stupid."

"Natalie, why did you answer the phone like that? You sounded like Minnie Mouse."

"Mom doesn't have caller ID on this phone, so I don't know who's calling. She's due for pest control, by the way."

"Natalie…" Paige changed her mind on going down the pest control path. "Mom left the hospital, you know."

"She did? Well, she's not here. Is she with you?"

"You were in on the decision to move her to a rehab facility, so…"

"I was?"

"You took the call."

"What call?"

"On Monday afternoon. You spoke with Mom's doctor."

"No, I didn't."

"Natalie, has there been anyone there with you since you moved in?"

"No."

"Are you sure?"

"Of course, I'm sure."

"And you've been answering the phone when it rings."

"So."

"Then you took the call. Maybe you weren't sober."

"I'll have you know I haven't had one drop of alcohol since I found out I was pregnant."

"No drugs either?"

"That's different."

Paige tried to remember some of the advice she'd read in the how-to-understand-an-addict articles. "Look, I'm on my way to this rehab place in Evanston. I'm almost there. I have to go to my office afterward, but then I'm going to come there. We need to talk."

"About what?"

"About you. I have to go. See you later."

"What do you intend to do about your opiate addiction?" Paige asked Natalie when she arrived at the house later that day. "You're pregnant. You've got to do something…for the baby's sake."

"The baby's fine. I'm the one with the problem."

"You're wrong, Nat. Those drugs go into your bloodstream and right into the baby's. He or she is at risk."

"I'm not that far along."

"You're showing, for God's sake. You've got to be at least five months."

Natalie shrugged.

"I've read up on it. All sorts of things could happen to the baby—going through withdrawal after birth, convulsions, seizures, stunted growth. Is that what you want for your baby?"

"So I'll stop. No biggie."

"You can't stop, and you know it."

"I can if I gradually taper down."

"You don't know how to properly wean yourself. Only a trained professional can determine that."

"You don't know what you're talking about. I've done it before. Plenty of times."

"And apparently that didn't work, because here you are, still on them."

"What do you care anyway? You never gave a damn before."

"It's not that I didn't care before. It was that—"

"Don't give me your stupid bullshit. You never cared about me."

"That's not true, Natalie."

"Right."

"You need to see a doctor right—"

"I can't afford a doctor."

"You can't afford *not* to see a doctor. And don't worry about the money. I'll pay for it. Or Mom will. One of us will cover for you when it comes to medical."

"How do you know Mom would pay for it?"

"Because I talked to her."

"You told her I was pregnant?"

"Yes, of course. We needed to—"

"That's *my* business, Paige. Not *yours*. If I want your help, I'll ask for it!" Natalie rose from her chair and headed toward the stairs to the second floor. "I knew this was going to happen. Stop meddling in my affairs!"

Paige gave her sister some time to cool down before she went to her room and knocked on her door.

"Go away!"

She ignored her demand and didn't wait for an invitation to enter.

"I just wanted to say that as much as you probably don't believe this, I am here for you. I'm on your side. The only thing I won't do for you is enable your drug and alcohol use. I care about you, Natalie, and I care about your unborn baby. I have the name of a specialist doctor in the area who said he could see you right away. Think about it. That's all I ask."

Receiving no response, Paige left the room and settled into one of the living room chairs. She had failed to reach Natalie. Maybe she would have better luck with Leland.

"Are we still on speaking terms," she asked him on the phone. Silence. "Leland, are you there?"

"Give me a minute. I'm thinking about how to answer your question."

"I'm sorry about dinner. It was clear that I had one thing on my mind and you had something else. I guess that should teach us that we need to be more sensitive to each other's…"

"Other's what?"

"Needs."

"Why did you hesitate with that word?"

"Because I'm not sure about yours."

"Can we start over?" he asked.

"Please."

"You're on. I will be sensitive to your needs…as of this very moment. But you might want to take advantage of it because I don't know how long it will last."

She chuckled. "You still have a sense of humor. I like that."

"How's your mom and Natalie?"

"They transferred Mom to a rehab facility. She's doing okay. Natalie, well, she has her share of problems, as you know. I'm trying to help her."

"But she's not a very willing recipient, right?"

"Right."

"Don't give up on her, Paige."

"I won't. Can we pick up where we left off talking about my father?"

"Dinner then?"

"Lee."

"Okay. I forgot. Where did we leave off?"

"You said something about a teddy bear, to check the teddy bear."

"Oh, right. He'd met this woman from India when he was in the service. He didn't go into all the details of his relationship with her, but at some point she sent him a bunch of precious stones."

"Now you're just teasing me."

"I'm not. She sent him a bunch of stones concealed in a stuffed teddy bear and told him to hold on to them until she could either come to the U.S. to claim them or send someone to do it for her."

"What kind of stones?"

"Other than calling them precious stones, I don't think he said. That, and that they're worth a small fortune."

"That's insane."

"I'm only telling you what he told me."

"Natalie and I looked all through Mom's house for a teddy bear but didn't find anything."

"If you do, remember who told you about it." He laughed. "Like I should get a share of the take or something."

"Fine," Paige said without much thought. "Now, I wonder if I have to worry about these two guys breaking in someday to try to find it…if that's what they were after." *Or maybe they already have.*

"Natalie told me they asked if they could have your dad's ring, for sentimental reasons."

"That's why they said they were here."

"The part about the ring could hold some truth. Ryan said the woman—I can't remember her name, it's been too long—told him to take one of the stones and have something made out of it for himself, which he did. He had the ring made."

"Could her name have been Qudrah?"

"Yes. That might be it."

"So *that's* how he got the ring?"

"That's what he told me."

"That's not exactly how the two guys who came here told it. Could these stones be stolen, do you know?"

"I don't think so. She told him she had inherited them."

"This story seems incredible."

"Your father got around."

"What else do you know about him?"

"Not much, but some wild things did happen at the casinos once in a while. I remember one time he went there with $500 in his pocket, ran it up to over twenty grand, and then lost it all on a single bet at the roulette wheel."

"That's crazy."

"Well, alcohol was involved."

"How come you never told me this stuff before?"

"In case you don't know, there's a male code of silence for some things."

CHAPTER 36

"What ever happened to my teddy bear, Mom?" Kayla asked Jessivel. "I haven't seen it since we moved out of Nana and Poppy's."

"I have no idea. Aren't you a little old for that?"

"I still like it. Reminds me of Poppy."

"Is that who you got it from? I forget."

"You don't remember? I saw it in Poppy's suitcase one day and started playing with it. I figured since he had given you that Care Bear when you were little, this one must have been meant for me. You don't remember him looking all over the house for it?"

"Not really."

"I hid it in my closet until I thought he forgot about it. And I never played with it when he was home."

"Well, there are still a few bags of stuff I never unpacked. It's probably in one of those. They're in my closet."

Kayla came out minutes later hugging the blue-eyed, dark-brown bear wearing blue-and-white-striped pants.

"That old thing needs to be washed. Throw it in the hamper next time you think of it."

Kayla examined the bear. "Looks okay to me."

"Just put it in there. I'm going down to the laundry room tomorrow."

"Whatever."

Jessivel mulled over what Cassandra had said about getting to know Paige better and understand her motives before discounting her. Since none of the job leads had panned out, maybe the time had come to do it. She called her.

"Yes, Jessivel, how can I help you?"

Her tone was cold and formal. Not the greeting Jessivel had expected or desired.

"Um...I just wanted to say hi and see how you were doing." As soon as she'd said it, she knew it was wrong, as they didn't have that level of relationship.

"I'm doing well. And you?"

"I'm okay. Looking for a job. Do you know of anything?"

"No. I'm sorry, I don't."

"I kind of lost my job at The Busy Bean."

"Yes, I heard."

"When I lost my temper at you."

"Mm-hm."

"So, you talked with Audrey about it?"

"She apologized for your behavior."

"I'm glad she did that. I apologize for it too."

"All is forgiven."

Jessivel didn't know how to turn the conversation into a more friendly one that might lead to Paige offering to help.

"Okay, then. Goodbye."

"Goodbye, Jessivel."

"You must have enough money by now for an apartment," Jessivel said to her mother over the phone later that day.

"I'm staying put for the time being," her mother whispered.

"But what about me and Kayla? Don't you care about us?"

"Of course I do. But you've got an apartment. So, what's the matter?"

"Are you kidding? This place is horrible! That's what's the matter. And I don't have a job, and—"

"Mrs. Perlman's neighbor is looking for a nanny/housekeeper. I could put in a good word for you."

"No way."

"What kind of a job do you want then?"

"A stupid barista job, I guess."

"And with that attitude, I'm sure you'll find just the right thing."

"Very funny."

"You know what you have to do, Jess, but you don't seem willing to do it."

"Kayla misses you."

"I miss her too."

"When's your next day off?"

Her mother didn't respond right away.

"Did you hear me?"

"I have tomorrow off."

"Can I pick you up?"

"For what?"

"To see us. Go to lunch or something."

"Okay. Pick me up at eleven."

Jessivel hung up hoping she'd have a better chance in person changing her mother's mind about getting an apartment. That would solve everything—a place to live without having to work her ass off in a job she hated. And if she lived with her mom, she could go out to a bar or somewhere without CPS getting involved. She could even get a part-time job to contribute something.

The next day, Jessivel had Kayla put on a dress that her mother had given her for her birthday two years previous and then spent time forming Kayla's hair into cute pigtails. When she finished, Kayla looked in the mirror.

"Mom! I haven't worn my hair like this since I was five."

"And Nana used to love it when you did."

"So?"

"So…we're having lunch with her today."

"So?"

"I want you to look extra nice."

"I look stupid. I'm taking them out," she said yanking on one of them.

"Leave those in! At least until after lunch."

"And this dress is stupid too. It doesn't even fit me," she said while pulling it in all directions.

"It looks fine. And it's only for lunch."

"This is so bogus. Why do I have to look like a baby?"

"Because Nana likes it. That's why."

"Why don't we have lunch where she lives? I want to see the mansion."

"Because we're going to a restaurant, that's why. Now go get that little pink purse she gave you and let's go."

"I'm not carrying that thing!"

"Why not?"

"It has Hello Kitty on it. She gave it to me when I was three."

"It wasn't *that* long ago. Go get it."

"I'm not carrying it!"

"Fine. Let's go then."

They entered the car and Jessivel said to Kayla, "Now I want you to act like a perfect little princess when we're at lunch. Whatever she says, go along with it. Tell her she looks nice. Tell her you miss her. Ask her when we can all live together again. Like a real family. That's it. Like a real family."

"In her room at the mansion?"

"No, that would have to change. Remember how we all lived in our house before? You want that again, don't you?"

"Sure. I guess. But I don't see what's wrong with where we live now."

"For God's sake, don't tell Nana that. Tell her you want to go to a different school, a better one."

"But I like my school."

"There are better schools, Kayla. You deserve a better school."

"I'm getting all A's and B's on my next report card, and I have a new best friend."

"You can do the same in a better school." She studied her daughter's hair. "Straighten the left one. It's too low."

"I hate these things," Kayla said rolling her eyes and tugging at the already-droopy pigtail.

Jessivel pulled up in front of the huge house where her mother resided and for a fleeting second felt like laying on the horn. But she didn't.

"Where should we go?" Jessivel asked her mother after she got into the car.

"How about Cassie's? I'm in the mood for their bread bowl soup." She turned around to face Kayla in the back seat. "What are you doing in that old dress? It's way too small for you."

"Told you so," Kayla snapped at Jessivel.

"And pigtails? What, are they "in" for older girls now? I'll never get used to these new fads. Well, they look hideous, to be honest."

"Mom made me wear them."

"And you're going to keep them in. They look cute," Jessivel said.

"What's wrong with you, Jess? Do you send her to school like this too?"

"There's nothing wrong with the way she's dressed. We did it for you, you know. You bought her that dress, and you used to love her hair like that."

"Right…when she was little. Maybe you should check out what the other girls her age are wearing, how they fix their hair. Get with it, Jess."

"Yeah, get with it, Mom."

Jessivel pulled into the restaurant parking lot feeling defeated. Once they were inside and seated, she made her pitch.

"You look tired, Mom."

"I do? I feel great. Never felt better, in fact."

"I think she works you too hard. Takes advantage of you because you live there."

"Not really."

"What do you do in the evening? Stay in your room?"

"I keep busy."

Jessivel tried without success to get Kayla's attention to give her a cue to pipe in with what she had told her to say earlier. "Kayla and I miss you." She gently kicked Kayla under the table.

"Ow!"

"Kayla, keep your voice down. Tell Nana how much you miss her."

Jessivel knew Kayla's eye roll would diminish anything she would say afterward, so she saved her from the embarrassment and spoke for her. "We both miss you," she told her mother.

"Of course, I miss you too. We'll have to do this more often. I was thinking about something you said the other day, Jess, about your living situation."

That got Jessivel's attention.

"You said Paige is in real estate. Owns her own business. I wonder if she could help you out with that. She must know of places that become available before anyone else. Or maybe she even owns some properties. You know, siblings help each other. I'm sure there would be something you could do for her in return. How well have you gotten to know her?"

More of the same advice she'd heard from others—something Jessivel didn't care to hear again.

"I don't know her that well, Mom."

"Who's Paige?" Kayla asked.

"Never mind. No one you know," Jessivel said.

"She's your mother's half-sister, Kayla. Your aunt. Didn't you tell her about this, Jess?"

"No…I didn't."

"Tell me what?"

"Nothing. It's adult stuff," Jessivel said, shooting her mother a what-are-you-doing? glance.

"I'm almost thirteen you know."

"Make it to eighteen, and you can call yourself an adult."

"I'll never be able to call myself an adult looking like this."

"Will you shut up about the dress and your hair?"

"Lower your voice, Jess. People are starting to stare," her mother said.

"People are staring because I'm almost thirteen and have these lopsided pigtails on my head," Kayla claimed.

Jessivel leaned in and said, "Look, Mom. I'm going to lose my apartment soon if I don't find work, and there's nothing out there for me. Are you sure you won't consider moving into an apartment or a house so we can all live together again?"

Her mother leaned in just as far. "When are you going to get it through your thick skull that we both have to work to support ourselves. The free lunch we had with your father is in the past. Gone. Over. No more. You're almost thirty years old. You have this beautiful child here to raise. Time to grow up, Jess."

Jessivel scrutinized her mother's face, then bored into it with her stare.

"Are you done eating?" she asked Kayla.

"No."

"Well, hurry up. We have to take Nana home."

"I'm sorry you don't see it my way, Jess," her mother said. "But it's reality, and apparently you need it shoved in your face in order for you to get it." Her scolding tone still held a level of concern. She turned to Kayla. "Kayla, dear, would you mind going to the restroom and washing your hands while I talk with your mother alone for a minute?"

"But I'm not—"

"Just go, please."

Jessivel's mother continued. "You may as well hear this from me. And I'm not going to repeat it…ever again. I don't know how much your father really loved us, but he did put a roof over our heads and food on our table. He pretended we were a family because he felt obligated to do so. His real family lived in a big house in Lakeview—Paige's mother's house now. We were something on the side he took care of so he wouldn't feel guilty or be exposed. The sooner you realize this and get over him, Jess, the better. And the sooner you grow up and be the responsible adult I know you can be, the better. You deserve it. Kayla deserves it. And I deserve it. I'm fifty-one years old and do house cleaning for a living. I can't support a family. You have to support yourself."

Kayla returned, leaving Jessivel no opportunity to respond the way she wanted.

The ride back to the Perlman home was a silent affair.

CHAPTER 37

"I'm not a child, Paige," said Natalie. "I think I can handle doing a few things for Mom now and again."

Paige's mother had strong feelings about having Natalie take care of her—as opposed to some stranger. But Paige had her doubts that Natalie could carry it off.

"It's more than that, Nat. She has to take her medications at the right time, she has at-home physical therapy, doctor's appointments, a strict diet. She may need help getting dressed, taking a bath."

"So? I can do all that. Contrary to your beliefs, I'm not inept."

"Have you given any more thought to getting yourself weaned off your meds, alcohol?"

"Believe it or not, I have. Can you give me the name of that doctor you talked about?"

Shocked at Natalie's response, Paige grabbed a scrap of paper, wrote down the name and number of the doctor she'd found, and handed it to her.

"Can we agree on something, Natalie?"

"What's that?"

"When Mom comes home, if you're ever at a point where you can't take care of her, will you call me?"

"And just why would you think I might not be able to take care of her?"

"You know what I mean. Too strung out on meds, alcohol, whatever—"

"How will I know?" she said laughing. "I'd be too strung out to—"

"That would be funny if it weren't so true."

"I'm getting help, what more do you want from me?"

"It's a start."

"You know her past," Paige said to her mother the next day. "She's an addict, and now she's pregnant. She's agreed to get help, but that doesn't mean she's going to be cured in a week and fully able to take care of you."

"You talk like I'm some sort of invalid. I don't need help...not that much."

"They're releasing you tomorrow. Natalie's first appointment with Dr. Gibbs isn't until Friday. I have to tell you, I'm nervous about this whole thing."

"You're nervous over nothing. I'm sure Natalie and I will get along just fine. Maybe all it will take for her to turn things around for herself is being home, with me."

Paige changed the subject, not at all convinced of her mother's analysis.

"Do you remember a teddy bear Dad brought home from one of his trips? The one Natalie ended up with."

"No."

"You don't remember? Natalie found it in his suitcase and started playing with it, and he got mad at her. Caused quite a commotion."

"What time tomorrow?"

"What time tomorrow for what?"

"Will I be released."

"Morning, I think. I'll have to check with the nurse. You don't remember the teddy bear?"

"I said I didn't. Why do you keep bringing it up? Can you check with them now?"

"Check with who about what?"

"What time I'm leaving tomorrow."

Paige asked at the nurses' station, then went back to her mother's room to let her know she'd be back at noon the next day to take her home.

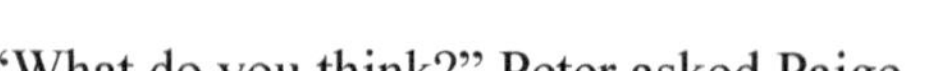

"What do you think?" Peter asked Paige.

"I don't know. You've taken me by surprise here."

Peter Alexander, owner of the strip mall where Paige leased her office space, had informed her that he and his wife were retiring to Boca and planned to put the property up for sale. He'd told her the asking price and wanted to know if she had any interest in buying it.

"What do you think of the price?" he asked.

"It doesn't seem to be too far out of the ballpark, but I'll have to pull comps and study the rent roll you gave me."

"No vacancies. That's a plus. And no one is in arrears."

"I know. But I'd still have to do my due diligence."

"Fair enough. I'll give you two weeks. Then I'm going to make it public."

"What about the other tenants? Do they know?"

"They will tomorrow, but you're the only one I'm meeting with prior to the announcement."

"Will you let me know if any of them are interested?"

"I highly doubt they will be, but sure, I'll let you know."

When they shook hands, he gave her a look she often got after shaking a man's hand—one of surprise that it wasn't your typical female handshake that instantly slips away as if it had never happened.

"You know the history behind the handshake, don't you?" he asked.

"No, I don't."

"It dates back to ancient Egypt. An open right hand was used by men to show they weren't carrying a weapon."

"Really."

"I'm glad you're not carrying a weapon," he said through a smile. "I would never want to mess with you."

Paige contemplated the deal. She had the money to invest in it, but so much needed to be taken into consideration before making such a decision—leases analyses, taxes, mortgage rates, the condition of the building in general and of the other tenant spaces. He had priced it well, and the location was good, not only for her business but for the others as well—close to public transportation, ample parking, high visibility from the street. She considered the other tenants—a sandwich shop, optometrist, pet store, currency exchange, nail salon, and a Catholic Charities resale shop. Lots to think about.

She spent time reviewing her assistant Olivia's proposal on new transaction software before leaving the office for home. She had nothing planned for the evening except to rest up for the next day when she brought her mother home.

Paige awoke from a deep sleep to the sound of "Bohemian Rhapsody" emanating from her phone.

"Where does Mom keep the friggin' spare key?"

"What?" Paige asked half-awake.

"The spare key. Where is it?"

"Natalie?"

"Who else would be calling you at two in the morning looking for Mom's key? Yes, it's me!" Natalie's slurred speech could mean only one thing.

"Where's *your* key?"

"If I knew that, I wouldn't be calling you, now would I?"

"Where are you?"

"I'm standing outside Mom's door, ready to piss my pants if I don't get inside soon. Where does she hide the spare key?"

"You have her spare key. Remember? That's how you got in in the first place."

"Can you just come here and let me in?"

"It's two in the morning, Natalie. Where have you been?"

"I know it's two in the morning. I just told you that. Okay, I can't hold it any longer. I'm going to pee on her front lawn."

"Please don't do that. Natalie? Natalie!"

Paige waited for Natalie to come back on the phone.

"Now can you come?"

"I'll be there in a half hour."

"Drive fast. It's cold out here."

Paige threw on a long coat over her t-shirt and sweatpants, grabbed her keys, and jumped in her year-old BMW, grumbling about her sister as she wound her way down Clark Street toward her mother's home.

"Damn that Natalie," she said aloud over the female singer on the radio. The day was going to be hard enough dealing with her mother's release without sleep deprivation thrown in.

When she arrived twenty minutes later, Natalie was sitting on the front stoop of the brownstone, her knees tucked up into her arms.

"Took you long enough."

Paige opened the front door without saying a word. Natalie followed.

"You're not going to lecture me?" Natalie asked.

Paige turned around to face her.

"Where have you been?"

"None of your business."

"Where is Mom's key?"

Natalie shrugged.

"Well, you had better find it or Mom is going to have to pay to have the lock changed."

"I lost it."

"Where?"

"Somewhere between here and where I went. Does that help?" Natalie snapped at her as she walked toward the stairs.

"You know, Mom needs someone more responsible than you to take care of her. Maybe I should hire a nursemaid for the both of you and be done with it."

"Go ahead, Miss Perfect. Whatever makes you geel food."

"You can't even talk. Are you drunk or high on meds?"

"Both, know-it-all."

"I hate you right now," Paige mumbled.

"Love you too, big sister," Natalie shouted.

"Nothing wrong with your hearing, I see. At least that's working!"

"You can go now."

Paige glanced at the mantle clock. Three-fifteen. With any luck, she would be able to fall back asleep for a few hours before heading to the rehab facility.

She walked out the front door, ignoring the loud thump that echoed from the second floor.

"Can't get out of here fast enough," Paige's mother said after signing the release papers. "Goodbye and good riddance."

"Seems to me they treated you rather well here, Mom. You look a hundred percent better than when you arrived."

"I didn't say they didn't treat me well. I just can't wait to get out. Go home. Sleep in my own bed. Have an old fashioned, if I feel like it. In the middle of the day, if I want. Let's go."

In the car, her mother asked about Natalie. Paige chose her words carefully.

"She needs help, Mom. I gave her the name of a doctor who specializes in drug-related pregnancy cases, but I'm not sure if she called him. I told her I'd pay for it."

"I'll pay for it. You shouldn't have to. She has to go for the baby's sake."

"Exactly. The fact that I had to convince her that she had to get medical attention is, well, beyond irresponsible. I don't know if she's that ignorant of the importance of seeing a doctor, or her brain isn't working right, or she just doesn't care."

"You're being a little hard on her, don't you think? She just needs a little guidance."

"She needs more than that. Just look at her!"

"I will when we get home."

"The drugs are affecting her brain, her thinking. She needs to get off them."

"Mm-hm."

"Well, I don't want to see her ending up having a 'drug baby'."

Her mother turned her head sharply toward Paige. "You think I do?"

"You're downplaying her problem."

"I'm supporting her. You're turning against her," her mother said.

"No, I'm not. I'm trying to help her. Don't you see that?"

Her mother's tight lips told her she probably shouldn't go any further.

"If you become her enabler, there will be no hope for her. Tough love, Mom. That's what she needs."

"Just plain love is what she needs."

"And you're going to need help when you get home. How is she going to help you if she can't even help herself?"

"I don't need any help, so that's not a problem."

"Mom, I watched you walk from the rehab place to the car. You're not that steady on your feet, even with the cane."

"You just got done saying I looked one hundred percent better."

"Well…you had a long way to go."

"Try being cooped up in that place for as long as I was, and we'll see how *you* walk. Anyway, they wouldn't have released me if they thought I couldn't take care of myself."

"And take care of Natalie too?"

"She'll be fine. Don't be such a worrywart."

"Would you like to know what she did last night?"

"Not really. But I think you're about to tell me anyway."

"She called me at two in the morning, drunk, locked out of your house. She wouldn't tell me where she'd been. Doesn't know where your spare key is. We're going to have to call someone to change the lock on your front door. God only knows who has her key."

"You've never lost anything in your life? I'll call a locksmith. No big deal."

"She peed on your lawn, Mom."

"Poor thing."

Paige continued the drive in silence, frustrated with her mother, convinced something bad would come out of Natalie living with her but not knowing how to change that course of events without upsetting the two of them.

CHAPTER 38

"Paige, this is Jessivel, and I need your help."

She had been vacillating between forgetting about Paige altogether and giving her another try. Desperation led her into calling her.

"Okay…what is it?"

"I screwed up, big time, yelling at you at The Coffee Bean, and now I can't find another job. I stand to lose my apartment if I don't find work, and then Kayla and I will be homeless…again." She struggled to hold back the tears.

"Are you looking for another barista job?"

"Yes."

"Where have you looked so far?"

"I went to Goodwill Industries, like you suggested, but that didn't work out."

"No? Did they tell you about the opening at The Daily Grind?"

"They did, but it was already filled, and it was only part-time anyway."

"Have you tried any online job-search sites?"

"I don't have a computer."

"They have free ones you can use at the library."

"To be honest, except for what I had to do in high school, I'm not very good on a computer. I've been on social media before but not for years, Craigslist once, but that's about it. I wouldn't know where to start."

She had to wait a few long seconds before hearing Paige reply.

"I have an older laptop I don't use anymore. You may have it, if you like."

The Internet intimidated Jessivel. She had struggled using it in school and since then had avoided it as much as possible.

"That would be…great."

"You're hesitating."

"I'm not very good on the Internet."

"I could bring over the laptop later today and help you with it if you want."

"Okay," Jessivel said, horrified that Paige would see her apartment, how she lived. She gave her the address, agreed upon a time, and then ended the call.

Jessivel peeked into Kayla's room, shrugged off the messiness, and spent some time tidying up the rest of her apartment. When she had done everything possible to make the place look decent, she plopped herself down and waited for Paige's arrival.

The harsh sound of the door buzzer caused Jessivel to jump. She fingered her father's ring on the chain around her neck before slipping it inside her shirt on her way to the door.

Paige wore jeans and a simple top—something Jessivel figured she had chosen to dress down for the occasion, down to her level.

They smiled at each other, awkwardly, before Jessivel took a step backward.

"Come on in," she said. She led Paige to the small kitchen table. "We can set up the laptop here. Would you like a cup of coffee or something?"

"No, thanks. I've got water in my bag."

Jessivel watched as Paige turned on the laptop and started clicking away.

"I like this site for job opportunities. It's called Job Find, and it works well both for job seekers and employers."

She scooted closer to Jessivel. "This site is pretty easy to navigate. Here's their main page."

"Can I be honest with you?" Jessivel asked.

"Sure."

"I'm not really following you. You're so fast on this thing."

"Don't worry. You'll get the hang of it. I'll write down each step, and if you get stuck, you can call me. Or get help from your daughter. Kids seem to have a sixth sense when it comes to electronics. After you've used it a couple of times, you'll be fine."

"If you say so."

"So, here is where you type in the job you're looking for. Barista, right?"

"Mm-hm."

"And you want to stay in Chicago, right?"

"Yes. Not too far from here."

"What is your ZIP Code?"

Jessivel told her.

"Okay. So, I'll type in five miles from your ZIP Code. That brings us to the next page. What salary range are you looking for?"

Jessivel shrugged. "I was making twelve dollars an hour at The Busy Bean."

"I'll put in ten to fifteen dollars per hour. It lets you indicate whether you want full-time or part-time. We'll keep both options open. And you are at an entry level, so we'll check that box."

"Sounds good," she said, knowing part-time wasn't going to cut it.

"Ready?"

"Sure."

Paige clicked on the "Find Jobs" box, and a list appeared.

"Look, here's a barista job not two miles from here with an opening. Oops, they require a full year's experience. Let's keep looking."

After they waded through this and two other websites, Paige asked Jessivel if she had a resumé.

"I have the one the social services worker put together for me."

"Does it include your experience at The Busy Bean?"

"No."

"Can I see it? I'll create one in Word for you that is up-to-date."

"In Word?"

"It's a program you can use to write letters, create a resumé, write a book, if you want."

"Could my daughter use it for writing reports? She has to use the school lab now."

"I don't see why not."

Jessivel fetched a copy of her resumé, and Paige created a version of it on the laptop. She showed it to Jessivel.

"Wow. That looks so…so professional. Where can we print it out?"

"You don't have a printer?"

Stupid question since I don't have a computer.

"Duh! Why would you have a printer with no computer. I'm sure I can find one for you in my office—we have a small inventory of computer equipment in our storage closet. But keep in mind that when you apply for jobs online, you will likely be attaching your resumé electronically."

Right.

"Tell me, Paige, why are you…um." Jessivel thought better of asking the potentially hazardous question weighing on her mind.

"Helping you? Is that what you were going to ask?"

"Something like that."

"Because we're family. That's what sisters do. And you know what?"

"What?"

"I kind of like you. You're pretty crusty on the outside, and you haven't exactly been welcoming to me, but underneath it all, I think you're alright." She paused before continuing. "I think you feel betrayed by our father. You think I've had it much better than you, and for that reason you resent me. And you're scared of your future. How am I doing?"

"Good so far."

"And you don't trust me, or at least you haven't up until now."

"Keep going."

"That's all I've got…except for one admission."

Here it comes. "What's that?"

"My initial reason for wanting to talk with you has to do with something that we haven't touched upon yet."

"More dirt on dear old Dad?"

"No. It's how he died. He had Huntington's disease. Do you know anything about it?"

Jessivel shook her head.

"It's a disease that affects the nerve cells in the brain. It can manifest itself in all sorts of ways—a person's thinking, body movements, speech. Many other ways. And it's genetic. Children can inherit it from a parent."

Jessivel momentarily froze while she absorbed what Paige had said.

"Do you have it?"

"I've been tested, and I don't have it."

"But I might."

"From what I've been told, there is a 50/50 chance."

"And you don't have it, so..."

"That doesn't mean anything. Regardless of whether I have it or not, you have a 50/50 chance."

"So how do I get tested…and is it expensive?"

"It's a blood test—they check to see if you have the defective gene that causes the condition. And if you can't afford it, I'm happy to pay for it."

"What about Kayla?"

"She won't need to be tested…unless you test positive."

"And then she'll have a 50/50 chance?"

Paige nodded.

"I want to be tested."

"Are you sure?"

"I'm sure."

"The reason I ask is because not everyone who suspects they could have it wants to get tested."

"Why not?"

"There are some things they can do to slow down the progression of it if detected early, but some people feel that since the disease can't be cured, what good would it do to get tested—it would just be something hanging over their heads, something to dampen their will to live."

"I'd want to know."

"That's how I felt too, but I wanted to make sure you understood it's a decision that comes with some ramifications."

"Either way."

"If you want, I'll make an appointment for you with my doctor."

"Speaking of Dad, my mom just told me he sold medical equipment for a living. Is that true?"

"Yes, he did. That's not what you were told?"

"Nope. Said he had to visit different construction sites, all over the country, to do inspections."

Paige shook her head. "Unbelievable."

CHAPTER 39

Paige's mother clung to her arm as they approached her house. "It's so good to be home," she said through a sigh.

Noticing the front door was ajar, Paige stopped short.

She held out her arm to keep her mother from entering the house. "Wait here, Mom. Something's not right."

"What is it?"

"The door is partly open."

Her mother pushed Paige's arm away. "It's just Nat's way of welcoming me home." Before Paige could stop her, her mother was inside.

"What the—"

Paige followed closely behind her. The first thing she noticed was the Kosta Boda vase, which had graced her mother's foyer console for as long as she could remember, smashed on the floor. She gasped at the ransacked living room—overturned chairs, sofa pillows strewn about, drawers pulled out of cabinets.

She checked the security system panel and found it in its normal "at-home" position. "Nat!" she called out. No answer.

Paige grabbed her mother's arm and guided her back outside. "You wait in the car," she said as she helped her down the steps. "I'm calling 9-1-1."

With her mother safely locked in the car, Paige called the police, who told her to stay in her car until they arrived.

"But my sister might be in there."

"And so might the intruder. Stay in your car and lock the doors until the police arrive. They're on their way."

It went against Paige's better judgment not to go in, but she did as told and joined her mother in the car.

"What about Natalie?" her mother asked. "Do you think she's okay?"

"Let me text her and see if she responds. I've been told to let the police—"

The sound of sirens made both of them jump. Two police cars pulled up, each carrying two officers. A female officer approached Paige's car. The other three went into the house, guns drawn. Paige rolled down her window.

"Are you okay?" the officer asked.

"Yes, we're fine. But I'm worried about my sister. She might be inside." Paige hadn't received a text back from Natalie.

"They're aware of that. Let's give them a chance to check out the house and see what's going on in there."

They waited in the car for the officers to clear the house. Several scenarios played out in Paige's mind. While she didn't think Tim and Hank were the type to break in her mother's home, she couldn't rule this out. They were interested in the ring, and they didn't walk away with it during their last visit.

It was close to twenty minutes before one of the officers emerged from the house. "Your sister is fine," he said. "Shaken up, but fine. The house is clear, if you want to come in."

Paige and her mother entered the house where they joined Natalie and one officer in the living room. They each gave Natalie a hug before sitting down.

Natalie sagged into a chair and sat limply with her arms clenched around her swollen belly. She didn't have any visible bruises or marks on her.

"Are you okay?" Paige asked Natalie.

Natalie nodded.

"Are you hurt?"

"No."

"So what happened?" Paige asked her.

"Some men broke into the house…tied me up…made a mess," she said, stumbling over her words.

"There is no sign of forced entry, Miss."

Natalie let out a quick snort. "Well, they got in somehow. I don't know."

"How many of them were there?" the officer asked.

"I said before I don't know," Natalie said, her left knee bouncing at a rapid speed.

"A few."

"Males, females?" the officer asked.

"Males. I already told you that upstairs."

"I'm just asking again so I make sure I understand. White, black, Hispanic?"

"White. I told you."

Natalie rubbed her wrists.

"Is there something wrong with your wrists?" Paige asked.

"They used duct tape on me."

Paige recognized the officer as one who had been there when their mother's house had been burglarized a couple of months earlier. "Do you think the two incidents are related?" she asked him.

"Could be, but I rather doubt it. The first one was an exceptionally clean robbery. Whoever was involved in that break-in came in looking for something specific and didn't mess up the place like this."

"Either way, that's two burglaries in less than three months. Have there been others in the area?" Paige asked.

"None recently. This neighborhood is exceptionally low on crime. Car break-ins mostly and not many of those."

"What happens next?" Paige asked.

"They'll finish processing the scene and then we'll do a walk-through to see if you can tell what's missing." He pulled out a notepad. "Who all lives here?" he asked no one in particular.

Paige responded. "My mother, Elaine West, and Natalie, of course. Natalie West."

"Who all has keys?" the officer asked.

"Each of us has a key," Paige said. "And in case Natalie hasn't told you this yet, she lost her key last night."

The officer looked up from his notepad. "Really? Where did you lose it?"

Natalie squirmed in her seat. "I'm not sure," she said, the pitch of her voice higher than normal. "I was out and lost it somewhere."

"Where were you?"

"What difference does it make? I don't know when or where I lost it."

"Well, did you have it before you left the house?"

"I don't know."

"Did you turn on the security system when you left?" the policeman asked Natalie.

"I may have. I don't remember."

The conversation continued without much more being learned until the officer asked Natalie one final question. "Would you mind coming down to the station where we can continue this discussion?"

Seeing the aftermath of someone having violated her mother's home, now twice, hit Paige hard—realizing that a stranger had gone through her belongings was unsettling to say the least. She proceeded to clean up the mess, knowing these emotions wouldn't go away simply by returning the physicality of her mother's home back to normal, and hoping she wouldn't feel this way every time she came here.

"I don't know why they had to take Natalie to the station," Paige's mother said. "She answered all their questions as best she could."

Paige disagreed and wondered if Natalie knew enough to ask for a lawyer if needed. "I'm not so sure of that, Mom. She was vague about the lost key and how she left the security panel. I wish now that we'd gotten a camera system. That way we would be able to see who came to the door."

"Maybe we should have gone with her," her mother said.

"Where?"

"To the police station."

"Wouldn't have done any good. They'll want to talk to her alone."

"Well, I think they're making a bigger deal out of this than they have to. Nothing was stolen."

"Your vase was broken."

"It can be replaced."

The way her mother was minimizing the situation baffled Paige. Like she was trying to shield Natalie from something.

"The fact that nothing was stolen makes me even more nervous. They could have taken any number of items, but they didn't. Why was that? And if they didn't find what they were looking for, will they be back?"

Her mother shrugged.

"Lucky for you, your safe is well hidden. We can thank Dad for that." Paige's father had had a floor safe installed under the carpet in their bedroom closet where Paige's mother kept her jewelry and other valuable items. It hadn't been disturbed during the first burglary. "Or do we need to check it?" Paige asked. She had always been curious as to what all her parents kept in there.

"Did you check it after the last break-in?" her mother asked.

"I started to, but when I saw the carpet hadn't been disturbed, I didn't go any further."

"Maybe you better look in it. Tell me what's in there…but don't open anything."

"Then how can I tell you what's in there?"

"Don't open anything sealed. The combination is my birthday."

Paige went upstairs to her mother's bedroom, pulled up the carpet on the closet floor, and opened the safe, which was roughly two cubic feet in size. She lifted out her mother's jewelry box and peeked inside at her mother's exquisite collection. Then she rifled through the papers, reached down to the bottom of the safe, and pulled out two sealed envelopes, one regular and one padded, neither one labeled. By its feel, the regular envelope appeared to contain papers. The padded one enclosed something else, hard to tell what.

Paige put everything back in place, locked the safe, and returned to the living room.

"Nothing was touched. Your jewelry box and everything else is fine."

"That's good."

"The sealed envelopes were still sealed, so—"

"How many?" her mother asked.

"Two."

"What color?"

"One brown and one white." *What difference does the color make?* "The white one was padded."

"I know of the brown one, and it should stay sealed," her mother said with resolve. "But let me see the white one."

Paige retrieved the bulky envelope and handed it to her mother.

She fingered it before giving it back to Paige. "Put it back where you found it."

"What's in it?"

"Nothing important," she said gazing past Paige. "Just something your father probably put in there."

When Paige returned, her mother mentioned a savings account she had in her name. "Was that bank book in there?"

"No, but when I retrieved your will from your desk, I saw a bank book in the same drawer," Paige said. "Do you mean that one?"

"Yes."

"A stash of quick money in case you need it?"

Her mother sighed. "My father gave it to me in case Ryan couldn't provide for me."

"Really? I didn't know that."

"There was never a need to say anything."

"Did you ever have to use any of it?" she asked, knowing there had been several withdrawals.

Her mother shrugged. "A few times. You may as well know this, Paige. I couldn't always depend on your father for everything. So, yes, I had to dip into it every now and again."

Paige wondered if any of the withdrawals had been for Natalie who was an expert at weaseling money from their mom. "That surprises me," she said.

"There may be a lot of things about…"

"What other things?"

"Nothing. I think I need to lie down for a while."

"You can't stay here."

"Why not?"

"It's not safe. That's two burglaries. And one missing key."

"Unrelated burglaries, according to the policeman," her mother insisted.

"That makes a difference?"

"They won't come back. They know what's here now."

"You're not making sense, Mom."

"Natalie will be here."

"Oh, that's comforting."

"Would you leave her alone? Imagine what she's going through right now. Being browbeaten by the police."

"I doubt she's being browbeaten. But she was tied up, for God's sake. She's not going to want to stay here either. You guys can come stay with me for now. I have plenty of room."

"I'm staying here. I just spent a month in a god-awful hospital room, and now I want to be home. End of discussion."

"It wasn't a month. Anyway, I'm not going to leave you here alone. I'll sleep here tonight."

"Fine. Do whatever you think is best."

Feeling the need to lie down herself, Paige found a set of antique bells on a rope her mother had hanging in the mudroom and draped them on the front doorknob in case she fell asleep and someone tried to gain entry, a trick she had learned after her divorce when she had first lived alone. Then, she curled up on her mother's sofa and closed her eyes.

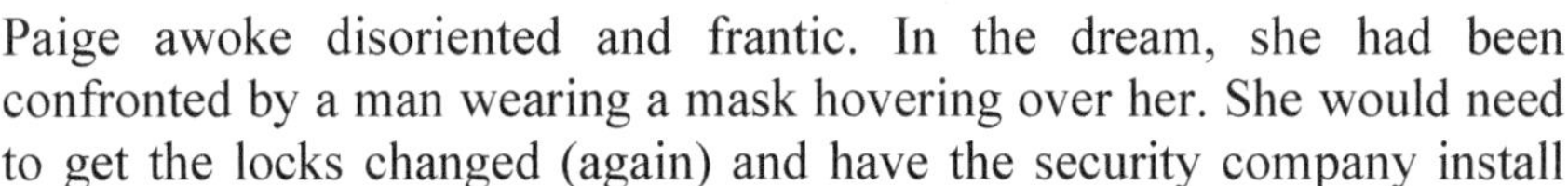

Paige awoke disoriented and frantic. In the dream, she had been confronted by a man wearing a mask hovering over her. She would need to get the locks changed (again) and have the security company install cameras as soon as possible.

An hour later, as she sipped coffee, she reflected on the two mysterious envelopes in her mother's safe and considered doing something unethical. *After all, who would ever know?* But, regrettably, that would have to wait.

Chapter 40

Paige appeared to be sincere in wanting to help, but Jessivel still couldn't stop thinking she had some ulterior motive that would become apparent later. And it nagged at her as to what it could be.

The news about her father's disease had freaked her out. Now that she had a better handle on "Googling," she typed in "Huntington's" on her new laptop. The symptoms and side effects were frightening—involuntary movements, difficulty speaking, trouble understanding things, memory lapse, bipolar disorder—and it could be a long, drawn-out illness.

She spent the rest of the day browsing job sites, finding the one Paige had recommended as the easiest one to navigate. She limited her search to jobs within a few miles, not as far as others had wanted her to search. She found three barista jobs worth consideration.

Kayla came home from school as she was finishing the last application.

"What's that?" she asked.

"My new laptop. Paige gave it to me."

"Can I use it too?" Kayla asked.

"For homework?"

"Yes, for homework," she said, rolling her eyes. "I have to do a report on the phases of the moon."

"Okay, but we won't have a printer until tomorrow." She grinned. "I applied for three jobs today."

Kayla gave her a high five. "So, do you like Paige now?"

“Sure.”

“Because you hated her before.”

“I never said I hated her.” *Not out loud, anyway.*

“You acted like it.”

“I didn’t know her, that’s all.”

“But she’s your sister. That’s what Nana said.”

“Half-sister. But I’m getting to know her as a friend first.”

“She’s your only friend, Mom.”

“I have other friends.”

“Yeah, who?”

“I consider Marlene at The Busy Bean my friend.”

“What color is Marlene?”

Jessivel mulled over her daughter’s question before answering. “Are you asking me what race she is?”

“No, what color is her skin?”

Jessivel hesitated, apparently too long for Kayla’s liking.

“You don’t know what color she is?”

“I don’t understand why you’re asking the question.”

“Color makes a difference.”

“And why is that?”

“Just does.”

“Are you asking about Marlene, or does this have to do with someone else?”

“Maybe someone else.”

“And who would that someone else be?”

“Maybe me.”

Jessivel had avoided having this discussion with Kayla up until now and still didn’t feel comfortable with it. “Your father was mixed race, Kayla. His father was Asian, and his mother was part white, part black.”

“So what does that make me?”

“Beautiful?”

“Mom, you know what I mean.”

“It makes you multiracial.”

“And what does that mean?”

"It doesn't mean anything, or it shouldn't anyway… Why are you asking this?"

"Because I don't know what to say when someone asks me what I am?"

"Kids at school ask you that?"

"I've had teachers ask me that."

"What? If anyone asks you what you are, teachers included, tell them you're a twelve-year-old girl."

"What if they ask me where I'm from?"

"Tell them Chicago."

"What if they ask me who's my daddy?"

"Tell them you never met him, that he—"

"When are you going to tell me more about him?"

"When you're older."

"How old?"

"How about eighteen?"

"How about now?"

"It's an adult subject."

"You say that about everything. There won't be enough days in the year to talk about all this stuff when I turn eighteen."

"I think there will be."

"My friends know all about their dads, even the ones who don't live with them. And Dylan's dad is in jail, and he knows all about it."

"Okay, what do you want to know?"

"Where did you live with him, at Nana and Poppy's?"

Shit.

"We…didn't get a chance to live together."

Kayla gave her mother a puzzled look.

"He died too soon?"

"Yes, that's it."

"Were you married?"

Double shit.

"We were planning on it."

"Where did he work?" Kayla asked.

"He was a mechanic. He worked on cars, in a garage."

"How did he die?"

"I told you before, in a car accident."

"What happened?"

"He was hit by a drunk driver."

"Do you have a picture of him?"

Jessivel had torn up the few photos she'd once had.

"No, I don't."

"Did you love him?"

"Of course, I did."

"Then why don't you have any pictures of him?"

"I just don't. I thought you had homework to do."

"Whatever."

Later that day, after Kayla had gone to bed, Jessivel cried over the man she had once loved, the man who had deserted her. She regretted the lie she had told Kayla about him being dead, and she knew that in time she would have to tell her the truth. Twelve just seemed too young. She had never fully understood why Jason, the man who had called her his "boo," had abandoned her when she needed him the most. How could she explain this to her daughter?

"Lousy bastard," she whispered through her sobs.

Jessivel's enthusiasm about finding a job soon dissipated when she didn't hear back from any of the companies she'd contacted. She said as much to Paige when Paige called to tell her she'd made an appointment for her to be tested for Huntington's.

"You can't get discouraged so quickly, Jessivel," Paige said. "It takes time to find the right job. And while the Internet is a great way to find one, not all jobs are posted there. You have to try other means at the same time."

"Like what?"

"Have you thought about walking into a coffee shop and asking to speak with the manager or owner? Fill out an application? Audrey told me you created that raspberry espresso yourself. That would be something to mention to the manager. Show them you're creative. Be assertive."

"I couldn't do that."

"Why not?"

"I don't know. I just couldn't."

"You want to find a job, right?"

"Yeah."

"Then you have to work at it. They aren't going to come knocking on *your* door. You have to knock on *theirs*. Word-of-mouth also works. Have you talked to people you know in the coffee industry?"

"Like who?"

"Former coworkers, for example."

"Yes, one."

"Try others. They might know of something. How about temp agencies?"

"Not sure what they are."

"Sometimes employers need someone temporary, someone they don't want to put on their payroll permanently. Short-term assignments. They go to a temp agency looking for someone. If the temp agency has you in their database, and your qualifications match the requirements of the job, they'll call you."

"But I don't want temporary."

"Temporary is better than nothing, right? You can do that until you find something permanent. And who knows, that temp job could lead to a permanent one as you make new contacts in the industry and meet people who may know of openings."

"This is way more involved than I thought."

"But you know what? The more you put into it, the more you'll get out of it. What's the old saying? 'You get out of life what you put into it.' That's true, you know."

"I never looked at it that way before."

"Just a little sisterly advice. Do you want me to go with you to your doctor's appointment? Maybe for moral support?"

Jessivel's immediate reaction was to say no, she could go to a doctor's appointment on her own. But after thinking about the nature of the visit and the fact that Paige had offered to pay for it, she thought differently. And furthermore, Paige's friendship was beginning to mean something.

"That would be nice. Will they have the results right away?"

"I remember waiting a long time. I'll pick you up a half hour before the appointment. Is that okay?"

"Yeah, sure."

Jessivel hung up and lay down on her bed to mull over the conversation. It seemed as though a lot was said despite its brevity. She considered acting on Paige's suggestion to walk into a coffee shop and ask for a job, something completely outside of her comfort zone. She talked with Kayla about it over dinner.

"What's so hard about that?" Kayla asked.

"Well, I'd be going in uninvited, looking to talk to someone I don't know who may be too busy to talk with me, and asking for something they may not have to offer. I don't know, I just find that awkward. And then you may end up talking to them in front of other people. Paige thinks I should try it."

"I'd practice it first."

"What do you mean?"

"What if I pretend to be the store manager and you knock on my door looking for a job."

"Hey, that's not a bad idea," she said to Kayla, giving her a high five.

After dinner, Kayla asked Jessivel to wait a few minutes while she prepared for the role play.

"Okay, I'm ready!" Kayla said through her closed bedroom door.

Jessivel knocked on the door.

"Come in."

Kayla's appearance threw Jessivel into a fit of laughter. Her hair was tied up in a knot on top of her head. She wore big-rimmed glasses from an old Halloween costume, Mardi Gras beads, and a long scarf wrapped around her neck several times. Her pant legs were rolled up to reveal a pair of Jessivel's platform mules she hadn't worn since she was a teenager.

"How can I do this with you dressed like that?"

"Close the door and try it again. You have to pretend I'm real."

Jessivel waited a bit to calm herself down. Kayla was so serious about this, she couldn't laugh again.

"Come in."

"May I speak with the manager, please?"

"I'm the manager. What do you want? I'm very busy, you know."

"I'll only take a few minutes of your time, ma'am. I'm looking for a job."

"What kind of job?"

"Barista."

"I'm sorry, but we have no openings."

"Okay. Bye."

"Mom."

"What?"

"That was terrible."

"I know. You could have been nicer to me."

Kayla rolled her eyes. "Boy, do we have a lot of work to do."

The following Friday, Paige arrived on time to accompany Jessivel to get her blood test. She greeted Paige at the door, eager to tell her about her discussion with the manager of Café Mocha.

"I did what you said and walked right in and asked for the manager."

"Good for you, Jess. That took courage."

"We call it *balls* in my neighborhood. Anyway, we had a nice talk, and she said that she was thinking of expanding her space into the empty shop next door, and if she does that, she'll have to hire at least one more barista and she'll keep me in mind," she said with enthusiasm. "I networked! Holy shit, I never thought I'd use that word in a sentence. Thanks for helping me."

Paige laughed. "We can learn from each other, you know. You know things that I don't."

"Yeah, right."

"Don't sell yourself so short."

Here it comes, Jessivel guessed. She wants something.

"Like maybe one day we can swap tales about our father. Over a glass of wine or something."

Jessivel suspected Paige was fishing for something—that would explain why she was being so nice.

"Maybe."

Shortly after they arrived for the appointment, someone ushered Jessivel into an exam room where they extracted a vial of blood. The nurse told her it would take six to eight weeks for the results.

"Why so long?" she asked.

"It's a lengthy process, and there are very few labs that do it, so they have backlogs."

"You okay?" Paige asked as they left the building.

"Yeah. But they said I won't know for six to eight weeks."

"I know. It's a long time to have to wait. Want to stop for some lunch?"

"I would but…no money."

"My treat."

Chapter 41

Natalie had been at the police station for several hours when she called Paige to tell her that she was ready to be picked up. Paige knew that when the police had asked Natalie to come to the station, it was an indication they thought she knew more than she had disclosed at the house. Paige wondered just how much more Natalie had told them.

"Are you okay?" she asked Natalie in the car.

"No, I'm not okay. I was tied up like a damn hostage for an hour at Mom's and now just spent three more hours being interrogated by the police!"

"What are they saying?"

"They asked me a million questions, then repeated the same questions with different wording to try to trick me up. After a while, I was so confused, I didn't know what had really happened."

"Do you think you need a lawyer?"

"I have no clue."

"Did they accuse you of anything?"

"They think I know who it was who broke in."

"Do you?"

Natalie hesitated. "Of course not."

"How did they leave it with you?"

"Just like in the movies. They said don't leave town or anything stupid like that."

"Well, the front door lock has already been changed, and I'm waiting to hear when they're going to install cameras."

"How's Mom?"

"This whole thing shook her up, but she'll be okay. Natalie, if the people who broke into Mom's house are the same people you owe money, they'll be back, and that's not fair to Mom to put her in that danger."

"What makes you think that's who broke in?"

"A lot of things point in that direction—nothing stolen even though some obvious things were out in the open that most thieves would have taken, for one. Let me ask you something. Why did you really leave Berwyn? Was it because they were after you for the money you owe them?"

"First of all, it's not *they,* it's *he.* And second of all…well, there is no second of all."

"It was him then, wasn't it?"

Natalie let out an audible sigh. "Someone connected with him, but I didn't tell the police that."

"You would have been better off telling the truth, Nat. Now they can get you for obstruction of justice or something."

"I didn't lie to them. Well, maybe just about the number of guys."

"That, and you didn't tell them all you knew, right?"

"Yeah."

"That's the same as lying, just so you know."

"You think you know everything, don't you? Try being me for a day."

"No, thank you."

Once home, Paige sat down with Natalie and their mother in the living room.

"I have a fundraiser to go to tonight, but afterward I'll come back and stay the night here," Paige said to them.

"What kind of fundraiser?" her mother asked. "Can't you skip it and just send in your donation?"

"Not really. I'm their guest speaker."

"Will you quit with the overprotective stuff already?" Natalie said. "We don't need you here. We're both adults, not children."

"The policeman I talked to said he'd periodically run a patrol car by here tonight," her mother said. "We'll be fine. Go to your fundraiser, and then go home. Get some rest, and I'll talk to you tomorrow."

"I'm going to engage the security system before I leave," Paige said. "Do you need for me to refresh how it—"

"Go, Paige."

"Double lock the door from the inside after I leave, and—"

"Go."

Feeling defeated and not at all comfortable with the situation, Paige left for home for a quick outfit change before going to her event.

Paige's cell phone woke her from a sound sleep.

"Help me," was the weak utterance on the other end of the phone.

"Mom?"

"I fell," she said in a voice as thin as air.

"Where's Natalie?"

"I don't think she's here."

"I'm calling 9-1-1, Mom, and then I'm on my way. Stay still until someone gets there. Mom? Mom, are you there?"

Paige called 9-1-1, threw some pants on under her sleep shirt, and flew to her car. "Goddamn Natalie," she muttered to herself as she sped through the streets. The glowing numbers on the dashboard clock read one-thirty A.M. What was Natalie doing out at this hour?

Stupid question.

She hadn't given Natalie the new house key—Paige and her mother had the only two keys that had come with the new lock—so if Natalie had left the house, she hadn't locked the door behind her. Unless she had taken her mother's key. She didn't want to think about the possible scenarios.

Her mother said she had fallen. The rehab facility had sent her home with a quad cane she was instructed to use. But knowing her mother's stubbornness, she suspected the cane hadn't gotten much use. She had rid her mother's house of things she could easily trip on or bump into, and she and Natalie had moved her mother's bedroom to the guest room on the first floor so she wouldn't have to navigate the stairs.

The paramedics had already arrived when she pulled up to the house. Paige threw the car in park and dashed inside.

"Is she okay?" she asked one of the paramedics.

"Are you related?"

"I'm her daughter."

"We're taking her to Midwest, if you want to follow us."

"How did you guys get in?" she asked.

"The front door wasn't locked, ma'am."

Paige quickly searched the house for her sister, just in case she was passed out in her room or somewhere. When she didn't find her, she grabbed her mother's purse and keys, locked the front door, and headed to the hospital. It wasn't until she was halfway there, she realized Natalie would have no way to get back in the house. Too bad. Being with her mother right now was more important.

She struggled to hold back the tears while anger built up throughout her body. Natalie's addictions were not valid excuses for her bad behavior, as her mother claimed. Of course, Paige realized Natalie's dependencies were bona fide disorders. She got that. But at some point, she had to take responsibility for them and do something about it. The "I'm not hurting anyone except myself" attitude she had was preposterous and selfish.

The looming red EMERGENCY sign above the massive revolving doors at the hospital's entrance brought both relief and anguish. Paige parked the car and sprinted toward the building, inhaling deeply as she braced herself for whatever news she was about to be given.

"My mother was just brought here by ambulance," she told the woman behind the desk. "Elaine West."

The woman looked at her computer screen for a few seconds and said, "Will you please have a seat in the waiting area? Someone will come out for you."

Paige sat uncomfortably as she watched people come and go, all in varying degrees of malaise. Fifteen minutes passed before a petite, middle-aged woman in scrubs approached her.

"Are you the daughter of Mrs. West?"

Paige nodded.

"Come with me."

Paige followed the woman through the secure double doors and into a long hallway of curtained rooms. She stopped outside of exam room 15.

"Your mother suffered a traumatic brain injury when she fell and hit her head," she said in a low voice. "She's conscious, and her vitals are stable. We're running tests."

"What kind of tests?"

"We first did what is called a Glasgow Coma Scale. This helps us assess the severity of the injury. Your mother scored a seven."

"Seven? Is that good or bad?"

"It's not terrible, but people with scores of eight and above have a better chance for recovery."

"Can I see her? Will she be able to talk to me?"

She pulled open the curtain to allow Paige into her mother's room.

"Mom?"

Her mother's eyes remained closed while she nodded.

Paige grasped her mother's hand. "You're going to be okay. The doctors are going to take good care of you here."

"Water," her mother whispered.

"Can she have water?" Paige asked the doctor.

"We'd prefer she didn't have any water. She's scheduled for a CT scan any time now, and we don't want her overhydrated."

"Sorry, Mom. Maybe when you return from the scan you can have something to drink."

Two young women in scrubs came into the room to take her mother to the imaging department. Paige was told she could wait in the lobby, as her mother was going to be transferred to a regular room after the scan. Paige pulled out her phone and Googled the Glasgow test while she waited. When she couldn't find anything more than what the doctor had said, she put her phone away and sat still, letting all the voices and commotion around her blend into one dull tone. An hour passed before she was greeted by a nurse who took her to her mother's room.

"Mom?"

Her mother nodded, eyes closed.

"Can you talk?"

She nodded again.

"When you fell, you hit your head. Do you remember that?"

"Headache."

"You have a headache?"

She nodded.

"Did they give you anything for it?"

She shrugged, then attempted to raise her arm, which didn't get very far before dropping back down to her side. "Ryan," she said.

"He's gone, Mom. He died months ago."

"I know."

"Then what about him?"

"Wanna."

"What did you say? Say it again."

"Light too bright. Tired."

A nurse walked in the room. "Are you Paige, her daughter?"

"Yes, I am. I think she just said the lights in here are too bright. I know she has a headache."

"We gave her pain medication for the headache. It might take a while to take effect." She went over to the light switch and dimmed the lights. "That should be better for her."

"How is she doing?" Paige asked.

"The reason she has a headache is because there's pressure inside her brain due to the fall. We're giving her diuretics to reduce it."

"Will she be okay?"

"We'll observe her condition for the next twenty-four hours. She's scheduled for an MRI tomorrow morning."

The nurse left the room. Her avoidance of Paige's question did not go unnoticed.

Still furious at Natalie for abandoning their mother, but feeling bad about her being potentially locked out, Paige swung by the house to put her mother's house key in the fake rock where Natalie could find it. She called Natalie's cell phone to give her a piece of her mind. The "service has been temporarily suspended" message enraged her even more.

When Paige returned to the hospital the next day, she learned her mother's condition had worsened. She tried to have a conversation with her, but her speech was so incomprehensible, it was almost useless. Still, Paige believed her mother was trying to convey something of importance to her, and so she kept at it until what came out of her mouth was abundantly clear.

"Your sister Wanda."

At first, despite its clarity, Paige was certain this wasn't what she had meant to say—Wanda was her cousin, not her sister. But when she repeated it, her mother's unmistakable words hung in the air for a moment and then echoed in her mind over and over again.

Wanda could only be her sister one of two ways—either Paige's father had had a fling with her mother's sister Bernice, or her aunt Bernice wasn't really Wanda's mother and her own mother was. She recalled Wanda's age being close to her own, just a few months' difference, which would rule out the latter. If this were true—if her father were Wanda's father as well—it would explain why her mother was estranged from her sister and why she refused to talk about it. It would also explain why her mother had asked her sister to leave her husband's funeral. And it would explain why she'd added Wanda's name in her will.

Oh my God.

Paige wondered if Wanda had known who her real father was all this time. She pictured Wanda in her head—they looked nothing alike, but then neither did she and Natalie nor she and Jessivel.

She and Wanda were half-sisters.

A nurse came into the room and said they were taking her mother down for another CT scan, leaving Paige to further contemplate the latest possible crack in her father's already damaged armor. She didn't know who he was anymore. The father she had thought she knew—the man who had had such a positive impact on her life—now seemed like nothing more than a foggy memory.

She attempted to calm herself down as she sat in her mother's hospital room, tried to regain her mental bearings and sense of direction, but the numbness she felt didn't allow for this. She questioned why she felt this way now and not earlier—why these betrayals by her father were hitting her even harder at this particular time.

She envisioned her father's two lives—his life as she had known it versus what had really gone on—side-by-side narratives difficult to contemplate, and even more difficult to comprehend.

Should I let go of the father I thought I knew?

A woman entered the room, introduced herself as Dr. Weidner, and sat down beside her. One look at her face caused a tangible sinking feeling in Paige's stomach.

"I'm so sorry, Paige. Your mother didn't make it."

Paige spent a few final minutes with her mother's lifeless body before hospital staff explained the postmortem procedures. Afterward, she walked to her car with considerable purpose, knowing how dreadful her mother's final hours must have been for her—physically, mentally, and emotionally. Anger built up inside of her as she drove to her mother's home.

"Where the fuck have you been?" Paige screamed at Natalie when she walked through the door, the little composure she'd been maintaining in the car fully collapsing.

"What are *you* doing here?" Natalie asked through a bloodshot gaze. She had on a jacket as though she had either just arrived herself or was about to leave again.

"Never mind why I'm here. Where have you been?"

"You look like shit. What happened? And where's Mom?"

"I'll tell you what happened," Paige said, adrenaline now surging throughout her body. "While you were out gallivanting around who knows where, Mom fell. She's dead, you asshole," Paige said, the sound of her own words making her realize just how unmoored she had become. "You were supposed to be taking care of her!"

"She's dead?!" Natalie plopped down on the sofa and held out her hands. "But she said she didn't need any help."

"You can't be that ignorant, Natalie. Any moron could see she needed help. What do you think that talk the three of us had was for? Did you listen to any of it?"

"What talk?"

"Are you kidding me? So you were high then and don't remember it?"

"Where's her purse?" Natalie asked.

"What?!"

"How am I supposed to live now?"

"I just told you Mom is dead, and your first reaction is where's her purse? Why don't you get your sorry ass out of here? Now!"

Natalie glared at Paige. "I live here," she said. "And I'm pregnant. You can't kick me out."

"Oh, yeah? Watch me."

Paige marched up to Natalie's bedroom, all the while practicing breathing techniques to relieve the tightness in her chest, something she had learned in yoga class. She entered her sister's room and armful by armful started throwing her things down the stairs, out of breath by the time she finished.

"Take your shit and get out of this house."

"I have nowhere to go. You know that. And it's not your house to kick me out of anyway."

Paige struggled to avoid stumbling over her sister's clothes and other belongings as she descended the stairs.

"I'm throwing all this stuff in your car and driving you to a motel. I'll pay for one month's rent for you to stay there. After that, you're on your own, sister."

"You can't do this, Paige."

"Oh, yes, I can. But wait. Maybe you'd rather spend the next month in jail…for obstructing a police investigation. What'll it be, Nat?"

While the pathetic-looking Natalie stood speechless in the middle of the living room, Paige scooped up her sister's belongings and proceeded to stuff them into the back seat of Natalie's car. When she finished, she snatched the door key that Natalie still had in her hand and put it in her pocket. "C'mon, you sorry piece of— Let's go."

"I'm not going."

Paige pulled out her cell phone and proceeded to call 9-1-1.

"Who are you calling?"

"The police."

Natalie told her to stop.

Paige stopped her call and looked up the number for a nearby motel.

"Now who are you calling?"

Paige left the room to complete the call.

"You're coming then?"

"Where to?"

"Just get in the car," Paige said as she got into the driver's seat of Natalie's car.

Natalie slid into the passenger seat.

"Give me your car keys."

Neither of them spoke for the first several blocks of their drive until Natalie finally broke the silence.

"So what happened to Mom?" she asked.

"I told you she fell."

"That usually doesn't kill a person."

"So now you're a medical expert?"

More silence until they reached the Rodeway Inn. Paige pulled up to Unit 8 and parked the car.

"What are we doing here?"

"This is your new home, Nat."

"I'm not staying here."

"You do what you want. I paid for thirty days over the phone."

"You've got to be kidding."

"Stay put while I get the key," she told Natalie after pulling the car key out of the ignition.

"Like where am I going to go?" she mumbled under her breath.

"You can go to hell for all I care," Paige shouted back at her.

Paige retrieved the room key from the office, opened the motel door, propped it open with a chair, and proceeded to empty the contents of Natalie's car into the room while Natalie stood by watching. When she finished, Paige left Natalie's car key on the bed and called for an Uber for herself. On her way out, she threw a hundred-dollar bill at Natalie, and said, "Here—go buy yourself some drugs."

CHAPTER 42

Jessivel spent the entire week on her job search, taking to heart all that Paige had advised her to do. When she met her mother for lunch, she bragged about what she'd done.

"Good for you, Jess," her mother said. "I knew you'd come around one of these days."

"Well, maybe all I needed was a gentle push."

"Or not so gentle," she said, a faint outline of a smile on her lips.

"C'mon, Mom. I came around. Can't we leave it at that?"

"Looks like Paige has had a positive effect on you. She's helping you leave the angry woman you'd become, something I couldn't do."

"She's not so bad."

"Maybe I could meet her."

"Really?"

"I think it would be interesting seeing you two side by side, both of Wayne's daughters."

"I don't think we look anything alike. And his real name is Ryan, you know. Ryan West."

"He'll always be Wayne Salter to me."

"Whatever."

"How's Kayla?"

"She's fine. Her newest obsession is an old teddy bear she said Dad gave to her."

Her mother's eyes popped wide open. "What teddy bear?" she asked.

"Some stuffed bear she said she got from Dad."

"He gave it to her?"

"Well, no. I think she sort of took it from his briefcase one day. Thought it was meant for her."

"What does it look like?"

"Why are you getting so hyper over some old stuffed toy?"

"What does it look like, Jessivel?"

"Calm down, Mom. I didn't even remember her having it until she brought it up. She went through some unpacked moving bags I had and found it."

"So, she has it now?"

"What's with you? Yes, she has it. It was dirty, so I washed it."

"You didn't."

"Okay, what's with the bear?"

"Nothing."

"Don't give me that crap. You're all uptight about this stupid bear. What's going on?"

Her mother sat in silence while she picked at her plate of food. "There was talk about a teddy bear in some letters Wayne got from the woman in India…or London. I forget where the hell she was. Anyway, I can't remember exactly what the letters said except that the teddy bear had striped pants."

"This one has striped pants."

"Then it's the same one. I think, but I'm not sure, this woman hid something inside the bear."

"Like what?"

"I don't know. If I remember right, she was vague about what it was."

"Like, what could it have been?"

"I'm telling you, I don't know. Drugs maybe?"

"Not Dad."

"I'm just guessing, Jess. I don't think so either, but Hannah thought at one time he might have been mixed up in drugs. All I know is that something was inside that he was to hang on to until she got back to him."

"So I'll look inside of it. But if it *was* drugs, I'm not sure what washing did to it."

"I have to get back to work. We better get going. And Jess?"

"What?"

"Promise me you'll call as soon as you open the bear."

"Honey, where's your teddy bear? Did you take it from the clean laundry pile?" Jessivel asked Kayla.

"His name is Asher, and he's under my pillow. Why?"

"No wonder I couldn't find it. Asher?"

"Asher Angel."

"I have no clue who that is."

"Andi Mack?"

"Who?"

"You're kidding, right?"

"Kayla, just give me the damn bear."

"You're not going to take it away from me, are you? It's bad enough you washed it. Now it doesn't smell like Poppy anymore."

"I just want to see it."

"Okay," Kayla grumbled as she stomped to her bedroom and returned with the bear. Jessivel pulled down the bear's pants and examined the handsewn seam down its belly.

"What are you doing?"

"Get me my sewing basket, will you?"

"What are you going to do to him?"

"Just get me the basket."

"No," she said as she attempted to rescue the bear. "You're going to ruin it."

"See this seam, all the hand-stitching? I'm going to slit it open and see what's inside. I can sew it right up again, same stitching. No one will ever know the difference."

"Why?"

"Why what?"

"Why do you need to see what's inside?"

"Nana seems to think Poppy was hiding something in there. Don't you want to see the surprise?" she asked, hoping it wouldn't be a baggie of drugs.

"What would he have put in there?"

"I don't know. That's why I want to look. Now, would you please bring me my sewing basket?"

"Fine."

Jessivel used a seam ripper to snip the threads down the front of the bear, then put her fingers inside the stuffed animal and felt around.

"That's gross!" Kayla said.

"It's just a stuffed bear, Kayla."

"Still gross. Anything in there?"

"I can't see or feel anything." She dug further, slipping her fingers into the bear's arms and legs.

"Good, now sew it up so I can have it back."

Jessivel did as asked, and when finished, called her mother to tell her the news.

"I'm not surprised. He, or someone, probably took out whatever was in there and did something with it."

"Please tell me Dad didn't do drugs."

"He didn't…not that I ever knew of anyway, but he did a lot of things I didn't know about, so maybe he did."

"Whatever was in there must have been important or valuable or something, don't you think?"

"When it comes to your father, I don't really know what to think. I gotta go, Jess. Talk to you later."

Jessivel considered her and her mother's conversation and what other secrets her father might have kept from them. Growing up, it never would have crossed her mind to ask her father detailed questions about himself. He was Dad. He was who he was. He traveled extensively in his job (or between families, she now knew), provided for them, treated them okay. Her only complaint was that while he was generous with his money, he was stingy with his time and attention. Still, there seemed to be no reason for her to ever raise serious questions about him.

After thinking about it, Jessivel couldn't name any of her father's friends, his hobbies, or even his favorite sports team. He had never talked about his life as a boy growing up, his schooling, his life in the military, or his earlier jobs. She had never considered that back in the day. Now, it made sense because he had another life…or lives. He *couldn't* give out many details.

Jessivel hadn't realized until now just how little she knew about her own father.

CHAPTER 43

When Paige called "the girls" to tell them what had happened with her mother, they offered to help with the arrangements and anything else she needed to do. While she appreciated their support, as with most things in her life, she felt more comfortable doing everything herself. Still trying to prove herself to her father? Perhaps.

Paige had asked her doctor to prescribe an anti-anxiety medication to get her through the next several days, even at the risk of falling into the same trap as her sister who believed there was a chemical solution to every problem. As she sat down to do the necessary tasks associated with her mother's death, she was glad to have the meds in her system.

She made a list of her mother's friends, acquaintances, and relatives and began making calls. Midway through the list, she thought of Leland and called him, remembering how upset he had been when she had failed to tell him about her father's death.

"Would you like me to come over?" he asked. "Just for someone to talk to."

She was reluctant to say yes. Next on her to-do list were the sealed envelopes from her mother's safe—something she had planned to do alone. And she wasn't sure having Leland there was a good idea in any case, not when she was in such a vulnerable state.

"No, I'm fine."

"No, you're not. I can hear it in your voice."

"You're right. I'm not, but—"

"I'm coming over, if for no other reason than to give you a hug and tell you how sorry I am for your loss. Where are you? Your house or hers?"

"Mine." She gave him the address. "Lee?"

"Yes."

"Thanks."

As she waited for Leland to arrive, guilt over her mother's demise surged through her. She hadn't taken the right precautions. True, if her sister had been home, sober, and attentive to her mother's needs, her death may have been prevented. But if Paige hadn't allowed her mother to be alone with an irresponsible addict in the first place, she may not be sitting here now dealing with the aftermath of her mother's death.

She stopped what she was doing and stared out the window, focusing on the birdfeeder outside the dining room window, until her eyes ached. When a bright red cardinal landed in the feeder, she lost it. Once the first tear emerged, the rest followed in an unbroken stream. She bent over her lap and let them fall, her only wish being that she had time to recover from her intense blubbering before Leland arrived. She didn't like for anyone to see her cry.

When he arrived, Leland pulled Paige into a familiar hug that she fondly remembered from when they were together, reminding her of how long it had been since any man had held her and made her feel like no matter which way she fell, he'd be there to catch her. His six-foot frame may not have been as compact as it had been back in the day, but it still felt good. Good and strong. Leland had never worn cologne due to a fierce sensitivity to it, and breathing in his natural scent brought back more memories. She relaxed in his arms as his able fingers slowly and methodically skated up and down her back.

After a minute, Leland released her from his embrace and looked directly into her eyes. "You okay?" he asked.

She brushed off his question with a wave of her hand and, after offering him something to drink, led the way to the living room.

He eyed the grand staircase to the second floor. "Nice place."

"Thanks."

"Kind of big for one person."

"Not really."

They settled in on her sofa in front of the elegant, warmly welcoming fireplace in the formal living room.

"I'm so sorry, Paige," he said. "Losing both parents in such a short period of time must be hard."

"It is. Mom's death came so suddenly. I wasn't prepared."

"I know, hon. I wish you weren't having to go through this."

His calling her "hon" made her remember that even when their marriage was on the rocks, he had still called her that.

"Thanks."

"Do you need any help with anything? The funeral arrangements. Taking care of business. When my dad died, I remember being overwhelmed with all that had to be done, and he didn't have that much." She had never known his dad, who'd died of colon cancer before she and Leland had even met.

"Thanks, but I think I have everything under control. I do need to decide what to do with her house though."

"Whether to sell it, you mean?"

"Mm-hm." The notion of losing all the memories made her wince, but then maybe that would be best given what she knew about her father—all her memories of him now tainted.

"Is Natalie still there?"

Paige took in a long, steady breath before responding. "I kicked her out."

Leland's eyebrows arched way up, but he didn't say anything.

"She was supposed to be Mom's caretaker. Instead, she was out somewhere, getting high on something probably, in the middle of the night, when Mom fell. She didn't have to die."

"You can't be sure of that. Maybe—"

"Really? You're taking Natalie's side?"

Leland threw up his hands. "Hey, I'm not taking anyone's side. I was just making the point that since you weren't there—"

Paige got up from her seat and walked away from him—the void in the pit of her stomach irritating enough for her to pop another one of the anti-anxiety pills. She hadn't counted on Leland questioning her anger toward Natalie. Now she wished he had never come over.

He joined her in the kitchen. "Paige?"

She kept her back to him.

"I'm sorry if I said something wrong. I didn't mean to."

"That's fine."

"It's not fine. I came here to give you some comfort, and now I've upset you." He walked up behind her and placed his hands on her shoulders. "I'm sorry. Do you want me to go?"

Paige turned around and buried her face in his chest. "It was all her fault," she said into his shirt. "She didn't have to die."

Leland held her until she was still again. "Do you want me to stay or go?" he said softly.

She bit her lip as she considered different scenarios, her mind at war with her heart.

"I have to go into the office to sign off on several deals on my desk."

"That's what's important right now?" he asked.

"And I have to…"

"You have to what?"

He squeezed her a little tighter.

"You don't have to stay," she said.

"I know I don't have to. I'm asking you if you want me to."

She kept her face buried in his chest, unable to look him straight in the eye, afraid if she did he would try to open up the heavily guarded areas of her heart.

"Yes. I want you to stay."

CHAPTER 44

Jessivel's joblessness became a more serious problem given the CPS hearing looming over her head that could affect custody of her daughter. She had followed up on every resume she had sent, but no one had any openings. As much as she hated the idea of a long commute, she recognized that now it may be necessary.

She called Paige for moral support.

"Are you okay?" she asked Paige over the phone. "You sound kind of funny."

"My mom died. I'm having a bit of a hard time with it."

Jessivel offered her condolences and asked if she needed help with anything, but Paige didn't seem receptive. If Paige didn't need her in a time like this, maybe she wasn't really family, after all.

"I'm sorry I'm bothering you, Paige. Just let me know if there is anything I can do."

"You're no bother, believe me. The funeral is Saturday, and there's just so much to think about." She told her the circumstances behind her mother's fall and how Natalie hadn't been there for her.

"I'm so sorry to hear that, Paige." She told Paige that she would like to come to the funeral to pay her respects, hoping it wouldn't be construed as an intrusion.

"I'd appreciate that."

"And I'd like to bring my mother. Would that be alright? Or do you think that would be inappropriate?"

"No, please do bring her. I'd like to meet her, and I think my mother would smile down on it. My impression was that she held nothing against her." Paige told Jessivel the place and time for the funeral service.

"I'll see you then," Jessivel said.

"Wait, you called me for something, and we got distracted."

"It was nothing."

"No, tell me. Really."

Jessivel told Paige about the upcoming CPS hearing.

"That sounds serious. Do you have representation?"

"Representation?"

"A lawyer or some other advocate to be with you."

"No. I didn't know I needed one."

"When's the hearing?"

"Tomorrow afternoon."

"That's not much time to find anyone, but I'd advise you to have someone there with you. Someone who knows the system. Have you found a job yet?"

"No."

"Hmm. That's not going to work in your favor. Look, I have a few things I need to attend to this morning, but let me see what I can pull together for you this afternoon. Maybe I can help. We'll see. I can't promise you anything, Jess, but I'll try."

"Are you sure? You must have your hands full with—"

"Don't worry about me. I'll be fine. I gotta go now. I'll call you either later today or tomorrow morning."

Jessivel hung up feeling stupid for thinking she could go into the hearing by herself.

Paige was clearly the smart one.

"I can't be there with you today, but a Mr. Eli Dabner will meet you there an hour before you're due in court," Paige said to Jessivel on the morning of her CPS hearing. "He's a family law attorney. I told him as much as I know about your case. You'll have to fill him in on the rest. And he's going to give you an offer letter that shows you are employed as of Monday. I really must go. Good luck. Call me later to let me know how it went."

She wanted to ask Paige questions, but she had hung up too fast. Just hours away from having to go to the hearing and being in the dark as to what was about to transpire caused a quivery twitchiness in her stomach that wouldn't quit. She had asked her mother if she could come with her, but she had declined because of some event at the Perlman residence that afternoon. The idea that Mrs. Perlman's stupid to-do would take precedence over a serious family matter that involved her granddaughter made her stomach act up even worse.

Jessivel eyed her watch for the umpteenth time—she had two hours before she had to get into her car and drive to the courthouse. The letter she had received stated no need to have Kayla present, so Jessivel had sent her to school without telling her about it. Now she wished she had her there for support.

The drive to the courthouse took less than twenty minutes. She wandered in through the front door where she showed the guard her paperwork. He pointed her toward the elevator and told her to turn left on the third floor to Court Room 3-12. Once she found it, she sat on the bench outside of the room, picking at her fingernails and hoping she wouldn't throw up or have to rush to the bathroom before the proceeding started.

An older man with slicked back hair and a paunchy stomach approached her. He introduced himself as Eli Dabner.

"I had little time to prepare for this, but it appears to be an easy, clear-cut matter. You didn't opt for representation when they notified you?"

"I'm not sure." She felt confused, like she didn't know what was going on around her even though she was right there.

"They would have sent you a letter telling you that you could attend the hearing with an attorney or one would be appointed if you couldn't afford one."

"I guess I didn't read what they sent me very well."

"No problem. Before I forget, here is Ms. West's offer letter showing you are employed by her firm as of Monday."

"What?"

"You didn't know about this?"

"She may have told me. I don't know. She hired me?"

"That's what it says."

"Doing what?"

He looked down at the letter. "Administrative assistant."

Whatever that means.

"Anyway, let's begin by you telling me what happened on the day CPS came to visit you."

They spent the next half hour discussing what happened and Jessivel's current situation.

"I'm not too worried about this hearing. They filed a Category III complaint against you, with no charges, so it will be pretty much the judge reading the CPS report and either agreeing with it or not. If he agrees with it, he can dismiss it, and everyone goes home. Or he can order subsequent checks on your home for a period of time—interviews with your daughter, family members, neighbors, etc.—to ensure as much as anyone can that there are no future threats to her safety."

"And if he doesn't agree with it?"

"He can call for further investigation, or if there is relevant evidence presented here today, he can order the child removed from the home."

Jessivel's stomach roiled. "He can't do that!"

"He can, but I don't see that happening, not from what I've been able to glean in the short period of time I've had to look into this." He paused. "Time to go in. Just follow my lead, and if you're asked questions, answer them honestly. That's all you can do."

Jessivel ambled into the courtroom and took her seat beside Mr. Dabner at a long wooden table facing the judge's bench. One by one, other people entered the room.

"How did it go?" Paige asked Jessivel later in the day.

"Okay, I guess. They didn't take Kayla away from me."

"Case closed? Nothing more you have to do?"

"CPS is going to keep in touch."

"With visits?"

"I think so."

"How was Eli?"

"Who?"

"The attorney I set up for you, Eli Dabner."

"Oh, he was fine. Thank you. But I can't pay you for him."

"Don't worry about it."

"And I'm not sure I understand the letter he gave me. The one that says I have an administrative assistant position at Castle Realtors."

"I did that to show the court you're employed, at least as of Monday."

"But I'm not."

"You are if you want to be. We should meet and talk about it."

"I guess we better because I still don't get it, but you've got so much on your mind—"

"Don't worry. I can make time."

They planned for Jessivel to come to Paige's office the following morning. In the meantime, Jessivel Googled "duties of an administrative assistant" and cringed—not only did she lack the necessary skills and experience, but the tasks listed didn't sound like ones she'd want to do.

"Okay, let's talk about the job I have for you here," Paige said to Jessivel when she arrived at her office. "I chose the title administrative assistant because it's broad in scope—it can mean anything. And before I go any further, if you're not interested, please say so. I'll understand, and I won't take it personally. Just keep in mind the court has a copy of the confirmation letter, so if you decide it's not for you, it's best you have another job lined up."

Paige was talking fast, and Jessivel struggled to follow her. She nodded, thinking it better to be a listener at this point.

"I have decided to buy this strip mall, the one we're in right now. There's a lot involved in buying retail property, so for the next couple of months, I'll need help with…well, someone to do things for me that have to do with the purchase and then afterward the management of it."

"You don't already have an assistant?"

"I do, but I already keep her busy with other things. I'm thinking this could turn into a permanent position."

"What kind of help will you need after you buy it?"

"Someone to take calls from the other tenants, collect the rent, manage the people we hire to maintain the property, help with monthly reports. Stuff like that."

"But I don't know how to do any of that."

"I'll teach you. Or someone else in the office will teach you. It won't be hard. Look, I'd never throw you into a job and let you sink or swim. We'd help you every step of the way. And then in time, I'm confident you'll be able to do things instinctively. What do you think?"

"I guess I'm not sure."

"It would be income until you find something else more suitable. Although, I must say I'd rather not invest in your training just to have you leave in a month or whatever. But that would be up to you. And I'd run into that no matter who I hired."

They discussed pay and benefits. Jessivel would be making significantly more than she did at The Busy Bean and would have health insurance in just thirty days. Jessivel agreed to give it a shot.

"And one more thing. I'm going to buy a small espresso machine for the break room. You'd be in charge of coffee."

Jessivel relaxed for the first time since arriving and smiled. "That I can do."

CHAPTER 45

aige checked her phone before getting out of bed. One text message.

coffee ready when u r

If someone had told Paige that twelve years after her divorce, she'd be waking up to her shirtless ex-husband in the kitchen making coffee for them, she would have called them delusional. But she did, and this morning she felt a little out of her mind for allowing it. Now, the day of her mother's funeral, she didn't know what she was going to do with him.

"You're sleeping later than normal, as I remember," he said to her as he poured their coffee. "Still take it black?"

"Twelve years is a long time, Lee. People change. Creamer is in the fridge."

"Yes, they do. Fortunately or unfortunately."

"Change is usually for the better…if you let it be," she said.

"Especially if you're the one who initiated it."

"Can we please not go down that road again?" she asked. "I thought we resolved this last night."

"Maybe *you* did."

The sensation in her chest that she'd experienced the previous night returned. This trait had always bothered her about Leland—he couldn't let go of something that hadn't gone his way. He hadn't been able to do that in their marriage and, apparently, he couldn't do that now.

"Lee."

"Paige," he said, using flirty eye-play to get her attention.

"You're hopeless."

"You could say that."

She'd needed him last night—his comforting words, the familiar feel-good spot of his body where she had nestled and become blissfully removed from the stress of her mother's death. No making out, no sex, just his presence. But then he had ruined it with talk about their relationship—past and future—asking her difficult questions that she couldn't or didn't want to answer.

"I would like to attend the funeral, if that's okay," he said.

"Of course. Visitation at ten followed by the funeral service."

"With you."

She didn't know where he was going with this.

"I have to go early to meet with the funeral director."

"What about Natalie?"

"What about her?"

"Will she be there?"

"I haven't talked to her since…" Paige had gone back and forth about telling her sister of the funeral arrangements, repeatedly asking herself if it was the illness that drove Natalie to her reprehensible behavior or something she could control.

"You should call her."

"Or if she cared at all, she could have called me."

She picked up her half-finished cup of coffee, dumped it into the sink, and walked away from him.

"Paige," he called after her.

"I'll see you later," she said to him halfway down the hallway, hoping that would be his cue to leave.

Paige's parents each had a smattering of aunts, uncles, and cousins still alive—all of whom were connected only by Christmas cards, births, graduations, and funerals—and Paige had notified them of her mother's death. Then, after giving it considerable thought, she had decided to call her estranged Aunt Bernice and her daughter Wanda. She called Wanda first, anxious about what her reaction would be to her call and wondering if she, her half-sister, would bring up their shared parentage.

"I'm so sorry to hear this, Paige. Your mother was a good woman. I always liked her. Look, I'm thirty-nine weeks pregnant and won't be able to attend her funeral, but I'll tell Mom about it…if you want me to. Unless you'd rather call her yourself."

"That would be great. Thank you, Wanda." She gave her details of the service, thankful for how the conversation had gone, but more curious than before if Wanda knew the identity of her biological father.

On the way to the church for her mother's funeral, it hit her that with the matriarch of the family gone, there was an obvious shift in the dynamic for the little family now left. "Change is usually for the better," she'd said to Leland earlier. Now, she wasn't so sure.

Paige had never given any thought to becoming an adult orphan—she was too young for that—nor had she ever considered losing her role as her mother's child. The impact of her father's death had been somewhat softened by Paige focusing more on her mother afterward—a distraction of sorts. And with Natalie now estranged, Paige sensed the lack of familial ties even more.

It all seemed so surreal. A stew of emotions churned inside of her—guilt, sadness, sympathy, and anger. A sick feeling curled in her stomach as she walked through the enormous double doors of the church in which her father's funeral had been held. She entered wishing she had someone with her to lean on. Someone like Leland. Leland—the man whose offer to accompany her to the funeral she had dismissed.

She met with the funeral director and then spent a final private moment with her mother. Afterward, she waited in the visitation room for the mourners to arrive, many of whom had attended her father's memorial service. An hour into it, Natalie arrived—on Leland's arm.

Stunned by their appearance together, Paige focused on her mother's hairdresser with whom she had been speaking, refusing to believe what she saw. Then, when her eyes forced her to look back at them—strolling through the room, appearing to be in deep conversation, arm-in-arm like a couple—everything around them faded into a blur.

Minutes later, still in shock that Leland and her sister had come together, she struggled to maintain a half-smile while she talked with her mother's next-door neighbor. She observed Leland and Natalie walk the perimeter of the room, half-listening to Mrs. Gaganshaw talk about how she and her mother used to have a glass of wine some afternoons…before five o'clock. *I could use one now, and it isn't even noon.*

Paige received sincere condolences from her staff members and many of the agents she employed. Tracy from the Backstreet Kitchen also came to offer consolation for Paige's loss.

Natalie and Leland eventually approached Paige. She took in a deep breath and reached out to hug her sister, the smell of alcohol making her gag. This, combined with the stiff embrace she received in return, she feared was going to be a harbinger of things to come.

Natalie wore a navy-blue pant suit that Paige recognized as their mother's. "It's nice you can fit into Mom's clothes," she said to Natalie, glancing down at the fabric of the outfit stretched over her blossoming stomach and wondering when she had taken it from her mother's closet. "Be sure to let me know if there's anything *else* you want of hers before I donate them."

"Drop the attitude, sis. And Mom said I could have this in case you're wondering," she said before walking away.

Paige doubted that was the case but saw no point in making an issue out of it.

She headed in the opposite direction of Natalie and Leland. When she spotted "the girls," she rushed over to them.

"Hey, sweetie, are you okay?" Sandy asked.

Paige pointed toward Natalie and Leland, arms around each other, conversing tête-à-tête.

"Is that your ex?" Valerie asked.

Paige nodded.

"Who's he with?"

"My sister."

"Huh? What's with them?"

"Who knows?" Paige said.

"Is she sober?" Gayle asked.

"Is *he*?" Valerie asked.

When Jessivel and her mother walked into the room, Paige left her friends to greet them. She gave Jessivel a hug.

"Thank you for coming. It means a lot to me," she said and meant it.

Jessivel introduced Paige to her mother, Crystal, and they also embraced.

The three chatted until other mourners interrupted them, at which time Jessivel and Crystal headed toward a seating area at the back of the room.

When the time came to enter the chapel for the funeral service, Paige swung by to where Jessivel and her mother were seated and led them to the front row to sit with her. Natalie and Leland soon followed.

"I suppose people would talk if we didn't sit together," Natalie whispered as she sat next to Paige. "Otherwise, I would sit as far away from you as possible."

"I love you too, Natalie."

Paige avoided looking at Jessivel and her mother, embarrassed by the unseemly verbal exchange she'd just had with her sister.

The service was felicitous, but like her father's, impersonal. The same balding, middle-aged funeral director wearing the same dull-brown suit stood at the podium and pretended to reflect on her mother's life as if he had known her.

Neither she nor Natalie had great singing voices, but Natalie must have thought differently about herself because she belted out the words to the funeral hymns louder than anyone else in the room, off-key and not in tempo, sometimes improvising the words, and clapping at the end of each one. Embarrassed for her and for herself, Paige stared down at the hymnal as she mouthed the words for the rest of the hymns.

Paige had invited certain mourners—some neighbors, close friends, and any relatives who had showed up—to join her afterward for lunch at a nearby restaurant. When it was time to go there, she realized she hadn't mentioned this to Leland and was hesitant about inviting "him" because it meant "them." She searched the room. When she didn't see him or Natalie, she called his cell phone.

"Did I tell you there's a luncheon at Ricardo's? I'm sorry if I didn't."

"No, you didn't." She heard him ask Natalie if she wanted to go there. "We'll see," he said before hanging up.

I did the right thing. Now, please don't show up.

At Ricardo's, Paige felt comfortable sitting with the people she considered her closest allies—Jessivel, Crystal, and her three best friends. They settled into chairs at one end of the u-shaped table configuration, in a windowless but otherwise cheerful room, where they engaged in small talk waiting for the others to arrive.

At one point, Crystal leaned toward Paige and said, "I hope I don't make you too uncomfortable being here, dear."

Paige placed her hand on hers. "Not at all, Crystal. I'm so glad you came."

"When things have settled down for you a bit, maybe the three of us can meet somewhere and get to know each other better."

"I'd like that."

The mourners arrived and stopped by Paige's chair to reiterate their condolences. The last two to arrive were Natalie and Leland.

"C'mon everyone, order up. Drinks are on the house!" Natalie said as she plunked herself down directly across the table from Paige. "Mom's dead, but we're not!"

"Oh, dear," Paige mumbled, loud enough for Jessivel and Crystal to hear. She glanced at one, then the other, and shook her head. "I'm so sorry," she said to them.

Natalie's behavior worsened throughout the meal—her voice getting louder with a significant amount of foul language laced in. Some of her drink sloshed out of her glass each time she raised it to her mouth, and when she talked, her words slurred to the point of barely being discernable. She clung to Leland as if she'd fall off the chair if she dared let go. Paige wanted to grab the drink out of her hand, for the baby's sake, but knew if she did, it would cause even more of a commotion in the room.

Leland appeared to be amused by Natalie's behavior at first, but after a while, he seemed more annoyed by it and tried to keep her in check by putting his arm around her and talking to her softly. This apparently irritated Natalie, and at one point, she attempted to get up to leave. After struggling on her feet for a few seconds, she went down.

Paige, who couldn't stand it anymore, apologized to the twenty or so people in the room while Leland scooped Natalie up off the floor and led her to the bathroom. The sound of her vomiting cleared the room except for her three friends.

"She's got a lot of nerve coming here like that," Sandy said. "But I don't understand why Leland and she are together. Do you?"

Paige shook her head. "No, I don't. And I don't really care. They can have each other."

"When is the last time you even saw him?" Gayle asked.

Paige hesitated.

"Paige?"

"Hmm?"

"How long ago was it that you saw your 'ex'?"

She looked past them. "Yesterday," she muttered.

"What!"

"He stayed the night."

Valerie gasped.

"You're kidding."

"We didn't have sex or anything. He was just there to…comfort me, I guess."

"But he stayed the night. In the same bed."

"Yeah, the big jerk."

When the girls finally got over the shock of Paige being with Leland the night before, they asked her if she wanted them to hang around until after Leland and Natalie had left the restaurant.

"No, you can go. They've humiliated me in front of others enough for one day."

Paige waited for the bill, head in hands, any previous thoughts of making amends with Natalie long gone. Disease or not, she had no business causing a scene at their mother's funeral. And shame on Lee for allowing her to do it.

Paige was reviewing the bill when Leland and Natalie finally emerged from the bathroom.

Natalie stared at Paige for a few long seconds, her suit amply stained with vomit residue. Turning to Leland, she said, "C'mon, honey. Let's get outta here."

CHAPTER 46

"So what did you think?" Jessivel asked her mother as they pulled away from the church.

"I like her."

"Who?"

"Paige, of course."

"And Natalie?"

Her mother gave her "the look," which Jessivel recognized as a warning that something hard-nosed was about to be said. "If she were my daughter, I would have dragged her outside by the ear and whupped her hide."

"I think Paige was embarrassed," said Jessivel.

"Who in that room wasn't? Shocking behavior. Shouldn't have happened."

"I have to admit that it made me feel good when Paige introduced me to people as her sister."

"I picked up on that too."

"So what did you think about seeing us side by side? Any family resemblance?"

"I can see she takes after her father. You take more after me."

◇

"Welcome to Castle Realtors!" Paige said to Jessivel on her first day on the job. "Let me show you where you'll be sitting."

254

Paige led the way through the office, with Jessivel feeling like a five-year-old on her first day of school. Paige introduced her to a few other employees before showing her a small cubicle not too far from her own office.

"You can put your bag in here," Paige said and then invited her into her office for the first portion of her new-hire orientation.

Paige explained the philosophy of the company, the services they offered, and a basic understanding of what Jessivel's duties would be. She added that Olivia, whom she had just promoted to Office Manager, would go over their policies and procedures, benefits, and the new-hire paperwork. She ended the orientation by saying, "I know this may not be exactly what you want to do for a living, and you may not stay long, but look at it this way—you can learn a lot about the real estate industry, different computer systems, and how to deal with a variety of people. You'll gain some skills that you can bring to other jobs. You'll make decent money, and who knows, maybe you'll really like it here. Fair enough?"

A bit overwhelmed by it all, Jessivel gave a quick nod in response.

"And now I'm going to ask you if you'll break in the new espresso machine and make me one of your famous raspberry lattes. I think you'll find everything you need in the break room. When Olivia finishes with your orientation, she'll show you our office management programs. In the meantime, I have a speaking engagement at Wright Community College this morning. If you need anything, Olivia is your "go-to" person." Paige gave her a welcoming smile. "Good luck."

When her first workday was over, Jessivel drove home feeling exhausted both physically and mentally. The job was so much more complicated and involved than her barista job, and she had doubts whether she had made the right decision accepting the position. But at least she didn't have to wait on people all day. And her being employed kept the people at CPS and CDFSS happy—a big load off her mind.

Paige had been patient with her, as had Olivia, and everyone else in the office had been nice, but that hadn't made up for how stupid she'd felt asking dumb questions, especially when it came to computer-related things. Like, "What does *reboot* mean?"

One big worry was that Kayla was now a latchkey kid. And too many distractions existed between school and their apartment door—mainly drugs, bullies, and boys—for Jessivel to feel comfortable. Kayla had blossomed into an attractive, sassy teen who didn't always use the best judgment—a lot like Jessivel herself had been at that age. Kayla typically got home from school at 3:45 in the afternoon. Jessivel used to get home before Kayla when she worked as a barista, but now she would be getting home at around six o'clock, two hours after Kayla. A lot could happen in two hours.

Today, Kayla wasn't home when she arrived, and Jessivel panicked. Her first day on the job and already there was a problem with her daughter. Her school backpack was on her bed, the jacket she had worn to school was also there, but Kayla was not. Jessivel looked out the window for her, then looked up and down the common hallway before picking up the phone to call the police.

The slamming of the apartment door caused her to jump.

"Where have you been?" Jessivel shouted at Kayla when she walked into the apartment ten minutes after Jessivel had arrived home. "I was about to call the police!"

"I was just down the hall. La-Keysha is in my class."

"Who's La-Keysha?"

"I just told you, our neighbor down the hall. She's in my class. She asked me to come over after school."

"You were told specifically to come right home after school and do your homework until I get home. What didn't you understand about that?"

"I don't have any homework."

"That doesn't mean you don't come right home. I didn't know what to think when I came home and you weren't here."

"Kinda like when I woke up that night and you weren't here. You mean like that?"

"Don't get smart with me," Jessivel said, knowing damn well her daughter had a valid point. "You're grounded!"

"You've got to be kidding."

"Rules are rules. You're to come home right after school. Alone. No friends over. No TV. No computer except for homework. Is that clear?"

"If I had a cell phone like all the other kids, I could have called to ask you if it was okay."

"Well, you can forget that. I can't afford one for you." If her father hadn't paid for her own phone a year in advance before he died, she didn't know if she could even afford one for herself. "And you could have used Mrs. Harding's phone. You know that."

"I didn't think of that."

"Did it occur to you to leave a note for me?"

"No."

"Don't you ever pull a stunt like that again, you hear?"

"Fine," Kayla said and stomped off to her room.

"And don't slam the door!"

Too late.

It was Friday, and Paige was arranging for an open house to celebrate her new ownership of the strip mall. When she asked Jessivel to work late on this day to help with the plans, she didn't hesitate to do so since she knew Kayla would not be home alone. Kayla's grounding had ended, and after meeting La-Keysha's parents, Jessivel had agreed to let Kayla attend a sleepover in their home.

At the end of their normal workday, Paige ordered pizza for everyone before they put in another three hours of working on plans for the open house. Paige called it a night at 8:30 P.M. She asked Jessivel if she'd stay a while longer so they could talk.

Jessivel sat quietly while the others filed out of the conference room, nervous about why Paige had asked her to stay. She thought she had been doing okay with her work.

"Thanks for sticking around, Jessivel," Paige said after everyone else had left.

"Did I do something wrong?" Jessivel asked.

"Not at all. I just wanted to check in with you to see how it's going. We haven't had the chance to talk much since you started here. So…"

"You are one busy lady, I must say."

"It has been a little hectic around here lately. That's why I need you! So, how's it going for you?"

"It's going fine."

"You don't sound too enthused," Paige said.

"Everything is so new."

The job had been working out okay so far—everyone there had been nice, helpful, and accepting of her and her lack of knowledge of the real estate industry. But after the newness of most tasks wore off, she found the work to be boring. Many days, she didn't see Paige at all except to say good morning, and when she did see her, Paige was completely immersed in her work with little time in between phone calls and meetings.

One aspect of her job Jessivel found interesting was tenant relations. It was only because everyone else in the office was in a staff meeting one day that she had the opportunity to deal with tenant Floyd Combs, owner of Maya's Deli, and according to those in the office who knew him, the grumpiest tenant in the strip mall. He came in agitated and barked his problem at her. Jessivel was able to calm him down and assure him she would take care of it. Later, after she sought help from Paige on how to handle his problem, she visited him in person to tell him how it was going to be resolved.

"Well, I'm getting good feedback from Olivia," Paige said. "She tells me you pick up on things pretty fast."

"I guess so."

"Not very excited about the work?"

"Well…I like dealing with the tenants."

"Even after having to deal with Floyd?"

"He's not so bad."

"I was going to ask him if he'd be willing to provide the food for the open house, but I'm not sure how to approach him."

"I got to know him a little, and I think he'd do it. I'll ask him, if you want."

Paige squinted and pursed her lips. "Okay, 'fess up. How is it that you get along with that old grump? No one else does."

She didn't respond right away, wondering if she should reveal what Floyd had told her about himself, even though he hadn't told her not to say anything.

"Well?"

"I don't know if you know this or not, but Floyd used to be rich…very rich."

"Really?"

"And he was once homeless. In that order."

"What happened?"

"Years ago, his wife and daughter were killed…murdered."

"Really."

"And he spent years and a lot of money trying to find out who did it."

"Did he ever figure it out?"

"No."

"Interesting. Wait a minute! Combs. I remember that case. It was the same year as the JonBenét Ramsey murder, and even some of the details were similar."

"That's the one."

"How dreadful. No wonder he's so grumpy all the time. How did you find all this out? You dealt with him just that once, right?"

"Twice. And then I bought lunch from him yesterday, and we talked some more."

"If you can get along with that man, you can get along with anyone."

After they tidied up the conference room and locked up, Paige walked Jessivel to her car.

"See this car?" Jessivel asked. "For a period of time, after Dad died, I lived in it…with Kayla. That was when I was coming to your soup kitchen. Every morning I woke up in that car, I felt like someone had stabbed me in the stomach with a knife. I was angry, frustrated, and feeling like a complete failure." Jessivel teared up. "Floyd and I have that in common."

They gave each other a hug that lasted long enough for Jessivel to realize how lucky she was to have Paige in her life.

"We better go," Paige said. "They're predicting a big thunderstorm coming through, and that sky looks awfully ominous right now."

Feeling good about the day and about herself, Jessivel headed home, eager to kick off her shoes and watch a little TV before going to bed.

She hadn't driven more than a mile when it started to rain—one of those lashing downpours that causes trees to take on new shapes and drivers to have difficulty staying in their own lane. Jessivel gripped the steering wheel with both hands and slowed to twenty miles per hour while the windshield wipers swiped full pelt to keep up with the torrential rain.

Suddenly, a figure appeared in her car's headlights. She pumped the brakes and stopped just in time to avoid hitting the woman who then stared at Jessivel through the downpour on the windshield. It took a moment for Jessivel to recognize her from the funeral service. It was Paige's sister, Natalie.

She rolled down her window, allowing sheets of rain to slap her in the face. She yelled to her. "Natalie! It's me, Jessivel. Get in the car!"

The woman remained frozen, her hands resting on the hood of the car. Maybe it wasn't Natalie after all. Now, she wasn't sure—the drenching rain obscured her vision.

Long seconds passed without the woman making so much as an eye blink. Jessivel rolled up her window, unbuckled her seatbelt, put on the emergency flashers, and braved the weather until she reached her.

"Natalie, is that you?" she asked her.

The woman nodded.

"Come with me into the car," she shouted as chards of rain pelted her in the face.

"I can't," she said.

"Yes, you can." Jessivel took her by the arm and led her to the passenger door, the rain pounding their backs. Once she had Natalie inside and the door closed, she ran around to the other side of the car and sidled into the driver's seat.

"Are you okay?" she asked her as she swiped the water off her own face. "Where were you headed?"

Natalie responded in a shaky voice, her stare focused on the dashboard and her words nearly drowned out by the rain hammering against the car's roof. "Paige's office. I ran out of gas."

"She's gone for the day now. Where do you want me to take you?"

Natalie didn't respond.

"Do you want me to take you to the motel where you're staying, Natalie?" she asked.

Still no response.

"Where's your car? Is it in a safe place?"

Natalie shrugged.

"Would you like to come home with me?"

Natalie turned to face her. "Could I?"

Jessivel put the car in gear and headed toward her apartment, holding her breath whenever the beams of the headlights disappeared behind a sudden downburst. She pulled up to a stop sign and looked over at Natalie—head hung down with a steady stream of water dripping from her hair into her lap—not sure what she was going to do with her once she got her into her apartment.

The rain had let up some when they arrived at Jessivel's apartment complex. Once inside, the first thing she did was retrieve an outfit from her closet she thought would fit Natalie. "Here, try these on. And then

I'll run down to the laundry room and throw our wet clothes in the dryer."

When Natalie emerged from the bedroom in the dry clothes, Jessivel asked her if she was okay.

"I'm okay. But my Mom's house isn't," she responded, her eyes downcast and her arms crossed over her stomach.

"What do you mean?"

"It's been trashed."

"What happened?"

"Someone broke in looking for Mom's jewelry."

"How do you know this?"

"Because I took them there to do it."

CHAPTER 47

Paige had just showered, changed into her pajamas, poured herself a Scotch, and turned on the TV when Jessivel called to explain what she'd just been through with Natalie, including telling her that their mother's house had been trashed.

"Natalie told me she owes money to a really bad character," she told Paige, "and he and some other guy came to her motel room and threatened her until she told them about your mom's jewelry."

"Not again!"

"She told them she didn't know where it was in the house, but they forced her to take them there. They held her captive while they ransacked the house and threatened to hurt her if she didn't come up with the jewelry, money, or something they could pawn to cover the debt."

"Is she okay?"

"Yes."

"Keep her there. I'll get dressed and go over to the house."

On her way to her mother's, enraged at yet another manifestation of her sister's imprudence, Paige called 9-1-1 to report the incident. Since they had not been made aware of it already, Paige figured Natalie must have successfully turned off the alarm system within the thirty-second window of them entering. Now, Paige felt stupid for not having changed the passcode after kicking Natalie out of the house. But how had she gotten in the house? Paige had confiscated her door key before dropping her at the motel.

The cool, damp October air made it feel colder than the actual temperature. Paige turned on the car heater to stop her shivering. She seethed over Natalie's behavior and didn't care how many demons she was facing. If anything valuable had been taken, like her mother's jewelry, Natalie would have to be held responsible.

The police flashers could be seen two blocks from her mother's brownstone. Paige parked as close as she could and rushed to the front door, where she was met by a policewoman.

"You can't come in here," she was told.

"I own this house," Paige explained. "I called in the break-in."

Paige showed the officer her ID and was allowed to enter, but not before she noticed a broken sidelight panel adjacent to the front door, the likely entry point for Natalie and her "friends." She glanced up at where she and the alarm system technician had discussed installing the security camera, work that had been scheduled for the following day.

The interior had indeed been trashed. Furniture was turned over, cushions strewn around, drawers and cupboards emptied. She asked if she could go upstairs to her mother's bedroom.

A policeman greeted her at the top of the stairs.

"I'm Paige West. I own this house. I'd like to see if the burglars touched the safe."

The officer accompanied her into her mother's bedroom closet where Paige lifted the carpet square and unlocked the undisturbed trapdoor to her mother's safe.

"I'm going to take this stuff with me, if that's okay," she told him, referring to the contents of the safe.

"Let me get a photo of everything first," he said. "Did you check in with the officer downstairs when you came in?"

"Yes."

He snapped photos of the safe contents along with one of Paige and asked her if she would walk the premises with him to see if anything was missing. When she determined that nothing was, she contemplated telling the officer that her sister had been present during the burglary but then decided against it. She wanted to hear the details directly from Natalie first.

Once the officers were gone, she texted Jessivel.

> r u still up? if so, pls call me

Jessivel wasted no time in calling her back.

"Where's Natalie?" Paige asked.

"Lying down on my daughter's bed."

"Can she hear you?"

"No, the door is closed."

"Do you know how she got away from these guys?"

"When they didn't find what they wanted, she told them that she had her mother's ATM card in her car and would withdraw as much as she could for them, so they took her back to her motel to get it. Once in her car, she slammed the door on one of the guy's hands and then sped off. She said she was driving to your office for help when she ran out of gas and abandoned the car in some parking lot. Then the rains came, and that's when I almost hit her."

"Can you peek in and see if she's asleep or awake? I'd like to talk to her. No, wait. Never mind. I'm going to come over. Is that okay?"

"Sure."

"I have to wait for the handyman to come and temporarily fix the window where they broke in, and then I'm on my way."

"Okay."

"Jessivel?"

"Yes."

"I'm sorry you've been dragged into this."

"No problem."

Jessivel opened the door for Paige and gestured toward Kayla's bedroom.

"Tell me who you owe money to," Paige said to Natalie. "I'll pay them. Anything to get them off your back and out of Mom's house."

"It's a him, just one guy. I don't know who the other guy was."

"Whatever. I'll pay him off."

"Where's her jewelry?" she asked.

"What difference does it make?"

"I just want to know. And half of it's mine anyway."

"Are you kidding me? Tell you what, I'll send you a bill for the damage to her house first, so we can subtract that expense from the half you think is yours. Oh, yeah, and the cost to change the locks. And the new security system. Now, tell me how to get in touch with this guy."

Natalie reached into her purse and handed Paige a crumpled piece of paper with a phone number written on it. Paige went into the living room to make the call.

"I will send you a certified check for the money my sister owes you. Just give me an address."

"Right. You want my Social Security number, too? Cash only, sista, and in person."

"Fine. Meet me at the McDonald's on Grand and Lincoln tomorrow morning at ten o'clock. You'll have your money," Paige said, surprised at her own courage, or "balls" as Jessivel would have put it.

"That's not how it works. We'll call you with the time and place. I have your number." The man hung up.

Apparently, Paige wasn't dealing with some amateur thug with whom she could call the shots. That scared her.

"I couldn't help but overhear your conversation. You're not going to meet this guy alone, are you?" Jessivel asked.

"He's going to call me with a place and time."

"You can't do that. It won't be safe."

"Let me see what he says first."

Paige went back into the bedroom to get more information from Natalie. "What kind of guy is this? A hardcore criminal? Is he dangerous? What if I give him the money and he doesn't stop there?"

Natalie shrugged.

"C'mon, Nat. I'm trying to help you here. Tell me who I'm dealing with."

"I don't know! I got these prescription drugs from this one supplier for a long time without paying him. Then this guy came after me. I don't even know who he is."

"What made you think you could—"

"You're talking to an addict, stupid. Don't you get that yet?"

"You're not making this easy."

"They kept telling me as soon as they got their money, they would be out of my life for good."

"If we can believe that. So what are your plans now? Find your car and go back to the motel?"

"I'd rather live at Mom's."

Paige drew in a long breath—that wasn't going to happen if she could help it.

"You're addicted to drugs and alcohol, both of which are expensive. You're irresponsible, pregnant, and broke. You are not staying at Mom's. What do you plan to do?"

Natalie looked down at the floor without responding.

"What about what's-his-name? Derek."

Natalie glared at Paige. "What about him?"

"Is he the father? Can he help you out of the mess you're in?"

"Nope."

"Nope, he's not the father, or nope, he can't help you?"

"Both."

"So who's the father?"

"It could be the fucking mailman's, for all I know. Are you happy now?"

"You need to go into rehab, Natalie. And not some thirty-day place, a real rehab where they'll know how to take care of you and your unborn baby. If I find a place that will take you, will you go?"

"Do I have a choice?"

"Sure. You can continue down the self-destructive path you're on and end up homeless or dead, not to mention what will become of your baby."

Natalie wobbled her head from side to side in a weary compromise between nodding "yes" and shaking "no."

"I'll go. I'll go," she said.

Waiting for the call from Natalie's "creditor" didn't take long. The man on the phone explained that the amount owed had increased to six thousand due to interest and told her to leave the envelope of cash in her mother's mailbox at precisely eight o'clock the following evening, and if she notified the police, or if anything went wrong, they knew where she lived.

Paige vacillated between complying with the caller's instructions and calling the police. Desperately wanting this goon out of their lives, and knowing that involving the police would only open up a new can of worms for Natalie and potentially herself, she decided on what she hoped wasn't going to turn out to be a foolish choice.

At eight o'clock, from the second-story window of her mother's home, Paige watched a silver sedan stop in front of the house next door.

A dark figure, with a hoodie concealing most of his face, calmly walked toward her house, and seconds later walked away with his hands in his pockets. She jotted down the license plate number, then tucked it away for future reference, if needed.

CHAPTER 48

"You can stay here, sleep on the sofa, whatever, until you go to rehab," Jessivel told Natalie. She felt sorry for her and wanted to help make her transition as painless as possible. "Tomorrow we can pick up your things from the motel, if you want. And find your car. Put gas in it. I have an empty gas can in my trunk."

"Why are you being so nice to me?" Natalie asked.

"We're sisters, or haven't you figured that out yet?"

"I know, but you have no stake in it, so—"

"I have to have some stake in it to help someone?" Jessivel asked, only to be immediately reminded that these were her feelings about Paige not that long ago.

"What about your daughter?" Natalie asked.

"What about her?"

"What will she think?"

"She knows about you. She'll be okay with it. Besides, I have a feeling it won't be that long before Paige finds a place for you. She's dogged when it comes to things like this."

"Looks like you know her pretty well."

"It took me a while." Jessivel grimaced at the pained expression on Natalie's face. "She's not that bad, you know."

"Try being her little sister."

"I have, remember?"

Natalie took a hard, obvious swallow. "Thanks for helping me," she stammered. "I know you don't have to."

Jessivel nodded, a fulfilling weariness running through her body. "You're welcome."

It was Saturday, Natalie's first full day of staying with Jessivel, when Paige called her. All Jessivel could hear was Natalie's side of the conversation.

"I've been thinking, and I'm pretty sure I can do this on my own," Natalie said after a couple of minutes. "I don't need to go to rehab. I'm not that bad. I've done it before."

"And it's too expensive."

"Well, I don't want to go. I've been to these before. They don't work."

"I'm not going, Paige."

"Why are you doing this to me? Your own flesh and blood."

Natalie squeezed her eyes shut. "You have no idea how painful detox is. I can't go through it again," she moaned.

Her body appeared to go limp as she listened to Paige. "Okay, I'll go," she mumbled before hanging up.

"What's going on?" Jessivel asked.

"She's sending me to a treatment center for pregnant women. A hundred frickin' miles from here."

"This is a good thing, right?"

"I've been to them before. They don't help."

"Maybe this one is different."

"I doubt it. She told me she's not paying the motel bill after the fifteenth and she's in control of Mom's house, so I don't have much choice."

"You have to think of the baby though."

"I know." A negligible smile unfolded on her face. "This baby needs me."

"You are so right."

"And it's something Paige can't do."

"What do you mean?"

Her focus went straight to her swollen tummy. "She can't have children."

Monday morning, on the day Paige was to drive Natalie to rehab, Jessivel discovered Natalie missing. She immediately called Paige and reluctantly admitted her failure to keep an eye on her.

"What do you mean, she's gone?" Paige asked.

"She left a note saying she couldn't go through with it." Jessivel paused before telling her the rest. "And she stole money from my purse."

"Damn her!"

"I know she's been hurting, physically I mean. And then last night she was acting really weird. Wouldn't eat. Wanted to be alone. Seemed to be on something, but I'm not sure. Maybe I should have called you."

"You don't know what time she left?"

"No. She was gone when I got up at six."

"Could you do me a favor and come with me to search for her?"

"Sure. What about work though?"

"The work will still be there when you return. And you'll be on the clock anyway."

"I won't do it if you pay me," Jessivel said. "She's my sister too."

Jessivel rode shotgun with Paige as they scoured the route between the Roadway Inn where Natalie was staying and Paige's office, searching for either Natalie on foot or her car, a bright blue 2003 Acura. Paige talked about Natalie while she drove.

"She's been going through this for a long time," she explained to Jessivel. Paige told her about the car accident that had changed Natalie's life.

"How long ago was it?"

"She's thirty-nine now, and she was seventeen when it happened, so twenty-two years ago, but I don't think she ever got over it. It was terrible in the beginning—she had nightmares, panic attacks, and on top of it, excruciating back pain from the collision. The worst of it for her I think was that she couldn't get the images of the accident out of her head, especially the paramedics carrying the child from where he had landed on the street to the ambulance, draped in a white sheet from head to toe."

"I'm sure that had to be hard."

"She talked about it in the beginning—how helpless she felt trapped in an awkward, painful position waiting for someone to extract her from her own vehicle. But later she clammed up whenever anyone brought it up, so we stopped talking about it. Maybe we should have persisted. I don't know."

"Look! Is that her car?" Jessivel asked.

Paige's gaze traveled to where Jessivel was pointing.

"Could be. Same color." She drove to the suspect car and parked.

Paige peeked inside and gasped.

"Is it her?"

"Yes." Paige tried the door. It opened and several mini liquor bottles spilled out.

"Natalie?"

When Paige got no response from her, she gently shook her. When she still couldn't rouse her, she tugged on her shoulder to see her face. Upon seeing the dried vomit plastered on her cheek, she called 9-1-1.

Waiting for the paramedics proved torturous—the dispatcher had advised them to remain calm, keep Natalie on her side, and not do anything else. Remaining calm wasn't possible.

When the paramedics arrived and examined Natalie, they told Paige they were taking her to Brighton Center Hospital where they had a separate substance-abuse facility. Paige and Jessivel followed them there. While they waited to see Natalie, Paige called the rehab facility where she had enrolled her and explained the situation. They agreed to have her transported to their facility as soon as she was able to make the trip.

Watching Paige come to her sister's aid allowed Jessivel the opportunity to see Paige in a different light. The only thing motivating her to help Natalie had to have been love for and devotion to her sister. No hidden agenda, no self-serving intentions. Just sincere allegiance to a family member in need.

"Paige?" Jessivel asked as they were leaving the hospital.

"Yes."

"Can we start over?"

"What do you mean?"

"You and me. Clean slate. Forget what a jerk I was in the beginning."

"So…does this mean you don't think I'm a tight-ass bitch anymore?"

Jessivel felt the warmth of blood rush up her neck.

"Like I said, can we start over?"

Paige smiled as she placed her hand on top of Jessivel's.

"Jess, you needn't ask."

CHAPTER 49

Paige leaned back in her favorite chair and stared at the two envelopes she had retrieved from her mother's floor safe, trying to muster up the courage to open the first one—the padded one, the one she suspected could hold the mysterious stones Leland told her had been her father's. She made a small slit on one end, then stopped to make a decisive call.

An hour later, she and Jessivel sat at Paige's kitchen table with glasses of wine.

"Ready?" Paige asked her.

"Let's go for it."

Paige finished cutting the top of the envelope. A dozen or so small colorful stones tumbled out onto the table followed by one larger, intensely blue one. They exchanged glances.

Jessivel picked up the large blue stone and rolled it around in the palm of her hand. "This is humongous. Do you think it's real?"

"I'm thinking these wouldn't have been in my parents' safe if they weren't. Let me see that one." Jessivel handed the stone to Paige. "If this is what I think it is, it's worth a small fortune."

"What do you think it is?"

"Alexandrite. Wait here a minute."

When Paige returned, she handed Jessivel a ring. "My parents gave this to me when I graduated from college. They told me it was insured for $10,000. It's not even a tenth the size of this one."

"Are you sure? They don't look the same to me."

"The one in my ring has been cut and polished. This one is raw."

"Wow."

"Now, it could also be glass—the one in the envelope, I mean. I'd have to get it appraised. There's just one catch."

"What's that?"

"The way Leland told me the story—and I don't know how accurate his understanding is—but according to him, our father met this Indian woman while he was I the service, and she smuggled these into the U.S. by stuffing them into a teddy bear by sending the bear to Dad."

"A teddy bear?"

"That's what he said."

Jessivel told Paige about the teddy bear Kayla had found in her grandfather's suitcase.

"What? The same one, you think?" Paige asked.

"Sounds like it. You said it had on striped pants, right?"

"Right."

"I opened it up based on what my mother had told me. Nothing was inside, but it looked to me like the seam I opened had been hand-stitched."

"Is the teddy bear you have big enough to hold all these?"

"Easily."

"Do you think your mother knows anything about the stones?"

"She said she didn't know what was inside of the bear, that it was something Dad didn't want her to know about."

Paige scooped up some of the colorful stones and rolled them around in her hands. "Holy shit."

"Paige, I've only heard you swear one other time!"

"Holy freakin' shit."

Paige had considered opening the other envelope with Jessivel present but then decided against it in case it contained something not relevant to her, something she didn't want to share with her or maybe anyone. She opened it after Jessivel left.

The envelope contained three documents, the top one a birth certificate for Andrea Meyers. "Who the hell is Andrea Meyers?" she asked herself out loud. She perused the rest of the information.

PLACE OF BIRTH: SAN DIEGO COUNTY, CALIFORNIA
CITY: SAN DIEGO, CALIFORNIA
FULL NAME OF CHILD: ANDREA ELLEN MEYERS
DATE OF BIRTH: JANUARY 1, 1976
SEX OF CHILD: FEMALE
FATHER'S FULL NAME: RYAN ALAN WEST
FATHER'S AGE: 23
FATHER'S BIRTHPLACE: CHICAGO, ILLINOIS
FATHER'S OCCUPATION: U. S. ARMY
MOTHER'S FULL MAIDEN NAME: ROSE LYNN MEYERS
MOTHER'S AGE: 31
MOTHER'S BIRTHPLACE: SAN DIEGO, CALIFORNIA
MOTHER'S OCCUPATION: HOSTESS

"What…another sibling!"

Paige reread the document. The girl had been born on the same day as she, in a different part of the country, but on the same day. *How weird is that!*

Paige set the other envelope aside as she took a swallow of wine.

Her mother must have known about this child—the birth certificate had been in with documents that would have been familiar to her. But then why hadn't she written this woman's name on her will as an added beneficiary? Didn't make sense.

Next was a typewritten letter addressed to her.

Dear Paige,

If you are reading this letter, it probably means I'm not on this earth any longer. And even if this letter is the last thing you've read of the things I left behind, you likely have questions. Here goes.

Paige glanced down to the bottom of the page expecting to see her father's signature. But it hadn't been signed by him. It had been signed by her mother.

I knew from an early age that I wanted to have children. I wanted a family, a nice family, something I didn't have as a child myself. So when I was told I couldn't have children six months after I married your father, I was devastated. I became depressed, so depressed that I thought of taking my own life.

Paige stopped reading and contemplated her mother's words. She knew her mother had had bouts of feeling down during her life, but nothing this serious. Had she felt so hopeless that it overshadowed the good things in her life, to the point of her believing suicide was the best solution? This concept was difficult for Paige to grasp for anyone, let alone her own mother. But what she didn't understand to even a greater extent was her mother's assertion that she couldn't have children. Obviously not true. She read on.

I didn't leave the house for months at a time. Your father and I became so distant—I didn't wonder if he would leave me, I wondered when.

One day, he came home from one of his business trips and said he had met another woman, Rose Meyers. I fell apart. After that, he was gone for some months, and I was ready to take a whole bottle of sleeping pills. But then he returned. With a baby. That baby was you. Had your birth mother not died of cancer a short time after you were born, I never would have known you, would have never seen your father again, and I'd have been dead at a much earlier age.

The shocking rush of truth kept Paige from reading on. She closed her eyes, and as she sensed her upper-body muscles grow weak, she gradually absorbed the impact of what she'd just learned.

I bless the day you were born, Paige. I feel like I saved your life. And I know you saved mine.

Paige shifted her position in the chair, dumbfounded by her mother's affirmation. Never had she had any doubt about Elaine West being her biological mother. She even resembled her—same facial features, same slim build, same curly hair. Her mother had raised another woman's child all these years—the child of her husband's mistress. Despite her mother's warm, loving words in this letter, she wondered how her mother truthfully felt about this.

Paige looked away from the page and wished she hadn't started to read the damn letter—maybe this was one of those things in life better not to know.

Your father and I stayed together, raising you, but we didn't have a traditional marriage. He spent more time with other women that he did with me. But we had our moments. After all, I gave birth to Natalie three years later. Doctors aren't always right.

She and Natalie were only half-sisters.

She imagined earlier times when both her parents were alive, remembering back as far as she could as a child. Nothing out of the ordinary came to light, no obvious signs other than her father being away on business so often, and even that wasn't inconceivable given his occupation.

I don't know how many other children your father had over the years. I do know of a son of Indian descent named Tamir who may now live in San Francisco, and I know about a daughter named Emma born a year after you whose mother's name is Francine Osterman. There's Jessivel, of course, and Wanda. Yes, Wanda. Your father had an affair with my sister Bernice after we were separated, and Wanda was born from it. There may be others.

Before he died, your father made me promise I wouldn't tell you the truth, so now I am betraying him. I should have had the courage to tell you all this in person, but I've never been a strong person. You probably know that.

Please don't disparage your father. I don't know why he did what he did. Maybe he wasn't satisfied with me. Maybe he was weak and when opportunities presented themselves, he took advantage of them without any forethought. Maybe he just liked having kids. I can't explain it.

I love you, Paige. I love Natalie. I hope you have a wonderful life and are able to help Natalie with hers. She's a good person and deserves it.

Love,

Mom

P.S. Your original birth certificate and the adoption papers are in the envelope. Andrea Meyers is the name your mother gave you at birth. Ryan agreed for you to go through a legal name change soon after he brought you home. And the bag of stones—very valuable. There used to be more, but your father sold them one by one so he could afford to support all the women and children in his life.

Paige rose from her chair, allowing the documents she held in her lap spill onto the floor. She walked to the open window that overlooked her backyard, calmed by the outside air softly floating in. She stared at a small dark opening that led to the forest preserve beyond her property, wondering what lurked in there, wanting to explore it, wanting to do anything to get her mind off what she'd just learned. The raw, empty feeling in her stomach and tightness in her chest led her to sit back down.

She questioned whether what she had now learned about herself was destined to be just one small part of her life, or was it central to her identity? Did family transcend blood? A sense of betrayal by both parents clouded her judgment. How could her mother have failed to tell her all of this when she was alive? To answer questions, provide support, offer more detail. How could she? "Not a strong person" didn't cut it.

Her scrambled thoughts made her head throb—a rapid, pulsating sensation in synch with her racing heartbeat. Everything she'd known to be true as a child had been built upon lies.

Her father had repeatedly told her when she was growing up that he'd wished on a star for her to be born. This previously warm memory now made her feel detached from reality and utterly cold.

CHAPTER 50

"Well, it's about time," Jessivel's mother said to her on the phone. She had told her mother about opening up to Paige. "I knew you'd figure it out one day."

"You could have enlightened me."

"Like you would have listened. You are one of the most headstrong, close-minded people I know. And the last person you'd ever listen to was me. Now, admit it."

"I was. But no more. I have seen the error of my ways, as they say."

"Good for you, dear. And another thing. I think Kayla may be following in your footsteps. Maybe it's time to show her the way too."

"You're right. You are absolutely right. You've always been right," Jessivel said with a hint of sarcasm, "but I never saw it back then."

"What was that noise?"

"Just a text message." She pulled the phone away from her ear and read the message.

can we talk

Jessivel was speechless for a few seconds, caught off guard by the words on the screen but more so by whom had sent them.

"Are you there?" her mother asked.

"I'm here."

They finished the call, and Jessivel reread the text message.

It was from Jason, Kayla's father.

It had been over twelve years since she'd heard from him, and even though he had abandoned her when she'd needed him the most, if she were to be honest with herself, she was still not over him. He was young then and irresponsible, and people could change a lot in twelve years. Still, if he wanted to talk about getting back together, she'd have to be careful, play it cool.

> Jessivel: ok
>
> Jason: where can we meet
>
> Jessivel: boothwater park?
>
> Jason: ok
>
> Jessivel: in an hour? by the fountain
>
> Jason: ok

She recalled how Jason used to like to see her in dresses, with her hair swept up, but now there would be no time before they would meet to shower and change. Today, like it or not, he'd see her just as she was when he'd texted her—in sweats and the Fendi t-shirt she had bought at a thrift store for $2.00. Maybe this was better anyway—she didn't want him to think she had dressed up just for him.

Jessivel perched herself on the edge of the wall surrounding the fountain in Boothwater Park, rehearsing in her mind how she thought the conversation with Jason might go, a scene she had played over in her mind many times—what he would say, what she would say back. She caught herself smiling.

She spotted a car pulling into the lot. A tall, slim man got out and headed for the fountain. When she recognized Jason, she felt a rush of joy, a feeling of everything being right in the world, something she hadn't felt for a long time.

He walked quickly toward her. The sight of him—his dark eyes and wavy hair—drew her back to her teens. His clothing choices hadn't changed much—worn-out jeans and a white t-shirt. When he got close enough, she saw he bore no smile, no expression at all. Was he just trying to play it cool?

"Hello, Jess," he said. He sat on the wall several feet from her, eliminating her anxiety about whether they would embrace when they first saw each other and what it would feel like after all these years.

She released the air that had built up in her lungs as she took in his appearance. Except for the sparse beard he now sported, he hadn't changed much from the last time she had seen him.

"It's good to see you again," he said.

"Good to see you too." Her mind quickly leapt to an image of being in his arms, feeling the strength of his body against hers.

"I'm here to talk about my daughter."

"What?" *His* daughter, not *our* daughter?

"You heard me."

She felt her breathing accelerate. For support, she grabbed onto the stone wall on which she sat, bracing herself for what he would say next, hoping for the best but prepared for something bad.

"What about her?"

"I want full custody."

"What? You have got to be out of your frickin' mind. You disappeared when you heard I was pregnant, I don't hear from you for twelve years, and now you prance in here wanting custody? What have you been smoking?"

"You're an unfit mother, Jess, and I'm concerned about her welfare." His demeanor remained calm, his facial expression indiscernible.

"Says who?"

"I still have friends in this town. They told me you've been homeless, living out of your car. I heard CPS was involved at one point. You've been fired from jobs, and my daughter was even arrested for shoplifting. Would you like me to continue?"

Jessivel drew in a long breath before speaking. "That's all in the past. We're doing just fine now."

"I heard there was a shooting in your apartment building last month. Is that a safe place to raise a child?"

Jessivel had heard that too, and when she'd checked it out with Hercules, he'd told her it was a kid shooting off a firecracker from his balcony.

"That was a firecracker, just so you know."

"That's not what I heard."

"And it won't be long I'll be moving into a house," she said without any truth behind it.

"I also heard you're buddies with Paige West."

"So?"

"So, she comes from money."

"So?"

"Maybe she could help you out."

"Just what are you getting at?"

"She could put up enough money for me to stay away from my daughter."

Jessivel stared at him, shaking her head in disbelief. "Get out."

Jason looked around. "Public park. I have just as much right to be here as you."

She started to get up to leave but then wondered what he'd do with her back toward him.

"Sounding better and better, isn't it?" he said.

"How dare you use *my* daughter to get money from me."

"Kayla, right?"

She didn't respond.

"Adam Wingate Middle School?"

"You wouldn't."

Jason got up and began walking away from her. "Try me."

"Oh yeah?" She stood up. "I'm married to a detective now, you know," she shouted after him, feeling ill-equipped to say anything more rational or meaningful in the moment. "And he is so not going to like this."

The next day, Jessivel drove to work and stopped in Paige's office before she began her first task of the day, planning to tell her about her encounter with Jason.

"How's Natalie?" Jessivel asked her first.

"Not good. Going through withdrawal is…not fun."

"When will she be transferred?"

"Thursday, if everything goes as planned."

"Have you seen her?"

"They suggested I didn't."

"I was going to ask if I could go see her, but maybe I shouldn't?"

"I don't know how she currently feels about you, but they told me she's referred to me as 'the goddamn bitch who put her there.'"

"Oh, no."

"I have to run. I have a meeting with my banker in a few, and then I'll be out of the office for the rest of the day at appointments. Do you and Kayla have plans for dinner tonight? Would you like to go out for some pizza or something?"

"Sure."

"Then if we could talk privately afterward, I have something I want to share with you."

The discussion with her about Jason could wait until then—looks like it would have to.

That evening, Jessivel, Kayla, and Paige had dinner at one of the local pizza parlors, Jessivel feeling anxious the whole time anticipating the upcoming topics of discussion—whatever it was that Paige wanted to talk to her about and Jason's threat. Afterward, Jessivel dropped Kayla off at her friend's house, and she and Paige went to her apartment.

"First of all, how do you feel the job is going?" Paige asked. "I know Olivia gave you that Excel spreadsheet project without much training."

"Okay, I think. I only forgot to save changes to the document once before closing it."

Paige paused before saying anything more, keeping Jessivel on edge. "Well, we think you're doing fine. My concern is that the longer you're here, the more we're investing in training, and I'm not sure you're in this for the long haul. I hope you are, but…"

"Ugh…I guess I'm not sure either, to be honest. I'm gaining great work experience, that's for sure. And I love dealing with the tenants and contractors. But the rest of it, well…"

"Tell me, how do you compare this to the barista job?"

"Better," she said without any hesitation. "I don't have to wait on people."

"So, let's just play it by ear. I'll give you as much tenant-relations work as possible, and we'll see where it goes."

"Okay. Is that what you wanted to talk to me about?" She readied herself mentally to tell Paige about her confrontation with Jason.

"No. Well, yes, but there's something else." Paige paused, gazed out the window for a moment, then cleared her throat. "My mother wrote me a letter before she died and told me something that shocked me…to the core."

Jessivel felt her pulse increase. "More news about Dad?"

"Well, yes and no." Paige hesitated before continuing. "She wasn't my biological mother."

"What?"

"Apparently, Dad had an affair with this woman who died shortly after I was born. I think he may have lived with her while my mom and he were separated. My mother, the mother who raised me, was told she couldn't have children. But she had wanted a child very badly, and so when Dad brought me home, she legally adopted me."

Paige dabbed her cheeks with a tissue as she told the story. When she finished, Jessivel got up and hugged her. "I feel so bad for you—to find out at this late stage."

"Funny thing, you're the first person I've told…and the first time I've cried about it."

"Let me guess. Up until now, you've been too angry to cry, or hurt, or maybe too confused."

"Exactly," Paige said as she wiped her eyes and blew her nose.

"Been there. Know exactly how you feel. Hey, what about Natalie? How did she come along?"

"Turned out the doctors were wrong. Mom got pregnant with Natalie three years later."

"Wow. So let me think about this. You, Natalie, and I have the same father but each of us has a different mother."

"That seems to be the case."

"Are you going to tell Natalie?" Jessivel asked.

"Not while she's in rehab…someday maybe."

"Well, you can count on me not saying anything…to anyone."

"Does Kayla know who her dad is?"

"Yes, but not the whole story. She's too young."

"Don't wait too long, Jess…that's my advice. I don't know about you, but at my age, hearing about all the things Dad did has been devastating. Maybe if I'd had some inkling of it earlier, it wouldn't be so hard to accept now."

"I don't know. That could go either way I think. Did your mom tell you why she never told you?"

"She said because she wasn't a strong person. She admitted in the letter to our father's infidelity. She mentioned you and Tamir. She also mentioned someone named Emma."

"So we have another sister?"

"Mm-hm. She gave me Emma's mother's name as well—I'll have to see what I can find out about them."

Paige paused before continuing. "And there's more."

"No shit."

"My cousin Wanda. She's also our half-sister."

"What? So she's not your cousin?"

"She's both. She's my mother's sister's daughter."

"Huh?"

"Apparently, Dad also had an affair with my aunt when he was separated from Mom." She choked mid-sentence.

Jessivel balled up her hand into a fist and punched her thigh. "I'm beginning to really hate that man."

"I still don't know whether I hate him or feel sorry for him."

"Really, Paige?"

"Don't get me wrong. I'm not condoning what he did. I'm just saying there had to be something wrong with him, something deep-rooted, to make him so deceitful." After she said it, she reflected on what her mother had said in her letter, which led Paige to feel her mother had been almost accepting of it.

"He was nothing but a lying, disgusting cheater, but I don't think I need to tell you how I feel."

"I know. And you have every right to feel that way. I have more."

"You're kidding."

"The stones. Turns out Mom knew about them. Said Dad would sell them periodically to, in her words, 'support all the women and kids he had.'"

"Wow. She knew all along."

"What about you—do you think your mom knows more than she's told you?" Paige asked.

"Probably. But she was one of the 'other women,' so it's different for her."

"I suppose."

"Too bad your mom's not alive to talk all this out."

"My feelings exactly. She died leaving me with more questions than answers."

Jessivel couldn't bring up Jason to Paige right now. The timing was all wrong.

That evening, exhausted from the day's events, Jessivel dozed off more than once in the chair in front of the TV, but once in bed, she had a difficult time calming her racing mind as she attempted to fall asleep. As soon as her head hit the pillow, snippets of her conversations with Jason and Paige came flying through the door to her brain. She had so wanted to share with Paige her encounter with Jason, ask her what she should do. But not after hearing what Paige had to say about her mother. The Jason conversation would have to wait.

CHAPTER 51

"Slow down, Natalie, I can't understand a word you're saying," Paige said.

"I lost her. I lost the baby!"

Natalie hadn't told Paige she was having a girl. "Where are you?"

"At this miserable place you sent me to."

"At the hospital?"

"No, rehab. I had a miscarriage in the transfer car."

Understanding her through the sobs proved difficult.

"I'll be there as soon as I can."

Natalie hung up.

Paige hoped that Natalie's abrupt end to the conversation meant she got what she wanted—Paige coming to her rescue—rather than something else, like *Go to hell. I never want to see you again.* She alerted her office of her plans and headed for Dixon, Illinois.

She had known Natalie's pregnancy would be at risk given her drug and alcohol abuse, and after discussing it with Natalie's doctor, she learned that getting her on a medically supervised Methadone regimen would be the best course of action. Miscarriages were more common for women on Methadone than women who were not taking the drug, but less than for women on opioids. Reminded of her own agony in losing Briana, Paige had no trouble empathizing with Natalie in her current state.

Mezzo Recovery House looked exactly like the brochure—a long, narrow driveway leading up to a large, white Victorian-style structure with a wraparound porch. She parked her car and rang the front doorbell. They were expecting her.

Paige was led into a massive living room, shown to a two-chair seating area near a fireplace, and asked to wait for Natalie. She scanned the room—a scene right out of a Norman Rockwell painting with a piano in the corner, built-in bookshelves on either side of the fireplace, a braided rug in the center, a comfy-looking sofa, and wingback chairs scattered about. She perused the book titles: *Pride and Prejudice, The Color Purple, Little Women, Great Expectations*. Many more classics, but none of which Natalie would likely ever read.

A woman in scrubs rolled Natalie into the room in a wheelchair. Despite her mournful expression, she looked relatively good—her skin wasn't flushed like it was when she was on something, and the drowsiness she so often displayed was absent.

"You look good, Nat. How do you feel?"

Natalie crossed her arms across her chest. "How do you think I feel? I feel like shit."

"Well, I think—"

"I just lost my baby, dumb-ass. Oh, right. You *do* know how that feels."

Paige let out a whimper and broke eye contact with her sister while she fought to calm herself down, the impact of Natalie's words distressful.

"Do you want to talk about it?" Paige asked.

"No."

"Is there anything I can do for you? Anything you need?"

"You can tell me that you're going to get me out of this place."

"Why? They're going to help you here."

"Maybe I don't want help now."

"But you *need* help, Nat. You can't deal with your addictions alone. No one can."

"I was doing fine until you interfered."

Her sudden calmness frightened Paige.

"I don't know what else to say."

"I never should have come up here," Natalie continued. "I was fine with my old friends, my life. It was great!"

"It wasn't great, and you know it."

"Don't tell me what I do and don't know. You can't get inside my head. And if you could, trust me, you'd be the first! And you have no right to judge me."

"I wasn't—"

"I know what you're trying to do. I've been through this before. Now that I'm sober, let's find a nice place for me to live, somewhere everyone is going through the same thing, just like me. A place to go before I enter the real world. No bars on the windows, but there will be rules. Lots of fucking rules. And weekly urine tests. Let's not forget those. Well, Paige, my dear big sister, I'm tired of peeing in a cup in front of someone. Give me my old life back."

"Do you know what drugs and alcohol do to your brain, Nat?"

"Oh, please do tell me about it."

"They affect how you think, what motivates you, your ability to make sound decisions."

"You're pathetic."

"Your values have been compromised, but you don't know that because that part of your brain has been damaged, hijacked in a sense."

"You don't know anything about it, so stop with the bullshit. I want out, and I want out now. I can walk right out of here anytime I want, you know. And then I'll go back to Mom's, and you can't stop me."

As soon as she felt marginally composed, Paige responded with her previously rehearsed speech. "You can't go back to Mom's. As executor of her estate, I have responsibility to protect the property, and it's not safe with you in it."

"I know my rights, you idiot, and I know she left half of everything to me, including the house."

"That's not quite correct—you get forty percent, I get forty percent, and Tamir, Emma, Jessivel, and Wanda each get five percent. And as executor, I have one year to distribute the assets to everyone."

"Wanda? Why her? And who the hell is Emma?"

"Our half-siblings."

"Wanda's our cousin, stupid."

"Correction. She's our half-sister."

"You don't know what you're talking about."

"Okay."

"And Emma?"

"Another half-sister."

"This is just bullshit. I'll take it to court."

"Good luck with that. Look, Natalie, I'd do anything for you—anything that would help you deal with your addictions and become an independently functioning human being. Anything. But—"

"You're all talk. You always were."

"But don't ask me to do something that will enable you to continue down this destructive path you're on. I won't do it. You're in an excellent facility here, and you're well on your way to recovery. Don't blow it now."

"You don't know anything. You don't know me. Send Jessivel here the next time. She gets me. If I'm still here, that is."

Paige remained seated well after Natalie had been wheeled away. How do you help someone who doesn't want to be helped? Is it possible to make someone want to help themself?

She considered the lost baby—Natalie had seemed somewhat receptive to help when the baby was alive inside her. It saddened her to realize that now that it was just her, she didn't seem as receptive.

<h1 style="text-align:center">CHAPTER 52</h1>

“So, Paige's family is more screwed up than mine,” Jessivel mumbled as she got undressed for bed, still shocked by Paige's story about her birth mother.

Her mind drifted to something Kayla had asked her the day before.

“When can we get normal, Mom?”

“Pray tell, what do you mean by normal?”

“You know. Like everyone else.”

“No one is exactly ‘like everyone else.’”

“Well, we're not like *anyone* else. But there are lots of kids in my class who are alike.”

“How so?”

“They have two parents, live in a nice house with their brothers and sisters, go on vacation. And have a dog...you know.”

“And that's your idea of normal?”

“Yep.”

“I suppose they've all been to Disney World too.”

Kayla shrugged.

“Is that what you'd want for our family? All those things?”

“Not the Disney World part. I'd rather go to the Grand Canyon...in one of those big motor homes. Erik and his family do that. Pretty awesome.”

“Well, good for Erik and his family. Save up your money.”

“Maybe we could borrow their motor home.”

"Yeah, right."

"I'll ask him."

"Don't bother. We couldn't even afford the gas."

That conversation got Jessivel to thinking about their future—something she had not given much attention to before. It would be nice to have a husband and go on vacations as a family. Have someone to talk to about their day. Someone to build a future with, create memories.

She answered her ringing phone. It was Paige.

"Olivia told me you went to go see Natalie this afternoon," Jessivel said to her. "How is she doing?"

"Actually, that's why I called. She lost the baby."

"Oh, my God, no. I know how much she looked forward to…"

"I feel terrible for her," Paige said.

"Me too."

"And that's the reason I called. Well, sort of. I went there, but she didn't want to see me. She would have rather seen you."

"Me?"

"She trusts you. Me, not so much."

"Well…I'm happy to go see her, if you think that will be helpful. I forget the town she's in."

"Dixon."

"Where's that?"

"Almost a hundred miles due west of here."

"A hundred miles? Is that still on this side of the Mississippi?" she asked with a laugh.

"Yes, not by much though. She wants out, Jess, but I think her being there at least thirty days, and most likely a lot longer, will do her a world of good. She's already past the withdrawal stage, so she has a good start. You could be what she needs."

"Why? You think I could convince her to stay?"

"She won't listen to me."

"A hundred miles is a long drive. I don't know if my car is that dependable."

"What if I drove you? You and Kayla. While you meet with Natalie, Kayla and I could do something else, get to know each other a little better. I *am* her aunt, after all."

"When would you want to do this?" Jessivel asked.

"Let me check with her primary counselor—I have a few other questions for her anyway—and I'll see what she thinks. I'll let you know."

Feeling in a familial frame of mind, Jessivel had the sudden urge to call her mom, just to chat.

Jessivel sat in the front passenger seat, Kayla in the back, while Paige drove the two hours to Dixon. To keep her occupied on the drive, Paige lent Kayla her Kindle with a few books on it she thought Kayla might like.

The two women talked about Natalie during the majority of the trip.

"I've taken hydrocodone before," Paige explained, "once for an extended period after I had surgery for a herniated disk, but I never got addicted. For some reason, it's been different for Natalie. Honestly, I don't understand how two people raised under the same roof can be so different."

From what Jessivel understood about addictions, they had little to do with how one was raised, but she wasn't about to say this to Paige. "When did you first realize she had a problem?" she asked.

"Not for a long time—she was good at masking the telltale signs. I think the first thing we noticed was a change in her appearance. She'd lost weight, stopped taking care of herself, poor hygiene. That had to have been two or even three years after the accident."

"Was she working?"

"After high school, she attended community college part-time and worked part-time in a restaurant. Right about the same time Mom noticed her weight loss, she dropped out of school and lost her job. She said she quit, but I suspect she was fired."

"What was she studying?"

"She wanted to be a nurse."

"What a shame. Has she ever talked about going back to school?"

"Plenty of times. That's one of her ploys to get Mom to give her money—she says she needs it to go back to school."

"But she never did?"

"Of course not. She used the money for drugs and alcohol. Mom and I had differing opinions on how to best help her. Mom gave her whatever she asked for."

"One thing I learned from one of my friends back in high school who had an alcoholic mother is that alcohol was bigger than her and even bigger than her love for her family."

"I believe that. I'm hoping Natalie is now acknowledging her addictions and she is on a road to recovery. I really want her to stay where she is. They can help her there."

"What does she say about her addictions?" Jessivel asked.

"What do you mean?"

"I mean, is she open about it? Should I be open about it when I talk to her?"

"In the past, talking to her about the problem was futile. She was in denial and had a history of lying about everything, to the point that I think she believed the lies herself. But now, I think and her counselor thinks we need to be open about it even if she isn't."

"I'm not sure what to expect, but I'll see what I can do."

"Well, we're here," Paige said. She turned to Jessivel. "Don't worry about Kayla and me. We'll find things to do. Call me when you're through."

Jessivel gave Kayla the standard be-a-good-girl lecture and exited the car.

"Good luck," Paige told her.

Jessivel entered the rehab facility unaware of how she would find Natalie and scared she wouldn't know how to handle the situation regardless of which way it went. If Paige, in all her wisdom, couldn't deal with her, how could she be expected to? But Paige apparently had faith in Jessivel, and for that reason, she would give it her best shot.

She checked in at the reception desk and was shown to a small conference room. Minutes later, Natalie arrived, looking like she'd just been through a hell of a battle.

"How are you, Natalie?" she asked.

Natalie shrugged as she swiped a long strand of hair from her face.

"I'm so sorry you lost your baby. I can't imagine how you must feel."

Natalie glanced up at her, her eyes bloodshot and vacant, not seeming to register what was being said to her.

"I wish I could help you."

Natalie tipped her head back, looked heavenward, and then let it flop forward. "I never set out to be this way, Jess."

"I know you didn't."

"I've never been comfortable with who I am," she said, her words deliberate and monotone. "Do you know how that makes you feel?"

Natalie's pupils were enlarged. Jessivel suspected she was highly medicated.

Jessivel shook her head.

"I'll never have what Paige has."

"Do you want what she has?"

"I don't know. I just know I don't want what I have, and I'm ashamed of myself."

"Why?"

"Look at me…I'm a mess."

"What *would* make you feel comfortable with who you are?"

"Being high helps."

Jessivel chuckled. "What I meant was—"

Natalie gave her a conciliatory smile. "I know what you meant." She glanced around the room, apparently momentarily distracted. "I've felt like an outsider my whole life. Even in my own family. It's like I'm two people—the good one and the bad one. The bad one always wins."

"You're not a bad person, Natalie. You have a chronic disease, and it needs to be treated. It *can* be treated. You know that, right?"

"That's what they tell me." She slid down in her chair, looked down for a brief moment, and then wiped her eyes with the back of her hand. "Nothing made me feel good as a kid. Then I discovered booze. That made me feel good. You call it a disease, but I'm not so sure. I think a lot of it had to do with Paige."

"How do you mean?" she asked.

"She always had more friends, better grades, ambition, things like that. She was the kid in school who wanted to sit in the front row. I was the kid who wanted to hide in the back. It felt like I was in her shadow most of the time, the problem child. More people referred to me as Paige's little sister than by my name. It was the 'little' part that bothered me most. There's nothing good about little."

"Did your parents compare you to Paige when you were growing up?"

Natalie considered the question for a moment. "No. They never did."

"So…"

"I did. All the time." She paused. "Still do."

Natalie shared with her several childhood stories to corroborate her assertion about Paige, stories with circumstances that Jessivel understood could have had a negative impact on her.

"But now, Natalie, I think you're in a good place here."

"I don't feel good being here."

"But it's safe here, and somewhere you can get the help you need."

"Some of the people here are weird."

"They're not only going to treat your addictions here, they're going to help you with any other issues you have, underlying problems that may have contributed to your medical issues."

"And the bed isn't very comfortable."

"You won't have to deal with Paige."

Natalie's face lit up.

"Can I tell you something, Jess?"

"Sure."

"I think of you as more of a sister than I do Paige. Thank you for coming to see me."

"You're welcome."

"Thank you for listening."

"Any time."

"And not judging."

"Okay."

"I'm tired. I think I want to lie down."

When a nurse came for Natalie, Jessivel texted Paige to let her know she had finished her visit. She waited outside to be picked up.

"How did it go?" Paige asked as soon as she entered the car.

"Okay."

"Just okay?"

Jessivel didn't know how much of their conversation she should share, especially in front of Kayla.

"Kayla, sweetie, can you use the headphones while we talk?"

"How come I never get to hear the good stuff?"

"You're not old enough."

"I'll never be old enough," she mumbled as she put on the headphones.

"How did she seem to you?" Paige asked.

"Tired. Alone. Sad. And highly medicated, it looked like to me."

"Her counselor told me she was on two medications to help with cramps and bleeding following the miscarriage, and they were considering putting her on an antidepressant as well. What did you talk about…if you don't mind my asking."

Jessivel hesitated before responding. "You, mostly."

"Me? Why me?"

Jessivel shared some of what Natalie had said she experienced growing up behind Paige, sugarcoating it somewhat.

"But I never treated her badly. No one did."

"You didn't have to—she was capable of beating herself up without any help from others."

"Does she still feel that way?"

"I don't think that's something that ever goes away, and maybe that's why she resents you."

"She has no reason to resent me. I've done nothing but…" Paige's voice trailed off, causing Jessivel to wonder what she was thinking or maybe recalling.

"I don't know much—I'm an only child with an only child—but I'm thinking that when you're in her position, when you feel like you're worthless and your self-esteem is in the toilet, dealing with those who have it all isn't easy. And when it's your sister, well, that just adds more insult to it."

"I never thought about it that way. I tried to put myself in her shoes, but apparently I didn't do a very good job."

"How could you?" Jessivel asked, having an aha moment of her own. "You've never been that low."

Jessivel considered telling Paige about Jason but decided against it, not with Kayla in the car. And Paige had enough on her mind without this anyway.

"And what did you two girls do?" Jessivel asked.

"There's a mall not too far from here. We window shopped, got to know each other. Stopped for a sundae. You've got a good kid, Jess," she whispered.

"Yes, I know."

CHAPTER 53

"What are you doing here?" Paige asked Leland when she arrived home.

"I tried your cell, but it went to voicemail. And I sent you a text."

She glanced down at her phone and saw she had multiple voice and text messages. "What's going on?" she asked.

"Can we talk inside?"

Paige opened the door and led him in. They settled in at the kitchen table.

"Now, what's all this about?" she asked him.

"Those two Indian guys."

"What about them?"

"They're fakes. They think those stones of your father's are worth a lot of money, including the one in his ring."

"How do you know this?"

"Do you have any beer?"

"No. Wine okay?"

"Will you join me?"

With some reluctance, Paige opened a bottle of wine and poured them each a glass, his a little fuller than hers. They sat across from each other, a bottle of red zinfandel between them.

"I couldn't get those two characters off my mind after hearing about them, so I called Natalie... How is she, by the way?"

"She lost the baby."

"Oh, no. I'm so sorry. How is she feeling?"

"She's in a place where she can get the help she needs. Why did you call *her*?" she asked. Why not me, she thought.

"And she's receptive to it?" he asked.

"Receptive to what? Why did you call her?"

"The treatment she's receiving."

"Is there something going on between you and Natalie?"

"Of course not. Why?"

"Well, she did call you 'honey' at Mom's funeral."

"She was drunk, remember? So she's okay being in this place?"

"So why did you bring Natalie to the funeral anyway?"

"Because she asked me to, and I thought if I ran it by you first, you'd say no."

"I wouldn't have said no."

"Well, I didn't know that. So, how's she doing?"

"For the time being, she's there and doing okay."

"That's good. She needs help. Anyway, back to why I'm here, I called Natalie and told her I'd do a little nosing around to see if I could find out who these two guys really were."

"Again, without checking with me first."

He shot her a sheepish grin. "Well, you have to admit, you haven't been very receptive of me, and…"

"And what?"

His face turned solemn. "I care about you, Paige. I figured maybe if I…wait a minute. Can I finish my story first?"

"Go ahead."

"Anyway, I didn't get very far trying to track either one of them down—of course, I didn't even know if they'd given you their real names—but I got lucky with their photos when I did a reverse image search for them on the Internet."

"How did you get a photo of them?"

"From Natalie's phone."

She had forgotten that Natalie had snapped a couple of photos of them when they were in their home.

"Where did you learn how to do that?"

"Ever watch the TV series *Catfish*?"

"No."

"That's where I got it from. Good show."

"So what did you find?"

"That they weren't who they said they were like I thought. The one who called himself Tamir is really Ivaan Bhoir, a man with a police record that includes identity theft. And the other one is really Dhruv Kahl. I couldn't find any dirt on him."

"Are you sure about this?"

"Look up their real names on Facebook and Instagram. You'll see their pictures. So I found Ivaan's phone number and called him."

"When did you get to be so gutsy? You wouldn't have done that when we were married."

"I didn't know how much I— Hey, you keep trying to get me off track."

"Sorry, go on."

"Anyway, I told him that I knew he was impersonating Tamir and if he wanted the police to stay out of it, he would tell me what he was after."

"You're incredible."

"Thank you. Wait…was that a compliment?"

"I'm not sure."

"That's when he talked about your father's ring, and that's when I took a risk."

"Dear God, do I want to hear this?"

"You tell me."

"Go on."

"I told him I wanted to be in on what he was up to, that I could probably help him. That you were my 'ex,' a real bitch, and—"

"Leland!"

"Hear me out, Paige. I actually did you a favor, and some day you're going to thank me for this…I think…I hope. Anyway, I told him that I wanted to get back at you at any cost. So the idiot falls for it and tells me what he knows about the stones."

"Which was?"

"That the real Tamir told him the stones had legitimately belonged to his mother, that she had inherited them from her rich uncle who had made a small fortune in the pharmaceuticals industry."

"And that pretty much matches what you told me my father had told you, right?"

"Yes. But I guess once the word had gotten out about her inheritance, friends and family hounded her to sell them so they could share in the wealth. After her house had been broken into several times, she sent them to your father for safekeeping."

"And that also matches what Dad had told you. But why did she smuggle them into the country in the teddy bear? Why so clandestine?"

"I don't know. To avoid declaring the value of them with customs and such. So there would be no paper trail for them maybe? So her relatives couldn't find them? I'm not sure."

"So they're not actually his…legally."

"Wait, there's more. After she did this, she was still getting harassed by others, and she told Ryan to just keep them, told him to do whatever he wanted with them."

"This all sounds so far-fetched. But let's backtrack for a minute. Neither one of them is my father's son, for sure?"

"Right. The one guy who claimed to be Tamir Noor was impersonating Ryan's son, the real Tamir, someone he'd met in a bar in San Francisco, I found out from him later in the conversation. Tamir had, after several drinks, told him all about the stones, who had them, and how he'd chickened out coming here to claim them."

"So Tamir Noor is the name of my father's son, for real? But not the guy I met."

"Right."

"What about the other guy?"

"He just came along for moral support, pretended to be another son."

"So how did you leave it with him on the phone?"

"After he spilled his guts, I told him if I ever caught wind of him pursuing this any further, he'd have to deal with the FBI."

"And he bought this?"

"Well, he may have thought I was an undercover cop."

Paige laughed. "Really. And why would he think that?"

"Well, I may have given him that impression. Anyhow, I don't think you'll have to worry about him anymore. He seemed really scared, begged me not to pursue it any further. Said he was on probation. I told him the stones were long gone, including the ring, and he said that was fine with him."

"You've changed."

He gently shook his head. "I'm still the same man," he said.

"More wine?" she asked, her head feeling pleasantly light.

"Don't mind if I do."

When they had finished discussing the two imposters and their attempt to get their hands on the stones, and while the wine flowed freely, Leland asked questions about her post-divorce life.

"I continued selling real estate, obviously. Ended up doubling my clientele and income in four years."

"I'm impressed."

"And then when the Garretts decided to retire, I bought them out. Went from being an agent to owning my own brokerage firm. I have seventy agents right now, most of whom averaged over $10 million in sales last year."

"That's a hell of a lot of commissions."

"My business model calls for high-performing, established agents."

"Of course, it does." He tilted his head and smiled. "So it looks like you have it all now."

"No. I may be the number-one woman-owned brokerage firm in Chicago, but I'd like to make it into the top ten of all Chicago firms someday. That would be having it all."

"Would it?"

"I just said it would."

"There wouldn't be a next goal? You'd be satisfied being, say, number eight in the city?"

Paige stared into Leland's eyes until it became uncomfortable.

"Just remember, it can get lonely at the top," he said.

"Okay, if you say so."

"Can I change the subject?"

"Please do."

He paused as a look of tenderness spread across his face, one that she'd never witnessed before, or at least not that she could remember. "I never stopped loving you," he said.

"Leland, we—"

"Look into my eyes. Tell me you don't see the love there."

She met his gaze, sardonically at first, but then with growing curiosity. The affection was there. She looked away, not wanting to see any more of his emotion and be pulled in by it, suddenly realizing that the door on this chapter of her life had never been completely closed. When her eyes met his again, she knew they may have been separated by the years, but they were still bound together by…something.

The next morning, Paige glanced at the chair on which her turtleneck sweater and jeans lay entangled with Leland's clothes. She closed her eyes and mentally recreated the moment when their naked bodies became one. During their lovemaking, there had been no past or future, only the moment. No self-consciousness…just pure ecstasy that had unraveled all of Paige's bedroom insecurities. Nothing felt forced or rehearsed as it had in their marriage. Nothing felt awkward. He was there with her because that was foremost on his mind. And vice versa. She stretched her arm over to his empty side of the bed to see if she could still feel his warmth, and then traced her finger across her lips as if his kisses still lingered there.

Paige allowed the soft pool of warm memories to continue until she was reminded of something Leland had implied during their conversation—that no matter how well she did in her business, she'd never be satisfied. His assertion bothered her, but not enough for her to stress over it now, not while he was here, not while she was still on high from the previous several hours.

The sweet smell of pancakes drew her into the kitchen.

"You used to always be the first one up," he said without turning around from his task at the sink, the atmosphere of the kitchen changed by his presence.

Paige fixed her gaze on his backside—one of her good Ralph Lauren towels lazily draped around his hips. His legs were more muscular than she remembered. The urge to creep up behind him and press her body up against his pulsed through her.

"What time is it?" she asked.

"Seven-thirty, sleepyhead." He turned around with two bowls of cut-up fruit and placed them next to the plates of pancakes on the kitchen table. "Hungry?"

She sat down. "Starved. When did you learn to cook?"

"Well…the day after you left me, I was sort of hungry. Correction. Several days after you left me, I was sort of hungry."

"Would this be the time for me to get out the violin?" she asked, regretting it when she saw the hurt look on his face. "Sorry. I didn't mean to be insensitive. I thought you were joking."

"Just so we're clear here, I don't joke about our broken relationship. Never have."

"Sorry."

"Can we talk about last night?" he asked.

Paige wasn't sure whether she wanted to talk about it and didn't respond.

"Is that a no?"

"No, it's not a no," she said. "It's just that I—"

"Did you mean what you said last night?"

"Of course I did." She was a little fuzzy on some of their nighttime conversation given the amount of wine they drank and the passion that had ensued. "Look, last night was good, really good, but I need time to think things through."

"I love you, Paige."

She wanted to verbalize the internal conflict she felt, but not understanding it herself, she didn't know quite what to say.

"Here's the thing, and I'm being brutally honest with you. If you and I were in our twenties or something and had just met, there wouldn't be even a shred of hesitation on my part. But we're not in our twenties, and we have history with each other. I'm not saying there isn't the possibility we can start over and make this work. I'm saying maybe we need to slow it down."

The color drained from his face. "There's someone else, isn't there?"

"No. There's no one else. I've been in a few relationships since we divorced, but never anything serious. I've been on my own ever since then. And maybe that's part of the problem—you get used to it."

"*I* never did."

"Can you give me some time to think this through? The last thing I want to happen is that we get back together and, for whatever reason, I pull out and hurt you again."

"There are never any guarantees."

"I know that." She paused for a moment, breathing in the delicious scent of the maple syrup. "Lee?"

"Hmm."

"Last night was good."

Leland left. Paige took a long hot shower, wrapped herself in a comfy fleece robe, and curled up in a chair with a cup of tea, comforted by the warm steam wafting up from it. She took a sip and let the hot liquid trickle down her throat.

She wished she had been able to relay to Leland in a more insightful way her reservations about starting up a relationship with him again but couldn't think of any better way she could have handled it. She had tried to be honest, with him and herself.

Being honest with herself—about her feelings and knowing what she valued and wanted in life—was something she hadn't learned to do until years after she'd left him. Or so she thought. At the time, she knew she didn't want to be in the marriage any longer but didn't understand why. Leland hadn't done anything wrong, hadn't treated her badly, nothing like that. All she knew was that she believed being a whole person instead of half a couple would be better. Being a third of a family unit when Briana was alive had been gratifying. But being half of a couple hadn't been.

And then, of course, was the difficult question he'd asked last night—would she ever be satisfied when it came to her work? She admitted to herself that as she achieved more success in her business, her self-expectations rose in tandem.

"It's lonely at the top," he'd said.

Now, as she reflected upon her life while married to Leland, compared to her current life, Paige understood for the first time why she had divorced him. She couldn't live with someone she didn't understand, and she couldn't understand him without understanding herself first. But that was then. Today was different. She dialed his number.

"Could you come over tonight?" she asked him.

"What's wrong?" he asked.

“Nothing. I just…”

“You just what?”

Something in her stomach fluttered. “I just want to get to know you better.”

CHAPTER 54

Jessivel cooked dinner for herself and Kayla before changing into her pjs and lounging in a chair in front of the TV. Her visit with Natalie earlier had left her with mixed emotions. On the surface, she had to feel sorry for her. She'd just lost a baby and was going through detoxing herself from alcohol and drugs. Each one in itself would be difficult enough to go through. The combination had to be overwhelming.

Her mixed feelings stemmed from not knowing how involved she should get with Natalie's problems. Shouldn't that be Paige's responsibility? She didn't know if she'd gotten through to Natalie that staying at the rehab facility was the best thing for her to do, and that had been her goal.

Natalie and Paige were her half-sisters. Jessivel still had a difficult time getting her head around this. They shared genes but were completely dissimilar when it came to physical appearance, personality, and lifestyle—not unlike she and the two of them. She definitely felt a bond with them, but not as strong or as meaningful she thought it would be had she grown up with them.

She went to bed agonizing over thoughts of Natalie, and later reminded herself that she had to talk to Paige about Jason before too much more time elapsed. Finding just the right time with her wasn't that easy.

◇

"When did you become an adult, Mom?" Kayla asked the next morning.

"Why on earth would you ask a question like that?"

"I have a paper due on Monday."

"On what?"

"When people transition from an adolescent to an adult."

"Why don't you Google it?"

"I did, and I know what the experts say, but I want to know when it happened to you?"

"When is it supposed to happen…according to the experts?"

"Biologically or psychologically?"

"What grade are you in?"

"Mom…you know I'm in seventh."

"Just checking. Give me both."

"Biologically, they say it happens to girls when they're twelve or thirteen, when they get their first period—making me one, you know."

Kayla had wanted to celebrate the event. For Jessivel, it felt like a slap of reality—her little girl was becoming a woman.

"I see. And psychologically?"

"Much later. It depends."

"On what?"

"On the person. One article I read said it's when you can take care of yourself, but I see flaws in that thinking."

"You do…what grade are you in again?"

"Mom," she said rolling her eyes.

"You seem older right now for some reason."

"So when did it happen for you? And what did it feel like?"

Not an easy question—Jessivel wanted to think about it some before answering.

"Earth to Mom."

"Give me a minute, will you? I want to answer honestly."

"It *has* happened, hasn't it?"

"Very funny. Yes, it has happened," Jessivel answered, knowing full well it hadn't been that long ago. In her mind and heart, she had felt like an adult the moment she stopped blaming others for her problems, her living situation, her life. "Probably when I had you," she lied. "That's when I became an adult. And how did it feel? It felt wonderful."

"Are you sure?"

"Don't you have other homework to do?"

"Fine."

That child is going to grow up to be someone. There was a time Jessivel would have ended that thought with *unlike her mother.* But that was another time.

"But I thought you liked it there," Jessivel said to her mother over lunch the following Saturday. They were in a small café Paige had introduced her to the week before. "Why are you leaving?"

"I have enough saved for a down payment on an apartment, like you wanted. I'm looking at a three-bedroom place in Woodlawn…where we can all be together again."

"What? But you kept harping on me to be on my own, carry my own—"

"That was when I couldn't support you. Now I can."

"But I listened to you. I—"

"You're still in subsidized housing, right?"

"Yes, but—"

"I can get you and Kayla out of there, as soon as next month."

"But I'm less than six months away from being out of there on my own, and—"

"It wasn't that long ago you were begging me to get a place where we could all live together."

"I know, but now things are different. Now I want to do this by myself."

"Is Paige helping you?"

"She gave me a job. You know that. She pays me well. But I earn every dollar I make. There's no handout from her, if that's what you mean."

"Mm-hm. That's very generous of her."

"I just said I earn what she pays me. Why are you making it seem like a handout?"

"You wouldn't have to work if you came to live with me. Not full-time."

"But I want to work. I like what I'm doing, well, most of it, and I'm learning a lot. Paige is even encouraging me to get my GED and then take a few courses at the community college."

Her mother shot her a smile. "I was just testing you."

"What?"

"To see if you really have changed, are ready to be on your own."

"And?"

"And I think you are."

Jessivel sat back in her chair and stared at her mother for a few long seconds. She bit her lip for a moment before responding.

"You could have just asked me."

"Mm-hm. I could have."

"Okay, so that was pretty clever on your part. I hope I'm as smart as you with Kayla when the time comes." She patted her mom's hand. "Are you really going to leave the Perlmans?"

"I'm thinking about it."

"You could get a one-bedroom, and then Kayla could still do sleepovers on a pullout sofa or something."

"I'd like that."

"Our company does that, you know, apartment rentals. Maybe Paige will even show *me* how to do that."

"You really have changed, haven't you?"

Jessivel nodded.

"I'm proud of you, Jess."

Jessivel picked up the tab for lunch. Afterward, she considered calling Audrey at The Busy Bean and all the social services people—everyone who had tried to help her before she was ready—and apologize for her past behavior.

The next day at work, Paige sat down in the side chair next to Jessivel's desk.

"What's wrong?" Jessivel asked. "You look… I don't know… Tired or something."

"Not tired. Suddenly, I'm missing my parents more than ever. Appreciate your mom while you can, Jess. She could be gone tomorrow."

"So now would be a bad time to tell you the stunt she pulled on me yesterday to prove to herself that I'm really getting my shit together, right?"

Paige laughed. "Probably, but you can anyway. Let's go get a cup of coffee—which, by the way, I never drank much until I met you. Now I'm addicted."

"Well, I hope that's the only bad habit you got from me."

"I swear more now too."

"My bad." It was so satisfying talking with Paige on this level, like a best friend. Paige made her feel comfortable regardless of the situation without any fear of being judged by her—she truly accepted her for who she was.

They headed toward the break room where Jessivel told Paige how her mother had psyched her out by suggesting she quit her job, move in with her, and all the rest. They both laughed about it.

"I like your mother."

"Oh, good one. Side with her."

Jessivel was about to tell Paige about her encounter with Jason when one of Paige's agents entered the break room. "Paige, Mr. Stiles is here to see you."

"You can send him in here."

A few minutes later, Gary entered the room. "So this is what you do all day—chitchat over coffee?" A teasing smile enveloped his face.

"Very funny. Gary, this is my sister, Jessivel. Jessivel, this is Gary, detective extraordinaire."

Jessivel felt the blood creep up her neck—hearing Paige referring to her as her sister got to her every time. She held out her hand to Gary.

"Nice to meet you, Gary," she said.

"Nice to meet you, too," he said, flashing her a broad smile. He turned to Paige. "I just stopped by to sign those documents." He glanced at his watch. "And it's lunchtime, so how about if I take you two gals out for a sandwich or something?"

"I've got a client I'm expecting in a few, but you two go," Paige said.

CHAPTER 55

"I'm going to run over to Volo Antique Mall this afternoon," Paige said to Jessivel over the phone the following Saturday morning. "I'm looking for an old dresser or sideboard I can convert to a coffee station for the break room. You know, for the espresso machine and stuff. Would you like to come? Help me pick it out?" She added, "And I'd like to buy you dinner for your birthday."

"Could we drive Kayla to her friend's house on our way?"

"Sure. I'll pick you up at three."

Paige had made the last-minute decision to invite Jessivel to the antique mall when she realized their relationship felt more like an old friendship renewed than the beginning of a new one. She couldn't explain the completeness she enjoyed with Jessivel in her life as someone she could share anything with and trust her with what she would do with it. She pondered this as she drove to pick them up, eager to see them, to catch up on important happenings in their lives, even if it turned out to be nothing more than what Kayla had been studying in school or how Jessivel handled the noisy next-door neighbor.

Kayla ran to Paige's car as soon as she entered the parking lot.

"Aunt Paige! Guess what!" she yelled halfway to the car.

Paige rolled down her window. "What is it, sweetie? Slow down. Watch for cars. Be careful."

Jessivel followed close behind her daughter, shaking her head. "Don't even bother," she said to Paige. "When she gets like this, there's no stopping her."

Paige was delighted to see this level of enthusiasm from Kayla. "So what are you so excited about?" she asked her after she had gotten into the back seat.

"I'm going to go to Oakridge Middle School next year and be on their varsity girls' basketball team!"

"Wow, when did this happen?" Paige asked.

Jessivel entered the car, still shaking her head. "It hasn't, and a lot of other things need to happen before it does."

"No, it's going to happen," said Kayla. "Do you know that their team went undefeated and finished first in the conference? First! Three years in a row!"

Paige glanced at Jessivel to gauge her reaction. "How did this come about?"

"When I finally had enough money to let her join the basketball team, and she learned they've been in last place five years in a row, she got the bright idea she wanted to go to Oakridge next year, home of the Flying Oakers."

"I'm going, Mom. One way or the other."

"Isn't Oakridge way north of you? Don't you have to live in the school district?" Paige asked.

"Yes, and—"

"We have to move anyway," Kayla blurted out. "So it's not a problem."

"This coming from someone who has no knowledge of what that will take," said Jessivel. "Turn left on Willow. Her friend's house is the green one on the right."

When they reached the house, Kayla bounded out of the car, backpack flung over her shoulder, and ran toward the house. Halfway there, she turned toward the car and shouted, "Thank you, Aunt Paige!"

"If she hadn't done that, I was going to yank her back in the car and make her come with us," Jessivel said.

"A fate worse than death, I'm sure." Paige cringed at her own words. Her daughter Briana would have been about Kayla's age had she survived her disease, and she couldn't help but wonder what it would be like to have her in her life today. A twinge of jealousy pricked her heart.

"Something like that."

They talked about Kayla's penchant for basketball and her determination to change schools.

"Do you think you'll be able to make that work?"

"Somehow I'll have to, or there will be no living with that child ever again. It is a much better school. Otherwise, I wouldn't even be thinking about it."

Jessivel's sigh caused Paige to ask her if she was alright.

"Something happened a while ago that has me worried."

"What is it, Jess?"

"It's Jason, Kayla's father. I heard from him."

"After all this time? What did he want?"

Jessivel told her about his wanting custody of Kayla unless she paid him off, and that he had mentioned Paige's name as someone who could afford it.

"What? For one thing, that's extortion. When did this happen?"

"Last month."

"You should have told me sooner. This is serious."

"I would have, but you had so much going on. It never seemed like the right time."

"Did he name an amount?"

"No."

"We need to go to the police."

"Did I tell you his father is a Chicago cop?"

"Great."

"So I told him I was married to a detective."

Paige laughed. "Why did you do that?"

"It was all I could think of at the time. I was so floored by what he was saying. As disappointed as I was with him for leaving me when he found out I was pregnant, I never would have expected him to do this."

"Sometimes you have to accept people for who they are rather than who you want them to be."

"Ain't that the truth."

"Speaking of detectives, I could ask Gary where you should go with this. He'll know."

Jessivel smiled. "Thanks, but I already have. He's checking out a few things first before he tells me what he thinks I should do. And I haven't heard from Jason since, so…"

The antique mall housed more than three hundred vendor booths on multiple floors in three connective buildings. Their motto "We aren't your stuffy grandma's mall; we are your *cool* grandma's mall," made it a place Paige liked to browse at least once a year. They talked while meandering booths crammed with a variety of glassware, books, lamps, furniture, and numerous other artifacts. But conversations that started out on one subject matter always seemed to turn into something to do with their father.

"Do you think it will always be like this?" Jessivel asked.

"You mean all roads leading back to dear old dad?"

"Pretty much."

"Well, it's the most obvious thing we have in common right now."

"Right."

"What about Gary?" Paige asked.

Jessivel shot her a quizzical look. "What about him?"

"Just wondering about the two of you."

"We're just talking business…about Jason."

"Mm-hm."

An hour later, after finding the perfect sideboard for the espresso machine, the two women left the antique mall and headed toward a nearby restaurant where Paige had made reservations.

"I hope you like it here. Their menu is limited, but everything is really good."

They struggled with small talk—searching for topics that had nothing to do with their dad—while they waited for their food.

"It's hard not to talk about him when we're together," Jessivel said.

"I don't think we should avoid him completely. After all, we can't change what happened."

"Like you said, it's what we have in common."

"Ugh…what I said was that's the most obvious thing we have in common. We have more in common than that."

"Like what?" Jessivel asked.

"Something more people should have."

"What's that?"

"Respect for each other's differences."

Jessivel turned to look past Paige for a few seconds, her expression genuinely reverent, in no way forced. "Paige?" she said.

"Yes?"

"I'm so glad you didn't give up on me."

"Me too."

EPILOGUE

"**C**an you give me a hand, Lee?" Paige asked. "I can't get these leaves in by myself." Guests would be arriving for Thanksgiving dinner in less than an hour, and Paige was running behind schedule.

"Be right there, hon," he yelled from the other room. "Changing Mia's diaper."

Paige and Leland had adopted now-eighteen-month-old Mia shortly after they had remarried.

"Then put her in her play yard, okay? I need your help in here."

"Was Natalie able to break free for today?" Leland asked her.

"'Break free' sounds like she's being held somewhere against her will. Here, help me with these table leaves."

"Sorry. Poor choice of words. So what about her? Is she coming?" he asked.

"Yes, she will be here. Her AA sponsor is driving her here."

"How many total?" he asked.

"Let's see. You and me. Natalie. Jessivel and Gary. Kayla. Crystal and Floyd. That makes eight of us, plus Mia."

"What about Wanda and her mother?"

"Aunt Bernice came down with the flu or something two days ago and is pretty sick, so they're not coming. Wanda's concerned about her and is staying with her temporarily."

"And I was so looking forward to seeing Wanda again so we could pick up where we left off last time with our differences about Donald Trump."

"I wish you'd keep your politics to yourself. Especially when it comes to him."

"So why all the leaves?"

"Just put them in. I don't have time for a discussion right now. Then will you baste the turkey while I iron the tablecloth?"

"Aye-aye, sir," he said with a slapdash salute.

"Smartass."

"Paige…little ears will hear you."

"Smartass," she whispered.

"You're a little scampy today," he said, patting her on the butt. "And I rather like it."

"You would."

"So, what are Jessivel and Gary up to these days? Are they still pretending to have a 'business' relationship even though all that nonsense between her and Kayla's father has been resolved?"

"Gary put me in touch with someone who's going to help me find the real Tamir and Emma. Did I tell you that?"

"You're changing the subject."

The sound of the doorbell made Paige jump. "Who could that be this early?"

Leland answered the door.

"Kayla," Paige heard him say. "Where's your mom?"

"Gary and Mom dropped me off. They thought maybe you could use some help, watching Mia, I hope. But I think they just wanted to be alone." She sighed. "Grown-ups." She bent down to pet Sadie, who was obviously excited to see her.

Paige did a double take when she saw Kayla enter the kitchen wearing tights and a short-cropped sweater that ended way above her waist and sporting what Paige hoped were henna tattoos on her hands.

"Where's the rest of your outfit?" Paige asked.

Major eye roll from the teenager.

"Aren't you supposed to wear a skirt or something with those?"

"It's the style, Aunt Paige. Everyone does it."

"How's basketball going?"

"Won our game last night. I scored seventeen points. Youngest player. Did you know I'm the youngest player on the team?"

"Yes, I think I remember hearing that…a few hundred times."

"Aunt Paige. Not a few hundred."

Paige laughed and patted Kayla on the head. "I'm going to come to your next home game."

"Yeah. Mom told me."

"If you would take Mia in the playroom and keep her occupied, that would be great," she told Kayla. "There's a new Mickey Mouse music thing in there she likes a lot."

"When are we eating?"

"Not for another couple of hours."

Kayla had that I-don't-know-if-I-can-wait-that-long look on her face.

"Would you like a snack?"

Kayla nodded with a wide grin.

"Help yourself to some fruit or cookies. You know where to find them. Hey, you're wearing the ring." Paige had not known Jessivel to have ever taken off their father's ring from around her neck. Now Kayla wore it.

"Mom lets me wear it on special occasions."

Paige had had it appraised one time when she told Jessivel she wanted to have it cleaned for her. The stone turned out to be a rare diamond worth more than $15,000. She added it to her own insurance policy but didn't share its value with Jessivel. Now that she saw her letting Kayla wear it, she thought better of it and made a mental note to talk to Jessivel about it.

A few minutes later, when Leland didn't join her in the kitchen, Paige called out for him. When she got no answer, she called him on his cell phone.

"Where are you?"

"I'm just pulling into the driveway."

"Where were you?" she asked, annoyed that he would have left the house with so much to do before the big meal.

She turned when she heard the side door open. Leland held a bouquet of fresh flowers—a mixture of carnations, zinnias, mums, and pepper berries all in autumn colors.

"I thought these might look nice on the table."

"How sweet." She leaned in for a lingering kiss and took the flowers. "If you keep surprising me like this, I may just have to keep you this time."

"I brought you flowers before. Remember?"

She looked him straight in the eye. "No, I don't. Was I that out of it?"

"There's no prudent way for me to answer that."

This was not the first time she'd been reminded how not ready she had been when she married Leland the first time.

"You're right. Will you give the turkey another squirt?"

A long series of giggles was heard coming from Mia's playroom.

"Mickey Mouse?" Leland asked.

"Probably."

"Kayla is so good with her." He glanced into the adjoining room. "Didn't she forget part of her outfit or something?"

"That's what they wear, apparently. My mom didn't approve of my wearing over-the-knee socks, clogs, and a crop-top either, if I remember correctly."

"Hmm. Could you recreate that look for me sometime? Maybe late at night, after Mia's gone to bed?"

Paige wrapped her arms around him from behind. "Maybe."

They continued working in the kitchen, chipping away at the list of food dishes Paige had planned.

"So how does Jess like living in your mom's house so far? Has she gotten over the fact that it's where her father's other family lived?"

"She's made it her own, so that doesn't bother her. At least that's what she says. And Kayla loves her new school, so that helps."

"How's the SUV working out for her?" Paige had given their father's SUV to Jessivel when Jessivel's car had needed repairs costing more than the car was worth.

"She loves it. Who wouldn't love that car? Dad bought it loaded."

"And how's Crystal doing with Floyd the Grump?"

"You better be careful calling him that. You're going to slip in front of them one day and—"

"There's a couple I'll never understand."

"Crystal and Floyd?"

"What do they have in common anyway? She's nice. He's not. And he's got to be at least fifteen years older than her."

"Yeah? So what do *we* have in common?"

"Hmm. We both like Pearl Jam."

"I outgrew them years ago."

"S'mores?"

"Too fattening."

"Making out in the back seat of my '64 Ford Mustang?"

"I had too many bruises from that."

"Hmm…there must be something."

"Help me with this pan. It's heavy."

"So why *did* you want me back, if we're so different?" he asked.

"To lift things, of course. And hang pictures. Oh, and to drag those stupid garbage carts out to the curb every Friday morning."

"You're such a romantic."

"I'm working on it."

"I thought you were going to say because of my stunningly good looks and hunky body."

"That too."

"We all know, of course, that I married you for your money," he said.

"The stones, right?"

"Yep."

"Well, at least you're honest about it," she said with a smile. After consulting with her parents' estate planning attorney to verify she and the other beneficiaries had legal rights to the stones, she sold them at auction, and dispensed their share of the profits to Natalie, Jessivel, and Wanda. She set aside money for Tamir and Emma and planned to give them their share as soon as she was able to locate them.

"How's JP's coming along?"

With some of the cash she had received from selling the stones, she started a construction project at one end of her strip mall to house an organization that helped homeless men and women and others who lacked relevant life skills to prepare for and find jobs. JP's—Jessivel and Paige's—had been Jessivel's idea, and she would be the one to manage it.

"If the weather holds out, enough of the outside construction will be done and they can work on the inside during the winter. If all goes well, we'll be open in the spring."

She sashayed over to him and snuggled into his arms, his strength making her feel safe, physically and emotionally. She absorbed the smell of him. "Only for the money?" she asked him.

"No, there were other things." He hugged her tighter.

"Like what?"

He patted her on her behind. "Now I'm not sure. All I can think of right now is—"

"We have too much to do, sweetheart."

"Mm-hm," he sighed.

"I love you, Leland Cushman." And that wasn't all. She loved their newfound intimacy—the emotional kind, the kind that would allow her to leap off that two-story building and know he'd be there to catch her…or at least break her fall. She had confided in "the girls" when she had first felt her heart going in that direction. After bombarding her with a multitude of questions, they had unanimously approved.

But as much as she reveled in the change in herself after reuniting with Leland, Paige didn't credit him as much as she did Jessivel with becoming her newfound self. Jessivel had been the one to set the example for her, something Paige hadn't realized until Jessivel talked to her on that level one day.

"I had built a wall around my heart," she had told Paige. "And that not only protected me from getting hurt, but it also kept me from understanding others. And then I met you and learned that no matter how someone appears on the outside, you can't judge them without knowing them. And you can't know them without letting down that wall."

"I love you, Paige West," Leland said to her. "What time are we going to Tracy's by the way?"

Paige continued to work one day a week at Tracy's Backstreet Kitchen. Without any prodding, Jessivel had joined her in the weekly ritual.

"Five."

"Everyone coming with us?"

"Kayla's going to stay here with Mia."

"Alone?"

"Lee, she's fourteen, almost fifteen."

"Okay, but—" The doorbell interrupted him. "Fasten your seatbelt, sweetie, here they come."

Book Reviews

I hope you enjoyed reading *The Ring* and will consider posting a short review on Amazon and/or Goodreads. Reviews and word-of-mouth referrals play an important role in helping authors promote their books, and your help in this regard is much appreciated.

E-Mail Subscriber List

Join my e-mail subscriber list www.florenceosmund.com/subscribe and you will receive:

- Entry in a monthly drawing for a copy of one of my books
- Notification of my future book releases
- A copy of The Ultimate List of Links for Authors
- Monthly notification of new blog entries (insight for authors)

Book Clubs

I love book clubs! If you belong to one and choose this or any other of my books for your monthly read, I'm happy to participate in your book club discussion. If you're local to northern Illinois or southern Wisconsin, I may be able to participate in person. If you are in some other part of the world, I can tune in by video conference or phone. Just shoot me an e-mail if you're interested—info@florenceosmund.com.

Florence Osmund

OTHER BOOKS BY FLORENCE OSMUND

NON-FICTION

How to Write, Publish, and Promote a Novel

FICTION

Nineteen Hundred Days

They Called Me Margaret

Living with Markus

Regarding Anna

Red Clover

Daughters

The Coach House

Osmund's books are available on Amazon
http://www.amazon.com/author/florenceosmund or at bookstores who
order from distributors IngramSpark or Baker & Taylor

About the Author

"I strive to create stories that contain complex characters and thought-provoking plots that challenge readers to survey their own values."

After a long career working for large corporations, Florence Osmund retired to write novels. Getting the rather late start in life as an author, she published her first book at the age of sixty-two. In the beginning, she made many mistakes trying to get established as an author, and she hopes her book *How to Write, Publish, and Promote a Novel* helps others avoid making the same ones.

Florence is a contributing writer for The Book Designer blog and book reviewer/assessor for indieBRAG, Awesome Indies, and Windy City Reviews. She continues to write literary fiction from her home on a small, tranquil lake in a far northern suburb of Chicago where she enjoys a wide array of wildlife who pay her frequent daily and nightly visits.

If you are a new or aspiring novelist, visit Florence's website/blog where she offers substantial advice on how to begin the project, writing techniques, building an author platform, book promotion, and much more.

E-Mail: info@florenceosmund.com

Website: http://www.florenceosmund.com

Facebook: http://www.facebook.com/florenceosmundbooks

LinkedIn: http://www.linkedin.com/in/florenceosmund

Twitter: @FlorenceOsmund

Amazon: https://www.amazon.com/Florence-Osmund/e/ B007ZQJC6U/

Goodreads: http://www.goodreads.com/user/show/8800692-florence-osmund